Winter Kill

China Invades Australia

By Gene Skellig

DEDICATION

This book is dedicated in part to past and future participants of the Commonwealth Antisubmarine Warfare competition known as "Fincastle", which in 1991 was held at RAAF Edinburgh, near Adelaide, South Australia. In particular, to the flight crew and ground crew of Royal Canadian Air Force 407 Maritime Patrol Squadron "Demons", Crew 7 "Moosemen"; to the crew of Royal Australian Navy (RAN) Her Majesty's Australian Ship (HMAS) Ovens, the Oberon Class diesel submarine that proved so elusive to the "407-7"; to the Royal New Zealand Air Force P-3C Orion crew from No.5 Sqn RNZAF Whenuapai, who ultimately won the competition; and to those scoundrels from the Royal Air Force, RAF, Nimrod crew and their "Liars Dice!" Special thanks to the RAAF Edinburgh's Wing Commander and to our hosts from No. 10 Squadron, and to the locals who gave us all such great experiences such as a tour of the vineyards of Barossa Valley and the Adelaide region in general. These experiences left long-lasting impressions of what Australia is all about.

ACKNOWLEDGEMENTS

The Winter Kill series, and my writing and publishing hobby, would not be possible without the encouragement and support of my wife and our four children. These wonderful, creative, people are a constant source of inspiration which I draw upon in my writing. As I plan my transition from service life to a semi-retired lifestyle as an author I am constantly amazed and reassured by the ease with which they embrace the complexities and challenges presented to them by the world which they are inheriting from us.

I am grateful for the huge contribution of my editor Michael McGee, and of my stable of 'beta readers' with a diverse range of expertise – Ron, Ben, Michel, Rand and others – who read various stages of the manuscript and provided feedback and suggestions to improve the readability and accuracy of the book.

i

DISCLAIMER

The characters and events portrayed in this book are fictitious. Any resemblance to real world events or person living or dead is purely coincidental or used fictitiously.

FOREWORD

Winter Kill – China Invades Australia runs parallel to the original, *Winter Kill – War With China Has Already Begun.* Available on-line at: http://www.amazon.com/dp/B0050D7E06 Whether you read *War With China* or *China Invades Australia* first is entirely your choice as both novels stand on their own. However, the author recommends reading *Winter Kill - War With China Has Already Begun* first, as it provides the geopolitical context and other 'big hands - small map' type of detail which would ultimately enhance your enjoyment of *Winter Kill – China Invades Australia.*

For best results, you may want to open a map application that will allow you to get to know the terrain where this novel is set. Imagine that you are personally involved in this crisis and you are the only one whose internet is still working. You can use internet resources to fact-check salient details and to study the terrain, and to seek out articles about real-world military preparations underway in far flung places such as Pakistan, India, Indonesia, Singapore, Australia, South Korea, Japan and other countries which see the rapid build-up of Chinese military forces in the region with increased concern. You may find, as the author suggests, that war with China has already begun and that a Chinese invasion of Australia could be on the horizon. An appreciation for these contemporary geopolitical and military trends will make your reading experience that much more intense. Your ear for snippets of news from the region will be that much more well-tuned to these real-world events.

CONTENTS

CAST OF KEY CHARACTERS

People's Liberation Army (PLA)

Major Gouling Fang — Little Dragon, veteran spy
Captain Zhao Yingting — Little Dragon
Colonel Huang — External Intelligence Directorate
General Bing — Supreme Military Commander, China
Colonel Hua — EA to Gen. Bing, Jinan Military District
Colonel Xu — External Intelligence Directorate
Colonel Guo — CO of air assaulters at New Zealand
Colonel Yip — CO of372nd Division, Charters Towers
L.Gen Leung — Army Group North (42 GA + 41 GA)
Colonel Wu — 2 IC to L Gen Leung, Charters Towers
Colonel Ma — CO of air assaulters, Queensland
Wan Shanyu — infanteer, 4th Btn, 370th Division, 42nd GA
General Sheung — Army Group South (65th, 38th & 41st GAs)
Colonel Jing — Commander 1st Armored Div, 65th GA

United States of America

Rylan O'Connor — CIA Station Chief, Canberra, Australia
Carl — Deputy Station Chief
James Webber — Secretary of State / Parker Administration
L Col Peter Weir — 75th Ranger Regiment, SOCOMD
Cheryl Weir — Wife of Major Peter Weir
Jake Weir — son of Lieutenant Colonel Weir
Major Joe Blakely — USMC/MARSOC LnO to Aus Army
Tannis Blakely — Wife of Joe
Agness Blakely — Blakely daughter, girlfriend of Sunny Yao
Sunny Yao (Yao Ming) — Son of Stanley, Chinese-American
Stanley Yao (Yao Ping) — US engineer working in Australia
Top Sgt Rick Rideout — Top Sergeant, 3rd Marines, MAGTFA
MgySgt Gary Gannon — Master Gunnery Sergeant, MAGTFA
Mattew "Matt" Blakely — Warrant Officer, Mt Weather EOC
General Upton (retired) — Matt Blakely's father-in-law, Altoona
Maggie Blakely — Upton girl, Matt's wife

Catherine MacInnes	– Upton girl, wife of Owen MacInnes
Owen MacInnes	– Mechanic, Richland Center, Wisconsin
Ian Morgan	– Mechanic, friend of Owen MacInnes
Beth Morgan	– Secretary to L Col Hurdman
LCol Hurdman	– CO, 1st Det, 829th Eng Coy, Richland WI.
Captain Jarvis	– Marine Air Ground Task Force Australia
Lieutenant Lion	– MAGTFA, Darwin, Area Logistics Officer
Colonel Millar	– 3rd Marines, M4 Log, MAGTFA, Darwin,

Australia

Captain Thorne	– 1 Cdo, Australian Special Forces
Sgt Wendy Hayman	– Military Police, 1st Brigade, 1 Div
Cpl Dickie Guay	– Miliary Police, 1st Bde, 1 Div, RAA
General Adams	– Commaning Officer, 1 Div
Nicholas Lenko	– Leading Snr Constable, NSW Police

Allied Military Personnel

Col Mike Latimer	– Canadian Military Attaché, Tokyo
Sarah Latimer	– Wife of Colonel Mike Latimer
Group Captain Patel	– Indian Air Force, Wing Commander,
General Singh	– Commander II Indian Armoured Corps
Commander Malhotra	– Captain(N), Indian convoy escort
Sqn Ldr Tanta	– Indian Air Force SU30MK1 pilot leader

Military Units

United States of America:
3rd Marines MAGTFA: Marine Air Ground Task Force Australia
DDG 114 *Ralph Johnson* – Air Warfare Destoryer, enroute Aus
DDG 111 *Spruance* – Air Warfare Destroyer, enroute Aus
DDG 116 *Thomas Hudner* – Air Warfare Destroyer, Darwin

<u>Australia:</u>
Forces Command HQ – Sydney, HQ Aus Defense Forces
HMAS Hobart   – Air Warfare Destroyer, Adelaide
Royal Australian Army (RAA)

     1st Division, "1st Div", combat ready formation

          3rd Brigade, 1st Division (Townsville, Queensland)

          1st Armored Regiment

          No.4 Field Artillery Regiment

     2nd Division, "2nd Div", reservists, low readiness

     1 Commando Division (Sydney), "1 Cdo", Special Forces
Royal Australian Air Force (RAAF)

     RAAF Base Tindal – F/A-18 Fighters, Northern Territory

<u>People's Republic of China (PRC):</u>
People's Liberation Army (PLA)
PLA Ground Force (PLAGF),
PLA Air Force (PLAAF),
PLA Navy (PLAN)
Beijing Military Region

     38th Group Army, Commanded by General Guo
Guangzhou Military Region (south-coast, Hong Kong, Macau)

     42nd Group Army – infamous for Korean Chosin Resevoir

     Special Operations Battalion

     124th Amphibious Mechanized Infantry Division

          370th, 371st, 372nd Regiments

     163rd Division

Jinan Military Region (General Bing's original command)

     20th Group Army, "all brigade"

     41st Group Army

          123rd Mechanized

          20th Division

PROLOGUE

LONG TERM STORAGE

Here we go, the Customs and Immigration Officer sighed quietly to himself as he scanned the rows of people lining up in front of him. This bunch would be arriving off the Qantas flight from Hong Kong. They might be a little better behaved than the passengers from other parts of the world. An increasing number of travelers seemed more desperate, more troublesome these days. But then, the whole world was different now.

The Officer straightened up and set his shoulders back, Australia's first line of defense from the relentless hordes. He motioned the man at the front of the line to come forward. The Chinese, very tall and gangly, lurched towards him awkwardly. He was young, in his late twenties, and fit-looking. But otherwise, he was a hopeless mess: an ill-fitting suit a few sizes too small, a tousled mop of hair with beads of sweat trickling down the forehead of his flushed face, clammy skin, and eyes darting left to right like a man at the gallows. The Officer took it all in and decided to give this one a careful check.

Four lines to the left, Major Goulong Fang progressed towards the front of the line. He turned his focus inward, trying to reach a Chi-Kung meditative state of equanimity. As he felt himself relax, his pulse and breathing slowing, he knew that his outward appearance had become a relaxed, unhurried, calm.

The passenger in front of him was waved to the counter, leaving Fang on-deck at the yellow line. He looked around at the other passengers from the Qantas flight from Hong Kong. A few lines to his right, he saw the nervous young Chinese being motioned to come forward. *Should have had some Chi-Kung training,* he thought of his compatriot.

"What is the purpose of your visit to Australia?" asked the inspector. Fang overheard, noticing the Officer's distinctive Australian-English accent.

"I am a student. It is recorded into my Academic Visa," the gangly Chinese stammered, holding open his passport to the page where a Student Visa was attached.

"How do you pronounce your name, in English?"

"Yingting-Zhao. Err, Zhao Yingting." The man replied, seemingly confused about his own name.

"Which is it, Mr. Zhao or Mr. Yingting?"

"I sorry for confusing. English naming is upside-downside from Chinese. I am in English Yingting. My name is Zhao."

Shaking his head at the tall young man's confusion, the inspector felt more confident in his impression that there was something wrong with the man. *Is he high? A drug mule? But the drug trade had taken such a back seat in security matters these days…*

"Would you please open up your suitcase, Sir?"

"By all means, Sir," said the bean-pole, fumbling with his keys and hastily undoing the tiny lock. Then he zipped open his suitcase while the immigration inspector took a more careful look at the man's student Visa.

Finding nothing out of the ordinary the inspector turned his attention to the contents of the suitcase. With his white-gloved hands, he gently probed the sides, top and bottom of the suitcase for hidden compartments. He took his time examining every detail of the Chinese national's possessions.

He squeezed the folded clothing gently but firmly, like a paramedic might feel a casualty's body for internal injuries. Nothing seemed unusual about the clothing, which was folded and packed with military precision.

"And what is this?" he asked, holding up a small porcelain statue of a top-knotted man dressed in robes and sitting on a throne, "This some kind of Buddha?"

"No Sir! That is Laojun, the Lord Laozi in his divine aspect," the man said with enormous pride.

"Is this an artifact, or some other culturally significant or valuable piece?" the Immigration Officer asked, uncertain if it was on the list of restricted imports.

"Not at all, Sir. It is simple tourist gift. I was….I obtained it at Jinan Province before my traveling here. I planning to giving it as gifting to Australian host family."

"Host Family?"

"Yes, Dr. Samulski Jack. His is familying my host stay. I am life with them to finished Diploma at Sustainability in Port Macquarie TAFE campus."

Looking unsure about the young man, the inspector turned the statuette over carefully in his hands. This seemed to make the man incredibly nervous, but when the inspector saw 'MADE IN CHINA' stamped on the bottom of the statuette, he realized that it was a simple tourist piece and not an archeological treasure.

The inspector stopped for a moment. *This character is just not right,* he thought to himself. *He's nervous like an amateur drug smuggler, but his luggage is clean... It's been through the x-ray and the sniffer-tunnel, and the man's already cleared the metal detector or he wouldn't have even been able to board the plane back in Hong Kong. But still...*he looked around. The other Officers had their hands full with the passengers coming up the other lines. People in the line in front of him were standing quietly, but he could sense their impatience. *Do I alert the shift super and risk another false alarm? On what, my hunch? I'll get another black mark on my record.* he thought to himself. *Or should I just let the bugger go?*

"Welcome to Australia," he said, handing the Laozi statuette to the man, who reached out for it reverently, with both hands. The Officer waved the next person up. Despite his misgivings, he had nothing to go on other than the man's obvious jitters.

Watching from just a few meters away, Major Fang wondered for a moment whether the Australian Customs and Immigrations Officers would pick up on the large number of such statuettes that were in the suitcases of many exceptionally fit young Chinese entering Australia over the last few days.

Having been briefed-in on his assignment to a much greater extent than less experienced *Little Dragon* agents, Major Fang knew that there were several hundred such agents making their way to their assignments across Australia, and that each of them had their own Laozi statuette.

Fang remembered when he had been given the details of his assignment directly from Colonel Huang, commander of Fang's unit within the External Intelligence Directorate. He had been given his own Laozi at that meeting; he remembered that his first impression of the statuette was that its face made him think of some of the Generals commanding the People's Liberation Army. *But why?* He had concentrated for a moment and then it had come to him: *it looks just like General Bing! Makes sense,* Fang reflected, *after all, the man was just elevated from commander of Jinan Military District to be the Chief of the People's Liberation Army General Staff, our supreme commander.*

Based on the role that the statuettes were to play in the operation, it now seemed obvious to Fang that General Bing was the genius behind OPERATION WINTER SNAKE. Of course, he would not share his deductions with anybody. That would be too risky, violating everything that Major Fang knew about OPSEC and INFOSEC. He could not share his insight with anybody. It was enough to be given such an important mission and the freedom of action required to carry it out. He knew that he was the right man for the job, which was more than he could say about many of the other *Little Dragons*.

Fang watched the tall, nervous Chinese, who had almost begged for the Australian Customs and Immigration Officer to detain him for looking suspicious, gather his things and move on hurriedly. *What a dead-head,* Fang thought. *Why would we have need of such a bumbler,* he reflected sourly. Then, as he watched the Chinese blunder hopelessly along, a head taller than nearly everyone else in the arrivals area, it made him stop and think.

Fang's meditations were abruptly stopped. The Chinese blunderer halted awkwardly, his upper body threatening to crash forward while his feet stopped in place. He was letting a large black man pass by. The man craned his neck up as the Chinese towered over him. He nodded and smiled in appreciation, and turned on his way. The Chinese kept looking at the black man as he walked away, quietly saying "Hac gwai," under his breath, with a sneer on his face. The husky black man passed, and then stopped to talk to a man in an airport uniform.

"Excuse me, Sir! Which way do I go for my connecting flight to Darwin?" he asked.

"Just follow the signs to the Domestic Flights, and then to your gate, C22. You can't go wrong, Mate!" said the agent.

"Thanks!" the black man said with a smile, hefting his green duffle-bag over his shoulder and lugging his suitcase with his other hand.

Fang picked up on the Canadian Flag sewn onto the black man's duffle bag, and another stuck on his suitcase. Has to be an American, he thought, probably from the 3rd Marines. Major Fang had taken great care to know the order of battle of all enemy formations within the Asia-Pacific area of operations, his personal Area of Operational Responsibility. He knew that when American servicemen travelled in civilian attire they were under orders to keep their American military identity a secret, to avoid being identified by terrorists and foreign intelligence operatives like Fang. The Canadian flag was a dead give-way, as was the black man's short-cropped, military haircut and extremely muscular build. The only thing that Fang found unusual was the soldier's friendliness. That was unusual for a Marine. *Maybe he really is a Canadian. Unlikely, but possible*, thought Fang.

He turned back to where he had last seen the tall Chinese. The fellow was gone, leaving Fang to stare into the empty space where he had been moments before. And then it hit him.

That tall guy must be from that basketball team from the 41st Group Army. Yeah, that's it! He's definitely that player from the 123rd Mechanized, in Guigang, Fang realized. *How could such a putz be part of such a prestigious unit as the 123rd? They're a ready-reaction force, crack troops. He must be good at something, I guess.*

Fang recalled the scandal several years before, when a Chinese military basketball team, the Bayi Rockets, had started a brawl with the visiting Georgetown University "Hoyas" from Washington, DC. As Fang passed through customs on autopilot, he thought about the scandal which had taken place during the visit of the American Vice President. He did not even worry whether the Inspector might notice the latex skin-patch covering the ugly scar on his face or ask to see the contents of his suitcase – and discover Fang's own Laozi statuette.

After breezing through Customs he retrieved his suitcase and moved through the arrival doors to the public side of the terminal. With the most dangerous phase of his mission now behind him, Major Fang first re-acquired and then kept an eye on the tall Chinese, keeping him under surveillance out of habit. *Yes, the bumbler made it through Customs, Despite his incompetence.*

Fang was good at spying on Chinese nationals abroad. Two years of deep cover for the External Intelligence Directorate, penetrating the Australian Falun Gong movement, had made Fang particularly good at monitoring Chinese nationals abroad.

Maybe if they had been up against an American military team, the brawl could have had some purpose. But to start a fight with students from Georgetown University – and to lose the game as well as the fight – had only brought shame to our nation. Maybe that goofy-looking bean-pole was the one who wound up in a neck brace. Hope he's better at espionage and recruiting Dragonflies than he is at sports diplomacy, thought Fang as he handed his suitcase to a taxi driver.

After watching the tall man depart in another taxi, no doubt headed for his assignment, Fang made a mental note of the date and time, along with the make, license, color and company name of the man's taxi. Fang then turned his attention to the next phase of his operation, already having filed away the arrival terminal observations into his highly organized brain.

Fang had a particular obsession with the most minute of details, a habit which had saved his skin on more than a few occasions.

1

DIPLOMACY

Three identical GMC Suburbans swooshed through the silent early-morning streets of Canberra. As the motorcade made good time on its way to the airport, two CIA agents had a speed-meeting in one of the vehicles. Time was ticking away quickly and the two men knew they had to make every moment count.

"Enough about the Secretary of State. Let's move on to other business," said Rylan O'Connor, Station Chief of the CIA detachment in Canberra, Australian Capital Territory. They led a small team that fed information into the CIA's Office of South Asia Analysis, OSA. As the eyes and ears for OSA in the region, they had a wide range of duties and travelled extensively. Typically, one of them would travel on assignment while the other would remain at the US embassy in Canberra. This made keeping each other up-to-date on various files difficult, so any chance for a face-to-face discussion - even a short car ride - was an opportunity to go over the most pressing files.

They had just finished going over the impact of some directives that had come in, from headquarters, when the Station Chief suggested they go over the regional issues.

"Good idea. We don't have much time before your flight. OK. So next is the Canadian Military Attaché in Tokyo," said Carl, the deputy Station-Chief.

"I'm still not sure if he presents us with much of an opportunity. What have you learned?"

"Well, his Military Attaché work has been quite boring, with nothing controversial at all. But then suddenly he was given this crazy new direction from Ottawa, and everything changed."

"You're talking about the currency play? Have the guys in Pine Gap intercepted any more on that?"

"Nope, but Tokyo Station has, from the Bank of Japan, and sources within the ruling Liberal Democratic Party. We have the BOJ's summary of activities of a few leading industrialists and bankers who have been paraded through the Canadian Embassy. It's all in the thumb-drive I gave you."

"So what's the short version?" O'Connor asked crisply, calculating that he had only a few minutes left before arriving at the airport to board the US Air Force Boeing 757. The corners of his mouth tightened in his habitual facial expression.

The Deputy Chief replied in a long, steady burst. His immobile, wide-eyed face betrayed little of the nervous energy that animated him. "They're throwing their new currency around like drunken sailors. They've made a series of deals that seem to have absolutely no due diligence, and no 'net benefit' to Canada."

"I thought as much. It's in line with what we got from Treasury. It's all about getting their new gold-backed currency into play on foreign exchange markets as soon as it's released."

"So what's our position? Is this against our interests, or not?"

"Washington still has not decided, but for now we have to leave this one alone. We may need some leverage on the guy. What do we have?"

"On the MA? Not much. Well, there is that boat project."

"Boat? I haven't read about that."

"He's been personally overseeing some sort of procurement project, with the Yamamoto Corporation. You know, the one that had that deal for access to ports in the Canadian Arctic?"

"I thought that one was dead, along with the rest of the Japanese economy."

"It was. But Tatsuo Yamamoto had this prototype, almost completed. Seems that they are using that as another way to pump twenty million or so into the Yamamoto Corporation."

"These are small numbers. What of it? What's the angle?"

"Don't' know yet, but Tokyo is working on it. There seems to be a personal nexus here."

"Why do we think that?"

"Because on two of the trips, he brought his wife."

"Well, it's not uncommon for a diplomat to take his wife on a side trip. Where to, Osaka, right? She probably did a bunch of shopping. Isn't she something of a culture vulture?"

"Yes, she is. But she did nothing. No shopping, and no visits to any other venues. Just the visit to the erection shop."

O'Connor let out a tight little laugh, as much as he would permit himself these days. Then he frowned at his subordinate, awaiting a definition of "erection shop".

"That's how it translates from the Japanese. It's where they finish off a ship, installing the mast and other tall items of the superstructure," replied the Carl.

"So what's so important about the ship? Why would a Military Attaché's wife be so interested in it?"

"That's what Tokyo is going to find out for us. All we know so far is that it has some unusual technology incorporated in the design, and that a one-in-thirty model of it has been tested in a wave pool. The thing is designed to survive sea-state five – typhoon-force winds. It seems to have some self-defensive features, but we've got almost nothing on it. It's not a military craft, however. Just some strange, tough little vessel. And we have no hint as to why the Military Attaché is taking such a personal interest in it. But it may be an opening. Other than that, the guy is clean, and we've got no leverage on him.

"So when do they hit the erection shop?"

"That's the problem. The security at the Yamamoto Corporation is tighter than at Fort Knox. They simply can't get in, without killing anybody, anyhow. "

"Is that it? Stalled? Or do they have a strategy?"

"They've asked the British for help. Apparently the Brits have some particularly capable asset in Osaka."

"Crap. I hate it when we have to ask the Brits for help. It always comes at a cost."

"True, but they sure do have some good spies, like that James Bond type we met in Moscow. Classy act, that guy."

Just before moving on to the next file, the Station Chief had an insight. The corners of his mouth relaxed, but his eyes narrowed.

"You know what, Carl?" he asked his deputy.

"What?" the subordinate said, without looking.

"With everybody going ape over the economic collapse that's hit the region, and all this talk about war, maybe having access to a sturdy little ship like that would be of personal interest to me, if I were in his shoes."

Carl looked up from his files. "Yeah? What for?"

"For getting the fuck out of Dodge."

The Deputy stared at his boss for just a second. This was getting close to laying it all out open, something seldom done in conversation at the Agency these days. Doing so could be seen as an acknowledgement of implied trust; or of weakness.

"I guess that would be an option," he replied to his superior. He trusted his boss; he knew he was a pro. Inwardly he felt relief.

"But is this guy some sort of End-Of-The-World-As-We-Know-It type of survivalist?"

"Not at all," the senior agent continued. "I've seen his file. He's a sharp guy, with a stellar career in their Air Force. And he's posted in the middle of an economic shit-storm in Japan. Maybe he's just got his eyes wide open, and knows how difficult it could become to evacuate his wife, and maybe his staff, if things take a sudden turn for the worst in Japan. After all, their posturing with China keeps getting more dangerous. But maybe that's our line. Talk to Tokyo, but I think we could set him up to be discredited as a survivalist nut, a doomsayer on Japan. If we need to pressure the Canucks on Japan, we could use him as a liability, an embarrassment. Anyhow, there could be something here."

The Deputy Chief looked back down at his files. "So what's next? You've got less than 4 minutes!"

The corners tightened on the Station Chief's mouth again. "We've got that Australian politician in Kuala Lumpur."

"Who, the one with the gambling problem?"

"Yea. We've got him eating out of our hands now. His handler says that he's obsessed with making a big score, but the guy never knows when to quit. He's into us for over a million dollars already, and we've documented lots of nasty sex with the whores we threw at him too."

"Great. But he's kept out of the press? And Canberra knows nothing of it?"

"Nothing. On both counts. The guy somehow keeps doing his job, and KLMP is not a problem spot for the Aussies. They've got their attention focussed on the Indonesian threat, and their problems with terrorism. So the guy's been left under the radar."

"So no change on the plan for him?"

"Well, we may not need to use him after all."

"Why not? Isn't the vote on their new White Paper coming up? Don't we need his vote?"

"That's the thing. Both sides of the Australian House of Representatives are getting very hawkish. The Prime Minister is not going to have any problems with the new Defense Spending bill, despite the hung parliament. So the controlling votes of the half-dozen Greens is now irrelevant. The bill will sail through."

"So we can save this asset for another day. Perhaps when our basing rights comes up again?"

"That's what Langley says. Our priority now is overcoming local opposition to our basing issues. We need to lay down another five to ten thousand men in Australia, along with some firepower which the Aussie citizenry will find contentious. So we have to make opposition to our personnel basing in Australia go away. That's what Sec State was in Australia for, but we still don't' know how successful he was."

"Well, for now, we have to assume that our risk tolerance is about to be reduced to near zero. We'll be expected to make sure that the Greens and other Commies here in Australia are shut down. We can't have any more of those protests, like we did when our last President increased the number of Marines up in Darwin. So how are we doing on the Green List, anyhow?"

"We've made progress on a few at the top, but it's very difficult to get close to the real ringleaders. They can smell us a mile away, and would turn any approaches into their own media opportunity. That's too risky for us, as we've been keeping a low profile here."

"Well, if I read the tea-leaves right, we are about to be given a free hand. Make some contingency plans for what we could do against the Greens and other long-hairs if we are given carte blanche."

"How far do you think we will go?"

"All the way. Money. Sex. Extortion."

"What's new about that? We're already doing that all over the place in Australia."

"Back it up with violence," said the Station Chief, coldly. He looked out the window at the scenery speeding by.

"Are you serious? If the rules of engagement change that much, you know that also means people will die," said the Deputy, concerned about the turn things may be taking.

"You have no idea. We've been frozen out of so many countries in this area, and Australia is absolutely essential now," O'Connor said, and then seemed to be taken away with his thoughts. He had already briefed Carl on how badly things had gone during his meetings in Jakarta with the BIN – Badan Intelijen Negara – Indonesia's intelligence agency. Despite gifts of another 24 Bell 412 and 36 UH-60 Blackhawk helicopters, medium range missiles and upgraded radar systems, along with fully outfitting the Indonesian Army Strategic Reserve Command with infantry fighting vehicles and artillery – over three billion dollars in military aid – the United States was losing the ear of the Indonesian political elites. They seemed to have traded their sovereignty for increased business and political ties with mainland China. Despite three years of personally cultivating his contacts within BIN, O'Connor had less than a half-dozen solid contacts that were still in the anti-Chinese faction of the Indonesian intelligence community. What with China building hospitals and airport runways in some of the more remote islands, and their generous infrastructure deals with Indonesian export sector, all but giving Indonesia free oil & gas facilities in exchange for long-term guaranteed supply, Indonesia was embracing China's growing influence. Despite a long history of proud independence, they were even participating in small but strategically worrisome joint military exercises with the Chinese navy. All of this flashed as a strained look on his face, before he resumed his reply.

"It's not official yet, just what I'm hearing from the guys with Sec State. The gloves are coming off, Carl, and we'll be the first to know. Work up some mischief against the top five Greens, their loved ones, anybody we can use to shut them down completely. Throw in some of the left-leaning media for insurance. We may have to throw one or two under the bus, Putin style, so that the rest of the media understand that anti-American sentiment is taboo. Like we did back home back in 2000, silence of the lambs, as it were."

The Deputy leaned forward in his seat. "Shit! That's serious interference in the Australian Secret Intelligence Services back yard. Do we engage ASIS on this, when the time comes?"

"Only if they ask. And they won't. Whether they get wind of it or not, the word is going to be plausible deniability. As long as their government is not implicated, they won't point at us either. So make it as quiet as you can, but don't worry about ASIS. They'll be told to turn a blind eye, or we'll poke them in the eye if it comes to that. Just be ready to execute – pun intended – when I get back from Washington next week. I'll have the Director's approval in hand," the Station Chief said, as the motorcade whooshed through the gate and rolled to a stop adjacent to the waiting business jet.

"Rylan, what's behind all of this? And I don't mean the geopolitics. What's coming? What's the event that'll stir things up?" Carl asked his boss, deep concern evident in his voice. At the last, O'Connor's emotions were finally to the surface. The impassive mask that had been his face throughout the trip had softened into an expression of worry.

The Chief leaned forward like a bull steadying itself for an impact. "Things are really heating up in Washington. What with what President Parker is about to do."

"What is that? She's already done so many radical things. From out here, it looks like her administration is desperate. Are things really that bad?"

"She's going to default on the Chinese debt."

"Oh. Shit," was all that Carl could say. He knew full well how badly that would affect the state of affairs within the region. "So will we be going to war with China?"

"Nope. That's the beauty of it. We're going to give them a shitload of the new G-dollars, like the Canadians are doing with their new gold-backed dollars. Only we'll be doing it on an unprecedented scale. China will come out of this smiling prettily, as we'll be quietly paying them off in gold while the rest of the world, and the US population back home, are stuck with the worthless old currency," O'Connor said, excitedly.

"Doesn't that mean that the shit storm is going to happen back home then? And not out here? We could be facing civil war if we screw our citizens, and reward China like that."

"Hey, don't look at me. I'd much rather go to war with China than fuck our citizens like that. But that's the plan. Avoid war with China at all costs, re-establish trade and commerce, so that our currency comes out on top. Then, once it's re-established itself as the global reserve currency, you know what comes next, don't you?"

"Yeah, sure, we go back off the gold standard, and try again with a fiat currency, get the printing press going full tilt. So how does it start back home?"

"Like the last time, in 1933."

"Confiscation of all privately held Gold in the United States," Cark said, with shock. "Holy Shit! That's it. That'll be the event that upsets the applecart. And I suppose the Chinese have already been told this?"

"Yup. Why do you think Sec State Webber was in Beijing before he came here?"

"So we've got nothing to fear from the Chinese on this? We just don't have the economic might needed to compete with them in their back-yard, so we have to save our economy without pissing them off. We try to balance them off through this network of military cooperation with our friends, especially Australia. Maybe later we'll be in a position to push back, but for now, we try to keep the Chinese addicted to our consumers – keep that 'Chimerica' relationship going. So, The real threat is our own citizens back home…" said O'Connor, with sickness in his stomach. He slouched back in his seat, deflated.

O'Connor got out of the vehicle without saying another word to Carl. With the Secretary of State now boarding, it was time for O'Connor and the other passengers to board, for the long flight back to the US.

As far as CIA operations in Australia, there really was nothing more to be said.

Secretary of State Webber was happy to be leaving Canberra. He had accomplished what he had been sent to negotiate and was looking forward to getting back to Washington, as much to be with his wife as to being back in the fray with the rest of the Parker Cabinet.

The 14 hour flight to LAX would be easy to endure, thanks to the comfort of the blue-and white modified Boeing 757-200 that had been something of a home-away-from-home for James Webber and his entourage for the lengthy Pacific Rim junket.

As he paged through the electronic documents on his laptop he reviewed the post-encounter notes his staff had generated during the trip. After reviewing them, and recalling the face-to-face meetings he had had in China, Japan, South Korea, Indonesia, the Philippines, Taiwan, Singapore and finally, Australia, he could not help but allow himself a bit of pride for the success of the mission.

While the truth of it would never see the light of day, the strategic objectives had all been achieved, and America's allies in the region had had an opportunity to press the United States for stronger military ties.

It was all about China. With last year's collapse of the old US currency, and the continued dislocations within the global economy after several years of lurching from one financial crisis to another, restoring trade relations with China – while at the same time attempting to contain China's expanding influence in the region – had been a delicate balance.

The secret currency-swap between the US and China, with the new gold-backed currency intended to bring much needed liquidity back into the badly broken trading relationship, was well received in China. Once the gold-backed dollar was announced in the coming weeks President Parker would be lauded for saving the world from total economic catastrophe. The new currency, the gold-backed US Treasury Dollar, or $G USD, would restore the dominant position of the US in international commerce, and start a wave of fiscal reforms the world over, with all major economies abandoning the Ponzi scheme of the fiat currency construct. At least for a while, anyhow, reflected Webber.

The trillions of dollars of debt denominated in Federal Reserve notes were about to be made worthless when President Parker outlawed the Federal Reserve cartel. This would amount to an absolute default on all sovereign debt. That's why Webber had been sent to Asia; to negotiate a secret deal with China and to mislead some and inform other allies in the region.

The Chinese premier had pretended to be surprised at the news, but also, strangely, was well prepared to discuss the mechanics of the currency exchange that Webber was to propose. They had immediately embraced the swap of worthless Federal Reserve Notes for the new $G USD, and promised to use the new gold backed "Dollar Gold" notes to maximum effect, in coordination with the President's coming announcement. They went so far as to provide Webber a copy of the text of the announcement which they would make, applauding the United States for taking such courageous action to restore global currency markets. It did seem strange to Secretary of State Webber that the Chinese had all of this prepared ahead of time, but he attributed that to the possibility of their having been given advance warning of the nature of the Sec State visit through diplomatic channels. He did not even consider for one moment that the Chinese had so thoroughly hacked into, compromised and otherwise infiltrated the communications systems of the United States as to have full knowledge of just about every important secret communicated between any agencies of the government of the United States.

For the Chinese, light-years ahead of the United States on state-controlled manipulation of information technologies, computer hacking, and espionage, nothing that Secretary of State Webber had to say had come as any kind of surprise.

What was surprising to the Secretary of State was the speed with which the hundreds of billions of $G USDs would be injected into the global financial system.

From what the Chinese had said, the money would first appear in contracts to get the profoundly under-utilized commercial shipping sector moving again, with global commodities contracts to be snapped up by China. The massive ships would once again be fully engaged in moving the commodities of the world to the dormant factories of China, Japan, Korea, and other Asian countries. Chinese economists had briefed that once the Chinese begin to spend the new G$, the Baltic Dry Index would show an impressive 40% jump in just the first two weeks after currency reform and currency swaps with China and America's other trading partners was initiated.

They went so far as to provide Webber with a summary of projected rises in stock market indices, and which multinational corporations would benefit most, just in case Webber 'had friends he wanted to reward', as the Chinese had put it.

While personally offended by the openness of the Chinese assumption that he would be so corrupt, he did not waste much time debating the ethics of it. He had immediately informed his friends and his broker, using the communications equipment aboard his Boeing 757 for a few personal calls. Of course, he made sure to call on a few CEOs in the investment banking sector, who he knew had also been briefed in on the new currency, hoping to curry favor with them by sharing some of the Chinese projections. *Could come in handy later, when I start fundraising for my presidential bid*, he thought to himself.

Returning his thoughts to the deft application of power and influence that he was at the center of, he thought about how swiftly the Chinese would do their part. He imagined the positive knock-on effects that the Chinese surge in commodity purchases would have on the commodities-producing nations, such as Canada and Australia, who would quickly ramp up production to fulfill the massive influx of orders from China. Even in the beleaguered US manufacturing sector, an unprecedented surge in orders for American-made automobiles – mostly SUVs and pick-ups – as well as commercial aircraft, would benefit the US economy right from the start. A series of large orders of vehicles, aircraft and other manufactured goods had also been penned during the Secretary of State's secret visit to China. It would be an economic stimulus of astonishing proportion, "economic shock-and-awe", as Parker had put it.

That had been two weeks ago.

By the time the Secretary of State had arrived in Canberra, still a dozen days before the official announcement, the global financial sector had already taken an uptick, likely due to the smaller surge of investments being made by insiders the world over who were positioning themselves to benefit from the official announcements to come. *Not a problem*, thought Webber, *as long as the general population does not catch on to the profiteering of those of us in the know. Who knows*, Webber rationalized, *maybe the profiteering would make the stimulus that much more effective.* Thinking like that really took the sting out of any ethical debate that may have been going on in his subconscious. *Maybe what I've done really is not wrong after all*, he thought to himself reassuringly.

President Parker had pinned her entire administration on the economic boom expected to follow the currency reform, when she had taken the gamble of essentially giving China and other creditor nations the bulk of the American gold reserves, in the form of the gold-backed currency. Were China to hoard the notes, or redeem them for physical gold, the new currency would fail just as the former president's "New US Dollar" had failed the previous year. Parker had determined that she would have to order the confiscation of all privately held gold bullion and coins, to coincide with the release of the new gold-backed currency. There simply was not enough gold left in the treasury to back the new currency. So they would have to put some Draconian practices into effect, imprisoning a few gold hoarders in the first few days, to put fear into the population at large and to motivate compliance with the confiscation order.

But now that the Chinese had promised to play their part, it was clear that President Susan Parker's gamble would work and that the new $G USD would instantly become the global reserve currency and stop the American slide into anarchy and civil war that, by all accounts, was otherwise inevitable.

Those economic and trade issues had been only half of the story. The corresponding military dimension, perhaps the more urgent motivation for his junket in Asia and Oceana, had been a much more delicate matter.

If global trade was about to restart, then the global trade routes would be where the dust would settle. If China were not contained, and American hegemony in the region were not restored, than China would have America – and the world – by the balls.

But with shortages of fuel, spares, and the draw-down of military personnel over the recent years of unproductive austerity; and automatic budget cuts having wreaked havoc over procurement and routine maintenance of their war-fighting apparatus; the American military simply did not have the global reach and expeditionary power projection capabilities it once had. The example of the USS Miami, a Los Angeles class nuclear powered attack submarine that had been damaged in a fire a few years ago, and not repaired due to budget cuts, was a prime example of an essential war-fighting capability that was simply allowed to go un-repaired. It reminded Secretary Webber of the decade after the fall of the Soviet Union, when the world's number two power had gone broke and allowed her once great military to 'rust out', her armed forces becoming a tragic joke.

And just as Russian President Ivan Valeriovich Dvorkin had begun when seizing power after the Putin assassination, President Parker and her cabinet had put the restoration of the American military as her highest priority, albeit after the restoration of sound money.

America was still the most powerful nation on earth, but no longer had the resources to offset China's massive military buildup. So by virtue of many small bilateral agreements with allies in the Asia Pacific region, the American 'pivot to Asia' strategy had been to build a grand alliance of nations who could each contribute key components of a power block, with American in overall command.

Taiwan and Singapore were still armed to the teeth, representing a constant annoyance to China. South Korea and Japan were staunch American Allies and hosted a robust American military presence.

A recent conflict between Japan and China over the otherwise worthless Senkaku/Diaoyu Islands had almost provoked a war that would have drawn the US into direct confrontation with China at just the wrong time. Washington had applied extraordinary pressure to convince Japan to back off, and let China seize the tiny, uninhabited rocks in favor of cooling tempers and garnering some good-will from the Chinese. To Secretary Webber, however, the move could have been as foolish as attempts to appease Adolph Hitler in the years prior to the Second World War. There had been one positive aspect of the Diaoyu Islands crisis, he reflected, in that the US had a pretext to beef up the Seventh Fleet and the number of troops permanently stationed in Japan and South Korea.

The impoverished Philippines, having had enough of Chinese espionage and heavy-handedness over disputed islands in the South China Sea, and Chinese moves to extract under-sea resources, had expanded their military ties with the United States, accepting billions of dollars in military aid which, comprised of small arms and transport capabilities, bolstered the number of men under arms who could be counted as solidly US-friendly.

Lacking the natural resources and strategic location of their more China-friendly neighbors in Indonesia, the Philippines were playing the only card that they had left, and improving the quality of life of their citizens just enough, through American food-aid, to hold their one hundred million citizens happy enough that they would not embrace the Islamicism that had so destabilized other south Asian nations.

In exchange, the Philippines agreed to work with the Americans on a few unique capabilities, keeping the potential conflict with China in mind, and had also agreed to provide additional bases for American Naval, Air, and ground forces.

Indonesia, located between Australia and the Malay peninsula, was the most strategic of the south Asian nations he had visited. It straddled the shipping lanes between the western Pacific Ocean and the Indian Ocean – the direct link from the Persian Gulf to Asia. Once a staunch military ally for the U S, Indonesia had become increasingly independent, charting their own course. Playing both sides for the maximum economic benefit, the Indonesians had continued to accept American military aid, but were far more involved with economic partnerships with mainland China. China would fund, plan, and construct major infrastructural projects in exchange for guarantees of long-term supplies of the agricultural, mineral and oil resources which Indonesia possessed.

The world's most populous Muslim nation, Indonesia's two hundred and fifty million inhabitants were becoming increasingly anti-American, resenting any effort to sway them from becoming a major economic and military presence in the area.

Despite his best efforts, the best that Secretary Webber could achieve on his 3-day visit was to have the Indonesians agree not to shut down several American factories, such as the iconic soft-drink factory in Jakarta that had been symbolic of American cultural dominance. For this, he had been forced to agree that the American Embassy in Jakarta would be moved from its prominent location on the Jelan Medan, at the south end of the Merdeka, to be relegated to second-class status and moved to the banking district along Jalan Kebon. It was deeply offensive to the

Americans; however, it did allow for a comprehensive re-design of the new embassy, which would allow for greatly improved security features. What really put salt into the wound was that the original US embassy site would be demolished by a Chinese-owned construction company. The contract to build a new, and by all accounts impressive, venue to rival the art gallery, museums, embassies and palaces of the embassy district would be another Chinese firm. And the new inhabitants of this glorious building would be a new Chinese Embassy.

When he had heard that, feeling the acceleration of the Boeing as it climbed out of Soekarno Hatta, the Jakarta International Airport, the sinking feeling that pulled him down into his seat was not due to the acceleration of the jet. It was his realization, *we are truly fucked in Indonesia.*

When word of this had spread throughout the aircraft, on the flight from Jakarta to Canberra, it took a toll on the diplomats. Fortunately, their visit to Australia had gone much better.

With Indonesia now solidly out of the American sphere of influence, Australia was now the most strategically important ally in the region. Also in close proximity to the shipping lanes from the Indian Ocean to the South China Sea, and with her treasure trove of commodities, Australia had agreed to commit the Royal Australian Navy and Royal Australian Air Force to a wartime role of interdicting of Chinese shipping. They had also agreed to increase the number of P-3C Orion antisubmarine warfare aircrews, to be ready to hunt for China's increasingly capable fleet of SSK diesel, SSN nuclear, and SSBN ballistic missile submarines.

Thinking of the naval warfare strategy, the Secretary of State put his mind to the question of Australia's problem with their Air Warfare Destroyer program. Only one of three *Hobart* class destroyers had been launched, with the second one falling even farther behind schedule at the Osborne Shipyard near Adelaide. With some of the hull modules manufactured at two other Australian shipyards and a few coming from as far away as Spain, there were all sorts of problems when the large blocks did not fit together correctly, completely stalling the project time after time.

The Australians had gone against the American's advice back in 2008, when they had chosen a Spanish hull design and attempted to cobble together enough shipbuilding capabilities in Australia rather than add their order to the renewed production run of the highly reliable American *Arleigh Bourke* class. With another 16 such hulls coming out of the shipyards in Maine and Mississippi over the coming years, enough to keep the shipyards working at least part time during these years of austerity, and with no major changes to the highly successful hull design, the Australians could have given the shipyard some much-needed orders and benefitted by avoiding all of the teething problems they were having, and they could have avoided a decade of delays and skyrocketing costs.

But the Americans had yielded to Australian diplomatic pressure to support the Australians' decision to go with the Spanish hull design and the overly complex arrangements with the three Australian shipbuilders involved. Yet the Aussies still wanted to use the American's *Aegis* combat system and the associated Lockheed Martin SPY-1D passive radar, fire control system and SM-2 Standard Missile family of weapons. This would give the new Australian fleet of three *Hobart* class destroyers an effective area missile defense capability for Task Group Defense, the protection of forces deployed ashore and an area and high value unit umbrella capability that could extend as far as 150 nautical miles from the ship.

In exchange for the technology transfer, the Americans had taken their pound of flesh out of the Australians, demanding increased basing rights in Australian territory. While the Australians were staunch allies of the United States, fighting side-by-side with the Americans in each and every war, their domestic political problems required that Americans not appear to operate anything like independent American military bases in Australia. For appearances sake, American military personnel had to be 'guests' on Australian bases, and to 'rotate troops' through short periods of time on so-called 'Combined Joint Exercises'.

Ever since the leaked contents of the secret version of Australia's White Paper on National Defense had disclosed to the world what the Australian military was expected to contribute to the American-led alliance, assisting with Air and Naval forces blockading Chinese shipping in the region, the cat had been out of the bag.

Everybody understood that the blow-back would mean that in the event of hostilities, the Chinese would retaliate against targets inside Australian territory. Not only had that leak enraged a sizeable proportion of the neutral-leaning Australian population, but it had also revealed the American's ambitions for increased basing rights in Australia, to go along with their increased presence in South Korea, the Philippines, and more recently, Vietnam, as a direct counter to expanded Chinese bases in Sri Lanka, Pakistan, Myanmar and now Thailand.

The irony was that the world's two largest economies and closest trading partners, with a deeply co-dependent fiscal and commercial relationship, were fast becoming a dangerous military rivalry. It was a dangerous game they were playing, and one side had the advantage of thousands of years of intrigue.

On a smaller scale, the Australians were also gaming the Chinese, supplying commodities to China while at the same time agreeing to increase their military commitments to the American-led containment of China. It was a ludicrous but very real and tense diplomatic dance which all parties avoided publicly acknowledging, pretending that by keeping the intense love-hate relationship with China unspoken, the ridiculous was somehow sublime. If not knowingly, then they were deeply self-deluded.

With strong public opposition to American bases in Australia, South Korea, Japan and in other Asia-Pacific countries, the American vision of establishing a network of bases and facilities, which could be ramped up and used at any time the Americans saw fit, was becoming increasingly difficult to achieve. The Australian request for the radar and missile technology transfer, and their choice not to purchase the two billion dollars' worth of ships from American shipyards, had presented Secretary Webber with a golden opportunity to strong-arm the Australians into quietly signing off on a secret agreement which effectively gave the Americans the right to move in and 'borrow' whatever space they required from any Australian defense installation anywhere within the Australian territory, but to do so in the guise of Combined Joint Task force exercises.

The first such expansion of the American footprint had been done years before, in the form of creating a Marine Air Ground Task Force Australia, "MAGTFA", basing 2,500 Marines on a so-called 'rotational' basis at the Royal Australian Army's Robertson Barracks facility in Darwin, Northern Territory, along with increased Aerial Port of Disembarkation, APOD, operations at RAAF Tindal, NT, and other RAAF airfields.

The deal also included dredging of the harbor and other improvements which amounted to a quiet expansion of the tiny Royal Australian Navy docks in Darwin. This would also allow for easier Sea Port of Disembarkation, SPOD, operations for the Marines from the Third Marine Division, as they rotated personnel and equipment in and out of Darwin from their bases in Okinawa and Hawaii. It was all about paving the way for Strategic Lines of Communication, SLOC – the air and sea pathways that could be used to deploy millions of tons of supplies and potentially tens of thousands of personnel into Australian territory, without being held up in negotiations and politics.

That had been the deal struck back in 2013, but the actual ramping up of the MAGTFA was only now taking place, along with a quiet expansion of CIA and other intelligence units footprints at 'space antenna' and other communications facilities scattered throughout Australia.

The expansion of the American complex at Pine Gap, near Alice Springs, was accomplished without any official paperwork whatsoever. The Australian government was that eager to have a larger commitment from the Americans, as Chinese dominance in the region was a profound worry for them.

Overall, the American diplomats had been happy with the arrangements and supported the Australian's naval program as it limped along. But with only one ship produced so far and an unending series of misfit hull blocks, integration problems and now legal conflict between the participants in the 'Sea 4000

Program', the Aussies were sorely lacking in missile defense capabilities and it now looked like the *HMAS Brisbane* and the *HMAS Sydney* would not be completed for another three to six years. That left *HMAS Hobart* as Australia's only operational air warfare destroyer.

Webber took off his glasses and gazed outside the window into the distance. *They will need the Brisbane and Sydney sooner than that.* He thought back with horror on very recent history, the conflict that had scarred and changed the world forever. The Middle East Nuclear Exchange, MENE, that had taken place when Iran and Israel had traded nuclear blows so suddenly, that had devastated the region. Then short months later came the far greater devastation of the nuclear war between India and Pakistan. Like shoppers at a year-end sales frenzy, every nation then rushed to get as much missile defense capability as they could get their hands on.

The jury was still out whether the American support to India, with stealth bombers and hundreds of cruise missiles, had provided enough of a first-strike advantage to limit the counter-strike ability of the new regime in Pakistan. 'Operation Peregrine Eagle', OPE, had been considered a success as it had achieved the goal of decapitating the Islamo-Fascists, loyal to Mualana Abdul Aziz and those of the Pakistani Army who had participated in the massive coup. But the fallout, particularly in India, had been devastating. Scores of Pakistan's one hundred and eighty warheads, mostly in the thirty kiloton range, had rained down on cities and bases throughout India. With the increased range of the Shaheen-II, and the increased accuracy and countermeasures of the Ghazvani missiles, the death throes of the short-lived 'True Islamic State of Pakistan' had delivered a terrible retribution on their Indian attackers.

And the world did not care. There was not even an uproar over the American support for the pre-emptive strike and the subsequent invasion of Pakistan by India. So while there were the predictable histrionics at the United Nations, there was not much of an international humanitarian response. It was as if, with the nuclear war genie now out of the bottle in two wars in less than 12 months, the world had largely accepted the notion that large scale conflict in far-away lands was unavoidable. With over two hundred million dead, the scale of the disaster in South Asia was beyond the ability of average people to come to grips with. They had largely put it out of their minds and focused inwardly on problems closer to home, such as the extremely high unemployment and social unrest that was threatening to tear apart the fabric of both Europe and the United States.

Despite the American complicity and active participation in the war between India and Pakistan, the world had largely turned their backs on that troubled Islamist nation. It was not so much that people did not care about the suffering of the untold millions of casualties from the radiation and from the conventional arms which India used to subdue Pakistan in the aftermath, it was just that they had heard enough grievous news stories originating from Pakistan over the years - and the many American and other NATO soldiers who had perished in Afghanistan. So the world had little sympathy, and was basically not concerned about the Indian annexation of the defeated Pakistan.

But the Chinese *were* concerned. With the Pakistani threat on India's left flank now neutralized, and with a massive re-construction and military mobilization now underway in India, China saw their South Asian rival as a major new threat. This was particularly underlined with India's now uncontested dominance over the Indian Ocean – the shipping lanes that were so crucial to the flow of the oil and mineral commodities that were the lifeblood of China's hungry economy.

So while the increased ability of India to project power in the region may have been the primary source of China's own need to increase their military presence in the area, and the corresponding decades-long build-up of Chinese military hardware, the Americans had no choice but to come up with a strategy to offset the imbalance and to preserve at least the notion of American dominance in the region. It was a very complex region, with a large proportion of global trade passing through the narrow choke point at the Strait of Malacca.

The Chinese strategy had been to build up military bases all the way from the Persian Gulf to the South China Sea. This 'String of Pearls' strategy represented a direct threat to American military hegemony in the region, and ultimately upped the risk of China emerging as the dominant military power in the strategically critical shipping route. Having evolved strong ties with Indonesia, militarily and economically, China was on the verge of locking up the sea-lanes. All they had to do was complete the build-up of a 'blue water navy' and base a sizeable enough fleet out of Indonesia, a development well within the range of possibilities, and China would be able to put the US 7th fleet out of the Strait of Malacca. And by aggressively expanding their Air Defense Identification Zone, ADIZ, as they had in late 2013, the Chinese were expanding the reach of their increasingly capable force of PLAAF fighter-interceptors, with SU27s and SU30s. The result was to cut off American, Japanese, Korean and Taiwanese access to a vast stretch of the air-space over the South China Sea.

The Australians shared the American assessment, and had accepted an increasingly active role in the strategic region. So Secretary Webber knew that he would be pressed for more American support on his visit to Canberra to meet with Australian defense officials. The Australian need for additional missile warfare defenses had been anticipated by Secretary of Defense, Joseph Alderman, and the Joint Chiefs. So the Pacific Fleet had been tasked with deploying three *Arleigh Bourke* guided missile destroyers to the region, which Admiral Beatty, Commander US Pacific Fleet, decided to send from 3rd Fleet, based in San Diego, rather than from the 7th Fleet, in Japan, so as not to diminish the firepower based in Japan to offset China's rapidly expanding naval presence. This was on top of the fact that there were now five Aircraft Carrier Strike Groups operating in the Asian Pacific theatre, with two Strike Groups dominating both ends of the Straits of Malacca.

As the Secretary of State recalled from the last briefing on the disposition of naval forces in the region, Carrier Strike Group 5 was on exercise with the Indian-modified Kiev class carrier,

INS Vikramaditya and her Battle Group in the Indian-dominated Bay of Bengal. *That will really piss off the Chinese,* he thought, as he visualized the CVN-73 USS George Washington Strike Group and the Indian Carrier Battle Group bearing down on the Chinese naval units stationed at the Chinese-funded and constructed dockyards in the Burmese port of Kyaukpyu.

But the strategic influence and ability to project power that a Carrier Strike Group offered came at an enormous financial cost, he thought to himself, recalling the CVN-78 USS Gerald R. Ford Carrier Strike Group, which was on its inaugural deployment somewhere in the Strait of Malacca. The first of the new X-Class of super-carriers, the cost of the Gerald Ford had come in at a staggering twenty billion old-style dollars.

With the collapse of the old US dollar, and President Parker's efforts to launch the new US Gold-Dollar, it would be a long time before the United States would be able to invest such colossal sums of money into new ships, let alone another X-Class carrier. This affected the Navy a great deal, as it drastically reduced the number of warships coming out of the shipyards.

Any contribution from the Australians to help control the Strategic Lines of Communication in the region was urgently needed by the US. If deploying some Air Warfare Destroyers to help protect the Australian Navy was the price to pay, the Americans would get far more in return. *The key is how it is all negotiated,* he thought.

Secretary Webber did not tell the Australians that *DDG 114 Ralph Johnson* and *DDG 111 Spruance,* were already being provisioned for deployment to Australia *and DDG 116 Thomas Hudner* was already passing the equator bound for an unscheduled port visit to Darwin, Northern Territory, Australia.

The Parker administration had decided to give the Australians the added missile defense capabilities but wanted the Australians to give them formal basing rights for a tri-service USAF, USN, US Army base in the Perth region, on the extreme west coast of the Australian continent. This would enable the US to have land-sea-and-air expeditionary power projection over the south Asia from the Indian Ocean to the South China Sea. It would be the American's second ever tri-service base, and would be modeled after the 87th Air Base Wing in New Jersey. The Department of Defense officials had recommended that they let the Air Force lead the planning for the proposed base in Western Australia, as the Navy and Army presence there would only be ramped up when required. The Air Force would have the largest footprint there on a day-to-day basis and would therefore be the most suitable branch of service to operate the proposed super-base in pre-war and post-activation modes. Hopefully there would be less inter-service rivalry than with the other super-bases, where resentment had seethed after the forced and poorly executed cobbling together of sister-services together after the last round of BRAC base closures.

On a personal level, Secretary Webber wondered if he was going to get any heat for holding shares in the engineering and construction consortium that would be given the three-year contract to build the super-base at Perth. In past years, up until the reforms that his President had ushered in, Washington was a great place to trade on such inside information, but President Parker – and Washington in general – had heard the American population loud and clear on such corruption. *I'd better liquidate my holdings in CHL before the stock goes up on the news. I'll still be up a lot. Better safe than sorry,* He thought, *besides, now I've got the Chinese tips to play – I'll make out like a bandit, and be well-positioned for my White-House run,* he thought with satisfaction.

With the super-base near Perth agreed to, Webber had decided not to press the Australians for a full-on USMC base near Darwin. *The current 'rotational' deal for MAGTFA is satisfactory for now. Maybe when the Australians become more worked up about the Chinese they'll beg us to formally base more Marines in the Northern Territory, so those negotiations can safely be put off for a few years,* he thought. *Once they put pen to paper on the Perth base, we'll reward them with the swift arrival of the three DDGs. In the meantime, I've got to keep the pressure on them to make the right decision and sign the revision to our Status of Forces Agreement. Once we have the new SOFA, we're in business. Their media can't even pry into the details of the Perth Agreement, because it all falls under their new 'Official Secrets Act'.'*

The US had given the Australians a ten-day window to communicate their decision, which should be in plenty of time for the *Thomas Hudner*'s arrival in Darwin. The tight timelines were necessary, as the Secretary of State would have to know the Australian answer before his upcoming trip to India.

Thinking of the thick India file he had not had time to review in depth, the Secretary of State felt a wave of exhaustion. He had not had more than five hours sleep any night in the past three weeks, and would only have a little over a week in Washington to catch up with the rest of cabinet. *Plenty of time to sleep when I'm dead*, he thought.

By reading the classified, annotated version of the 'Early Bird' every morning before breakfast, however, he had maintained a fairly up-to-date grasp of world events, and had paid some attention to what little the international media had to say about the status of disaster response in the aftermath of the Indo-Pak war.

Of course, in the United States, the loss of over two hundred million souls in India was only given lip-service, as many people actually believed that India had been overpopulated to begin with. He personally found that sort of attitude to be repugnant, and his heart went out to the poor victims of the nuclear war. His sympathy was equally given to the Pakistanis and the Indians, as he did not hold the civilians responsible for a war that was started by the Islamo-Fascists who had seized control of Pakistan and her arsenal of over 200 nuclear warheads. *Well, that war was actually started by India - but they had no choice*, he corrected himself.

He knew that the actual purpose of the meeting in India was really all about supporting the reconstitution of the Indian military, and not at all much about relieving suffering for the hundreds of millions of desperately poor, wretched civilians who were dying in India and Pakistan from the effects of the war.

The rapid restoration of the Indian military, after so many of their bases were destroyed in the war with Pakistan, was the anchor in the American strategy to contain China in the region. Without an effective Indian military, China would only be emboldened to increase their presence at their bases in Myanmar, Pakistan, Sudan, Thailand and soon, Indonesia.

China's attempt to secure their own supply of oil and other commodities from the Persian Gulf and Africa were in direct conflict with American interests in the region, so the proposed American super-base in Perth, and possibly one in India, were crucial to American long-term strategic goals.

Fortunately the outgoing administration had done a good job with the heavy lifting on these files, which ensured a smooth transition for the Parker Administration to continue these initiatives. For his part, the Secretary of State was confident that he would be able to conclude an agreement with the Indians. He had worked with some of their top military personnel before, in the ramp up to Operation Peregrine Eagle, which had paved the way for the Indian invasion of Pakistan.

Secretary Webber looked forward to meeting with Group Captain Patel, whose assessments on Chinese intentions seemed bang-on to the Parker administration. Hopefully he would have the ear of the incoming administration, especially with the risks posed by the incipient failure of Pakistan.

Having once been an Air Force pilot himself, Secretary Webber was impressed with India's steady build-up of Russian manufactured IL76-M air refueling tankers, and the upgrades the Indian Air Force had made to their Russian SU-27 and SU-30 fighters. So little was known about the true capabilities the Indians had added to the very reliable and super-maneuverable Russian multirole fighters, but recent exercises with Indian SU-27s working with American F-16s in Alaska had proven that the Indians knew what the hell they were doing and had been, before the Indo-Pak war, on the verge of becoming the world's second most powerful Air Force.

Webber slipped his glasses into his shirt pocket. Having put the Australian file out of his mind, and also having begun to look forward to getting back to Washington before his trip to India, Secretary of State Webber allowed himself to recline his comfortable seat back, and fall into a deep, unworried sleep.

SecState Webber had been asleep for about two hours when an aide woke him up, calling him up to the communications cabin, just aft of the cockpit.

Webber rubbed his eyes to get the cobwebs out.

"Take it slow, Colonel Redmund. I'm not even awake yet. What's up?"

"Sir. We got new orders. There's a copy of the message coming off the printer now, but it's quite simple. We're diverting to India. We'll be landing at Hyderabad in six hours." Webber stiffly pulled himself out of his chair and made his way to the communications cabin.

Reading the message with a frown on his face, Secretary Webber had read enough to know the gist of it. "What will our arrival time be in local time?"

"Uh, about noon, Sir."

"Shit!" said Secretary Webber, as he read the message: INDIA HAS COMMUNICATED THEIR INTENT TO CARRY OUT A RAID ON CHINESE WARSHIPS BASED AT KYAUKPYU IN THE BAY OF BENGAL. THEIR INTENTION IS TO DESTROY ONE OF CHINA'S SIX JIN CLASS SSBN BALLISTIC MISSILE SUBMARINES. THIS WOULD BE AN ACT OF WAR, AND MOST CERTAINLY PROVOKE A NUCLEAR RETALIATION BY THE CHINESE.

He read on: "IT IS UNCLEAR WHY THE INDIANS ARE CONSIDERING SUCH A DANGEROUS ACTION. IT MAY BE IN RESPONSE TO INCREASED PLA PRESENCE IN THE INDIAN LADAKH AND ASKAI CHIN PORTIONS OF THE TIBETEN PLATEAU. THE PLACEMENT OF CHINESE TROOPS IN THESE INACCESSIBLE MOUNTAINOUS AREAS HAS REKINDLED TENSIONS BETWEEN THE TWO MOST POWERFUL NATIONS IN THE REGION. OUR ASSESSMENT IS THAT THE INDIANS DO NOT INTEND TO CARRY OUT THE STRIKE AT KYAUKPYU. THEIR LIKELY INTENT IS TO PRESSURE THE CHINESE TO WITHDRAW THE JIN CLASS SUBMARINES OUT OF THE BAY OF BENGAL, IN

MUCH THE SAME MANNER AS PRESIDENT KENNEDY STARED DOWN THE SOVIETS OVER THE CUBAN MISSILE CRISIS. THEIR STRATEGIC GOAL SEEMS TO BE TO DENY THE CHINESE ACCESS TO THE BAY OF BENGAL WITH THEIR MEDIUM RANGE MISSILES. WHILE WE SUPPORT THIS GOAL, YOU ARE DIRECTED TO ENGAGE THE INDIANS TO ASCERTAIN WHETHER THEY WOULD ACTUALLY DESTROY A JIN CLAS SSBN, OR WHETHER IT IS THEIR INTENT TO BLUFF. IF YOU DETERMINE THAT THEY ARE INTENT ON ACTUALLY DESTROYING A TYPE 094 SUBMARINE, YOU ARE AUTHORIZED TO WARN THE INDIANS THAT THE UNITED STATES WOULD TAKE MEASURES AIMED AT MAKING SUCH AN ATTACK IMPOSSIBLE. WE DO NOT WANT TO SEE WAR BETWEEN INDIA AND CHINA, AND WILL TAKE EXTREME MEASURES TO PREVENT SUCH. S.P. PRESIDENT."

"What is it, Sir?" asked one of Webber's diplomatic team.

"Go ahead and read it for yourself." Webber said, handing the cable to his senior staffer.

The member of Secretary Webber's diplomatic team read the message quickly. "Holy Cow! Am I reading this right? If the Indians really mean to destroy a Chinese sub, are we are going to attack *India* to stop them?"

"I'm not certain that is what we will do, but we have to make them believe we are prepared to do exactly that."

"But Mr. Secretary, they are our allies. We need them to do just this, to push back against the Chinese. As far as I see it, if they can pressure the Chinese to pull their Type 94s out of the Bay of Bengal, isn't that the type of pressure we want India to achieve?"

"Sure, but you have to look at it from the Indian perspective. It worked when they actually did something like this to Pakistan in 1971. And more importantly, they just won a nuclear war with Pakistan. Despite the terrible loss of life and damage to their country, India has come out of this in a stronger strategic position. They may actually believe that war with China will somehow work out well for India. So I agree with this assessment. India may actually intend to sink the sub, and we do have to stop them. If that means we bend their arm, great. But if it means we have to destroy one of their SSKs, diesel subs, then we will do that if we have to."

"But Sir, if we take out one of India's SSKs then we will be at war with our ally. Besides, the Indians can just use one of those *Brahmos* hypersonic cruise missiles – their Air Launched Cruise Missile – to take out the Chinese SSBN in Burma. They could launch one from one of their warships at their navy base in the Andaman Islands. So taking out their attack sub would be ineffective".

"True, but if we convince them that we will degrade their military capabilities to avert a war, then they may agree to make the whole thing just a bluff," the Secretary of State said, not sure how he would achieve that.

"You know as well as I do that the Chinese are great poker players. They won't be pushed around by a bluff."

"I know, Pete," said Webber, looking beaten.

"This could get nasty in a hurry."

2

BANISHMENT

When he logged on to check his email on the computer in his cramped office at the Ranger School, Major Peter Weir had a momentary burst of excitement at the subject line of an as yet unread email.

It was his AI, Assignment Instructions. For a moment, he decided to print it off without reading any of it, so that he could share the joy of first reading the good news side by side with his wife, Cheryl. After eighteen years at his side his wife had earned it. She had thrown herself into the full range of activities that the spouse of an up-and-coming officer is expected to do, both inside and outside of the US Army officer's wives community. So now that he was about to be reassigned, Peter Weir knew that he owed a great debt to his wife, and the best way to begin to repay that debt would be for her to be the first to read the AI message.

They both hoped that he would be reassigned to 3rd Battalion, 75th Rangers just in time for 3rd Bn's rotation into the breach as the Ranger Ready Force, as one of three identical, rapidly-deployable special operations battalions. With the 3rd Bn about to rotate into the high-readiness role, ready to deploy anywhere across the globe within 18 hours, it was the best place to be for an officer as eager to face the ultimate command challenge – sudden, unexpected, and unrehearsed engagement with some ruthless enemy.

The 75th Ranger Regiment was well known and highly respected for their specialized skills ranging from air assault, direct action ops, infiltrations and exfiltrations, personnel recovery and so on - the full spectrum of special operations - but what was little known outside the Ranger community were their 'new talents' which amounted to a revolution in special operations thinking.

The Rangers were re-inventing themselves into post-asymmetric warfare specialists, ready to wage war – and interdict the enemy – in more nebulous circumstances that defied traditional definitions. And it was more than simply adapting the latest technology into their range of special equipment. It was more than using battle-space sensors and communications technologies to accelerate their OODA loop to the n'th degree – they could already 'Observe, Orient, Decide, Act' in a much tighter spiral than just about any potential adversary. No, the real revolution was in better *understanding* the battle-space context.

Simply put, the global war on terror had taught the Rangers that developing linguistic and cultural understanding required more than mere lip service, as the ability to assess the battle-space now required special ops forces to understand their opponents from their own perspective, quite alien to how North Americans typically see the world.

To be truly effective the world over, the 75th Ranger Regiment had begun to cultivate cohorts of regional specialists who could understand a variety of foreign languages, such as Russian, Hindi, Farsi, Arabic, Indonesian, Mandarin, Cantonese, Tagalog and Malay.

And Major Peter Weir was one of this new breed of Special Ops experts. He had spent the last four years studying and making himself an expert on one of the more prominent potential adversaries – China. While his grasp of Chinese was still quite rudimentary, his understanding of their cultural and historical influences was impressive, even to the native Chinese instructors who were guiding him. Teaching would be the wrong word, as Major Weir was given a great deal of freedom in how he approached his assignment, and he was autodidactic enough that his 'teachers' quickly found themselves in more of an advisory, supportive role.

On the strictly military side, he had become something of an expert on the order of battle, history, and the TTPs – Tactics, Techniques and Procedures - of the three million strong People's Liberation Army.

Getting his arms around the great diversity of the five main branches of the PLA – their ground forces, the PLA Navy, PLA Air Force, their strategic missile force and their reserve force had proven to be overwhelming, so Peter had focused on the command structure of the PLA, on the macro level, and also studied the highest readiness units, special operations forces and other rapid-reaction formations on the micro level.

His research amounted to a detailed, highly classified study of the highest readiness units that had been going through considerable changes over recent years, with particular emphasis paid to the People's Liberation Army's best equipped and most well trained 38TH Group Army, Beijing Military Region, the new "all brigade" 20th Group Army, Jinan Military Region, and, of course, the highest readiness units of the 42nd Group Army, Guangdong Military Region – of North Korea/Chosin Reservoir fame so deeply entrenched in American military lore.

He had submitted his analysis, aptly entitled "The New Red", over six months ago. Other than his CO's initially positive comments, he had received no further comment back from the chain of command. *Surely that won't hurt my chances,* Peter thought. *If anything, they should put me in as an A5 Planner with 3rd Battalion, where I can get involved in updating plans for and awareness of the Chinese threat – put some action into the 'pivot to Asia'.*

An assignment to such an operational unit, given his exceptional track record as a Major with the 75[Th] Ranger Regiment, could be accompanied by his promotion to Lieutenant-Colonel. And promotion had been on his mind for the last two years, not so much for the prestige and pay increase, but more for the range of topics he would be able to engage in as a light-colonel. As much as he enjoyed being a senior instructor on loan to the 4th Ranger Training Battalion, at the Ranger School in Fort Benning, Major Weir yearned for the more strategic cutting-edge side of the Special Operations world the he belonged to with the 75th Ranger Regiment, a special ops force of the US Special Operations Command, SOCOMD.

As he laid out in "The New Red", his own assessment was that the next war would be in Asia. He fully supported the US military's Pivot to Asia and had been carefully putting together special skills, including language training, that could help move his career along in the right direction.

He felt certain that the powers that be had noticed him, and would find a place for him as an operational planner with 3rd Btn, 75th Rangers. Perhaps they'd make him Deputy Chief of Staff, Operations. DCOS Ops would be perfect, but Major Weir knew that there was a risk that he had over-done his specialization on China and risked being reassigned to the Regimental Special Troops Battalion. That could still result in promotion, as there were lots of O-5s, lieutenant-colonels, in the RSTB, but it would probably result in a desk job and not a front line combat command role – therefore the end of his career progression.

Either way, he thought positively, *the promotion's got to be in the bag this time. The only question is what and where.*

But as he retrieved the message from the printer, and folded it so that he would not accidentally read any of it, Peter had a moment of doubt.

What if I have been passed by? What if I'm reassigned to yet another school, or some other garrison post? What if, God forbid, I have already hit my terminal rank? he thought. *Cheryl will be devastated. She has her heart set on being a general's wife, like her mother was. And her father would be so disappointed.*

Peter banished the negative thoughts from his mind by taking stock of all the reasons his promotion was assured, and his reassignment to a career-enhancing position was certain.

He knew that the US Army had borne the brunt of the savage cuts to defense spending in recent years, *but the Army has been cut to the bone as it is – they can't cut us anymore. And with guys retiring or taking those early retirement offers there's got to be some great billets opening up all over the place. And I'm due for mine.*

As he looked back on the highlights of his career, and the consistent way he had been moving along with his professional development, putting a tick in every required box – on time or ahead of his peers – he knew that he had done his part in the "up or out" career stream. Certainly he should do just as well as his buddy Steve had done.

Major Weir hung around at the Benning Brew Pub pretending to enjoy a beer. Some of his buddies teased him for refusing to tell them what his Assignment Instructions were, but he insisted on discussing them with "C-in-C-House" first. But while he sat and sucked back his brew, he began to worry again.

He had almost decided to give in to the temptation and read his AI message, when his pal Steve arrived to share a pint with him, and then give him a ride home. They had carpooled for years, for the chance for the best friends to have some time together each day and to save a few bucks in the process.

Saved from the pressure from the other officers, Major Peter Weir was somber and clearly in no mood for chit-chat. It was not just that there were NCO's around, making discussion of an officer's career path inappropriate. Had there still been an Officer's Club on base, where he could more openly talk career, he still would not have felt much like talking about it. But he was more than willing to listen to Steve's own good news, even if he was not willing to reciprocate.

Years of experience told his friend to leave it alone and just drive Peter home. Steve guessed correctly that Peter was upset about his reassignment, but he knew better than to pry. Sooner or later Peter would let him know.

For his own part, Steve had already shared his own Reassignment Orders with Steve, at the Brew Pub, and really appreciated the sincerity in Peter's congratulatory comments.

When Steve slowed his car to a stop in front of Peter's Married Quarters in the sleepy neighborhood on the far side of the sprawling base in Fort Benning, Georgia, the change in pace seemed to wake Peter from his reverie.

"Sorry, Steve. I should have told you on the way here. I got my Orders."

"I thought as much. You get just the AI, or the full PCS?"

"Come on, you know how long it takes for that stuff." They both knew it usually took months for a Permanent Change of Station message to come out of the Personnel Reassignment Work Centre."

"That's how it used to be. But let me tell you, ever since that last RAR back in 2012, the Orders have been flying out of the PRWC like you wouldn't believe."

"RAR?" asked Peter.

"Rapid Action Revision – you know, to our beloved Department of the Army Regulation 600-8-11? Reassignment – Personnel - General?" Steve said, as he stopped the car. He had an encyclopedic skill at rolling off Regulation titles and numbers that sometimes stopped Peter in his tracks – he had trouble keeping up with the guy. "How long since your last reassignment – three years, right? Well, a lot has changed in how they administer our reassignments now. Don't you read the revisions to Admin Orders?"

"Yeah, right. As if I have the time for that," Peter said, shifting uncomfortably. He didn't want to appear behind the loop, not even to Steve. "It's really not been on my radar, what with my focus on the Chinese. What're the important changes?"

"Not much, really," Steve's voice changed to a monotone as he quoted Army regulations, *"The Reassignment processing begins upon receipt of Assignment Instructions and ends with the issuance of Permanent Change of Station orders in accordance with Army Regulation 600–8–105..."*

"Knock it off, Radar O'Reilly! I know the regs!" He had read them. Just not as closely as Steve, apparently. It rankled him a bit, and he was already chafing over the uncertainty he was feeling. "Just tell me what's changed, will you? Otherwise I'm going in there blind, and you know how Cheryl is about this sort of thing. Come on, make it easy on me. What's changed that matters to me?"

"Well, if you don't like what's in your AI, you can't pull a compassionate as easily as before, that's for one thing. Now you'd need a colonel / O-6 endorsement, at least in the case of outside the continental US - based unit." Steve looked Peter in the eye and with emphasis added: " – if that's what we're talking about." Steve paused a beat, waiting for Peter to react to his fishing. But no response came, simply because Peter still did not know what was in his AI. Steve carried on. "And you have to ask for an involuntary foreign service tour extension in lieu of an operational deletion or deferment now. Oh, and they also added an internal control evaluation to cut down on CO's playing favourites and re-shuffling the post-plots. Now only the DCOS G1 has the authority to approve exceptions or waivers."

Peter understood what that meant, "So no matter what my reassignment, I'm stuck with it. No room to maneuver anymore?"

"Sorry to say so, but yeah, that's how it adds up now. Of course, you could throw the medical. They've also added that PRWC's have to incorporate our medical readiness classification into the reassignment process, but that's based on your med status *before* you get your AI, so not much you can do with that. Even playing the family crisis card, and any other compassionates, is basically a non-starter these days."

"Why all these changes? They having more trouble fitting pegs into holes, or what?"

"No, Pete, it's all about *velocity*. How fast they can move people about. They keep changing our strategic focus. One day it's the 'pivot to Asia', the next it's cranking up readiness in eastern Europe. Now it looks like they're trying to do both. That's what I think is behind these changes, they have to be able to reassign us faster, in weeks rather than months."

"Like we are on a war footing again?" A year or two back Peter would have asked a question like this with a gung-ho, ready-to-jump attitude. The eagerness of the soldier was still there, but there was a slight weariness tinged with dread in his question now. Too much had happened in the world lately; the subtle shifting of attitude was creeping across military men everywhere.

"Exactly, buddy. Steve said with bravado, but his eyes shared the same attitude. "So what gives, where are you going?"

"Can't say. Don't know. Believe it or not, I'm not going to read my AI until I'm with Cheryl." He stared down in his lap as if preparing for a profound disappointment. "I don't have a good feeling about it. I think I'm going to lose my promotion."

In the silence that ensued Steve shut off the car and sat with his best friend, unsure of what he could say. He knew how keenly Peter felt about this, and how much he wanted to please Cheryl and everyone else. *Everywhere else, Peter was solid as a fuckin' rock,* Steve thought, *but when it comes to Cheryl...but what can I say to Pete about that?* Deep down, everybody was getting a little scared these days. *But who would ol' Pete have to look to for strength if not his pal Steve? I gotta help the poor guy, somehow.* Steve was too good a friend to ignore what Peter was going through. No, it was his place to buck him up, give him the spirit to do what had to be done.

"Into the breach, then, buddy," Steve said, suddenly, before elbowing Peter sharply in the ribs to break him out of his funk. "Get the hell out of my car and call me when you need to get drunk!"

Peter turned to Steve, surprised. "Screw you too, pal!" he laughed. It worked.

"Get out of here, ya bum," Steve smiled.

After meeting her husband Peter at the door and giving him her customary, passionate kiss, Cheryl gave him the 'I'm annoyed with you' look.

"So were you celebrating with the boys at the Brew Pub while I was dying here, or what?"

"No, Sugar, I had to wait for Steve. He was held up with the CO. You know what? He got the Russia Desk at the Pentagon! Svetlana will be so pleased."

"That's a good move for them, right?"

"Oh yeah, he'll be a full-bull within three years in that job."

"So what's he got to complain about?"

"He has to go on another one of those solo deployments, so another six months away from Svetlana and the twins before he can take the job."

"Where to?"

Peter shrugged. "Can't say." Cheryl understood, she'd heard Peter say that simple phrase before. "Somewhere he can bump up his Russian language skills to 'working proficiency' before he takes the desk job in Washington," he offered to her. It was the best he could give her. Peter could not divulge the actual assignment his buddy was given, that of spending two months in pre-deployment training and then ultimately another four months inserted into the Russian version of the United Nations Military Observer Course.

As a foreign officer in the RUSUNMOC program, Steve would have a great opportunity to rub shoulders with a few dozen Russian officers in Solnechnogorsk, the sprawling Russian military base outside of Moscow.

Ostensibly an opportunity to contribute to a Confidence and Security Building Measure, CBSM, and polish-up on his Russian language skills, it was really all about putting Steve in the Solnechnogorsk region. While he was officially going to be attending the harmless UN-related course at the Russian Federation's 'Higher Officer's Academy, VYSTREL, he would also have a plausible explanation for spending his off-duty time poking around the roads and towns in the Solnechnogorsk region at large.

Despite being an Army officer with no overt connection to USSTRATCOM, Major Weir understood the significance of his pal's assignment. He and Steve had both studied the Russian military earlier in their careers in preparation for duty as Arms Inspectors. The two Rangers were supposed to focus on the security protocols the Russian Federation were developing to watch over the warheads stripped off of the missiles as part of the START-III treaty, but that had been cancelled after the Putin assassination, when the relations with Russia had taken a turn for the worse as Russia went through another period of instability.

Peter knew that the bunker where Russian President Dvorkin would evacuate to in time of war, the massive underground complex of 1st Missile Attack Warning Division, just happened to be buried deep under the Vystrel Academy in Solnechnogorsk, where the innocent-seeming RUSUNMOC program was hosted.

Peter did not envy his buddy's assignment, as he now saw the Russian angle to be something of a dead-end, career wise. The heady days of the Cold War with Russia were over. Russia would never be strong enough to compete with the USA. To Peter, the Russians were the 'old red'. But he could not discuss this with his wife, as Steve's assignment was highly classified, and even he himself already knew more about it than he should.

"Inside Russia, I bet," she guessed, accurately, before moving on to what really mattered to her. "So what did we get? - Tell me. TELL ME!" She jumped at him, laughing like a little girl on Christmas morning.

"I can't tell you. I have to show you."

After fighting her off for a few seconds, as she dug her hands into his shirt, his pants, and mussed his hair as if she were giving him a body-cavity search, he pulled out the AI message from the breast pocket of his fatigues.

"Here it is. I haven't read it Cheryl, so I don't know if it is good news or not."

Cheryl released him and moved back a step. Their world went dead quiet in that moment. Her eyes bore into his with a meaningful intensity.

Her voice was low but it cut through the stillness. "Go ahead. Read it out loud. You tell me where we're going."

Peter began reading out loud, and then froze, silent, with the paper sagging in his hands. Cheryl hesitated for a moment, then snatched the document and read the message for herself. It was in ALL CAPS, confusing to read at first, even though she had read several of her husband's previous career related messages.

After scanning through several lines of incomprehensible addressee lines, she read out loud: "Assignment Instructions, Weir, Peter, Major, Serial Number… blah blah….Sydney, Australia! What the fuck is this, Peter?"

"Give it back," he grabbed the message from her and read it again more carefully, from end to end.

Cheryl was sideswiped by this. Australia might as well have been the moon to her. "Is this some kind of mistake? What does that do for us? You said it would be a front-line unit. What is this, another school or something? What's that going to do to Jake?- It'll ruin his university plans! What…?"

"Stop! Let me work through this a second," Peter snapped at his wife, uncharacteristically, but it had no effect on her.

"You gotta call the CO. Better yet, I'll call his wife," she said, her voice rising with her increasing panic. "This has to be all about all your bullshit with Gary, you guys were way too outspoken about Ranger Training Battalion being ordered to admit women to the Training Brigade back in 2013."

"That wasn't it," he replied. Peter and Gary had never said a thing about women as Rangers, only that it was bad policy to direct that RTB to pass all the female candidates, regardless of performance. That would have made it impossible to flush out any under-performing candidates. They felt that such policy would have been a cancer to the profession and they spoke out about it. *Sure, it may have been a dicey move in a politically-correct climate, but it couldn't have screwed me here — could it?*

"Yeah, well, you screwed us somehow, Pete. And this shit reassignment is the consequence," she accused him, remembering her father's disappointment at her husband's activism. *I'll never be a general's wife now!* she thought, tears welling up on top of the anger still pulsing in her face. She threw her forearm across her face to hide her tears.

Peter would sooner have faced a dozen enemy hand-to-hand than disappoint Cheryl. In the Army he was as manly as the rest of them, but with his wife he was vulnerable. He was determined to stay calm. "Enough! Just let me think," he said, his eyes poring over the document. "Don't go jumping to conclusions. This could be good..."

"What do you mean?" Cheryl asked, her voice thick with despair.

"This is a LnO posting."

"What's that?"

"Liaison Officer. This is way more important than an S5 planning billet. Don't worry. It could ultimately lead to a Military Attaché assignment, as a full bull Colonel. This really is a stepping stone, Cher."

Cheryl lowered her arm from her eyes and looked at him.

"Explain," she commanded.

"I'm going to work as the US Army Liaison to the Special Ops Command of the Australian Army for the next three years. I'll be officially attached to 2 Commando Regiment, and serve as their deputy Ops O, based in Holsworthy. That's in Sydney — a world-class city. In fact, it's the hometown of your favorite actress, from that film we watched last week. Anyhow, you'll love it there, so will Jake."

Speechless, Cheryl Weir was skeptical, and just looked at him with an expression that said: "Bullshit!"

"This is an important job. I'll be sharing tactics, techniques and procedures, helping them with their exercises, and being the link between our 75th Rangers and their Special Ops Command. That puts me in the loop with their four-ringers and above on a daily basis. I'll be reporting to General Wattley directly. No, Sugar, this is actually good news for us."

"Well, if you say so. I personally think Steve and Svetlana are going to get their Colonel's way faster, using that Russian angle. Maybe you should put more effort into learning Chinese," she said.

"Why?"

"Well, you and Steve used to joke that if you learned enough Russian then you could get a job with the Red Army when they take over. But now that the Russians are in such a mess, and it's all about China, maybe we should map out your career prospects with the People's Liberation Army," she said, sarcastically.

Peter continued to scan the document and suddenly he relaxed. He looked up at her with a little smile.

Cheryl saw his sudden change. "What?"

"Aren't you going to congratulate me?"

Her brow furrowed more deeply. "For what, this career-ending banishment to the outback?"

"No, my dear. I think you better read paragraph 10 again," he handed her the message and then went over to the bar to fix them a couple of drinks.

Unable to believe her eyes as she read it over and over, she stammered: "So this means…"

"Yup. I leave Ranger Training Battalion a Major, and arrive in Australia a Light Colonel. I got it, Sugar Pie, I'm promoted!"

Later that night, after making love to the wife of a Lieutenant-Colonel, soon-to-be LCol Weir sat at his desk in the study, and poured over his atlas. He looked at China from the Australian perspective and wondered how it must feel to the twenty five million Australians to have over a billion Chinese so nearby, so hungry for their resources, and so capable of simply coming down and taking what they want at any time.

What have I gotten myself into? He thought, taking a long drink of whiskey before going back to bed.

Days later, after the shock of the unexpected posting to Australia had sunken in, Major Weir got into a discussion about China with some of his friends in 3rd Btn, 75th Rangers, who would be next in rotation for the high readiness duty as the Ranger Ready Force.

"So if we ever do go to war with China, how are we set for Chinese language in 3rd Battalion?" Peter asked.

"I know we have some Chinese names on the rolls, and I'm sure at least some of them speak Chinese. We've probably got at least a dozen Chinese speaking Rangers. Mostly comms types, actually," said the unit's S1, Personnel Admin O.

"What about white guys? Have we got any white guys who speak Chinese?"

"Actually, Pete, now that you mention it, I don't think we do, at least not with the Officers. I've read all their pers files and something like that would have stood out. Mind you, I was not really thinking about China. Maybe I could go through them again, or get the CO to approve a call for Chinese speakers within the unit. Too bad you're not going to be with us in the 'third'. So what are you thinking, Pete? – getting some of the boys to do some professional development with China in mind? Could be a good idea…. "

When Major Weir got home that night, he found that Cheryl had out-done herself cleaning the house and meeting him at the door dressed as if they were expecting house guests. Her excited, friendly manner made him feel like the astronaut in the 70's show, *I Dream of Jeannie,* by the way she seemed to be so eager to please. He sensed that she had begun to see herself as a Colonel's wife, fully embracing the obligation to be ready at the drop of a hat to entertain other senior officers, generals and the occasional diplomat. *She certainly has adjusted fast*, Peter thought.

At about the same time as Peter and Cheryl Weir were getting used to their news, in their military home in Battle Park, Fort Benning, another military family was having a similar conversation in their nearly identical military home in the military housing community at Joint Base Lewis McChord, in Washington State.

The two families had never met, living on opposite sides of the country, and yet they had a lot in common. On the other hand, the differences, between the Ranger Major and the Marine Corps Captain were stark; they lived in completely different military cultures.

For Captain Joseph Blakely, his Permanent Change of Station Orders were not a surprise. He knew that the 3rd Marines were looking for augmentation to fill a variety of positions as they ramped up their numbers in the Marine Air Ground Task Force – Australia, MAGTFA, pronounced 'MAGTAF'. They also had to back-fill positions made vacant in Okinawa and Honolulu, where the bulk of the personnel assigned to the MAGTFA came from.

Also up for an operational tour and hoping for one that would fit his career plans, Blakely and his wife knew right away that their posting to Darwin, Australia was career-positive. It meant a promotion to Major fully a year ahead of schedule. After three years with USSOCOM's 1st Special Forces Group out of Joint Base Lewis McChord, JBLM, Captain Blakely had yearned for a better assignment.

His current job was leading a small detachment of US Marines fitting into a larger US Army formation. His USMC Special Operations Capable Force Recon Detachment was MARSOC's contribution to a larger Special Operations force, 4th Battalion, 1st Special Forces Group, a formation of "Green Berets", in the US Army, and not part of the USMC itself.

Leading a USMC unit of any size is an honour. However to have his unit embedded with Green Berets of the US Army, with their lumbering, constrained operating procedures, frustrated

Captain Blakely and his Recon Platoon to no end. He felt completely cut off from the fold of the USMC, as did his men. He was orphaned from other Marines, both geographically and in terms of mission.

The one thing he really did enjoy about working with the US SOCOM was their focus on Foreign Internal Defense, or what was more commonly known as "counter-insurgency". The doctrine of working closely with a nation to help them fight off an occupation or insurgency had great strategic appeal for the United States. This was especially true in the context of the 'pivot to Asia', where the seven or eight US-friendly "Host Nations" in the Asian Pacific region were hoped to fight off the Chinese. So supporting Foreign Internal Defense, FID, was expected to be a force multiplier for the US. In this larger picture, despite his misgivings as a Marine, Captain Blakely found common cause with his US SOCOM counterparts, along with other intangible benefits as a professional Special Forces operative, but that was not enough. He missed being with his fellow Marines.

Other than the forty men of his Force Recon Platoon, the only other Marines he saw on a daily basis at JBLM were the Marines from 4th Landing Support Battalion, USMC, also based in Fort Lewis. However, these Marines were not part of US SOCOM, and were really focussed on sending logistical support to the 3rd Marines more than getting involved in any deployments or direct action.

Blakely and his Force Recon men wore their USMC pattern combat uniform, "MARPAT", on a daily basis, and looked so different from the vast majority of soldiers and airmen at JBLM that they occasionally had comments from "the locals." When shopping in the PX, for example, Blakely had experienced people asking him if he was a visiting soldier from some foreign country. It was one thing to have anonymity, and not be identified as special forces, but it was another thing altogether not to be seen as an American serviceman. Of course this would never happen in a community serving a USMC base, like 1st Marine Division's Camp Pendleton, in San Diego, where Marines truly were at home.

Over a Jameson, double – neat, like his father the barrister drank when thinking through an upcoming court appearance, Captain Blakely sipped at his Irish whiskey while he thought about the pro's and con's of his Permanent Change of Station.

For any other captain, an accelerated promotion to major would have been enthusiastically embraced. The PCS detailed a three year assignment to a place called 'Robertson Barracks', in Darwin, Northern Territory, Australia as US Pacific Command, USPACOM, Host Nation Liaison Officer, HNLnO, within MAGTFA.

Being permanently assigned, even moving his entire family to live in Australia for the next three years, and working as the link between the Australian Army and the 3rd Marines, would have been seen as positive to just about any other Marine captain, but not for Joe Blakely.

The problem was that it took him out of SOCOM, out of the Special Ops world, and back into the Marine Corps proper. And that meant being confronted with hostility, alienation and animosity – not from the host nation military or the civilian population, the Australians, but from his very own USMC because of his recent Special Ops employment with MARSOC within SOCOM.

As a member of US Marine Corps Special Operations Command, MARSOC, Joe Blakely had been out of the mainstream of US Marines and thrown into a bizarre and artificial unit which, from the perspective of pretty much every other Marine, was an insult to the Corps.

The problem was one of reality versus self-perception for the Marine Corps. The reality was that the USMC had been under-represented within US Special Operations Command, USSOCOM, where the pre-eminent special forces of the various branches of armed services of the United States were managed. At the core of USSOCOM was the US Joint Special Operations Command, USJSOC, comprised of units such as the US Army 1st Special Forces Operational Detachment - Delta Force, US Navy Seal Team 6, and the US Air Force Special Tactics Squadron. However, in addition to the more specialized and well integrated units of USJSOC, USSOCOM at large drew from the Special Operations Commands of the US Army Ranger, US Air Force Special Ops Command, US Navy Seals, and, since 2006, the US Marine Corps Special Operations Command, MARSOC.

Captain Blakely had been with MARSOC for six years, and accepted the requirement for MARSOC to exist. But it flew in the face of Marines Corps self-perception. Blakely, living within this dual Marine – SOCOMD reality, had at first been surprised to encounter animosity from regular Marines, who saw themselves as part of the elite of the elite of US armed services; each and every Marine, in fact, was a special forces caliber soldier. To the Marines at large, MARSOC simply did not need to exist – as personified by MARSOC operators like Captain Blakely – as it implied that the rest of the Marine Corps was somehow less capable than those Marines attached to MARSOC; as if the MARSOC Marines were the 'first amongst equals'. Hence the insult.

Eventually Blakely accepted that bridging the gap between MARSOC and the rest of the USMC was way beyond his pay grade, and a problem that he did not have to deal with while working within 1st Special Forces Group at JBLM. But now that he was being reassigned to a front-line Marine unit, he had to come to terms with it.

His thoughts seemed to have stalled, bogging down on the question of his own re-integration into the fold, so he turned his attention to the LnO job itself.

Technically, he was being re-categorized as a "Miscellaneous Military Occupation Specialty, Category II, 8248 Foreign Area Officer, East Asia (Excluding PRC)". This meant that he had to develop a deep understanding not only of the Australian military's structure, Order of Battle and general operational procedures, but he also had to become intimately familiar with ORBAT of each and every power in the US Pacific Command Area of Operational Responsibility.

The USPACOM AOR was immense, with essentially one half of the world's population and seven or eight significant militaries to consider, starting with the largest, China, with 1.4

billion people and 5.2 million in uniform; and India, with 3.5 million in uniform out of a greatly reduced population of just 800 million remaining of their former 1.1 billion population in the aftermath of the Indo-Pak war. Next came Taiwan, with 25 million people and 2 million in uniform; to Indonesia, with 240 million people and 1 million in uniform; Singapore, with 5 million people and 500,000 in uniform, to the Philippines, with 105 million and 320,000 military; to Japan, with 130 million people and 280,000 soldiers; and a host of smaller powers with considerable military capabilities.

To top it all off was the most important consideration: the strategic needs of the United States of America. Soon-to-be Major Blakely did not know much at all about the region, its militaries, politics or issues. But he did know that the US had long recognized that the region was a potential powder-keg, well beyond the capabilities of the US, even with the 3rd Marines and the 7th Fleet, to contain. As a result, President Obama back in 2011 had begun to "rebalance" US foreign policy in what was termed the "pivot to Asia". Much of this centered on the fact that the region was now the economic center of the world. However, on the strategic military side it was all about knitting together alliances with western-leaning - albeit somewhat totalitarian in nature - nations in the region. Each was a potential problem for China. Other than India, however, none were in any position to stand up and compete with China directly. Hence the strategy of building a regional alliance to box China in.

So while the strategic importance and intellectual challenge of his new assignment had great professional appeal, it was actually the personal dimension that gave Capt. Blakely the most trouble.

Captain Blakely knew that he had to suck it up, deal with the hostility and win back his place amongst the Marines at large. So as he drained the last of his drink in the quiet of his study, his mind began to work at a furious pace. Before he even realized it, he had formed a strategy which he could implement even before his new assignment began. Inspired, he now knew what actions he should take at the outset in order to return to the fold and to quickly establish himself within the closely knit community of the 3rd Marines; to quickly and unambiguously eradicate the stigma of having been with MARSOC, while still being effective as the US SOCOM and MARSOC Subject Matter Expert, SME, for his liaison role with the Australian Army.

To this end, he cast his mind to the few encounters he had had with men from the 3rd Marines. *The only guys I know from the 3rd Marines were those two guys from that exercise in Germany. What were their names? Gammon? No, Gannon. He must be a Master Gunnery Sergeant by now. And his big black side-kick, what was his name? Oh yeah, Rideout. Strange one, that guy. You'd never expect a man that muscular to be so philosophical, and yet so crude! Rideout would have actually fit in well with the psychological warfare guys in SOCOM. Anyhow, earning the respect and, frankly, the support of Staff Non-Commissioned Officers like those two will be essential,* he thought. *The SNCOs are the key, both to my own reintegration into the Marines and to shaping the Marines rotating through MAGTFA to be effective in support of Australia, the Host Nation. So really,* he realized, *my mission is to draw some SNCOs into the mindset of counter-insurgency, Australia style, adapting Marine Corps Standing Operational Procedures, our SOPs, to be more line with how we approach it in MARSOC. Getting them into the right frame of mind, way outside of their normal comfort zone in the 3rd Marines, will help me accomplish both sides of my mission.*

What I really need to do is talk to that Thorne guy from 1 Commando, Australian Special Forces, before I ship out. I need to get the skinny on who the incoming SNCOs will be for the next rotation into the MAGTFA in Darwin. I'll get Thorne started on them, quietly, without broadcasting it to everybody, as long as I get Chain of Command concurrence from the 3rd Marines...

As he thought about the shaping operation he was conjuring up for the SNCOs, Joe thought about the normal requirement to run such things past the Chain of Command, CoC, in 3rd Marines, and then decided that it might be better not to. *I'm going to be a Liaison. That means consulting with my peers in the Host Nation, like Captain Thorne in 1 Cdo, giving advice meant to ensure the success of our mission – that of not screwing up our welcome in Australia; that of working well with the Australian military to prepare them for war. I won't have to clear any of that advice through the 3rd Marines CoC. More likely, I will back-brief them on it when I am on the ground in Darwin. Besides, if Thorne goes with the plan, it'll be his operation, not mine.*

I'll get him to go after Rideout, if he's on rotation to Darwin, because a guy like Rideout, if he is a Top Sergeant or Master Gunnery Sergeant by now, will have enough influence to make or break it between the Host Nation and the Marines. Rideout is the key....

Lost in her own thoughts about packing up the house and getting the Blakely family ready for the unexpected move to Australia, Tannis Blakely went into the basement to check on Joe. He was busily typing away on his computer, composing an email, and looked up with a happy expression on his face as he hit 'Send' and then turned around to face Tannis.

Tannis noticed a change in her husband's mood. He had somehow cheered up, from the moodiness he had shown for hours, since sharing the news with her about the reassignment. After a few hours in his study in the basement, not quite a 'man cave', it was his sanctuary, and a place where Tannis usually left him undisturbed.

"Why are you suddenly so happy? What's up, Joe?" Tannis asked, noticing the bottle of Jameson, which seemed about a third lower than the last time she had seen it.

"Nothing, Tan. Just thinking about the new assignment, and what I have to do. I'm actually getting into it, you know, what the job will entail, how I can use what I have learned these last three years with SOCOM. You know, 'soldier stuff'.

"Well, I think you need to take some time away from that, and use your 'situational awareness' here at home," Tannis said, motioning upstairs with her eyes.

"What?" he asked, and then got up to follow Tannis up the stairs. He was blindly heading into a crisis which he had no intelligence on.

When he saw his daughter in tears, madly typing away at her laptop on the dining room table, and seeing the small face of the man she was communicating with, he understood immediately.

Seeing her father, she abruptly folded her laptop screen, and turned to face her father.

"This really sucks, Dad. Can't you do anything about it?"

"Aggie…" Joe stammered, unsure what approach to take. His 16-year old daughter, Agness, was clearly distraught, and it had something to do with her boy-friend.

"Well, it is true? We really are moving to Australia? Dad, can't it wait a couple of years, till I'm 18? I could go to university, like Sunny. Then you could just leave me here."

"I thought Sunny was in Grade 11. He's more than a year from university.

"Duh," she said, rudely. "He is *now*. But he will be in university next year, Dad. So obviously when I'm 18, and get into university myself, he'll already be a sophomore at UW.

The Blakelys were a modern family, and had no particular problem with the fact that Agness was sexually active with her boyfriend, Sunny Yao. Sunny was a very polite and trustworthy young man, and had shown that he had something of the respect and honor that his father, Stanley Yao, clearly had tried to instill in his only son.

Over the years, the Blakelys and the Yaos had gotten along very well, both families hoping that their children would not rush headlong into the marriage that was clearly in their future. Both Sunny and Agness had excellent grades and were likely to be awarded scholarships to the University of Western Washington.

Stanley Yao and Joe Blakely often wound up playing racquetball at the local YMCA, both men finding themselves looking for a match on the 20-minute 'buzzer' court, where players could find opponents on a drop-in basis. Not quite pals, they got along better than neighbors, what with the strong relationship that their kids were in, and the common values they shared in terms of wanting only the best for their kids.

Thinking about the young Chinese-American boy, and his father, reminded Joe of something that Stanley Yao had told him a few weeks ago.

"Wait a minute," Joe said, perplexedly, "What about their move? Aren't the Yao's moving soon as well?" *Maybe that will make it easier on Agness to move on, if Sunny is also moving,* he thought.

"Moving? Sunny didn't tell me anything about that. He's just come back from seeing his mom, in Oregon, and wanted to meet with me to give me some bad news. I was in the middle of telling him about your Orders, and that we have to move to Australia this summer, when you came up…" said Agness, suddenly yanking her laptop cover back up, no longer afraid that her parents would read her private correspondence.

Moving politely out of the line of sight to Agnes's laptop, Joe and Tannis made themselves busy by the coffee maker, and quietly talked while Agness typed franticly on her laptop.

"When we were kids, we'd just use the phone," said Tannis. "What's all this about Sunny moving?"

"I'm not sure, but Stan said that he may have to leave for some new job someplace. He was not sure how his son would take it, and he was not sure if he was going to accept the job, but had seemed to want to give me a heads up that there could be some drama between our kids over it," Joe said, quietly,

"Why didn't you tell me?"

"Because I forgot. Besides, he asked me to keep it under wraps until he made a decision. No point getting the kids worked up over it, if he decided not to take the job."

"Where was the job?"

"I don't know, but it was with some mining firm, Broken Hill Properties, I think."

"BHP!" shouted Agness. "Based in….dah-to-dah-dah…Australia!" Agness had logged off from her chat with Sunny, and left her computer open, displaying a Map. She sat upright, looking like she had just won the lottery.

"What? BHP? Australia? What do you mean?"

"Mom, Sunny's bad news, that he was setting me up to hear, is that he and his dad are moving to Australia! He was all upset about how to tell me, and wanted to tell me in person, but when he read my blast about our news, just now, he told me everything. Look at the map. Sunny's going to be at this boarding school, in this little town called "Charter's Towers". It's not far from Darwin, Dad, where we're going!" Agness said, excitedly, showing her parents the map on the computer.

"So where's Stanley going to be, if Sunny is going to be in Boarding School in Charter's Towers?" Joe asked, looking carefully at the map.

"All over the place. That's why he's dumping Sunny at some sort of posh boarding school full of rich ex-pat kids – paid for by the mining company. His dad's going to be evaluating lots of mining companies that BHP might buy, or something, so he'll be travelling all the time. Sunny loves the idea, and so do I. Sunny says that we could go to university in Sydney. And until then, we"ll be able to see each other on the weekends!"

"Uh, Aggie, do you have any idea how far it is from Darwin to Charter's Towers?" Joe asked,

"Can't be far, a couple' of hours' drive…" Agness replied, looking at the computer. "Oh. Shit. Dad, is twenty-three hundred kilometers far? – in miles?"

"Oh yeah, that's like, fifteen hundred miles, Aggie. About two days of hard driving.

Not the least bit discouraged, Agness switched gears. "How long in an airplane? Two hours?"

"More like three."

"OK, what's the airline there?"

"QANTAS" said, Joe, relieved that his daughter was now on-board with the move to Australia.

Momentarily frustrated at her laptop, Agness asked "I can't find them. What am I doing wrong?"

Reading the "Q U A N T A S" that Agness had typed in the search window, Joe smiled, remembering the rejection letter that an old friend of his had shown him. His buddy, a former Marine Corps pilot turned civilian, had gotten a rejection letter that had pointed out that the guy had misspelled the company name in his application. The airline had poked a bit of fun at him, correcting his spelling while at the same time clearly rejecting him: "There's no 'U' in QANTAS," Joe said

"That's weird. Oh, that works, Dad. 'Queensland and Northern Territory Aerial Service, Q-A-N-T-A-S," said Agness, "wonder if that works in Scrabble."

Tannis and Joe watched over her shoulder as she quickly searched for airfares between Darwin and Charter's Towers.

"That's not too much," said Tannis. "I think Dad and I can spring for a few flights, for you and Sunny. Maybe on long weekends, or school breaks. What do you say, Joe?"

"Sure. As long as you're doing well at school. I know Sunny will." Joe said, to which everybody laughed. Sunny was an honor-roll student, every bit the stereotypical Chinese student, kicking ass on his white classmates. That he was second-generation Chinese, and spoke Chinese out of respect for his family, he was not the slightest bit Chinese at his core. Actually named "Yao Ming" in Chinese, Sunny's Birth Certificate listed him as "Sunny Yao". His classmates didn't even know his Chinese name, and they knew his father as "Stanly Yao", rather than "Yao Ping", the Chinese version. But Sunny was every bit an American, with the same loyalties, prejudices and ambitions as his white classmates.

Blakely had been up against the Australian commandos a number of times in a variety of international competitions, and found them to be at par with the best of the US Army Rangers and the Marines from MARSOC. What he liked and respected most about the Australian Special Forces was their relaxed, confident manner. He attributed it to the lack of high-ranking men along with them on international exercises and deployments, as if the Aussies thought of Sergeants and Captains as sufficient supervision for the men, with no need of superior officers to watch over them. He knew that that was true, of course, having seen the disruptive influence that even his new rank of Major could have when an O4, Major, turned up to look in on the small, closely knit specialist teams that participated in such competitions.

In the weeks and months before his deployment, as he read-in on the Australian military and their geopolitical context, he became eager for the assignment to begin

But before he left, he wanted to see his only living relative. Using the two weeks of annual leave that he had left to burn, so the Blakely's of Washington State went back to Pennsylvania, and stayed with Matthew and his wife. While there, the two brothers talked shop quite a lot, both being military. Near the end of the trip Matt brought Joe, Tannis and Agnes along to his father-in-law's sprawling acreage in Altoona, Pennsylvania, the Upton farm. Joe and his family had been there before, as the Uptons, Matt's in-laws, had unofficially adopted the two Blakely brothers years ago, when their parents had died, so Joe considered himself part of the extended Upton family, and seeing all of them before his assignment in Australia was almost as important as the one-on-one time he had spent with Matt.

It was a special occasion indeed. Fourteen family members seated in the three joint-combined tables extending from Upton's kitchen well into the family room. For Old General Upton, it was a rare occasion to have his four daughters, his two sons-in-law, children, and guests like Joe, Tannis and Agness filling his overly large ranch with the noise and activity that the old General loved. The collection of his kin and guests made him feel that he was a true patriarch.

This is what makes a life, Upton thought proudly as he looked out over his family. *To see my family here tonight, healthy, happy and prospering.* He sat back and let his son in law, Matt Blakely, bring up the subject of his brother Joe's assignment to Australia.

Joe had recounted the news of his assignment, promotion, and the good timing that it turned out to be for his daughter. There were smiles all around the room at the great news. Then, the mood became more serious as Joe got into the details.

"So one part of my job will be helping the Australians improve their amphibious capabilities, and come up with some Joint - Combined exercises for them to try out the new landing craft and other kit we have given them,"

"Why Joint combined?" asked one of Joe's sisters.

"*Joint* refers to more than one branch of service, in this case, the Australian Navy and the Australian Army. Their Special Forces, mostly from 1 Commando Regiment, are actually Army troops, not like the Marines. In any case, that's where the 'Joint' comes from. *Combined* is when you have forces from more than one country – the 3rd Marines representing the good ol' US of A – and, in fact, for some of the exercises that I understand are being planned for the months after we get to Australia, there'll be a small but important presence from the Indian Army and the Indian Air Force, so it really is 'Joint-Combined' on many levels," Joe said, proudly.

"That sounds like bread and butter for the Marines, but how does that bring in your Special Ops background?" asked his older brother, Warrant Officer Matthew Blakely, Major Joseph Blakely's older brother.

"Not much, at first. It's one of those 'walk before you run' things. They have to learn more about amphibious assault – and our version of manoeuver warfare, before we mix in the role of recon and other special forces. But eventually, if the focus is preparing them for war with China, Australia will have to have better asymmetric warfare skills."

"What for? To help liberate places the Chinese could invade in Southeast Asia? Or are you talking about a Chinese occupation of Australia?" asked Mat. "Is that really the reference scenario we're really talking about here? Shit! That would be bad. Very bad."

The room fell silent. With General Upton and the two Blakely boys all being current or former military personnel, and with the old General's other son in law, Owen MacInnes having served for a short stint in the US Army Reserves, the daughters and wives around the table all had a degree of awareness regarding military matters, everybody around the table understood how serious Joe's comment really was.

"What's the population of Australia, twenty million?" asked Owen.

"Twenty five," replied Joe.

"And how big is their army?" asked Owen, who had given up on military service after his single tour in Iraq, in favor civilian life. Always worried about his brothers in law still in uniform, he still had the military edge and bearing, only no longer drank the Kool-Aid.

"Thirty thousand soldiers," said Joe.

"What is that? – A British style over-strength division? I mean, how many in their army, all-in?"

"No, that's it, Owen. That's their whole entire army, all-in. They have another thirty thousand in their active and standby reserves. It's quite simple, really. Their fighting force is their Forces Command based in Sydney, essentially made up of various units of their 1st Division scattered across the country, which is where their deployable and highest-readiness units are drawn from for expeditionary deployments. Their 2nd Division is basically their home defense force, made up of reservists."

"So what about their Special Forces, are they part of this 1st Div?" asked Warrant Officer Mat Blakely.

"No, they have a brigade-sized Special Ops Command. Those are the guys I will be working closely with, when I'm not busy with their fish-heads and the Forces Command guys, coordinating their exercises with Marines of the MAGTFA in Darwin. At least, that's how it all looks on paper. What it will be like for real, once I am established, could be another story altogether. But the Orbat of the Australian Defense Force is really quite simple. They are a puny force, and responsible for a massive territory," Joe said, ominously.

"And the Chinese have what, two million in uniform?"

"I was just getting into that with the M2, Marine Intelligence guys. The Chinese have seven military regions, with about twenty military districts, and about twenty Group Armies in various states of readiness," Joe said, matter-of-factly.

"What's a Group Army?" asked Agness, not normally interested in military jargon, despite her father's best efforts. It was as if she had blissfully ignored years of shop talk around the home. But all of the serious talk about China as a threat had made her become interested in knowing more about it.

Something in her intuition told her that it was important information, and could have something to do with her future with Sunny Yao.

Joe Continued: "A Group Army is a military formation, generally self-sufficient, with integral logistical, aviation and other support. Some are well-rounded for the full-spectrum of conflict, basically like the Marine Corps, except that these Group Armies each have an area they specialize in. So in a war, they would combine them in ways that fit the specific battle space and strategic plan. A Group Army can have up to one hundred and sixty thousand soldiers, give or take."

Doing the numbers in her head, Agness was shocked. "So they have around three million soldiers."

"That's about right. But what's even more shocking, considering their mass-conscript style of doctrine, is the real number."

Agness didn't wait. She didn't want to know the answer, but she couldn't bear not to know. "What's the 'real number', Dad?"

"The number of men and women fit for military service," Major Blakely replied to his daughter, with everybody else at the table listening intently.

Agness frowned. "Why is that important?"

"In a mass-conscript army, like the Soviets had in World War Two, and the Chinese are still organized as today, the actual soldiers are not valued that highly. They are expendable – like bullets. We saw this in the Korean War, such as in the Chosin Reservoir with the Chinese 42nd Group Army. They just kept pouring men into the fray, with us mowing them down like crazy, until we ran out of ammo. You see, they can afford to take massive losses, and just keep throwing more and more men – and women, actually – into the war until they overwhelm you."

"Attrition warfare," commented his brother

"That's right, Matt. So given that most able-bodied men, and a surprising number of women, will have rotated through and served for at least a few years in the PLA, the number of people suitable for military service is like a kind of massive reserve of expendable soldiers. And China, like the Soviets fighting the Germans, is willing to take unimaginable losses.

Agness took it all in with dread. "So what is the number?"

"Three hundred and fifty million. Counting able-bodied men. Six hundred million, if you count the women."

She tried to fathom it. The numbers simply beggared belief, but Agness tried to picture so many people in a war, and rejected it on some level: "But Dad, there's no way they would throw away that many lives, just to win a war."

"True, but it does give you a sense of how deep their reserves truly are, and that if it ever came down to it, they could just keep throwing bodies at us until our puny numbers – exceptionally trained and well-armed as they are – would be overwhelmed."

Agness stared at him and through him, slowly coming to grips with the terrible possibilities ahead. Her questions ended as she took in what could be coming. She was not alone in her foreboding. Others stared awkwardly into the food on their plates.

Changing subject to more technical matters, Owen MacInnes broke the uncomfortable silence. "You said 'high readiness'. So they have expeditionary forces, ready to go?"

"Oh yeah, even if China has not been an expansionary power, something has been changing in terms of their Order of Battle. They've been ramping up their military spending, at an average of ten to twelve percent every year since about 2000. While we've been cutting our spending by about the same amount every year since 2012," replied Major Blakely. "They've been building up their military capacity in a very stealthy way, developing their manufacturing capabilities in terms of commercial shipping and aviation technologies, and not broadcasting the military applications of these productive capacities. Just like the Germans did in the 1930's.

"That's why we need those alliances. Kind of like the Allies against the Germans in World War Two. Indonesia alone would add 240 million citizens, but I think they're more in the Chinese sphere of influence these days. At least we have India, with a billion people, well, at least 700 million or so left after their war with Pakistan. Anyhow, they are very anti-Chinese, 'cause of the can of ass-kicking the Chinese opened up on them in the 1960's."

"So if the Chinese are the new Germans, the big threat to everybody, then who are the new Russians? – The Russians?

"No, Matt, I think it really is the Indians who are the new Russians in that context. Even with their losses in the Indo-Pak War, they're the ones who can throw massive numbers of soldiers into a war. So if attrition is what you mean, yeah, the Indians would play that role this time around," said Joe.

"So who are the Australians in that analogy? The Polish?" asked Owen.

"Are you kidding?" said Matt.

"No, seriously, the Poles killed like 30,000 Germans in the opening weeks of the German invasion of Poland. Nowhere near enough, but quite respectable given that they still had cannon and cavalry, and were up against a new form of warfare, like tanks and motorized infantry, right? The Poles fought heroically for a few weeks. And from what I've read and seen on the History Channel shows, if the Allies had thrown in with the Poles early on, and not let Stalin and Hitler divide Poland between them, it could have made a huge difference," said Owen.

"Well, maybe," commented Joe. "We could debate that. But no, the Aussies would have to be the Russians in that context."

"How so? - I don't' get it. They've got *zero* population, and the Australian climate is all desert there, not winter and forests."

"I don't mean it that way, Owen. I mean in terms of *territory*. All the other countries in the region are relatively small and heavily populated. But Australia is massive. It's a continent on its own, something like twenty-five hundred miles across. That's like from Berlin to Moscow *twice over*. And in warfare, real-estate is everything. It would take a huge number of troops to occupy so much space, and the defenders could trade off space for time, like the Russians did," said Joe, passionately.

"I suppose, if they are not defeated outright at the start. But with such puny forces there to start with, how could they expect to stand up to the Chinese long enough for their vast territory to make a difference? After all, the Chinese could throw just a half-dozen Group Armies at it, and completely overwhelm the Aussies," said Mat, with a dose of skepticism. "After all, aren't the Australian cities – and military units – concentrated along the east coast, from Sydney up to Brisbane? What's to stop the Chinese from overwhelming them at the outset and then simply marching across those thousands of miles of outback at their leisure?"

"Me and 2500 other Marines, for a start," said Joe. "And some very nasty special ops tricks I'm supposed to train the Aussies about. After all, I *am* a specialist in Foreign Internal Defense and counter insurgency," said Joe, with pride.

"Only in that case, you and your Aussie 'mates' would be the insurgents," said Matt Blakely, grimly.

Owen pondered at what that would mean. Would it be anything like the Russian front in World War II, with partisans ruthlessly hunted down and entire towns being massacred? He recalled the terrifying photographs he'd seen in the history books and TV shows.

General Upton gazed over his family at the table around him. *What terrible events does the future have in store of us? Will this be the last time we're all together?* he wondered, after all that they had just talked about. A scholar of military history, the old General knew that ominous clouds were coming.

3

BILLABONG

Master Sergeant Rideout was on a rampage, and his long time buddy Master Gunnery Sergeant Gannon would soon be on the receiving end of it. Their friendship dated back to Rideout's first terrifying days in the Marine Corps as a recruit at Parris Island. It had been eighteen years since Rideout first planted his feet in the yellow footprints inlaid in the parade square, his first day in the Marine Corps. Within weeks, when others had tried unsuccessfully to bring Rideout into line, Gannon had been the first man to ever knock him down in a fist fight and since then their friendship had only deepened.

Therefore it was only logical that the two men still used each other as punching bags from time to time. Only now, as Staff Non-Commissioned Officers, SNCOs, harsh words had largely replaced the fists. But when it was necessary to let off some steam, the two Marines sought each other out.

Rideout stormed into Gannon's office and barked at his pal sitting at the desk. "What the fuck is the matter with you, Gary?"

"Elaborate, asshole," Gannon shot back.

"I mean, why did you pawn this detail off on me – you're the Master Gunnery Sergeant around here, and I'm just a lowly Master Sergeant. So the 'making nice with host nation' crap, this 'Ack–Limey–Tization' detail is your problem, not mine!" shouted Top Sergeant Rick "Ride" Rideout.

With a crooked smile on his face, 'Master Guns' leaned back in his chair as if he was about to enjoy what would come next.

"Have you read the tasking? – I mean, *carefully*?"

"Sure. It says I have to go on a two-week tour with a couple of Australian Army military police. What the fuck is that? To get some 'local knowledge'. I can figure this place out on my own. They do speak English here you know. Well, sort-of, anyhow."

"Ride, you missed the *salient* point here."

"Cut the crap. You're no more well educated than I am, so don't try to impress me with Officer vocab. This is not some piece of shit memo here. What's your point?"

"The prominent, jutting out, relevant term in that tasking is 'integration' of Marines into the host nation military community."

Master Gunnery Sergeant Gannon deliberately left out his conversation with the Australian Special Forces Captain Thorne, who had spoken to him about the true nature of the task. That it had something to do with the new USMC LnO to the Australian military command, some newbie Major Blakely, inbound from MARSOC, was enough to convince Master Guns that it was an unavoidable task that he had better embrace from the start. He was pretty sure that he had met the new LnO some time back on an exercise in Germany, and recalled a degree of confidence and determination that engendered his respect. So when the MAGTFA Administration Officer gave him the personnel selection criteria for the assignment requested by the ADF's Forces Command, he knew just who do assign. *Besides,* he had thought, *it's exactly the sort of mind-fuck that Rick Rideout really needs, maybe the antidote to his crudity and penchant towards that high risk behavior of his.*

"We're Marines, Gary. We don't *integrate*. What sort of shit is this? Sounds like Air Force fag talk. The only time I integrate is when I am on top of, behind, or underneath a woman."

"Getting warmer," said Gary, unable to hold back his smile.

Ride stopped cold. "A woman? This is about a woman?" He was now on full alert. "Now you've got my attention!"

Over the years, the two men had made it a habit of steering each other towards any golden opportunity to nail down an impressive, exotic, or acrobatic woman that would also represent something of a challenge. It was not so much about getting each other laid, but about putting them on the hunt for a woman worthy of some monumental or impossible pursuit.

More often than not it got the men into some sort of trouble, or at the very least, a memorable adventure.

"Read the names again, Ride."

Rick read the tasking order more carefully. *You are to report to Sergeant W. Hayman, of 1st Brigade...*he read.

"Your lips are moving, Rick!"

"Is this the Sergeant from our in-brief last month?"

"The one and only."

"Hymen?"

"HAY-man, HAY, Man," Gannon corrected.

Sergeant Rideout dove over the Master Gunnery Sergeant's desk and grabbed his head in a vice-like grip. Master Guns Gannon tried desperately to free himself, but Top Sergeant Rideout was stronger, and laid a disgustingly wet 'doggy kiss' on Master Guns' face.

"Yuck! I hate it when you do that."

"Just my way of saying 'Thank you' in advance," he grinned wolfishly as he stepped back from the desk and righted himself. Gannon wiped his face and considered climbing over his desk to have at Ride, but he thought the better of it, and maintained his composure.

"I'm going to tag that beautiful Aussie six ways from Sunday," Ride announced proudly.

Knowing what he knew about the assignment, Gannon thought about saying something to the contrary but decided to let Ride enjoy his fantasy a little longer, as it would likely be his last in a very long time. So he played along. "Like you did that security guard in Fiji? What did she say to you at the airport?"

"Va–Raaa–Waa! *It means she wants to fix you, boy*!" Ride said, imitating the accent of the other Fijian security guard at Nadi International Airport, who had explained what the large, sexy black woman had said in her native tongue, offering the Marine a 'Fijian handshake'. Ride still had a few of the scars in his back from her long finger nails. He wore the scratches down his back with great pride.

"I still don't believe you went with her. She was a monster!"

"Oh yeah!" Ride replied, enjoying the memory of his weeks with Shasta, and their nights dancing at the Black Marlin Bar in the resort his unit has been billeted at during the exercise. "She was a fine specimen, with more stamina than any other women I have ever been with."

"You still in contact with her?"

"No fuckin' way. Are you kidding? How would it look for the boys if their Top Sergeant settled down with just one woman?"

"Yeah, that would be the end of the legend, and the book."

"That's right. There would be no more chapters in: '*The great schtupping spots of the world*,'" he said, without even a pretense of modesty. That the boys were always ribbing him about adding "new chapters" to the book with each exploit only egged him on to score even better the next time. He loved the notoriety, and thought that it bolstered his effectiveness as Master Sergeant.

"Hey, what was that expression she had, about me?"

"The one they use in Fiji for useless idiots?"

"That's the one. Something about 'eat him'?"

"*Put him in the pot*!'" he said, with the accent.

"So I'm now three up on you. You still have not delivered anything tasty my way, in over six months. Have you lost your touch, Ride, or are you just getting greedy?"

"Yeah, I know. I'm still working on your Chinese order," said Ride, of Gary's long standing goal of bedding a beautiful Chinese woman.

"Anyhow, shouldn't you be somewhere?" asked Gary, looking out his window at the parking lot where an Australian Military Police SUV was just pulling into a parking spot.

As the two buddies stood there, looking out the window, Sgt Wendy Hayman got out of the left, passenger, side of the Land Rover just as the sun broke out from behind a cloud.

The sunlight made her blond hair suddenly golden, transfixing the men with her beauty just as she had held the theatre of newly arrived Marines when she had briefed them on the Robertson Barracks Standing Orders, alcohol policy, local ordinances and long list of 'things not to do while in Australia'.

She was stunning.

"Uhh…!" was all that came out of Rick's mouth as he gawked out the window. He gulped in amazement as he gazed with longing at the vision before him. Then he pulled himself together. "Thank you, Gary," He said reverently, as if he was thanking God for a gift from Heaven. That was all he could say before heading out to meet her, now enthusiastically embracing his task of integrating with Host Nation military personnel.

When Top Sergeant Rideout reached the parking lot and approached Sergeant Hayman, Gunnery Sergeant Gannon was still watching from his office window. As he did so, the ridiculous image of Rick Rideout and his Fijian girlfriend running naked across the resort's golf course in the middle of the night, his junk flailing about like a fish-whacking club as he chased after her, flashed across his mind.

Quite a Marine. But that nudity thing keeps getting him into trouble, Ride just can't help but show off his monstrous cock, Gary thought to himself. But when he saw his large friend standing close to the Australian MP, Gary wondered if the petite woman could handle the large black man who now had her in his sights.

Ten days later, after touring a variety of very sleepy Australian Army posts up and down the Gold Coast, from Sydney to Cairns, Master Sergeant Rideout had largely given up on his quest. The problem was that his quarry was so professional and serious, keeping to their itinerary without deviation, that he had no opportunity to work his charms on her. They spent six to eight hours a day on the road, first covering the vast distance from Darwin to Sydney, and then shorter distances but with multiple stops at armories, bases, outposts, and a few notable landmarks along the way up the east coast, from Sydney to Brisbane and the Gold Coast.

In the evenings, while he was left on his own in whatever barracks or hotel had been arranged for him, she and her Corporal were always busy or had private commitments of some kind, and did not seem to want to elaborate on them.

This frustrated Top Sergeant Rideout to no end, and made him want 'Windy' Wendy Hayman that much more. *Perhaps it's that faggy Corporal Guay, the driver, who is making it 'three's a crowd'*, he thought, as they pulled out of the small town, Charters Towers, on their way back across the endless plains of northwest Queensland on the narrow two-way Flinders Highway. With 2370 kilometers between their current position and the MAGTFA at Robertson Barracks in Darwin, Ride felt like a hostage who was in for some serious torture.

The Aussies he had met on the tour had been very welcoming and seemed to have the beer light on every afternoon, along with the ubiquitous BBQs, which was one aspect of Australian culture that Rick really appreciated. He had enjoyed Grade-A Australian beef and kangaroo, along with lots of barbequed garlic bread and a wide variety of beer and wines. But this had not quenched his thirst for sex.

And then the most remarkable thing happened.

As Corporal Guay drove along the sun-baked A6 highway, approaching the small town of Richmond, Ride realized that he was actually enjoying the trip, getting to know Australia and the relaxed 'caravan culture' lifestyle that these somewhat crude, yet relaxed and friendly people enjoyed.

For once in his life he was enjoying the company of a beautiful woman, and the seemingly gay man, without feeling the need to fuck the woman or distance himself from the gay man.

It was at that moment when he truly relaxed and embraced the Aussies, that he felt a strong connection with the place. His nine-month rotation with the MAGTFA now looked like a pleasant, perhaps all-too-short, assignment.

As he watched the endless sea of golden grassland and parched tundra pass by he thought about taking a week or so off, and going out on his own for an Australian 'walk-about', where you head out with no destination in mind and embrace the people and experiences that life presents along the way.

In his somewhat philosophical reverie, his normal degree of USMC alertness had been abandoned, so he did not pick up on the subtle clues that could have warned him about the conspiracy that was taking place around him.

As he sat there, looking at the map book, he did not pay any attention to the silent communication that was taking place between the driver and Sergeant Hayman, or the secretive nods the two exchanged as they agreed that *the time has come*.

He had not picked up on what they were up to when, at a gas-station stop in Richmond, the Corporal had deliberately shielded from Ride's view the packages he had picked up from a business just around the corner from the gas station, while Sergeant Hayman had fuelled the SUV. So he was totally unprepared for what came next, after the trio had driven another hundred kilometers to the west from Richmond.

Suddenly the Land Rover lurched off the road and bounced across the rocky tundra.

As he flailed for something to hold onto, he looked at the driver with wild-eyed surprise.

"What the fuck!? What are you doing? Stop the car!"

"Relax, mate, we're almost there."

"Where?"

"The end of the line. HOLD ON!" said Corporal Guay as he steered the Land Rover onto a large rocky dome-shaped outcrop and headed right for the cliff at the far side.

"What are you doing!" shouted Master Sergeant Rideout as he grabbed hold of the hand-grip above the door and stared in disbelief at the rocks as they grew large in front of the windscreen. The Land Rover took flight, and flew off the rock dome towards the rocks.

"Wheeee!" shouted Sergeant Hayman, as if it was all a great deal of fun.

Gravity took hold of the Land Rover and its wheels came into contact with the scoop-shaped path on the far side of the precipice. As the vehicle settled heavily onto its springs, Corporal

Guay steered violently to the right and the vehicle swerved away from the rock face which, an instant before, Top Sergeant Rideout thought he was about to be splattered upon.

With his heart racing and bouncing around some place between his teeth and his throat, Ride saw that the Land Rover had landed in some kind of trench that had been invisible from the rock dome. The narrow channel led towards a curving line of trees ahead.

The trees seemed greener and more vibrant than the dried-out, parched trees that he had seen in the dried-out creek beds and sandy gullies along the side of the endless, arrow-straight highway.

For a fleeting moment, he attributed the sudden vividness to the near-death experience he had just been through, and was just about to comment when the Land Rover came to a sudden stop and the two Aussies leapt out of the vehicle as if in a panic, leaving the Marine sitting alone in the vehicle, dazzled.

He could not believe what he was seeing.

There, in front of him, was his beautiful Australian blond stripping out of her clothes.

That Corporal Guay was also stripping off his 'uni', was lost on Ride. He couldn't take his eyes off of Sergeant Hayman. But the beautiful woman, now in her panties and bra, was not the only beautiful sight. Beyond her, beckoning even more invitingly than a woman's spread legs, and somehow offering to quench an archaic, basic need in his soul, was what he would later describe as an oasis.

He was momentarily frozen between two worlds: one, the disciplined world in which he had to restrain himself, be the embodiment of technical proficiency and high moral fiber as a Senior NCO in the United States Marine Corps; the other, the ancient, basic, natural humanity that this magical place was awakening in him.

"Come on, mate! Get out of your uni! If you don't have a 'cozzie' then go in your skivvies! Last one into the billabong is a Dag" shouted Corporal Guay.

With that, the two Aussies ran bare-foot over the sandy ground towards the cliff's edge.

Ride watched Hayman's firm ass jiggle athletically in her stark white panties and he saw her final foot-plant on a rock from which she propelled herself into the air, tucking her legs up under her bottom before disappearing from view.

The concussion and sudden spray of water into the air from her perfectly executed cannon-ball, and Guay's own dive off the ledge, broke Top Sergeant Rideout out of his trance, and into motion. Somehow stripping out of his clothes on the run, he stripped completely naked, inspired to abandon all modesty as he threw himself into the inviting pool.

After shouting in satisfaction when he breached the water's surface and swimming around for a while in the refreshingly cool water of the billabong, he climbed out of the water and sat on a large, flat rock. The billabong truly was an oasis, with the joyful sounds of Sergeant Hayman and Corporal Guay reverberating off the rock walls at the far end of the long, boomerang-shaped lake. Ride was in his own head-space, communing with a long lost friend – the earth herself.

Still nude and completely unashamed, he enjoyed the feeling of the water beading off of his muscular body as the warm sun dried him. His love for nudity was generally hard to satisfy as a Marine, but here in his oasis it felt absolutely appropriate. Being nude out in the unexpected and very private place in which he found himself made him feel more grounded than he had in a very long time. He felt as though he had gone native, and was better for it.

For a glorious few minutes he sunned himself inclined on the rock looking and feeling very much the Barberini Faun statue he had first seen while on deployment in Germany. The statue of the mythological Satyr, the powerfully muscled god-like being of ancient mythology, had made a strong impression on him when he had seen it in the museum district of Munich. Ever since he had first seen it, it had been something of his personal avatar, the image of a fully satisfied, heroic figure reclined in naked splendor, relaxing in the sun.

The mood changed suddenly when Corporal Guay and Sergeant Hayman returned from the water, and sat in the grassy area near Ride's rock.

They could see that Australia had gotten to the man, and that he was forever changed. But they were a bit surprised to see an American so comfortable with his own nudity.

"Mate, any chance you can find some togs to cover that donger up? It's rather large and frightening," said Hayman.

It took Ride a minute to understand, and then he felt suddenly awkward. He had crossed the line, having mistakenly thought that that Sergeant Hayman's panty-clad swim had meant that nudity on his part was somehow appropriate.

He covered himself and got up awkwardly to retrieve his clothes. He returned a minute later wearing his shorts.

"Sorry if I offended you, Wendy."

"It's not me you offended, I actually don't mind seeing a digger's dongo. No, it's my little Corporal you scared with that doodle of yours," she said, with a smile.

Rick looked at Corporal Guay, not sure what to say.

"Relax, mate, you're not my type."

After ten days together, Sergeant Rideout still did not know for sure if Corporal Guay was gay or not, and had to ask.

"So are you gay, or what?"

Guay snorted in disgust. "I'm gobsmacked you're asking me that question, Mate,"

"Why?"

"Well, even if you Yanks get all wobbly about gays, and pretend that you don't have any poofs in your military, it's not something we care about one way or the other in ours. We've got some, but who cares? That's their business. As for me, Mate, you asked, but I'm sorry I have to let you down. I go for the Sheilas, Mate."

Feeling even more embarrassed, Ride looked at Sergeant Hayman.

"Isn't it dog's balls, Ride?" she asked.

"What does that mean?"

"Obvious, mate. Isn't it obvious?"

"What?"

"Corporal Guay and I are lovers. He's my bloke," she said, taking Guay's hand in her own.

Ride looked at her, then at Corporal Guay, and then back at her, trying to take it all in. "I had no idea. I actually thought he was gay."

"A poofter? My Dickie? You are a Drongo, aren't you? I knew you were a Root Rat, always looking at me like you wanted to get your hands on my Mappa-Tazzi, but I thought you knew that Dickie and I were 'having a naughty' every chance we got."

Rick noticed a cringing expression in Cpl Guay's face, as if something Sergeant Hayman was saying had made his stomach turn. *Something's not right here, and it's not about their relationship*, Rick thought to himself.

Having some difficulty following the Australian slang, Rick was relieved to finally understand why he had been left alone so often on the trip, and it made him feel a lot better.

He just smiled, and shook his head, fairly sure that 'having a nasty' meant having sex, Australia's version of American's 'doing the nasty'.

After some small talk about what a billabong really was, he felt the need to be on his own for a while. Comprehending all the Australian slang was too much of an effort, and with his recent social faux-pas in mind, not to mention that the prospect of bedding Sergeant Hayman had just been ripped from his future, Top Sergeant Rideout needed some alone time.

"I'll be back in a while," he said, and then he got up to explore the terrain beyond the billabong, on his own, to think about what it was about the place that made him feel so attached to it.

Working his way up from the billabong, he found himself back at the top, facing the boundless desert. A long, flat horizon was bisected by scattered hills in the distance. Otherwise it was the endless tundra of the Outback.

Rideout strode athletically across the desert plain, feeling the hot breeze on his face, cooling the sweat running down his forehead. His pace slowed as he walked, changing from that of a marching Marine to one of a serious desert traveler, going in rhythm with the land. *You have to go slow but steady to keep from sweating so much,* the voice in his head told him.

A bird floated in the sky above, part of a dance. Rideout spotted a dog in the distance – a mangy little coyote, he assumed. The dog stopped and looked at Rideout. Rideout stopped and looked at him. Then the critter scampered off, leaving the Marine looking on after him. *Good thing it was just him, if he had a gang they could have chewed me to bits, the little buggers,* he shuddered. He heard a bird's cry above him. He looked up and saw the same bird circling around him. It was as if the bird was laughing at him.

Ride decided he'd better head back to the billabong. He turned in a full circle. He couldn't see any sign of the billabong or where he had come from. He controlled his sudden sense of surprise. *Look down,* he thought, *there should be tracks.* But the ground was too rock-hard. *What the fuck? Fuckin' Aussie country,* he thought for a moment, reverting to his old Marine mind-set. He turned, slipped on a loose rock and crashed to the ground.

He painfully, slowly got back on his feet. He had fallen hard. *That's hard ground, this could support a tank without making a lot of tracks,* he thought. *Look where you're going,* called in his head. He stopped cold. Had someone spoken to him?

At that moment the desert flooded over him. It was big, huge, bigger than he was, and it did not care if he fell down or died here. It simply *was.*

All the training, all the bases, the endless big talk of his fellow Marines, the constant swagger, the drill, the life – out here, it was as if the land spoke firmly to him and said: *That is nothing; this is all.*

He was alone. No buddies to joke with, no one to back him up. Here it was just him and the land. Sure, he'd been on road trips and been alone in the massive Wyoming plains; hiking in the Rocky Mountains and a hundred other places in the world. But something about the Outback shook him to the core. Its sheer starkness called to him and challenged him. *Aren't so big now, are you, little man?*

No, I am not little, he said to no one and everything around him. *I can learn if I have the time, and I can survive here.* He stood tall and faced the desert before him. *I am Man.* The thought hung strangely in his mind, as if spoken from his ancestral consciousness.

He would have been lost in his thoughts if he had not been interrupted by the call of that same bird. He looked up at the winged creature that seemed to float away, calling back to him as if to follow. Which he did. He walked steady and sure, not the march of a Marine, but that of a man, like men who had walked across this land for thousands of years. He followed the path the bird was taking, and suddenly, there it was.

The billabong. He had been so wrapped up in this strange trance that he had forgotten that he was lost. But not anymore. *That was strange*, he thought, *Must have been the heat. I better not tell the others.* Determined to shake off this experience; he returned to the persona of one Master Sergeant Rick Rideout, USMC.

He made his way back down the slope to the idyllic paradise to rejoin the couple. It was clear to him that they had 'had a nasty' while he was away, judging by the bits of twigs and grass in Sergeant Hayman's hair and the mischievous smile on Dickie's face.

Ride was feeling great, despite his earlier embarrassment. In spite of the heat and the exertion of his hike, the experience had left him with a strange euphoria.

His mood improved even more when Dickie handed him a cold beer.

"Have a coldie, Toppo!"

"Thanks, Dickie."

After opening the can and enjoying a few long gulps of the cool '4X Gold' beer, he watched Dickie pull another can of beer out of a long white sock.

"What's with the sock?"

"You see a coolie around here?"

"Cooler? No, now that you mention it. So how did you keep the beer so cold?"

"Keep it cold? It was warm when we bought it back in Richmond. No, mate, I *cooled* it here, while you were out on your walkabout."

"But how did you get it so cold so fast? This is as cold as a fridge."

"Well, how would you do it in America, if you were out in the never-never without a coolie?" Dickie asked.

Looking around, Ride thought he had the answer.

"The billabong? I would put it in the water to cool it down."

"Wrongo, the water temp is at least 20 degrees centigrade."

"So how'd you do it?"

"Old bushman's trick. It's really good oil, actually. You just put your can of grog in a sock, pour some warm water on it and set it out in the breeze for half an hour. As the air evaporates the water off the sock, it sucks heat out of the can."

"That really works?"

"Too right. Works like a charm. Dirty pond-water, even piss works well on the sock. As long as you have a breeze you can get your beer to cool down to about five degrees centigrade in about half an hour. Even in a hot breeze like today you don't need a Freemantle Doctor, just air moving across the wet surface of the sock and physics takes over."

"Latent heat of evaporation," added Wendy, "for the water on the sock to evaporate, it has to suck energy out of the can."

Looking up at the hot sun and enjoying another long sip of cool beer, Ride thought about the physics of it.

"So would it work on bottled water too?"

"Sure. But maybe not as good as for an aluminium can."

"You mean 'aluminum'."

"No, mate, we say 'al-you-min-i-um', cause we speak the Queen's English. But the technique works on plastic water bottles just fine. You see it every day on the highway."

"What do you mean?"

"Remember that pack of banana bender cyclists we saw yesterday?"

"Yeah."

"Didn't you see the socks on their water bottles? All the cyclists use this technique. They generate their own wind by cycling, and always have cold water close to hand."

"Got any more warm 'grog'? I'd like to try it for myself."

"Sure, in the Rovie. Help yourself, Toppo. The breeze is dying down, so you might want to tie them up in the trees to get more air flow."

Refrigeration technology, Ride laughed to himself as he sat back against a tree after setting up a few wet socks with beer cans in them, hanging from a tree. *How long will we have to wait for the beer to cool?* he asked in his head. *Who cares*, he answered himself, and laughed out loud. *What a day*, he thought as he rolled his head around and looked at the sky above him, *What a country*! He was alive, here in this place and he was glad.

Half an hour later, Ride retrieved the cans of beer that he had hung. They were nice and cool.

As he helped Dickie set up the small portable BBQ rig from the Range Rover, Rick felt at ease with the young man and not the slightest bit embarrassed about his earlier gaffe.

But he did have some unfinished business with the man.

"That was quite a stunt you pulled, scaring the crap out of me like that!" No one but no one scares 'Ride' Rideout. This was a major deal to a proud Marine.

"That's how we do it in the outback, Mate."

"What do you mean?"

"Initiation. We don't' share our secret places with just anybody. And this one is one of our favorites. It's something of a tradition to only share these sacred places with people of good character."

"So you've decided I'm of good character?"

"Yes, Mate, you've passed the test."

"What test? What did I do to pass it?"

"When you stopped being such a Root Rat, and just relaxed and enjoyed yourself like a regular bloke, you became human again." For a moment Ride felt awkward that he'd let the "proud

Marine" in him slip back in at the start of the conversation. Dickie did not seem to notice this, and continued. "But we knew it would be tough for you, cause you're doubly cursed."

"How so?"

"Well, first of all, you are a Seppo."

"Seppo? I think I heard that a few times in the bars down in the dockside area, in Darwin. What's it mean?"

"The sailors were taking the piss out of you, Mate. They were calling you a 'Septic Tank' – rhymes with 'Yank', get it? Septic Tank – Yank: 'Seppo'."

Turning a bit red at the thought of not having knowing that he was being insulted, Ride got his hackles up a bit: "What's wrong with being an American?"

"Oh, nothing. 'S'truth. But your American way of life makes you see things, and act on things, as if you are in a great big rush to get somewhere, to do something. That makes you less receptive to just *being*."

"Sounds very philosophical. Are all Aussies like you two?"

"Well, it's not as if we are Buddhists here, but we *have* inherited a close connection with the land."

"Inherited? From whom?"

"First of all, from the abos – the aborigines, Mate. You have your native Americans and Spanish: we have the aborigines. Their culture reverberates in the Australian soul, and it is a constant reminder to us that we may walk on this land but our footprints here are ephemeral. That sort of puts it all into perspective for us.

"But that's not the end of it. Our connection with the land goes much deeper than what we learned from the aborigines. You see, today, our connection is more with our forefathers, who broke their backs taming this unforgiving land. You have your cowboys, and we have our pioneers. You cannot imagine some of the horrible conditions they faced, disease, drought, starvation and the ever-present scorching sun. Yet they persevered, and transformed this land into the bread-basket of Asia, second only to your California in terms of the diversity and quality of our agricultural output. So our connection with this land, what makes it sacred, is very close to home. It's quite literally in our blood."

Ride thought about that for a while, and how different he felt just sitting around and 'being' at the billabong. He remembered how insignificant the desert had made him feel, yet at the same time was inspired enough to rise to its challenge.

"What's the second curse?" he asked.

"Well, I don't mean to offend, but you *are* a Marine."

For just an instant, Top Sergeant Rideout, USMC, felt provoked, but he did not say anything. As he reflected on it, he thought the comment might have something to do with the way that a Marine is 'always on', always hyper-aware, and ready for anything. *Maybe that's the point here*, he thought. As he let himself relax again, he felt the wires that held him together as a Marine, the ever-present tautness, fade into the background. It was almost mystical.

It made his real life, as a Marine with the 3rd Marines, seem very far away, and yet he knew that it was still there, at the core of who he was. As though he were on a well-deserved vacation, getting some much needed down-time, 'decompressing' as they say in the Marine Corps. He felt that he was being restored somehow. But there was more. The desert had broadened his own definition of who and what he was. It was as if the Outback had welcomed him with its mysterious, silent call.

"I think I understand, Dickie," he said, looking slowly around at the magnificent country and the bright, blue sky overhead. It all seemed to take him into a one-ness and give him a feeling of belonging. He thought to himself, *I've got to remember this moment in my mind, like a photo in an album – I don't ever want to forget this.* He turned to Dickie and smiled. "Thanks for sharing this sacred place with me. I can feel it, you know."

"I know. This is the sort of thing that makes Australia so magical. You don't have to be a greenie to know it. The land is *alive* here, that's 'London to a brick'. And if you treat it with respect, interact with it like a loved one, it will protect you."

Such feelings were strange to Ride. After all, he was a kick-ass Marine. If he let these strange thoughts take over, he wondered if he'd float away like that bird that had led him back to the billabong. But he shook himself back to his old self.

Putting back on his USMC persona, Ride spoke to Dickie with newfound respect.

"This Australian thing with the land, how does it affect you as a soldier?"

"Good on ya, Toppo! Bulls —eye!" said Wendy, who had been hanging back while the boys had had their conversation. "Now you've got it. This is what I was tasked with getting across to you."

Ride spun around to face her. "*Tasked?* By your higher headquarters? Are you kidding me? Your chain of command is *that* philosophical?"

"No, Toppo, they're as figjam as any other chain of command. Once you get to those lofty rank levels you're far removed from the trenches. That's universal in any military. No, Mate, Captain Thorne, from 1 Commando, set this up. He figured that we need to reach a few of you senior NCOs on account of your role in herding kittens in your MAGTFA unit. We've had trouble in the past with your mob not treating our land, and our civilians, with the required amount of respect. So for our diggers to work with your lot, we have to get this through to you."

"So the message is, treat Australia with respect?"

"That's right, mate," she said, seriously, "Make sure your boys understand that they are welcome guests here, abide by the Robertson Barracks Post Standing Orders – especially regarding the constraints and procedures for the exercise areas, weapons ranges, and interactions with our civilian population." She was suddenly the serious, professional again, speaking with purpose.

"So all of this, this grand tour of your facilities, this initiation to your sacred billabong, this was all about having us understand and abide by your rules?" he said, incredulously.

"Maybe now would be a good time to cut out the bush-talk, Wendaye," Dickie said, over-emphasizing the "AYE", saying her name, Wendy, with an over-the-top Australian twang.

And then he got it. What had been gnawing at his subconscious for the entire trip. Now it made sense. He thought back to a number of times when he had been introduced to the Australian Army and Special Forces units they had paid a visit to in their tour. Each time, Wendy would start with some incomprehensible slang that now seemed to be a cue for the local Aussie soldiers to speak the same way. It now dawned on Sergeant Rideout that *the bush-talk was part of the charade, part of the entire exercise. And now Dickie wanted her to cut it out, as if the job had been accomplished. But what job?*

"Good on'ya – er, good idea, Dickie. Time to cut the crock-talk," she said, and then continued with a different air about her, far more serious: "Yes. We have a problem here in Australia, and this MAGTFA experiment with your lot simply must succeed," she explained, in what seemed to be another language altogether, English! To Ride, it was like one of those seamless transitions in a movie, when the character switches from some foreign language to English, without skipping a beat.

Wendy continued in normal English, with only a mild, and easily understandable, Australian accent. "The majority of our civilians don't want Americans basing here in Australia, especially you hard-charging, hard-drinking, womanizing Marines," she said, winking at Rick with a smile. "When your guys have leave, and get off their faces and beat up our prostitutes, they demonstrate that they simply don't get it. Take for example that serving wench from the meet-and-greet we were at with the zoomers of the R-Double-A-F over in Tindal; you remember her?"

Top Sergeant Rideout grimaced with the recollection. "Yes. I had to staff the paperwork on the expatriation of one of my men for that mess."

"Well, that 'mess' is a perfect example. She may have been a simple serving wench, and proud of her tits, but when she wrote "407" over her tits, she was just being hospitable to that Canadian P-3 Crew. And even if she was pissed as a parrot and gave your man a welcoming kiss, it was not an invitation to be raped."

"It was not a rape…"

"Bullshit. The Wing Commander may have been able to make the civilian charge go away so as to avoid another diplomatic incident, but it was a persistent, unwanted sexual advance resulting in unwanted and fairly rough sex I might add. And the way she was simply tossed out of the barracks like garbage after all, with nobody watching out for her, was quite frankly, disgraceful. And to make matters even worse, the girl was a Lemon, so having unwanted sex with a man was even that much more offensive to her."

Ride sighed, knowing that what she said was essentially true. The young private had gotten her extremely drunk and then screwed her, in what he later bragged to the men of his platoon as a state of near unconsciousness. Back home in the US, it would have been described unequivocally as a rape.

"You know as well as I do how bad it would have been if a journalist had gotten wind of that," continued Sergeant Hayman. "So what we have here is a cultural problem. Our women are comfortable with their sexuality. Maybe it goes with our men being a bit more crude and loud-mouthed than you Americans are, but when our women show off their breasts, they are still decent women who must be treated with respect. Our diggers – our soldiers - they know this, and they know where the line is drawn, but you Yanks don't seem to get it. And as for our sex-trade workers, your lot treat them as whores, whereas here in Oz, at least in Queensland and the Northern Territory, prostitution is legal and our sex trade workers are protected by the law, so when your men bugger off without paying, or they mistreat the prostitutes, they offend all of Australia. These little incidents on their own are not all that important, but when they interfere with the strategic picture, they become immensely important. I don't need to remind you of your 3rd Marines' litany of problems at Okinawa," she said, seriously, and then lightened her tone as she continued. "But those of us in the military, we understand why you are here, and we appreciate you more than you can imagine."

The reference to Okinawa hit Top Sergeant Rideout in the gut. It had been one of his mentors, Colonel Rogers, a man he deeply respected, who had fallen on his sword in the interests of the 3rd Marines. Rogers had been stripped of his command for the depraved actions of one of his men. The disproportionate punishment of the CO had been meant as an example, so that there would be zero tolerance for misconduct by Marines in Okinawa, and provide a foundation for a concerted effort to regain the trust of the local Japanese population who had been on the brink of kicking the 3rd Marines out of their home base.

So he understood the connection between the behavior of the men and the strategic interests of the United States of America. But as for the strategic situation in Australia, Ride did not have the full picture. He knew that the increased numbers of Marines rotating through Darwin was important to the US, but he wanted to know more about the Australian point of view – why Americans would be appreciated at all.

"Why is that?" he asked,

"Because we know what's coming with the Chinese," she said, sincerely. "Sooner or later, this entire region is going to war and we'll be right in the middle of it. And your lot are going to spill blood with us. *Here*. On this land," she said, digging her hands into the earth where she sat, "in this sacred place - and a very long way from your loved ones back in America," she concluded.

After a long moment of silence, as he smelled the earthy odor of the soil she had disturbed, tasted the sharp bite of pitch in the air from the nearby gum trees and felt the warm air brushing his cheek. He understood her completely.

I've got to make sure the boys understand what this is all about. This is no swan, no time to whoop it up. This is more like what the 1st Marine Division of X Corps faced in the Chosin Reservoir in '50, he thought, after kicking ass on the Chinese 42nd PVA, the 25,000 men of the 1st Marines, along with the 41st Royal Marine Commando and elements of the US 3rd and 7th Infantry Divisions, a combined force of only 30,000 men, suddenly faced off against 120,000 men of the Chinese 9th army, who had surrounded the UN force, he recalled of his studies of the terrible winter war in North Korea. Had it not been for the heroics of the Marines, and the support of 1st Marine Air Wing and the navy pilots from

Task Force 77 in interdicting the influx of Chinese forces and in resupplying the Marines, we would have faced the same lack of provisions, fuel and ammunition that proved fatal to the Chinese. Ride shuddered at the thought of so many Chinese from the 59th PVA in particular, who had perished as much from starvation, frostbite and exposure as from the ferocious assault by the 1st battalion, 7th Marines at Hill 1419, and other battles in the desperate winter warfare that the Marines engaged in during the breakout from Yudam-ni.

For Sergeant Rideout, the lesson learned was the essential role played by logistical support, ensuring that the front-line units have everything required to remain combat effective and not leaving units stranded and unsupported. That had been the take-home point. The winter war with the Chinese in North Korea had always been a particular fascination for him as a student of modern warfare. It provided so many great examples of how leadership and the actions individual soldiers could play a vital role in the larger campaign. He drew on these examples when coming up with training scenarios for his men, but had never before – not even in Iraq or Syria – been in a time and place where defeat of an American or allied force was comprehensible.

But now, here in Australia, with only a small number of Marines to augment the modest Australian military, he had a profound sense of certainly at the core of his intuition that not only was war with China coming fast, but that how he personally prepared his men, motivated them, and shaped their character would make the difference between life and death for his men, and victory or defeat for these remarkable Australians.

As he looked at his new friends, and felt a deep and growing bond with them and their unusual country, he knew that the coming struggle would be even more desperate than Korea.

Marines will die here, with these fine people. This is truly sacred ground. And who knows how much time I've got to get my boys into the right frame of mind, to face off against overwhelming odds, with insufficient support, and where the actions, the life, and the sacrifice of each and every Marine could make or break the entire campaign. This is not the time or the place for fucking around, Top Sergeant Rideout decided.

4

LITTLE DRAGONS

Sea Port versus Aerial Port: Lieutenant David Lion made a mental note to bring up the difference in how things were being done at the Sea Port of Disembarkation, SPOD, versus the Aerial Port of Debarkation, APOD. The squids from the US Navy seemed to rely more on hard-copy paperwork that accompanied the freight through the SPOD, unlike the online records used by the Air Force APOD that he was used to in his normal work, managing intermediate logistics support to the Marine Aircraft Wing back at his home base in Kaneohe Bay, Hawaii. He knew not to complain, however, as Major Bantry had made it clear that a lot of things would be done differently in the Marine Air Ground Task Force Australia, MAGTFA.

The Major seemed quite content to let the stores pile up in the warehouses and dockyards while negotiations with the Australians dragged on, rather than to push the issue and get the gear moved onward. It was as if the Major was more concerned with process, making sure that a master list of the facilities needed for MAGTFA were included in the SOFA, before the backlog of incoming goods was addressed. Lieutenant Lion thought: *it might be more appropriate to sort it out in execution, using contingency procedures, perhaps even damage-control center methodology. When the plan goes to shit, we have to use contingency operating procedures rather than to try to amend an already irrelevant master plan...*

The sheer quantity of equipment flowing into the port of Darwin and the air base, Tindal, was astonishing. It comprised not only the supplies for the in-coming rotation of Marines from

Okinawa and Hawaii for the beefed up MAGTFA, but also a range of 'contingency material' that the planners at USPACOM were shoving down their throats – and much of that was not even earmarked for the Marines of MAGTFA.

One element of the latest such shipment was a set of four sea containers loaded to the gills with 'Flexible Solar Power Stations'. Lieutenant Lion had heard about these during his advanced logistics course at Quantico. He knew that the solar power rig had some advantages over power supplied by diesel generators. They would reduce need for supply convoys and they were quieter and more compact. This would theoretically help patrols' mobility and save space for other supplies. But he also knew that there were drawbacks, such as the lack of power source when the sun was not shining and the long time required to recharge batteries. He had accepted his instructor's conclusion that the flexible solar power units were not well-suited to Marines on the go, and not 'recon friendly', but they certainly could have some applications in the sun-baked outback of Australia. Whatever the case, he just had to make sure that all the components stayed together as the load was broken down. It would be impossible to track things down afterwards, and he knew that now, or later, it was his responsibility to un-fuck the logistical mess that was unfolding on a daily basis. Maybe the shipment of batteries for the 119F's had been packed with the flexible solar rig, rather than with the accessory pallet for the Diesel unit, he thought as he read the papers.

Lion made a mental note to ask the Logistics Officer from the Australian Army to send the four sea-cans to the assembly area in the 'back 40' of the sprawling Robertson Barracks, in the outskirts of Darwin, but he knew that that was only a temporary solution. Ultimately, the containers would have to find a better home. He put the paperwork back together and made the two-hole punches at the top of the bundled pages, and added them to yet another classified folder full of shipping papers.

It was just one of a hundred decisions he made on a daily basis, attempting to impose a little USMC order on the chaos at the crowded port city. There just weren't enough personnel in the Combat Logistics Company to handle the massive influx of equipment coming off the ship; what with supplies, rolling stock and other material for no less than a dozen different USMC units being deployed into the Northern Territory.

Before returning to his log-plot, Lieutenant Lion thought about the classified folders he had been building up; folders that had come with each sea container, vehicle, tri-wall or other shipping container that arrived from San Diego or Joint Base Lewis McChord and other log bases in the immense USPACOM AOR. But basically, it was just paperwork; mountains and mountains of paperwork.

Lieutenant Lion knew that a careful analysis of the shipping paperwork would have revealed the scale of the pre-positioning scheme. Therefore every snippet of information about these war-fighting supplies was treated as Top Secret, even if, on their own, each individual shipping label was either Secret or merely Unclassified. As busy as he was, he did not fall into the trap of using his computer to track the material, as he had been specifically forbidden to use any networked computer for anything other than routine work. Major Blakely, the new Liaison Officer, had convinced Major Bantry, the S4 Log, that the USPACOM material must be treated as though it were not even there. With the Australians' poor record of electronic security, using paper copies was the best way to keep the details from showing up in the local media or by being hacked by foreign intelligence operatives. It made sense to Lieutenant Lion, but it also made his life that much more complicated.

It was already difficult enough. Not only was it impossible to simply establish their own USMC base in Australia, due to local political issues, but also, the 3rd Marine Expeditionary Force – especially Marine Logistics Group – were stretched to the limit.

As much as Lieutenant Lion found the confusion and inefficiencies created by the non-standard practices to be annoying, he understood why it had to be this way. Everybody in the Corps knew that the strategy for the Western Pacific and South Asian region was to maximize the number of areas where the USMC and the American military in general had local knowledge, by basing or rotating numerous small units, negotiating 'Status of Forces Agreements', SOFA, and by steadily habituating the locals to a persistent, non-problematic American presence.

As one of only a few dozen personnel who were actually stationed in Australia, living in Married Quarters with their dependents unlike the bulk of the MAGTFA who rotated in on a short term basis to Darwin from their permanent stations in Okinawa and Hawaii, Lieutenant Lion knew that his job had a strategic role. Perhaps it was not as much of a strategic role as the USMC LnO, Major Blakely, who was in direct liaison roles with the Australian military units and their high command. However, just by virtue of being in place for the next three years, the young logistics officer had to take a long view on his task. For the bulk of the MAGTFA, on the other hand, the focus was the deployment - force generation - force employment - recovery - redeployment cycle that Marines were so well known for. Their battle-rhythm was all about showing up unannounced, kicking ass in combat or masterfully demonstrating their combat arts in hair-raising exercises and maneuvers, and then sorting out their kit and making themselves scarce.

In the two-week pause between deployments, the rotating-in Marines were passing through either the 'Sea Port of Disembarkation', SPOD at the Darwin dockside, or if they travelled by air, through the 'Aerial Port of Disembarkation', APOD, at the Tindal RAAF air base farther inland, directly south of Darwin. The out-going Marines passed through the very same dockyard and airstrip on their 'Embarkation', through the SPOE and APOE. It was easy to tell the men apart, as the incoming men typically had a bewildered look about them, not knowing which way was up in their new Area of Operational Responsibility, AOR; whereas the out-rotating men seemed to be much more comfortable with their surroundings. Both groups were always spic-and-span, their kit properly squared away in USMC tradition.

Lieutenant Lion's job, as the resident 'movements' subject matter expert in MAGTFA, was to sort their logistics out, making sure that the right kit, fuel, food, water, ammunition, weapons systems, combat service support, telecommunications equipment, office supplies, transportation support and, most importantly, personal kit, pay and mail arrived where it was expected, at the appointed time.

Lion's job was difficult enough on a routine deployment, where the entire operation was self-contained and largely planned and executed from a supporting base, such as his own home unit, Combat Logistics Element, 1st Btn, 3rd Marines, out of Camp Courtney, Hawaii. But with MAGTFA, having to use the constellation of warehouses, storage facilities and aircraft hangars loaned to the Marines by the Host Nation, Australia, and to comply with the Robertson Barracks Post Orders somehow wrapping around the 3rd Marines own Standing Operational Procedures, the red tape and problems were greatly magnified.

Were it not for the help of the two long-term SNCOs from 31st Marine Expeditionary Unit, out of Camp Hansen, Okinawa, Lieutenant Lion would have been overwhelmed. But Master Gunns Gannon and Top Sergeant Rideout had time and time again helped the young logistics officer, mostly by steering him toward the right contacts within the Royal Australian Army, RAA, in the Darwin area, and the Royal Australian Air Force, RAAF, at the air base a few hundred miles to the south. He was on his own with the squids, but the compact nature of the sole Royal Australian Navy dockyard in Darwin made it easy to figure out who was who in the zoo.

The one thing Lion found strange about the two SNCOs was that they had none of the "in-and-out" mentality that reflected the rapidly changing world of typical Marine deployments. Rather, they seemed committed to settling in and making long-term friendships, close bonds, and something strangely like 'fitting in' to the Australian military community. It was almost as if Master Gunns and the Top Sergeant were planning to stay here for a significant period of time. *Perhaps the rest of their lives*, he thought, and then shook his head.

Lion thought about the way Gunns Gannon was putting so much time and effort into working out all the little snags which came along, taking care to resolve each and every issue into a good long-term solution rather than simply overcoming some particular obstacle before moving on to bigger things. Top Sergeant Rideout, similarly, was all over any Marine, at any rank level, who crossed the line and made any sort of trouble with the Aussie military personnel and, even more so, their civilians.

Likely from the influence of the two SNCOs, Lion had noticed, there was a subtle but notable tightening of the behavior of the Marines rotating in from the 3rd Marine Expeditionary Force and elsewhere. Once indoctrinated by the briefings and seemingly omnipresent SNCOs, the men were behaving at their best, and with an air of seriousness that he could only put down to the rumor that Gannon and Rideout were preparing the men for war – real war, where men died, and never saw home and family again; where every hour off-duty, every safe day or quiet night of sleep, was one of your last.

As he followed the thread in his own mind, Lion started to wonder, *who will the enemy be? China? Indonesia? India?* He had no idea. *I've got to take more time to read the daily INTSUM*, he thought, suddenly more concerned with his own poor understanding of the regional threats. *If war is coming, I better get my act together, especially on the caches – Major Bantry is wrong to put those off. If we go to war suddenly, here in Australia, we'll need fuel, food, ammunition and spares to be safely tucked away farther inland. Leaving it all stockpiled at the Darwin dockyard and hangars at Tindal is a single point of failure. I gotta get working on moving that stuff out to the notional dispersal sites, farther inland. Like those solar-power generators, they shouldn't be sitting in the sea-can graveyard at Robertson Barracks. They should be forward deployed to the dispersal sites from the get-go. Maybe I should go around Major Bantry, and talk to Major Blakely about getting some log support from Australian 1st Brigade, and their Combat Service Support Battalion. Cut through the red tape, and get the trucks moving.*

At just that moment, Major Blakely and Major Bantry were having a heated discussion about the very same thing. At first, Bantry had tried to show his strategic grasp by laying out all the problems with the as-yet unfinished revisions to the Status of Forces Agreement, SOFA, that was supposed to spell out in great detail all of the support, facilities and freedom of movement that Australia was going to give the MAGTFA. However, Major Blakely was pressing him to get on with the job of moving the USPACOM contingency supplies onward, despite the incomplete SOFA.

"Look Bantry, it's your fucking job to get those convoys on the road," Blakely snapped. "It's my job to work with the Aussies to get you whatever square footage you need in whatever bum-fuck little towns the S5 planners have identified as suitable dispersal sites. And I'm telling you for the Nth time that the high command of the R-double-A-F and the R-double-A are responding promptly to each and every request we have made. They are with us on this. They want the stuff tucked away in the outback, and they don't care if it's the 3rd Marines, the 7th Marines, the US Army or their own militia who end up using this stuff when the time comes. They just want it out of sight and secure. Your dog-fuck of an assembly area out behind Robertson Barracks, and that colossal pile of stuff in the hangars at Tindal are definitely not secure, nor are they invisible. I'm surprised the local media are not all over this – it's only a matter of time before we have protesters at the gate, and international press asking us what all the material is really for, for Christ's sake!"

Major Bantry understood what Blakely was talking about. As much as he wanted a perfect SOFA to get signed off, even he had to admit that the incoming material was becoming a circus. And he knew that it was his fault that it had not been forwarded onward to the dispersal sites. He understood that the idea was that this would ensure that America had an easily expandable footprint which they could mobilize follow-on forces into when the strategic situation required. In the case of the Northern Territory of Australia, this meant pre-positioning sufficient war-fighting stocks of ammunition, equipment and material to support a Division of US Marines, nineteen thousand men, which would be drawn from the 3rd Marine Expeditionary Force in Okinawa, the 3rd Marine Regiment in Hawaii, and if needed, reinforcements from 7th Marines, in San Diego and attachments from the other units of the 1st Marine Expeditionary Force in Twentynine Palms, California.

But the lack of American bases meant that the equipment had to be squirreled away at existing locations in Australia where there already was an American presence, or in warehouse space 'loaned' to the Marines by the Australian Army.

Bantry gave in. Not as someone deflated by failure, but as a professional strong enough to snap-to and change course when required. "OK, Joe, I'll go along with you on this. Just as long as you get the Aussies to push the facilities' footprints and capabilities to me. I'll send the convoys to the bare bones sites, along with as many traffic techs and movements people as I can spare. But in each and every case the Aussies will have to set up local support, engineers, heavy equipment and general duty personnel to help break down the loads, sort out the facilities in terms of deficiencies, required maintenance, structural issues and security overlays - and handle the PA suppression too. If I can assume all of that, then, OK, I'll get the trucks rolling."

Blakely appreciated the cooperation and returned the familiarity. "Thanks, Ken. You'll have it. So how soon can you get the first convoys out the door?"

"How about a week?"

"Sorry, that's not good enough," Major Blakely pressed, suddenly back into hard-ass mode, "The Aussies were expecting to see convoys rolling right off the ships and right through town. I want to see some advance parties out the door tomorrow night, with the larger convoys to follow within 72 hours. Can you accomplish that, or do we have to take this up with Colonel Millar?"

Bantry sighed at the thought of the ass-kicking that he would get if he had to interrupt Colonel Millar from his meetings with RAA's 1st Division, their Training Command, in Brisbane.

"No, there's no need to bother Colonel Millar. I really should have gotten to this point on my own. And no," he continued, his back up at Blakely's nagging. "I'm not going to get into some pissing contest with you. I'll give the orders tonight, but there's going to be some problems caused by the way things have piled up. If we do it your way, and push things up the road in haste, there's bound to be a lot of stuff that goes to the wrong place. Deliberate planning will be out the window. You know that, don't you?"

"Yes, but far better to have it dispersed and screwed up than all piled up here and screwed up! So great, get on with it. I'll be at my desk with the Aussie's 1st Brigade by 0600 hours, to help coordinate. Just give me one of your junior officers to help with liaison and load-planning. Have him report to me by 0700 hours, OK?"

"Sure. I'll send you Lion."

"Great. I know that kid. He's got a good head on his shoulders."

Three days later, after some challenging days getting the advance parties to their dispersal sites, the backlog of sea cans and trucks began to disappear from Darwin and Tindal. It did not take Major Blakely and Lieutenant Lion very long to become intimately familiar with the 'bare base' facilities at such strange sounding places like: "Weipa, Exmouth, and Derby".

Lacking sufficient guidance on the USPACOM contingency material, they had to rely on their own judgment. So they had fallen into a habit of sending first-line command-and-control related supplies to the facilities in Bachelor and Katherine, which were considered far enough south of Darwin, yet accessible from the few road lines of communication to constitute fairly accessible contingency stores. The facilities dispersed in the remote communities of Northern Territory had been loaned to the MAGTFA HQ Battalion by the Australians until more centralized, secure facilities could be constructed for the storage of the war-fighting stores. Similarly, the second and third-line items were being stockpiled in more distant, similarly non-descript warehouses in the remote communities farther along the 1500 kilometers from Darwin to Alice Springs.

For the more sensitive equipment, such as Information Management material and certain types of ammunition, from depleted uranium 0.50 caliber rounds to vast quantities of C4 and other Explosives Ordinance Disposal resources which required climate controlled and high-security storage facilities, Alice Springs was seen as the most strategic destination, not only because it was located virtually in the center of the Australian continent, but also because there was a great deal of infrastructure already there and under US control.

The American-operated facility at Pine Gap, some eighteen kilometers from Alice Springs, was ostensibly a Satellite Tracking Station, but that was only part of it. The facility was actually a multi-agency, multi-purpose installation, hosting a surprisingly robust Central Intelligence Agency presence with a variety of communications eavesdropping and analysis capabilities comprising the core of the South Asian intelligence gathering operation for CIA Headquarters, Langley Virginia.

The facility was built around an ECHELON system of Cold War origins. ECHELON was part of the SIGINT efforts of the "Five Eyes" signatory nations to the UKUSA Security Agreement: Australia, Canada, New Zealand, United Kingdom and the United States of America. Capable of intercepting land-lines, satellite transmission, computer networks, internet traffic, microwave and other forms of information transmission, the ECHELON system has been operating with impunity since the Congressional Oversight Committee and House Committee on Information Security were shut down in the later years of the Obama administration.

With so much information now wide open to the American and "Five Eyes" SIGINT operators at Pine Gap, one might assume that the analysts had their finger on the pulse for all of the South Asian AOR. Nothing could be farther from the truth, however, as the 500 or so American and allied analysts and support personnel were simply inundated with information flow. As such, the facility at Pine Gap was going through yet another expansion; gently but persistently pushing the Australians into giving the Americans more and more space that was entirely under American control; habituating the Australians to accept that there were more and more spaces within the facility that the Australians simply could not go into and were not to ask about. It was the closest thing yet to sovereign territory of the United States within Australia, like the US Embassy, in Canberra.

This meant that the 'special' loads could be inspected or accessed by the Americans without observation by the host nation, Australia. Some of the contents were not to be shared with the Australians, so they could not be stored in any facility not completely controlled by Americans – which left Pine Gap as the only suitable destination, despite the 1500 km distance from Darwin.

It also fit with some of the contingency plans, many of which called for the Americans to take the lead for Command, Control, Communications, Computers, Surveillance and Intelligence, C4ISR, in support of an allied effort which, ultimately, would see American military forces dwarfing their Australian allies. However in peace-time, the US had to be subtle in gradually expanding the footprint of the NSA, CIA and other intelligence gathering entities that became ensconced in the American-controlled facility at Pine Gap.

It also looked good on the map. It was right in the center of the massive Australian landmass, with Highway A87, known as Stuart Highway, bisecting the Australian continent from Darwin in the extreme north, through Alice Springs and Ayers Rock in the barren center, and on to the sleepy city of Adelaide and the wine producing regions in South Australia.

Major Blakely knew that Major Bantry was right about the likelihood that some of the material would have be brought all the way back to Darwin or redirected to some of the smaller dispersal sites in the smaller communities, once the dust had settled. *If it ever would*, he thought, *but security now is worth the inconvenience later.*

While Major Bantry and Major Blakely worked out the big picture, Lieutenant Lion was responsible for the nuts and bolts of the logistics coordination. After getting word that Bantry was getting things moving, he wrapped up the latest batch of paperwork for the air movements team at RAAF Tindal before getting started with re-jigging the convoy load planning, to fit the now accelerated pace that Bantry and Blakely were hastening.

In comparison to the mess of sea-cans, vehicles and other stockpiles, the day-to-day aviation related spares he dealt with were much simpler, going straight to the sprawling gravel parking area by the old hangar on the military side of Darwin International Airport, which the Aussies had provided to Marine Aviation Logistics Squadron 24, MALS24, 'The Warriors'.

Lieutenant Lion's counterpart there, the sexy red-haired Captain Allison Falkner, was having no problem keeping up with the hand-off from Lion, of the arriving stream of spares for the helicopters of the 1st Marine Aircraft Wing. David Lion envied her in a way, as she still had a few months before the two CH53E Super Stallion heavy-lift helicopters and their crews would arrive on a C-17. All she had to do was herd kittens to support the eight Twin Huey's, two C-12's – basically the same as a Beechcraft Super King Air 200 - and the twice-weekly arrival of C-130 Hercules transport runs from Marine Corps Air Station Futenma, on Okinawa, Japan.

For the really big APOD activities, such as C-17 and C-141 flights, personnel and freight were to be offloaded at the RAAF base at Tindal, about 200 miles south of Darwin, where the Marines occasionally rotated a squadron of FA-18 hornets and the occasional F35 for trials with the RAAF. There had already been a few sea containers Lion had sent on to Tindal, with heavy items such as engines, wheels and other spares for the Air Force, and, of course, the constant two-way stream of Marines rotating into and out of the Australian AOR.

From a logistical point of view, the rest came by sea. The heavy equipment, Light Armored Vehicles and variety of special-purpose engineering equipment trundled off Military Sealift Command's Large Medium Speed Roll-on / Roll-off ship, USNS Soderman, at the docks in Darwin. The Ro-Ro had finally arrived at Port in Darwin. With so little room to work with at the navy pier across from the Darwin Convention Centre, Lieutenant Lion had to keep things moving.

As it was, the influx of military equipment had turned Kitchener Drive into a veritable parking lot. It infuriated Lion and the rest of the logistics staff standing up the MAGTFA that the geniuses at 3rd Marine Regimental HQ considered the Vehicle & Equipment Prepositioning Ship to have arrived 'in time' for the Joint Combined Exercise that was scheduled to start on June first. But the two weeks the Logistics Company had had to offload, trans-ship and deliver the equipment to the boys in 2nd Battalion, 3rd Marines was just too tight. The equipment still had to be inspected, serviced, and staged before it could be used in the upcoming 'Exercise Rope-A-Dope' with the Australian Army.

The Marines themselves had arrived weeks before and the Top Sergeant had put them through some sort of orientation in the Australian outback. When they came back to Robertson Barracks they expected that their Light Armored Vehicles, Humvees and other vehicles had arrived, been serviced, fuelled and were sitting ready to go in an assembly area. Despite the challenges and unrealistic deadlines the loggies faced, they accomplished the task. Their late nights and considerable personal initiative, as always, were invisible to the rest of the Marines, who only noticed their logistics support personnel when something went wrong.

As much as he felt that he was single-handedly bringing order to the chaos involved in standing up an entire Marine Air Ground Task Force, Lieutenant David Lion was not the only person working furiously under tight timelines, grappling with the minutest of details of the locations of military and civilian strategic stockpiles, critical infrastructure, industrial installations and the intricacies of how Australian military units functioned.

After his direct flight from Hong Kong, ostensibly to study Agriculture at the University of Newcastle, Zhao Yingting had felt like a hero. He had been on dangerous missions before, including a daring insertion into Sudan before the civil war, to control a Sudanese warlord who played a role in removing opposition to the Chinese acquisition of foreign oil companies in Sudan's oil producing areas. Were it simply a corporate matter, officials with China's state-controlled commodities investment firms would have simply used US currency to secure the assets by bribing corrupt officials. But in Sudan, as in many troubled third world countries, China had recently taken to deploying ruthless and very talented spies with vast sums of money to secure the more active local influence of the dominant warlords, so that China's future access to the area's commodities would not be interfered with. And with the old US currency having become about as useful as toilet paper, the currency of influence and promises required a more intimate touch. This often required agents such as Zhao to be inserted into the equation, in support of sophisticated operations to remove or install the right sort of warlord – one who could be managed effectively in pursuit of China's strategic interests. But Sudan had been a walk in the park compared to his current mission.

Here in Australia he would be alone, without the direct supervision of more experienced agents as he had enjoyed in Sudan; none of his embassy's support team to back him up if things got out of hand.

On the way to Australia, he had been excited at the prospect of showing his superiors what he was capable of doing. But as the plane approached the airport, he started to get scared. He sweated and his hands began to tremble; this was Captain Zhao who, through what he believed was his great talent and obvious destiny, had believed himself to be the perfect man for the job.

Originally a product of a fortress garrison in Jinan Military District, Captain Zhao Yingting showed great promise as he rose through the ranks. When he led a team of eight special forces operatives of the People's Liberation Army Ground Forces in an international military skills competition held in Slovakia in 2009, the then junior sergeant's team had gathered in an impressive eight first-place finishes and four second place finished in the fifteen-event competition. Soon after, he had been deep-selected into the PLA Officer Corps as a rising star, and ultimately honed as an agent in the External Intelligence Branch of the PLA's 42nd Group Army, based in Guangzhou Military Region, along the extreme south-coast of China.

With Hong Kong and Macau within the Guangzhou region, the 42nd Group Army had been given additional resources to identify, recruit, and cultivate skilled agents to be sent abroad – ostensibly as simple students out of China's most open, westernized cities.

Through several years of study abroad, Captain Zhao Yingting had worked hard to improved his stilted English, but had plateaued below the 'working proficiency' level. He simply was not linguistically gifted. On the other hand, he had been fairly successful when he had been tried out as an external spy, influence peddling in Sudan, and more recently infiltrating expatriate Chinese communities in England. Periodically he had been brought back to China for advanced training and attempts to develop him into more meaningful competencies. He had excelled at studies in computer science, showing promise as a hacker, but was not quite good enough for the elite hacking units of the PLA. The problem was his lack of social skills. He blundered his way through relations with teachers, peers and superiors.

Upon closer examination, his psychological profile proved him to be too insecure and emotional, ultimately unsuitable as a cyber-warrior. Extremely tall, he was a gangling young man who stood out in a crowd, as he towered over everyone around him. While stumbling and bumping into things wherever he went, he somehow had prowess on the basketball court. That is, until his run-in with the Georgetown team. On one hand, he could be aggressive and even vicious; on the other hand, it was noted by his superiors, Zhao had a harsh streak that could show itself at inopportune times, raising his profile when it was least desired.

Zhao might not be quite the person for a very important mission, they had determined.

Yet in the frenzied shuffle and secrecy in assigning agents ruthless enough for OPERATION WINTER SNAKE, somehow he had slipped past the checks and balances and been selected as a Little Dragon. It takes a bureaucracy as big as the PLA's, or any other large military for that matter, to fit such a square peg into a round hole.

Zhao had just returned to China after a particularly dangerous, 'no-notice' mission, assassinating an Iranian official in London - to great praise from his Commanding Officer back in Guangzhou City. The hasty execution of the Iranian diplomat had led to collateral damage that other Chinese agents had been forced to quickly clean up. This had made his continued presence in Great Britain too risky for the Chinese state, so Zhao had been concerned about whether there would be consequences for his mixed performance. But with Australia now higher on the Chinese agenda, Captain Zhao intuited that he might wind up down under, or some other place he could continue to develop his English language skills. But as the weeks wore on without a new assignment, he had begun to worry.

He had been sitting idle at a military university up in Jinan province for several months, and had begun to feel that his career had come to a grinding halt. But then he had been summoned to the Headquarters of Jinan Military District for a briefing that was so secret even his commanding officer did not know that he had been called in. After he had been briefed-in and given his mission orders, he had not even been allowed to return to the Jinan Military Academy, where he had been treading water.

He had been moved around for a variety of specialized training sessions, where his ability with a range of communications and computer systems were brought up to speed, with a particular emphasis on systems operated by the Australian military. Strangely, he had also been given a winter survival course, up in the mountains of Mingyon Glacier, Yunnan Province. It had seemed ludicrous to him to focus on winter survival skills and alpine conditioning. He chalked it up to the occasional inefficiency of the training systems in the People's Liberation Army. *What use will I have for winter survival skills in Australia?* he had thought.

Yingting Zhao had been ordered not to discuss, or even think about the mission itself, not even to his closest compatriots in Special Ops Battalion, Guangzhou. He had also been ordered to relocate his wife and son to a remote village outside of Nanning, where they were required to stay until called for.

Zhao did not really know much about his mission, other than the highly motivational and philosophical material that he had been spoon-fed in the in-brief. Oblivious to what he was getting himself into, Zhao had eagerly soaked up what a more reflective thinker would have recognized as nationalistic propaganda dressed up in purposely distorted Chinese mythology.

What Zhao had been told of his actual mission was that he would deploy to New South Wales, NSW, on a Foreign Student Visa, and spend three months settling into a predictable and low-profile routine as just one of many Chinese students among the 40,000 students of the North Coast Institute of the Technical and Further Education, TAFE, campus at Port Macquarie, NSW. One detail that had been stressed was that he must take special care with a small porcelain LAOZI statuette. It had been handed to him after an inspirational speech about Yinglong, the 'responding dragon', that would ascend Phoenix-like from the ashes of a destroyed world and restore China to its rightful place, the ascendant master of the earth.

Captain Zhao had been told to watch for the Yinglong signal, which had not been explained in detail, other than "you will know it when the time comes. It will relate to that first girlfriend of yours, in your village".

Fei Yen, flying swallow, Zhao thought.

"Her name, in conjunction with the Yinglong, will be your activation code. Until you hear the Yinglong signal, you must not break open the Liwu, 'gift'."

He was told to build a small network of friends, from the local Chinese community, who he could call upon for 'a great adventure', and to know as much about his assigned area as possible, but not to be seen as gathering intelligence. Just be ready to switch into high gear, when the time comes.

Zhao had reached out to accept the 'gift' with reverence, as much out of his enthusiastic agreement with Colonel Huang about China's destiny, as out of his commitment to treat the statuette with great care simply because he had been ordered to do so. It would be the most important item in his suitcase, and his entire mission hinged on his getting it through customs upon arrival in Australia. After that, he was to keep it intact for months, until he was activated, and then that he would break it apart to reveal a sheet of paper hidden inside. If it were discovered by Customs and Immigration, even if they had it translated, it would appear to be nothing more than a poem, written in archaic Chinese, that had been preserved inside the statue as some sort of prosperity trinket. His story was that it was a gift that Yingting brought from China to give a professor or other lucky recipient, in gratitude for their kindness or hospitality.

Now, after three months of hard work at the Port Macquarie TAFE campus, Zhao had built a reputation as a hard-working student that was surprisingly socially active for a student from China. His professors found him to be infinitely curious about everything Australian, devouring every opportunity to explore, visit, or talk about a wide range of agricultural, manufacturing, and commercial enterprises. Still, the professors noted his social ineptitude, Yingting Zhao being the initiator of many an embarrassing incident. Good on paper, they thought, but in person, as in a job interview or post-graduate screening, he'd never pass muster.

Still, his intellectual curiosity seemed to be well balanced with his vigorous fitness regime, which was unlike other Asian students. Yingting spent hours upon hours cycling up and down the hilly roads in the many forest parks inland from Port Macquarie. What he did not understand at the time was that those early rides, which he had been ordered to do before he left China, had merely been training for the much larger tour he would ultimately take, along with another agent who had been put in place in Southport, farther up the coast, in Queensland.

After being activated and breaking open their Laozi statuettes, and wiping lemon juice over the archaic poem to reveal the orders, written in invisible ink, the two "Little Dragons" had immediately understood the importance of their missions and why there had been so much emphasis on physical training back in China; the reason behind all the paranoia about operational security.

As per their orders, they had sought each other out, using the code-words and duress codes they had been given. The two soldiers had never met before, but recognized the experience, focus and confidence that told them that they were peers. Intensely dedicated to China, the professional spies rolled up their sleeves and got down to work without wasting any time socializing or enjoying the many distractions available to them in Australia.

Together, they had spent ten days cycling from Newcastle, New South Wales, to Southport, Queensland - but not along Highway One, the coast road, which would have been a mere seven hundred kilometers. Rather than the easy route, they had been ordered to follow a specific route and to stay at specified locations along the way. Their route took them as far inland as Bourke, NSW, and Cunnamulla, QLD stretching their journey to over two thousand kilometers of sun-baked, neck-burning, tongue-drying torture.

The athletic soldiers loved it, putting in up to two hundred kilometers per day. Fortunately they did not have to carry much in their panniers, other than a few changes of clothes, water, and a range of energy snacks. Unlike touring cyclists who they met on the road, who had saddle-bags loaded with camping gear or had their equipment carried by a support vehicle following them, the Chinese agents operated independent of any support and yet travelled extremely light, knowing that they would find food and lodging every night. To the recreational cyclists they encountered, the two Chinese men seemed a bit odd - one man being extraordinarily tall and thin, like a twig; the other short and muscular, like a tree trunk.

Their task was to pay a surprise visit, to check on the status of two dozen other Little Dragon agents. Most of these agents were low level agents who had not been given anywhere near the level of operational details as Zhao and his counterpart from Southport. But each had been given a clear tactical objective, from a military installation, piece of critical infrastructure, civil defense or law enforcement agency, or simply an operationally important cross-roads. During their inspection tour they were shown the digital photographs, maps and detailed record of observations of personal movements, timetables and other aspects of the regional Little Dragon's assignments.

They were also briefed on the number and status of each of the dozen or so "Dragonflies" that each Little Dragon had been ordered to recruit in their assigned area. Most of these Dragonflies were Chinese expats who happened to be in the community assigned to the Little Dragon, such as legitimate international students or businesspeople who had no idea that China was about to make an audacious move for Australia's commodities. What they did understand, when carefully felt out by the Little Dragon who had identified them as potential recruits, was that once they had been approached they really only had two choices: enroll in the local network of Dragonflies that the Little Dragon was putting together, *or face the consequences.*

Invariably, these Chinese citizens, with loved ones back home in mainland China, knew what that meant. The few who showed even the slightest hesitation to do their part for the cause had been unceremoniously murdered.

Very few Dragonflies were recruited from the general population of Australian Chinese, however. The exceptions to this rule were a few unhappy young Australian Chinese, found to be susceptible to the intoxicating propaganda, or to drugs, sex, alcohol, or a variety of other 'perks' the Little Dragons tempted them with and were recruited. Zhao had met a few of these Australian traitors, and he despised them. He saw what they were doing as a reflection on their character. In his mind, their disloyalty to their birthplace was not erased by their vigorous enthusiasm for the Motherland, the *Zuguo*. *But they could have their uses*, he had decided, *even if I would not personally trust a single one of them. They're not really Chinese anymore, after all.*

The final topic discussed with each of the regional Little Dragons in Zhao and his stocky counterpart's two areas of operational responsibility were the 'key players' in the community. In most cases, the Little Dragon had built up detailed files on the most influential civic officials, military personnel in the area, industrial and commercial players, as well as the more influential members of the Australian-Chinese community. A great many of the 500,000 ethnic Chinese citizens of Australia would be deeply conflicted when the time came, so the Little Dragons been ordered to generally avoid approaching Australian-born Chinese directly, other than to gather intelligence on them for use during later stages of the coming invasion.

Captain Zhao was generally pleased. However he did encounter a Little Dragon, in Dubbo, who seemed to have fallen off the rails, expressing concerns about what was about to happen. As per his orders as a regional commander of what was essentially a 'Fifth Column', Zhao had taken the man out to a remote area, along with one of the man's more promising Dragonflies. Once in the secluded area, Zhao pulled out a pistol and pointed it at the Little Dragon.

"On your knees," he hissed at his comrade, who obeyed in confusion. Then Zhao pulled a short cord from his pocket and, handing it to the Dragonfly, simply said, "Do it."

The Dragonfly immediately understood what that meant. Without a word, the young novice wrapped the cord around the Little Dragon's throat and began strangling his mentor. Zhao watched with pleasure, smiling as the Little Dragon struggled in his death throes. The Dragonfly, executing his former recruiter, would then take over his mission, the blood on his hands proving his loyalty to the cause.

After completing the regional inspection together, the two Little Dragon agents parted company and turned their focus to their own tactical missions; in Zhao's case, at Port Macquarie. He did not know why Port Macquarie was so important, as it really was not much of a port at all. Certainly it could not accommodate a ship with much of a draft. It seemed to Zhao that the town was no more than a pleasant little city of 44,000; a sleepy, retirement-oriented place. There were no military units in the area, no industry, and no port facilities to speak of. There was not even a rail line. But his orders had been clear, and from the Port Macquarie district at large he had generated a list of thirty potential Chinese to work on, out of which he had generated a half-dozen Dragonflies which he trained for the assignment of to the coal terminal in nearby Newcastle. He was satisfied that this 'Team One' understood their mission: the requirement being to wait for the mysterious Yinglong signal, and to link up with follow-on forces who would arrive soon after on a Ro-Ro that would pull into the Coal Terminal full of heavy armor. It would be their job – and that of their Australian dockyard workers who Team One was to take prisoner – to offload immediately upon arrival.

Zhao then turned his attention to training up Team Two, the section of Dragonflies he had selected for his task at the Port Macquarie airport, which was expected to be a much easier task. However, out of his desire to be praised for his good work by the senior officers that he would encounter at the second site, he wanted to be with Team Two when the time came.

Perhaps his two assignments in Port Macquarie would prove to be more important than they appeared. He hoped, anyhow. *Secrecy is the key*, thought Captain Yingting Zhao. *We have to be ruthless in defense of operational security, until the appointed time...*

The sort of man most feared by Captain Zhao and other Little Dragons was out there, albeit several steps behind the curve.

His orders came from the Strategy Unit of the New South Wales Police Force's little known Operations Group, which was responsible for evaluating the national dimension of global trends affecting the diverse range of Australian cultural communities. Many of these, such as the Chinese community, were considered 'closed communities', which were notoriously hard to penetrate. But for Leading Senior Constable Nicholas Lenko, the assignment seemed tailor made.

The product of the marriage between an Australian diplomat and a white woman born and raised in China, Nick had been raised with his mother's native language and cultural sophistication and his father's citizenship and name as his birth-right. But it was not until he was sixteen years old that Nick's parents finally repatriated to the Sydney area, upon his father's retirement from the Diplomatic and Consular Corps.

On his father's advice, he had kept the Chinese aspect of his upbringing a secret, at least from the other recruits and instructors he had encountered at the NSW Police Academy. The information was disclosed on the Enhanced Reliability Screening form, when he had first applied for entry into the ranks of the NSW Police Force, along with the details of his residency and employment over the previous ten years. However he simply had not broadcast this to other police at large. And why should he? There was clearly an anti-Chinese sentiment in Australia and he did not want to be singled out for being half-Chinese.

To all intents and purposes, he was a typical Caucasian cop, fitting in well with the other highly trained cops in the Operations Division. Administration, on the other hand, knew all about his fully bilingual status – trilingual if you consider that he was equally adept in Mandarin as in Cantonese.

Nick had long expected that his Chinese skills would eventually open some doors for him, but had wanted to establish himself as a police officer so that he would never be accused of playing the race card. As a result, when he was first approached by Chief Superintendent Waroway for a special assignment that required his unique characteristics, he had agreed. When told that he would be required to keep his linguistic abilities secret, even from other NSW police officers, he had become even more enthusiastic. It was a perfect fit.

Nick saw the short-term assignment as a chance to make his move towards the Operations Group Strategy Unit's Asian cell without broadcasting that this was his ultimate goal. As it was, while the OGSU had conceived of the operation it had been tightly controlled by the somewhat paranoid Chief Superintendent in charge, who trusted few with operational information, and trusted Information Systems – computers and electronics – even less.

As a result of Chief Superintendent Waroway's paranoia and Leading Senior Constable Lenko's own secrets, essentially nobody knew the true nature of his assignment – not even the section within the People's Liberation Army, Jinan Region, who were assigned to monitoring the operations of the New South Wales Police Force to the minutest of details. In other areas, it would be accurate to say that the PLA personnel monitoring foreign police forces had a better grasp on specialist police units operations than the units themselves often did.

The assignment itself was rather pedestrian. He was set up as a 'mature student' at Macquarie University, Sydney. Not to be confused with Port Macquarie, the small port city about 300 km farther north of Sydney along the NSW coastline, Macquarie University was one of Sydney's three most important universities.

Lenko's task was to attend a full-time course-load as if pursuing a degree in network administration, all the while watching for visiting Chinese students who seemed to be particularly socially active or were doing a lot of things that were not strictly related to their studies. The assumption behind his task was that the spies amongst the visiting Chinese students would be found to be talking to more people than the stereotypical studies-focused workaholics that genuine students tended to be.

As a cover, the Chinese spies might be interested in photography, have large networks of friends, travel more than the others and have more money to spend on their activities. Other cues to look for were English language skills that were above average from the get-go, competencies like leisure sports or driving a vehicle - things which could hint at someone being a highly trained operative.

After four months, Leading Senior Constable Lenko was updating the master list of names that he had identified as warranting special attention. As part of his protocol, the routine was to send the names and student ID numbers 'through the wash' in the university's computer system, activating certain data-mining 'bots' through the Associate Dean level of access which Waroway had obtained for the operation. This allowed Nick's computer to retrieve information on each subject, such as grades, attendance records, use of cafeteria debit cards, the timings of the subject's entry and exit to the university's swipe-card access-control doors at the sports complex, libraries, laboratories and dormitories along with other information. It presented a virtual picture of the life of a visiting student, which usually fell within a predictable bandwidth of modest social activity, frugality and generally successful academic performance. But as he scanned the rows and columns to see that the data-mining was keeping up to date, Lenko recognized a pattern.

Several of the students he was tracking had had their grades and attendance drop off sharply in recent days. Intrigued, he looked more carefully at each subject's profile, picking up other cues. After cross-checking with the data set from the previous month, and then going two months back, Lenko used another police application to access the credit card data from one of the erratic subjects, and found that the student had used a credit card to rent a car. Upon further investigation, a few mouse clicks really, he found an open-ended hotel reservation at a ski resort in the hills.

Skiing, in April? But the ski season has not even started yet! he thought to himself. *This is strange. There is no way the guy could attend his university classes in Sydney from all the way up in Kosciuszko Mountain.* Lenko checked the student's academic timetable, rolling the calendar forward into mid-May: *He's got five major exams to prepare for. What is this, some kind of study retreat then?*

The next day's lectures provided Nick an opportunity to observe the subject, or suspect, more likely – *only suspected of what?* Nick thought, as he took a seat a few rows below and to the left of the man, in the lecture hall. It was not his normal seat, but he often made a point of sitting in different rows so that he could listen vicariously to Chinese conversations. Leading Senior Constable Lenko assumed that he would not be noticed.

He did not hear much, but by the hushed tones that the subject's circle of friends were speaking in, Nick knew that he was on to something. He surreptitiously snapped a picture of the group of students with his cell phone and did not look in their general direction until the end of the class.

As he walked past the group, he smiled at a pretty Asian girl who had just joined the group. She had looked into his eyes and smiled at him, as if she liked him. He had seen her around the campus a few times but she was not on his list. *Probably a non-player, but wow, great boots!* Nick thought to himself, feeling excited at having some more faces to link to his primary subject – *known accomplices* – he had already categorized them as in his mind.

With the Nancy Sinatra song playing in his head, he made his way back to his apartment in good spirits. *These boots were made for walking....*

Once settled at his desk, he logged onto the secure server and began to run searches on the subject's associates. He found that there were similarities in the unusual behaviour, particularly for three of the subject's friends, who had made similar vehicle and hotel arrangements. All had booked themselves into comfortable, kitchen-equipped suites at resorts well outside of the Sydney area, and all had rented large, expensive SUVs.

Nick was just spell-checking the final draft of an executive summary of his findings and excitedly added some new information – that they had all been spending a great deal of money at the Mountain Equipment Co-op, Columbia Sportswear, and Trek & Travel when he heard a knock at the door.

Distracted by his thoughts, he failed to follow his normal security protocols and simply peeked through the keyhole. Seeing an attractive young co-ed that looked familiar and very cheerful, Nick pulled the door open immediately.

He suddenly regretted not having his Glock 27 in hand, as he became aware of three men he had not seen through the keyhole. They pushed past the pretty Chinese girl and shoved Lenko backwards into his Macquarie University Village apartment. As he struggled to get free and the men pinned him to the floor and covered his mouth, the young woman checked to see that nobody had noticed.

Facing sideways on the floor, he watched as her high-heeled boots danced back into his suite, the door closing behind her with a solid 'clunk' that punctuated the suddenness of his change of circumstances.

He finally placed the girl's face in his mind's eye, and the boots confirmed it. The song was no longer in his head, as he had nothing to be cheerful about any longer. He had gone from hunter to prey, and he knew it.

He knew that he was going to get laid. *That sexy little bitch from Beijing, Jiao, always dancing around in her high boots, she's really getting turned on by all of this. Letting her come along for the ride on this abduction is going to seal the deal! She's going to be so wet,* thought the Dragonfly who had been pleased to see his own name feature so prominently in the cop's report.

Sitting in the passenger seat while a more junior Dragonfly drove the van, he enjoyed riding shotgun on the caper. Three others of his cell rode in the back along with Jiao on the bench opposite the cop, taunting him mercilessly while he sat, hooded, and chained to the floor.

At one point Lenko began to struggle, and became difficult to subdue. They over-did it a bit with the kicks to the anonymous lump under the hood, and knocked him unconscious.

As Lenko lay on the floor of the van, wetness and blood darkening the fabric under his mouth, they soon arrived at their destination.

They took Lenko to the abandoned Dunlop factory in Alexandria, a few kilometers west of Bondi Beach, in Sydney. One of the Dragonflies was a photographer, and had discovered the location online as a great place to shoot pictures of urban decay, graffiti, and acres of abandoned industrial buildings.

It was also a great place to find some privacy, where a man's screams may be heard, but would not draw all that much attention. Even if the police were called, it would take them hours upon hours to search the sprawling wasteland, even if there were a good reason to waste precious resources on such a call. More likely, the Dragonflies knew, the police would not come at all.

The Little Dragon at the centre of a group of two dozen Dragonflies at Macquarrie University had picked up on Lenko's surveillance when he saw the man pretend to be ignoring him while taking his picture with a smart phone. Trained in spotting counter-intelligence, he had long suspected the man was a cop, by the way he watched everybody and everything that was going on in the lecture hall, his eyes always moving like a sentry. So when the Little Dragon had checked in with his regional commander, Scarface, as he thought of the Major from the PLA, he was aware of the seriousness of his discovery.

In less than an hour, Major Goulong Fang had dispatched two other Little Dragons to reinforce the Macquarie University agent, and had given him clear instructions.

After hours of torturing Leading Special Constable Nick Lenko, they knew a great deal of his mission and his operational practices. The Macquarie University Little Dragon personally returned to Lenko's suite to mitigate the potential damage. He soon discovered that Lenko had been truthful in giving up his log-in codes and passwords in the course of his torture.

After reading the draft report on Lenko's laptop, he set to work. First he deleted his name, and three others from his group, ensuring that he removed all supporting documents and other data about their grades, spending habits and credit card transactions. He then inserted alternative names and some additional narrative about there being some cross-over between the now wholly revised list of suspects and their activities in the Bondi Beach and Exchange districts. He rewrote Lenko's conclusion to state that *the subjects do not appear to be foreign intelligence operatives at all, but rather part of a network of international students who buy and sell research papers, essays and other academic materials which they fraudulently submit as their own work*. His final recommendation now read that their names and the evidence should be provided to the legal advisor for the university, and that further surveillance within Macquarie University does not appear to be warranted.

But then he hit a brick wall, and had to call the men holding Lenko at the Abandoned Dunlop Factory site. After hanging up, they forced Lenko to tell them how he sent in his reports. By this time the torturers had figured out Lenko's weakness – his attachment to his testicles – which gave them a quick and easy lever they could pull on, or in this case drive nails into, when they needed Lenko to be more detailed.

Knowing that he had betrayed his country by giving in to the torture, and after having experienced unimaginable physical and psychological pain, Lenko seemed to welcome death when it finally came. His tormentors enjoyed taunting him, telling him something of the changes made to his report as they tried, unsuccessfully, to get him to beg for his death.

What the Little Dragons did not see in the tortured expression on his face was the deep satisfaction that Nick Lenko had hidden from view. He knew that they had not considered that he would have a duress code procedure. A special trick taught to him by one of his instructors in OGSU was to leave a duress word in a report, in this case the phrase "she was tardy", and not to remove the phrase until the moment before sending the report.

Lenko knew that when the analysts in Canberra picked up on his duress code as still being in place they would flag his report as having been sent under duress. That he would be long dead before the Immediate Response Team was sent to check up on him in his flat in Macquarie University Village was of no consequence to Nick. He knew that he was going to die; it came with the territory. But that fact was made easier by the knowledge that the preliminary draft of his report, sent a half hour before he had been interrupted, was without the duress code. It was already in the hopper in his secure cloud account.

So what these fuckers deleted from the report, and what they inserted into the falsified final report, would provide useful intel, he thought, as he saw a man who had recently joined his torturers, a man with an ugly scar on his face - not one of his Macquarie University subjects - moving towards him brandishing a knife.

Nick Lenko did not feel the blade cut across his throat, but he felt a change in the tension in his neck with his cheeks and tongue suddenly feeling as though they had been lifted or were free-floating. The hot, wet, feeling of his own blood pouring over his chest was the final sensation.

General Bing, as always, paid close attention to the briefing. But by the look on his face, he was pleased, despite the news presented to him by Xu.

Of the hundreds of Little Dragons inserted into Australia in the months and weeks before the Yinglong signal, and the six other regional Little Dragon commanders, only two had gotten themselves into any serious trouble. One, assigned to monitor personnel at the RAAF base at Edinburgh, South Australia, had chosen his accommodations poorly and had elected to set up shop in a four-star hotel rather than to rent a modest apartment as per his orders. The fact that he had been given cash, gold coins, and a couple of virtually infinite credit cards had gone to his head and he had decided that his mission meant that he was important enough to warrant the additional expense. He had booked himself into the prestigious Thistle & Clarke Vineyard Hotel, in the Barossa Valley, some 25 km northeast of Adelaide, South Australia.

He had done a fine job documenting the order of battle of the RAAF base at Edinburgh, just west of Adelaide, and even plotting out the residential addresses of the Wing Commander and senior staff as well as each and every one of the Aircraft Commanders from the P3 Orion maritime patrol aircraft of No. 92 Wing, the experimental aircraft crews of the Aerospace Operational Support Group, and the senior officers of the land forces unit co-located with the air base, the 7th Btn, Royal Australian Regiment. His photographs and notes on the fuel farm, engineering plant and other support infrastructure were first rate, and the sixteen Dragonflies he had recruited were loyal to the cause, ready to strike the dispersion airfield which the Australian aircrew were expected to be deployed to when Adelaide is destroyed.

The problem was that he had pinned all of his tactical materials onto the wall, in an impressive montage of espionage. And when the cleaning staff of the hotel had become sick and tired of his rudeness, and the fact that he had kept a "do not disturb" tag hanging off his doorknob for several weeks, they had brought their complaint to the owner, Mr. Clarke himself.

Mr. Clarke did not knock when he opened Mr. Kuang's suite. He had previously noticed the strange comings and goings of a parade of thuggish looking Chinese in the past two weeks, and had had enough of it. A Chinese thug attempted to stop him from entering the suite, but Mr. Clarke, a former soldier, having served in Iraq with The Australian Army's 2nd Division, had no problem pushing the little Chinese aside and walking into the suite to look for himself and see what was going on in *his* fine establishment. Mr. Kuang was not in the suite.

When Clarke saw the intelligence materials on the wall, he recognized its importance and took immediate action. The Dragonfly was no match for the big man, who trussed him up like a sheep, tying his hands and legs together with a telephone cord before speed-dialing the South Australia Police with his cell-phone.

"Mackie, it's Jocko Clarke. Better get a bunch of coppers out here to the hotel. And call in the military. I've come across a right nasty bunch of Red Chinese who mean to do us harm."

"You're not taking the Mickey out of me, are you?"

"No. God's honest truth, Mate. Real spies. I'm looking at pictures of the base at Edinburgh. Maps with all sorts of military symbols, pictures of our Air Force personnel, and of 7[Th] Battalion, Royal Australian Regiment. Heck, here's one of Wing Commander Rawlings, looking fat as ever!"

Two hours later, when he strolled into the hotel foyer and several unfamiliar faces locked onto him, Kuang, the Little Dragon, knew that he had screwed up royally. His mind raced, thinking of what to do, whether it was time to bite down on his suicide tooth or if he should try to link up with some of his Dragonflies and attempt to carry out his mission anyhow.

He chose poorly, electing to turn around and attempt to flee rather than to kill himself while he still had the chance. Caught by his arm as he darted forward, he was spun around and sent crashing into the wall. As he got to his feet, the last thing he saw before he passed out was a big fist smashing into his head.

When he came to, he looked up into the meaty face of an Intelligence Officer from the Royal Australian Army.

"Where am I?" He asked, feeling a strange void where the suicide tooth had been.

"You're in the Base Hospital, Mr. Kuang. And you are in a lot of trouble," said the Intelligence Officer, smiling at the contorted expression on the Chinese spy's face. "What's the matter, missing something?" he said, holding up a plastic bag with the suicide tooth in it.

Kuang jerked his hands in a futile attempt to get his hands on the tooth, only to feel his hands yanked back to the side of the bed by the steel hand-cuffs linked to the bedside rails. He tried to kick and squirm, only to find his legs also bound to the bed frame.

"I'm not telling you anything!" he said, angrily, but the Intelligence Officer only smiled.

"No worries, Mate. You've already told us enough. We've already tracked down most of your thugs. We still haven't figured out what you're on about, but it seems clear to me that you're not here to study agriculture, so we've got you for immigration fraud, to say the least."

Agent Kuang relaxed a bit at that. *Maybe they don't know what's going on. Maybe I can hold out long enough, and it won't matter. The loss of my suicide tooth may not even be such a problem - I could be freed in a matter of days,* Kuang thought.

After seeing the momentary look of hope on his prisoner's face, the intelligence officer took it all away.

"Oh, I guess there's also that espionage thing. Sorry, but we're going to have to send you back to China, hopefully along with that list of names you left for us in your hotel. What are they, a network of spies? PLA? Or some other branch of the Chinese government?" he asked, rhetorically. "So when were you going to make your move? What were your intentions here? You gathering intelligence on our P3s? Or is it our Army you're here to spy on? No matter, we'll know soon enough."

The RAAF intelligence officer was not as confident as he had put on. Despite all the photographs and other material the Chinese spy had left for them to discover in his hotel room, there was nothing there that told them what his actual objective was. *Well, there might be*, he corrected himself, *once they come back from translation services at HQ in Canberra.* For now, all he knew was that the man was a Chinese national who appeared to be collecting information on the military units in the Adelaide area, and appeared to be part of an extensive network of "Little Dragons" and "Dragonflies".

The few available Chinese-speaking officers in the South Australia Police Force had been overwhelmed with the sheer volume of the documents, but had determined that Kuang was part of a major espionage operation. Until more Chinese speaking resources could be brought to bear on the documents, all they could do was try to sweat some information out by 'interviewing' the prisoner.

Other than the indecipherable Chinese documents, the one thing that the RAA Intelligence Officer and the South Australia Police officers on site had been able to determine was that the man had gathered a considerable stash of survival gear, firearms & ammunition, and, strangely, winter weather gear. The rented SUV he had been driving was loaded to the gills with food supplies, fuel canisters and camping gear. It was as if the man was prepared for an extended stay in the wilderness of northern Canada in January, not Australia in May.

Clearly the capture of the Chinese agent was important. *How long has China been doing this? Are they doing it all over Australia? What does it all mean?* the Intelligence Officer wondered, but he knew that it would take some time to properly interrogate the subject and analyze the documents discovered in his suite. And whatever they learned would probably be suppressed, for diplomatic reasons, just as the incidents of Chinese hacking of Department of Defense computers in the USA had been for years. It seemed to him that the Americans, and therefore the Australians, were afraid to provoke China by raising the issue of what was clearly a major state-sponsored effort to hack into military and business computer systems without restraint. *Why do we sit down and take it up the arse from these buggers?* he thought, as he contemplated the implications of such a concerted network of spies.

It made him think of the level of espionage and counter-espionage he had read about war-time Europe. *Perhaps this would prove to be the 'red-handed' discovery that would break it all wide open, put Chinese espionage onto the national agenda. Time will tell.*

In the mean-time, a Priority Intelligence Report had gone up the Australian military chain of command and had been promptly shared with the CIA chaps up in Pine Gap. *Maybe the Americans could put it together with whatever else they had on China,* he thought, as he looked down on the worried looking spy.

5

DRAGONFLIES

This is the most critical phase, thought Colonel Hua, as he scanned the bank of television feeds and computer displays from his central workstation in General Bing's command post, forty meters under the Jinan Military District Headquarters. Once OP PLAN LIWU, "The Gift" began in earnest, and the shooting started, the future emperor of China and his staff, including Hua, would have to monitor events from the much more secure site east of the Shihe Reservoir in the Shihekou Delta region. Colonel Hua, as General Bing's Executive Assistant, the 'Command EA' – equivalent to a western general's Chief of Staff - had been to the snakes-den site many times in the past three years as OPERATION WINTER SNAKE took shape.

Each time he entered the complex he felt an almost religious sense of awe, not at the great accomplishment in engineering, but at the role that the facility would play in history. The humility he gave himself credit for was a false one, however, as Colonel Hua was far more than a mere sycophant – he was a zealot. He had taken the notion that General Bing would become the greatest Emperor in history, revived the ancient Chinese glory and morphed it into an incipient religion, a cult of personality centered on General Bing. He saw himself as a future spokesman for the movement; a high priest, in a sense.

The pleasure he felt as he thought of himself in those terms was rudely interrupted when the Senior Colonel in charge of the External Intelligence Directorate watch-keepers piped up.

"I think we've got a situation here, Command EA! We're going to need the General in here for this," said the Colonel responsible for monitoring the agents abroad, throughout OP PLAN XIAOLONG, "Little Dragon."

"Colonel Xu, go ahead and brief me. I'll decide if what you have to say warrants interrupting the Snakehead," Colonel Hua said, as if speaking to a subordinate. He had long ago begun to throw his weight around, talking down to superior officers as if it were he, not General Bing, who determined who would be the next example.

Senior Colonel Xu thought about how Colonel Hua had more often than not been the one to pull the trigger, as in the case of the traitorous Dr. Sun Tingting. The learned Doctor was the climate scientist who had once been crucial to the planning behind General Bing's vision of depopulating the earth in order to ensure China would have a liveable climate in which to enjoy ascendency over the rest of the world. But when the climate scientist had tried to warn the world of the coming nuclear winter and the severe climate change and associated mass extinction of the human race – the winter kill of the human race - he had been unceremoniously executed by a bullet from Colonel Hua to the back of his head. That, and more recent summary executions, had kept Xu and the other senior staff from pushing back against the repugnant Colonel Hua. It had been a mistake, many of them were coming to understand; each time they did not respond when Colonel Hua spoke out of his station, his personal power and megalomania only increased. *You are a truly despicable little man,* thought Dàxiào Colonel Xu. *We'll take care of you sooner or later, if the General does not tire of you first,* he thought.

Xu answered Hua's arrogant response. "Whatever you say, Shàngxiào," the Dàxiào Colonel sneered, drawing a harsh, but fearful look from the Shàngxiào Colonel Hua. Equivalent to an American Colonel, or OF-5, Hua was one full grade below the Dàxiào Colonel Xu, who was equivalent to an American Brigadier General, or OF-6.

Ignoring his distaste, Xu briefed Hua. "The board is all clear except for two Little Dragons. That one in Richmond, British

Columbia, continues to display high-risk behavior and is behaving as though he were fully autonomous. He's been parading his Dragon Flies in and out of his hotel room as if he were a Drug Lord, and sooner or later he's going to attract too much attention – if he has not already done so. You know how it is when a foolish man has a little power and lets it go to his head," he said, and then looked meaningfully at Colonel Hua. "I recommend that we close him out and reassign his Dragonflies to another Little Dragon in the Vancouver region. I don't suppose you want to authorize that on your own authority as the Commander's EA, do you, Colonel?"

"I'll let you know in a minute," said Colonel Hua, taken aback by the man's open hostility. The insult was not lost on Hua, who saw the Brigadier as his most serious rival. *Once we move into Phase Three, I'll pin the responsibility for any major screw-ups from the Little Dragon operation on Xu, so it'll be better to let him make his recommendation directly to the general – after I pre-empt it, by expressing my doubts as to how well Xu is managing his spies,* Hua thought with satisfaction.

"Move on to the other problem, Colonel Xu."

"Right. Well, we have a new problem, in Adelaide, South Australia. Seems we have lost contact with the Region Lead, Kuang. He had been an effective and stable Little Dragon, from all accounts. And up until now there hadn't been any warning signs – no counter-intelligence, no conflict with civilians, and a steady stream of useful intelligence on the Australian air base at Edinburgh, near Adelaide. And now, suddenly, 'poof'! He's disappeared. We can't even raise any of his Dragonflies, and the man we sent in to check on his hotel has not reported back."

"What's this, we may have lost one in Adelaide?" interrupted the Shàngjiàng-grade Colonel-General Bing, equivalent to an American 4-Star, OF-9. Now, with the sudden death of his predecessor, Bing was China's Supreme Military Commander. General Bing had arrived in the middle of Colonel Xu's briefing.

For a terrifying moment, Colonel Hua worried that the General may have heard some of their earlier exchange, but then he relaxed when the General walked past him and placed his hand on Hua's shoulder in the customary way, before taking his seat in front of Hua's workstation. Hua would have purred if he were a feline; he was so happy to have the General's touch.

"He must have run into some sort of trouble. And if you can't raise his Dragonflies, then the problem must be local law enforcement, or perhaps even state or military counter-intelligence. Not good, Colonel Xu," said General Bing, pleasing Colonel Hua to no end. "But there's no real mission risk, right?. It'll take days for them to figure it all out and work it through their chain of command, and we've only got, what, 36 hours?"

"Yes, Shàngjiàng," said Xu.
"Speaking about those Australian Long Range Maritime Patrol Aircraft, how about the Maritime Patrol base in New Zealand?" Bing asked, following up on a previous discussion of the surprisingly capable P3C Maritime Patrol Aircraft flown by the New Zealanders.

Xu spoke with authority. "We now have a Dragonfly in place with 5 Squadron, the girlfriend of the pilot-lead, name of Major Brant, on their P3Cs. All four of 5 Squadron's MPA are unserviceable, and there won't be any patrol presence in that sector for the next 72 hours, so that operation has been a success. They won't have to tip their hands early, interfering with the MPAs, because they can't fly anyhow. So now they can focus all their energy on taking out the Takapuna Beach armory, and the police detachment. The base itself, at Whenuapai, will be taken by air-assault only, Sir, as you recall. You went with my recommendation that we not risk activating their Wing Defense Forces by having the Dragonflies attack the base prior to the arrival of Colonel Guo's assault teams," Colonel Xu reminded General Bing, and then swallowed uncomfortably in the ensuing silence.

General Bing was not the slightest bit concerned with the rudeness of Xu's comments. He was well beyond that, thinking about the tricky job Colonel Guo's initial wave of assaulters would have dealing with the security forces bound to come across to the Devonport sector in response to the air-landing assault on the Whenuapai airbase.

"How are we doing with getting a team in place to shut down Auckland Harbor Bridge? Colonel Guo is going to need that link shut down so he can clear out Devonport and the east sector before moving in on Auckland once his follow-on forces arrives at Base Whenuapai," said General Bing, demonstrating his detailed knowledge of every aspect of OPERATION WINTER SNAKE, in this case, the Supporting Plan that would achieve the subjugation of New Zealand.

"That continues to be a concern, General. We have not had much luck with the Chinese community in Auckland. They're mostly second and third generation from Mainland Chinese immigrants, not the younger crowd from Hong Kong and Beijing. So they're turning out to be very hard to corrupt.

"Staging the follow-on forces through Fiji will be no problem," Xu continued, "As we have two good teams at Nadi. So that's how I recommend we mitigate any problems with the Auckland Harbor Bridge, if Little Dragon Guanglie can't get enough Dragonflies ready in time. We'll delay the capture of Auckland, if we have to, until Colonel Guo has enough of 38th Group Army's follow-on forces in place. Meanwhile, he'll have picked Devonport and Takapuna clean of military stores and suitable transportation; Guo will be ready to outfit the follow-on forces. No, Sir, New Zealand is not a big worry. I'm more worried about what's going on in Adelaide. If the Australians generate good intelligence in time and raise their readiness – even if they don't have the full picture – we could be facing a disaster in that sector."

"I agree, Colonel Xu. So I hope, for your sake, that your Little Dragon in the Barossa Valley has not screwed up too much," General Bing said, ominously, before moving on. "Do we have any good news out of the Australian AOR?"

"Certainly, but most of that could be summed up as 'according to plan'," Colonel Xu said with his customary efficiency. "However, there is one notable success you may find interesting. It seems that a police special agent investigating Chinese nationals at Macquarie University showed some interest in our Little Dragon in the south-central Sydney area, one of

Major Zhang's. You may recall him? He's the one we call 'Scarface', on account of the deep scar on his face?"

"Oh yes, I remember him. He seemed to be a very capable young man. What's he done?"

"Well, when he got word that one of his Little Dragons was in trouble he took quick and decisive action. He put together a team and they killed the cop and not only expunged all of his data, but he also planted some clever misinformation into the cop's chain of command – and pinned the murder on academic cheats. So not only was the police attention diverted from our operations, but the police forces wasted valuable time and resources barking up the wrong tree."

"Well done. Make sure you keep an eye on this Major Zhang - Scarface – I want him to be given increased responsibilities, and if warranted, accelerated promotion," Bing directed.

"My thoughts exactly. We'll put Zhang on deep-select for Zhōngxiào," Xu said, fully intending to promote the ruthless and efficient Major Zhang to the equivalent of Lieutenant Colonel, or OF-4.

General Bing paused, noticing one of his best friends, General Leung, had arrived. "Good, Leung, perfect timing. Colonel Xu has been briefing us on OP PLAN XIAOLONG. Let's move on. Brief us on the status of Little Dragons preparations for the assaults on the real prize, the east coast of Australia. I am sure that General Leung would like to know what sort of reception his Colonel Ma will have," commanded General Bing. He arched his back and felt his muscles stretch. He looked around the room with a satisfied, confident smile.

In the fusion Centre at the American Controlled CIA installation at Pine Gap, near Alice Springs, an Australian intelligence analyst was discussing recent intel with his CIA counterparts. He had taken to bouncing everything off of them, openly sharing all intelligence, hoping to glean even a little of the 'close hold' American intel as it related to Australia. More often than not it was a one-way street, as the CIA still had not gotten over the last set of leaks out of the Australian defense community. *The Yanks simply don't trust us with information critical to our own national security,* he thought. *But there's nothing for it. We have to give them everything and try to infer their take on it, at the very least.*

He had just received input from the Australian military's J2, Intelligence Branch Officer, in Canberra. The Intel had been generated from police and military reports out of the Barossa Valley area, just outside of Adelaide.

"This does not fit our assessment of the Chinese," the ranking CIA analyst said. "So we shall assess it as spurious, probably an overzealous ranger in the outback down there."

"I don't understand," the Australian responded sharply, "How can you dismiss this as a mistake? Our boys down there are not idiots, you know. And this is coming in from a variety of well-respected professionals – both civilian and military. They know what the hell they are doing, and they have loads of electronic and paper documentation in hand."

The CIA analyst looked up from the paper he was reading. "I didn't mean to insult you. We are guests in your country, after all, so I don't mean to insult the host. But your boys have it all wrong. It does not fit China's strategic aims. Case in point: the Chinese efforts to hack our military and commercial systems are part of an arms-length, paranoid habit of seeking to gain advantage without having to invest or develop for themselves. It's right out of Sun Tzu, where if you can defeat your enemy without engaging in battle, then you have truly won, or something like that."

The American continued: "On the industrial side, they want technology which they simply can't generate, and then they can manufacture massive quantities of it as knock-offs and flood the market with cheaper and only slightly inferior versions. This strategy has given them phenomenal growth rates and is a winning formula for them. They started this with toys, decades ago, and then they moved into more and more sophisticated consumer goods, plastics, and finally sophisticated electronic devices. And this applies to military technology as well. Take the original American-made M14 rifle for example. The Chinese knock-off, by China North Industries, "NORINCO", sells here in Australia for about $500 dollars and is almost as good as the original American version, which sells for $2,500."

The Aussie was becoming annoyed by this bloodless know-it-all. "So what's your point? Are you saying that this is an acceptable situation? Isn't that what's responsible for hollowing out the industrial base in the United States, the closing of factories, and the export of jobs?"

"Yes. That is my point exactly. It is a losing situation for America, and a winning formula for China," he said, with a smile.

The Australian frowned for a moment, not understanding why the American would smile about being taken advantage of by China. "I don't' get it. What does that have to do with your assessment of the Intel from Adelaide, that clearly establishes that there is an active network of Chinese nationals, likely PLA, spying on military installations and personnel?"

The American leaned forward in his chair and gave another one of his annoying, superior smiles. "OK. I'll spell it out for you. They are already winning the war, and have been for years. They've got us by the balls, with our debt and our trade deficit. So why would they screw that up by such a hostile act? I mean really?" He started speaking faster and more loudly, buoyed by his own mental processes. "A network of HumInt assets? Armed agents, preparing for what, a tactical mission? China is about to attack your little air base? For what purpose? To start a war? To bring about an allied, anti-China trade war? Why would they do that when they could get whatever they want on the internet? And starting a war? No way. They don't have an expeditionary air force now do they? Have you ever seen a Chinese C-17? THEY DON'T HAVE ANY!" he nearly shouted. "They've only got about 20 IL76Ms, but that's it, in terms of strategic airlift. And to go to war with Australia they would need literally hundreds of heavy-lift, Antanov-A124 or some other C17-type aircraft." He immediately shifted from shouting to a fast, flat monotone. "So as of right now, they could not fight an expeditionary war, therefore your Intel is wrong."

"But what about sea-lift? Couldn't they come by sea?" asked the Australian officer.

"Sure, but not in the numbers they would need. Maybe they could take New Zealand, if they could get there with a Brigade Group or stronger. But with the 7th Fleet in the Malacca Straits, and with all the satellites we have watching their military bases, we would know about their mobilization long before it could set sail. And as it is, they only have what, two carrier battle groups now? And very few of the specialty ships you would need for an amphibious invasion. And they don't have any long-range bombers or air-to-air refueling aircraft, so their air power is no threat."

"What about missiles? Couldn't they take out our forces, and your 7th fleet with missiles, or nukes?"

"Sure, if they want to commit suicide. They have some ICBMs and something of a SLBM capability now, and some pretty good SSK diesel subs and a new class of SSBNs - Jin class, I think they're called - but they are still no match for the US Navy. Besides, to fight a war here in Australia they would have such enormous supply lines, easily cut with our allies in the Philippines, Japan, Singapore, Taiwan and so on. Heck, all it would take is a small increase in our naval presence in the region and a few divisions of Marines on top of what we've got up in Darwin already, and Australia would be virtually impregnable to the Chinese. And even if they could make landfall, and establish a beachhead somewhere on your continent, there's no doubt that your Army, Navy, Air Force and Militia would throw them back into the sea," said the CIA analyst, confidently. He leaned back, pleased to be able to spout off after long hours of staring into computer monitors. At last, being able to show off his superior knowledge.

The Australian was not impressed. He set his hands on his hips and leaned slightly forward toward the American. "Well, I'm not willing to dismiss this Priority Intelligence Report from my mates in South Australia so quickly. So I hope you won't mind if I formally ask you CIA buggers to earn your keep for the years of operating your listening post on Australian territory, and put your gear to good use for our interest for a change," the analyst said, his face turning purple and his blood vessels swelling at his barely suppressed rage. "I am formally asking you to generate us an IMMEDIATE update on the Chinese order of battle, the disposition of their forces at this time, and a complete Intelligence Assessment of the threat of an attack or any other hostile act by the Chinese upon any of the forces or territories of Australia," he said, clearly intent on going as far up his national chain of command as he needed to, to get the CIA to provide the comprehensive analysis that only the CIA was capable of conducting. *Americans!* he thought to himself.

The CIA analyst realized that the request was not just a trial balloon from a disgruntled Australian liaison officer. It was really coming from their military headquarters in Canberra, through the man's liaison role to the CIA facility in Pine Gap. Therefore, it was Australia speaking.

With big, blank eyes, the American glared at the Australian. "OK, buddy. You got it. I'll throw out common sense and thirty years of expertise on all things Chinese, and go back to first principles," said the analyst, with some annoyance. But then his face brightened up. "You know what, it wouldn't hurt if I pressed a few buttons back in Langley on this, get them spun up a bit and see what they come up with," he said, already applying his analytical talents to the problem. "I'll run it up the pole for you! It'll be fun, even if I already know that it's a waste of time," he said cheerfully, and then added: "It'll take about 18 hours, what with it being the middle of the night back home. Meanwhile, I have to ask for a similar level of effort from you in exchange."

"Effort? What do you want me to do?" asked the LnO. He was thrown off balance not only by the CIA analyst's rattling speech, but by the American's quirky manner of shifting from detail-oriented arrogance to bright-eyed smiles, on a dime.

"I'll need an update from you on your own disposition of forces and your HHQ's ConOps and contingency plans for a full-on invasion by China. You do have such a plan, don't you?"

"You know damned well we do. You and I have gone over the 2009 White Paper before. You know all about our plans to increase our subsurface fleet to 12 hulls, and the manner in which they would be used for anti-shipping, surveillance and strike," said the LnO with annoyance.

"I'm not talking about that naval fantasy. Thanks to your overly free press everybody knows you can only staff two of six subs now and you are years away from having a credible sub-surface-centered defense strategy. I'm talking reality here. The here-and-now, come-as-you-are. What you proud Australians will do if you wake up *tomorrow* hearing angry men shouting Chinese in the streets. Your civil defense plans, national mobilization for a war of national survival."

This definitely threw the Australian off balance. "I don't think we have anything like that. Are you seriously asking me to ask HHQ in Canberra if we have a plan for….for what, a no-notice, organic mobilization for insurgency operations against a surprise Chinese occupation?"

"Yeah. That's what I am asking for. If you seriously think it is even *possible* that this PIR from Adelaide has any basis in fact, then you are entirely fucked. The Chinese, if they ever come here to do you harm on a grand scale, will have figured out a way to remove your allies from the equation and to somehow move a million soldiers here in a hurry. They'll swarm over your defenses like they did to us at the battle of Chosin Reservoir in 1950."

Silence hung in the air for a long moment.

The LnO sighed, thinking of withdrawing his request, but he could not let go of the notion that the PIR from Adelaide was an important bit of information. It needed to be acted on with a sense of urgency.

He ground his teeth. "OK. I'll do it. You ring Langley and sharpen your pencil and I'll talk to the J5 and look into our CONPLANS," he said. The Australian then left the CIA Fusion Centre and made his way to his office in the a modular trailer just outside of the American-controlled portion of the comms facility at Pine Gap. He felt a little smaller after this last exchange with the CIA; leaving him feeling like a guest in his own country. As if Australia had already been lost.

He looked up at the wide blue skies, deceptively peaceful and quiet. *What if the Chinese really are coming? That would be a real pickle.*

6

BY LAND IF NOT BY AIR

Owen MacInnes may not have had that much experience in the few years he had served the Army Reserves, but he still considered himself to be a military man. So when he had been visiting his wife's family in Altoona, Pennsylvania, he had tried to fit in. With her retired General of a father, and a long-serving Warrant Officer as her brother-in-law, the conversations around his wife's family's dinner table tended to have a military dimension.

The Upton family home was originally owned by a large farming family, but when they had fallen on hard times and been forced to sell the farm, a young Major Upton had bought the property, planning for his retirement from the US Army. His retirement had been postponed several times over the years, and re-considered after the birth of each successive daughter. Had the General had sons he would have retired and become a rancher, his life's dream. However he had postponed his retirement four times, with four daughters and no sons, and continued to advance in the Army until he retired as a Brigadier General with 30 years of service.

General Upton, retired, had built his long dreamed-of ranch, and tried to become a farmer. In fact, he had been operating an effective little hobby farm, but without sons to back him up he had limited the scale of his ambitions – but he had not abandoned his dream. As a result, the Upton family home was something of an under-used resource which could, with the right sort of men, become a thriving dairy farm, orchard, or other agricultural enterprise.

But the General, with only two of his four daughters married off, still lacked the manpower. Still healthy and active, he was willing to wait as long as it took for one or more of his girls to pick up his lead and become interested in the ranch. Until then, he and his wife, Fiona, would make use of the excessively large home as the center of the Upton extended family. But with only two sons-in-law the General had to really stretch the term "extended family", in order to have a really satisfying family gathering.

To this end, and perhaps out of a desire to delude himself into feeling that he had the large family he had always dreamed of, he often invited Joseph Blakely, the brother of his daughter Maggie's husband, Matthew Blakely, to round out the table.

It was still strange for General Upton to think of Maggie, as anything other than an Upton. *Too bad I couldn't have had him take her name*, he thought to himself, '*Warrant Officer Matthew Upton*' *would have had a ring to it.*

Thinking of his daughter's husband, and the man's brother, Major Joe Blakely, made him worry. They had all enjoyed each other's company for the last week, but it had been punctuated with the departure of Joe, Tannis and Agnes for their Change of Station to Australia. That they had made time to visit with Matt and Maggie, and the Upton family at large, had been greatly appreciated. But everybody knew that it would be the last large family gathering for quite some time. Major Joseph Blakely and his family were not expected to have any entitlement to Leave Travel from Australia to the US for their three year assignment, not in the current financial state of the US Army.

But what had made it worse for the old General was what his son-in-law, Warrant Officer Matthew Blakely, had disclosed to the family in one of their late-night discussions around the kitchen table.

Without divulging any secret information he had been privy to in his duties at the Mount Weather Emergency Operations Center, WO Blakely felt that he was free to discuss his take on the dangerous path that President Parker had put the United States on, what with the confiscation of gold and other radical financial measures that she was putting into place.

When the conversation had turned from military matters to social and economic ones, Owen MacInnes finally found a place for himself in the conversation with the old General and the Blakely brothers. It was hard enough for Owen to get involved in conversations, what with his civilian status and old General Upton's seeming hatred for Owen. But when it came to discussing how the general population at large saw the confiscation of their gold, the extraordinary bank levies, and the new requirement to register their fire-arms, for once Owen was the subject matter expert and the military men had actually listened to his perspective for a change.

They had talked long into the night; the topic was what to do if a major crisis tore apart the fabric of American society.

"If it gets really bad, then this farm would be a great place to ride it out, General," said Matthew.

"Sure, Matt, if you don't work in the world's most well-equipped bunker," said his younger brother, Joe, not entirely in jest. The two brothers had often debated whether it would be better to take one's chances on the surface rather than being trapped. No matter how well appointed, an underground tomb would wear on the mind, the brothers had agreed.

"As for me, I know that I'll be stuck in Mount Weather for the duration. That's why I'm so happy Maggie has a place to head for, where I know that she'll be safe."

"Have you and Maggie discussed what she should do if it gets hairy on the roads? Who she can turn to for help along the way?" asked Owen.

"Not really. It's only a hundred and twenty miles from our home in Winchester to the ranch here in Altoona," said Matt.

"And how far from this bunker you work at, Mount Weather, to Winchester.

"Why?"

"Oh, just thinking," said Owen, not wanting to share his thoughts. He did not have a very good relationship with his wife's father and did not want to be presumptuous. For her part, his wife, Catherine, had stood up for him. That had only made things worse for Owen with old General Upton, and had culminated in the young couple choosing to hold their marriage in their home in Richland, Wisconsin, rather than at Catherine's father's ranch in Altoona, Pennsylvania.

The Upton family, and a good contingent of friends from the Altoona area had made the nearly 800 mile journey to see Catherine and Owen get married, but the General had not forgiven his son-in-law for what he took as a personal insult.

"So what's your plan for societal collapse, Owen? Are you a survivalist? Got your own 'bug-out' plan to some cabin in Wisconsin Dells?" asked Joe Blakely.

Unsure if the major was making fun of him, Owen tried to change the subject. "Yeah, right. As if Catty and I could afford a place in the Dells. I just hope it never gets that bad. Out where we live there are some real nut-jobs, armed to the teeth and ready for social collapse. I pity the poor cops, or soldiers, who try to maintain law and order if it ever comes to that. You know, many of them see the federal Government and men in uniform like you and Matt as the enemy," Owen said.

"Well, I expect that it will be different depending on the circumstances," said Matt. "If the government can keep it together, the citizenry will stay in line. But we've certainly had a few situations lately, like that scare in some small farming community down in Kansas, when the banks were down for that day – remember? Everybody became convinced that the financial collapse had come, just because the town's three banks were all closed due to some kind of computer virus?"

"I didn't hear about that one. What happened?" asked Joe.

"Well, a few locals got out their guns, figuring that it was 'open season' on 'open carry', and deputized themselves to save the supermarket from hoarders. Turned out that things were fine until they showed up on main street with their guns. Then all sorts of panic took over, and there were some shootings. By the end of the night some grocery stores had been looted and the gas station was on fire. Even some of the cops got wrapped up in the panic and filled their squad cars with cans of food and cases of water. If it weren't for some very disciplined US Army Reservists who mobilized a company to support the Sheriff, just on a phone call from the Governor, things could have really gotten out of hand." Matt looked meaningfully at Owen, who appreciated the nod to Army Reservists.

He's trying to help me with the General, thought Owen. "Yeah, well, if you get the right sort of Reservists. Some units really know what they are doing, and others are no more than little empires for their CO's," said Owen, with an undertone of anger that the two Blakely's suspected had something to do with the abrupt end of Owen's short-lived career with the US Army Reserves.

7

BYPASSING CUSTOMS

John Oxley loosened his tie with his right hand as his left steered his car along the airport road. He had just finished his evening shift at the small regional airport in Port Macquarie and was on his way home. He'd processed a Citation business jet that had arrived, on schedule, at 0300hrs, and was on his way home for the day. There were no other international arrivals on the books for the overnight so his replacement should be able to enjoy the standby-duty period at home, asleep, on the recall posture.

A bit of work, but really not enough to justify the three of us, Oxley thought to himself. It was about as busy as normal for this sleepy area on Australia's east coast. It was still an open question whether the three personnel of the Australian Customs and Border Protection Service would keep their jobs, what with all the cutbacks in the public sector. There was just not enough maritime and aviation related customs work to keep the small detachment busy. Most likely, "Ox" knew, the Port Macquarie unit would be rolled up into the Newcastle office, and at least two of the Customs Inspectors would be declared 'redundant', or relocated to the Sydney office.

What the fuck!? Driving along Tuffins Lane, he had almost reached Hastings River Drive when he looked up over the river and saw a Boeing 737 turning final, about to land.

In the moonlit night he did not recognize the flowery livery of the jet and it was too dark for him to make out the registration number as the aircraft passed directly overhead. What surprised Oxley was that the aircraft was in a left-hand circuit for Runway 21, which was against the rules. Aircraft were supposed to approach straight-in, over Hastings River, or in a non-standard, right hand circuit for Runway 21. But this one was doing it all wrong, which could only mean one thing: they weren't local.

Ever since the runway had been expanded a few years back, more and more airlines had been using the airport, bringing in charter flights who wanted to avoid the inconvenience of changing planes and clearing customs in Sydney.

But all such flights had to be arranged well in advance, so that Ox or another Customs Inspector could be notified and refueling, parking and a host of other airport services could be coordinated. Otherwise there would be nobody at the airport, at least not until after 0700hrs. All of that was the Port Macquarie Airport Operations Manager's responsibility to deal with, but Ox knew that in the end the passengers would be allowed to disembark and enter the terminal to clear customs, so he reluctantly turned around and headed back to the airport.

As he drove around the terminal to his parking spot he could only see the tail protruding over the one-story terminal building as the jetliner taxied back along the runway for the parking spot on the main apron.

As he drove, he rechecked the schedule. *Nope, nothing expected today. Better call Kirkie.* He speed dialed the tower controller as he pulled his Prius over into the reserved parking space, but did not get out of his car. As he listened to the phone ring he saw the airliner turn unexpectedly off the runway and head east along the narrow taxiway to the rows of small general aviation hangars east of the terminal and parking apron. The main wheels of the large aircraft barely fit on the narrow taxiway as the Boeing 737 continued along and then nosed-into a smaller parking apron which normally only small business jets and charter aircraft operated from.

"What kind of idiot would..?" he began saying out loud, and then the phone was answered.

"Tower, Charleswood speaking."

"Kirkie! Ox. What the hell is that jet doing on Charlie-Two?"

"I don't know, I'm gobsmacked up here. They landed NORDO, and still won't answer on either the MF or Ground."

As Ox and Kirkie talked, Ox noticed an enormous black American-style SUV driving through the parking lot and pulling up at the far end of the terminal building. No sooner had it come to a stop than all four doors opened and more than a half-dozen Asian men spilled out of the vehicle.

"Hang on, Kirkie. I think you've got some company. There's some blokes heading towards your side entrance."

"I see them. Hey, are those guns?"

"Holy Shit! Yes, they've got rifles, and looks like some hand-guns."

As he spoke, Ox looked at the airliner again, and saw the door opening. Moments later the forward emergency chute deployed and a bright orange air-inflated slide sprang out from under the port-forward door of the airliner. Uniformed soldiers began leaping out of the aircraft, sliding down the chute.

They seemed well trained to Ox, as each man in turn reached out to help the next soldier to his feet at the bottom of the chute, and then moved aside to make way for the stream of men coming after.

"Is this some kind of exercise, Kirkie?" he asked, over the phone.

"No, Ox. I'm ringing the Air Force now but there's no answer. I can't raise Air Traffic Control or the LAC either."

"No worries. There's Constable Buchanan now, in his Nissan."

Constable Buchanan had been monitoring the airport frequency in his New South Wales Police Force cruiser, after the Local Area Command, LAC, had received numerous complaints about the airliner violating local noise abatement ordinances.

As Buchanan pulled up to the terminal, three of the men from the black SUV turned towards him. He had no sooner stepped out of his vehicle when the men began firing at him. He ducked just in time. Bullets tore into the hood and front panel of his vehicle. With scarcely a moment to comprehend what was happening, the young constable hunkered down and rushed to the rear of his vehicle.

At the other end of the well-lit parking lot John Oxley saw it: two men were firing at Buchanan and another half-dozen were heading upstairs towards Kirkie up in the airport tower. Something clicked in his head. From deep inside, perhaps from his time with the 41st Battalion, Royal New South Wales Regiment, Ox switched into combat mode. There was no doubt or confusion in his mind. He knew exactly what was happening. The men trying to break into the tower building and the soldiers pouring out of the 737 were here to do harm to his friends.

Ox jumped into action, but not out of flag-waving heroism. All he could think was: *My mates are in danger!* He gunned the gas pedal and accelerated around the north end of the parking lot, speeding straight at the two gunmen who were shooting at Buchanan.

The gunmen looked around too late. All they saw was the "bush basher" bars mounted on the car's front end as it smashed into their legs, propelled them into the air and shot them into the brick wall, their heads splattering grey matter and bloody fluids all over the wall.

Ox rushed out of his car to Constable Buchanan's side, and found him unscathed. The constable jumped to his feet, looking wildly around. "What the fuck is going on here? Is this a terrorist attack?"

"It's big," Ox answered, as he motioned Buchanan to follow him. "All those men on the airliner are armed. And a bunch are having a go at Kirkie up the tower right now!" He picked up one of the rifles the dead men had dropped on the pavement, and handed it to the constable and then picked up the other one for himself. He looked at it for a few seconds with a quizzical expression on his face and then nodded to himself after figuring out the 'full-auto-off' lever. The rocker was full forward, in the 'full-fire' mode. "Let's go!" he shouted, his commanding voice jolting the bewildered constable up and into action. The two men then rushed through the door of the tower staircase.

The door had been blown off of its hinges, leaving a yawning hole leading to the stairs. *They're already up there,* Ox thought as he cautiously took the first steps up.

With Constable Buchanan backing him up the Customs Inspector led the way up the stairs, unsure if there were many rounds left in the rifle's magazine. He paused to take another look at the assault rifle in his hands and recognized that it was a Norelco M14, but with a much longer magazine than he had seen at the gun club. *That's gotta be a thirty-round magazine! Good, there must be a few rounds left,* he thought, as he turned the first corner. He could hear some commotion above, as though someone was trying to bash down a door.

Three hundred yards away, Colonel Ma stood in the cockpit of the Boeing 737 that had been pressed into service along with hundreds of other passenger aircraft as part of OPERATION WINTER SNAKE. The careful preparations had been time-consuming but now the painstaking effort was coming to fruition.

Brigade Commander for the East – Central Occupation Sector, centered on Port Macquarie, Colonel Ma wanted to be with the first wave of assaulters from the 121st Mechanized Infantry Division, 41st Group Army, and to be on-hand to witness the men's performance in this, the most critical of the eleven airfields in General Leung's forces hoped to capture in the first few hours of Day One.

He was as relieved to be on the ground as his men were. They all knew that the most dangerous part of their mission was not the prospect of ground combat in Australia but the likelihood that a number of airliners would be shot down by Australian air defense forces before reaching their destinations. He knew that as long as at least one of the three aircraft designated for this particular objective made it through they would most likely achieve all four of their Port Macquarie area tactical objectives.

His aircraft was the largest, with a full company of Chinese Special Forces personnel to disgorge. The next aircraft, due in another ten minutes, was a Q400 with only one platoon, and then a Fokker-50, modified with extra fuel tanks, transporting another platoon of his men.

If all three aircraft made it unscathed, then when General Leung arrived with the command element three hours later there would be almost two hundred men in place. That should be sufficient to hold their four objectives long enough for follow-on forces, which should arrive within the next five to eight days.

As he watched his men assemble on the fly while disembarking, he was proud of them. They had trained intensely for their mission without knowing how it fit into the larger strategic vision. Now, as they seized the engineering plant, fuel farm, hangar-line and other facilities on the east side of the regional airport without encountering any resistance, he turned his attention to the airport terminal itself.

From where the aircraft was parked, even when he opened the pilot's window and stuck his head out, Colonel Ma could not see all of the terminal building. He saw a section of his men making their way there, but for some reason they were ducking behind parked cars in the parking lot and not running flat out as they had been trained. *Are they be under fire*, he wondered? He was unable to hear anything over the shrill noise of the aircraft's Auxiliary Power Unit.

Colonel Ma was about to head back and go down the chute when he took a quick look to his right, between two hangars, and saw two police vehicles approaching a section of his men who were making their way across Boundary Street for their objective – his future base of operations – Newman Senior Technical College.

It had seemed strange to him at first that he was to set up Battalion Headquarters in what was essentially a high school, but when he was shown the floor-plan of the modern facility, with dormitories, kitchen and recreation facilities for the large number of residential students from outlying areas, he recognized the utility of the place. Its close proximity to the airport, where his forces would be disembarking, was an added benefit.

But they needed to capture the facility quickly, and establish a secure perimeter.

To do that, the section tasked with storming the facility had to get past what looked like three or four NSW police officers who had responded to calls from the airport security personnel.

They were supposed to have been taken out by the Little Dragon and his Dragonflies, Colonel Ma thought, with annoyance, as he watched the skirmish unfold. It quickly became apparent that the fire team were not long impeded by the police officers; they took them out with a few short bursts from their Type 95 assault rifles without breaking their stride. *Well done, boys. Keep moving!* he thought, as he turned to exit the cockpit.

On the deck of the control tower, Kirkie Charleswood could feel the adrenalin. He was not afraid, but if he thought about things a bit he would have been. What kept him going as he unraveled the fire hose and prepared his other weapons was the idea: *I'm not alone. Ox and Constable Buchanan are coming. I've got a chance!*

He kept an eye on the closed circuit TV cameras, first at the street-level entrance and now at the final security door, just below the narrow staircase up onto the tower deck itself. He saw that there were five or six terrorist trying to break down the reinforced door to the tower deck. Ox and Buchanan had already taken out two of the attackers, and were moving up the stairwell. Kirkie hoped to make things difficult for the attackers. He had just enough time to go turn open the tap and firmly grip the nozzle before the water pressure attempted to flail the hose out of his hands. He held on and waited.

As expected, the moment the door was torn off its hinges, his attackers lobbed a couple of grenades up onto the tower deck. The concussion was deafening, but Kirkie was not hurt, protected as he was by the line of heavy metal filing cabinets he had hid behind up against the rear wall of the tower deck.

Now it's my turn! He thought, as he twisted opened the nozzle, sending a powerful spray of water ahead of him as he moved in on the stairwell.

He saw a surprised look on the face of a Chinese-looking man, who was thrown backwards down the narrow staircase by the force of the water, bowling back on the two men behind him in the process.

As Kirkie moved the water-jet from man to man, he aimed at their faces as much as possible to keep them blinded and out of action. *Come on, boys, get up here!*

When he heard an uproar a few flights above him, with men screaming in Chinese and the roar of water spraying all over the place, John Oxley realized that Kirkie, was using a fire-hose on the attackers. Constable Buchanan must have realized it as well, because he was right on Ox's heals as he raced up the final two flights of stairs to the administrative deck immediately below the control tower deck.

It only took a moment to see what was going on. Five men in various stages of inundation were picking themselves up off the floor or attempting to crawl out of the way as an intense, sharply focused jet of water played on each of them in turn, sending them back down onto the floor in a scramble of arms and legs. A couple of them were firing in the general direction of the source of the water.

Ox and the constable opened fire on them, killing four of them before they even knew that they had been flanked. As he moved in on the last man, Ox signaled 'cease fire' to Buchanan, seeing that the sole remaining attacker had lost his weapon and had his hands raised to protect his face from the water.

"Shut it off, Kirkie! We got' em!" Shouted Constable Buchanan as he took out a pair of hand-cuffs and secured the assailant's wrists.

"What the hell do we do now?" asked Buchanan.

"Kirkie, get the hell down here!" shouted Ox, who then grasped the bewildered man by the upper arms and yanked him to his feet.'

"Bugger me, but you're a tall, skinny bastard!" he said, as he shoved the man towards the staircase.

"You don't' have to tell me twice, Mate!" said Kirkie, as he reached their level. He grabbed the man's other arm and helped Ox drag the man down the stairs.

As they exited the staircase they saw a group of soldiers at the far end of the parking lot, moving their way.

Constable Buchanan fired off a few rounds; Ox had abandoned the rifle in favor of taking their captive.

The heavily armed soldiers all ducked behind cars, despite the fact that constable Buchanan had only fired three or four rounds before his Glock 22 was empty. As he reloaded, Kirkie and Ox shoved their captive into the back of the assaulter's black SUV, which still had the engine running, the keys in the ignition.

As bullets began to hit the rear of the SUV and the brick wall opposite the vehicle, Constable Buchanan began to drive them around the west side of the terminal and out onto the taxiway, turning north and putting the terminal building between the advancing soldiers and themselves.

"Jesus Christ! What the hell is going on? Were those Indonesians, or Chinese?" asked the constable as he drove through the security gate in the chain-link fence and swerved onto Tuffins Road, heading towards downtown Port Macquarie.

"I'm sure they're all Chinese. This guys' mates we met in the tower, and those soldiers, must be working together."

"So we are under attack by the Chinese?"

"Yeah, Ox. And I think it's worse than that."

"What do you mean, Kirkie?"

"Just before I left the tower I overheard an emergency broadcast on Guard frequency. It was from the Army. They were ordering a full national mobilization of all Armed Forces, Reserve Units and Civil Defense personnel. They said that Canberra, Sydney and Melbourne have been attacked with nuclear weapons from Russia and that there are reports of attacks in smaller communities across Australia."

"Are you serious? Nuclear war with Russia? National mobilization? What? Are we at war with Russia or with China? Where did all of this come from?"

"Obviously it's a complete surprise. It doesn't really matter if it is Russia or China. Maybe the Russians are using some of those Asian looking Russians from their far east. Maybe they're in it together, but those soldiers are definitely Chinese. "Where we going?" asked Buchanan, slowing the SUV to a stop at Hastings River Drive.

"What do you mean? Turn right, head for the LAC. What were you thinking? - leave town?"

"No. I guess not," said the young constable, now clearly shaken by the turn of events. His hands were shaking, despite the firm grip he had on the steering wheel.

"Calm down, Peter, we're OK. People are counting on us, and we're not going to let them down. And you are a visible symbol of authority, so you need to pull yourself together and stand tall. Are you with me?" asked Ox, reassuringly.

"Yes, Mr. Oxley. I am. It's just…it's just so unbelievable."

"There's no way the Chinese will get away with this. The whole world will come down on them like a ton of bricks. I bet the Yanks are already all over them, nuking the bugger out of them. All we've got to do is deal with any of them that have landed here, and take care of our own. The rest of the world will take care of the big stuff."

"So what do we do?" he asked, as he turned left off of Gordon Street onto Hay Street and then pulled into the narrow driveway past the fire-hall, and arrived at the back parking lot of Local Area Command, North Coast District Headquarters of the New South Wales Police Force.

"Bugger me! GO!" Shouted Ox.

Constable Buchanan accelerated past the group of Chinese soldiers and Asian men in civilian clothes who were standing around outside the LAC office. The soldiers had been told to expect the black SUV, the Control Tower team, at some point so they did not open fire on it until they saw that it was full of white men, not fellow Chinese.

Bullets ripped into the vehicle as Buchanan steered around the rear of the building and then out across the grass in the back yard, smashing through the hedge and bouncing through the back yard of the Port Macquarie Workwear property.

One more hedge went under their wheels and then they burst out onto a well-manicured lawn and then onto Murray Street beyond.

"They've already captured the LAC? Bugger!"

"Head for the Depot!" said Ox.

"What, on Munster?"

"Yeah. Good on ya. If anybody can fight these guys, it'll be the guys from the 41st Battalion," said Ox.

"I don't know. If they've got the airport and the LAC, then they've probably gone after the armory as well," said the constable, as he turned off Church Street and headed up Munster.

All three men looked ahead and saw another group of Chinese soldiers getting out of civilian vehicles, moving in on the building, firing as they advanced the local reserve unit depot.

"Mate. I think you had the right idea after all. Get us the hell out of town. Head inland. We have to get ahead of the Chinese."

"Too right!"

Ox thought of another place. "Make for..." He paused, changing his mind. "No! Don't turn that way! There's probably more of 'em coming from the airport. Head down Lord Street, and take the long way 'round."

Ten minutes later they had reached the small community of Wauchope and found that the local detachment of the New South Wales Police Force was intact.

The community must have gotten word that war had broken out, but the detachment's five or six police officers were clearly in the dark as they attempted to settle the growing crowd of citizens who had gathered in the parking lot outside the small police station.

The otherwise quiet night air was interrupted by the roaring engine and squealing tires as the black SUV screeched to a halt in front of the crowd. The citizens of Wauchope turned to look at the men inside.

Sergeant McCreary, the NSW Police Force detachment commander, stormed up to them, about to shout at them for reckless driving. Ox got out of the vehicle, dragging his prisoner with him. He threw the Chinese to the pavement, getting everyone's attention. McCreary recognized Oxley and decided to shut up and let him speak.

In the perhaps fifteen minutes since World War Three had broken out, John Oxley had abandoned his civilian personality of a friendly Customs Inspector, and had re-activated his long-dormant persona, that of a confident and aggressive infantry Warrant Officer, 41st battalion, Royal New South Wales Regiment. He did not need any paperwork, permission or invitation. His country was at war. *Besides*, he thought to himself as he prepared his words, *a general order to mobilize Australia's armed forces has been given*. He was needed.

"Take a look at this man" Ox said, pointing to the man he had just thrown to the ground. "He's our enemy. Himself and a planeload of his kind, Chinese soldiers, have just taken over Port Macquarie."

"Bonkers!" a man spoke up from the crowd. "You can't be serious! I mean, we heard that we've been attacked, that there are a half-dozen mushroom clouds over Sydney, but how can the

Chinese be here already in our little county? There's nothing important hereabouts. This can't be happening so fast!"

"Listen, there's no time to debate. My name is John Oxley. I'm going to tell you what's going on, and what you need to do, and you are going to do as I tell you. You got it?"

"By what authority?"

Recently self-re-enlisted Warrant Officer John Oxley walked up to the man who had spoken out, someone he did not recognize. The man stood in front of the others, hands on his hips, as if he was entitled to get his way.

Ox did not answer the question. He punched the man square in the face, sending him reeling back into the crowd. His mates grabbed hold of him, helped him up, and kept him quiet. *Probably one of those hobby farmers who has moved to the region after a life of selfishness in the big city,* Oxley thought to himself. Ox was angered by the type, more interested in arguing than doing their part.

NSW Police Sergeant McCreary was impressed. "Go ahead, Mr. Oxley. You've got our attention. Tell us what's for."

"Thank you, Sergeant McCreary."

"Folks. Australia is at war. This is not an overseas war, like Afghanistan or Iraq, which had nothing to do with Australia. It's not like the great war, where so many of our young men shipped off to join the Australian and New Zealand Army Corps, ANZAC – to die for the folly of British officers at Gallipoli. No, friends, this is on our homeland. Our homeland has never been invaded before, so we have no historical precedence. But what we are facing is what they call a 'war of national survival', and the Chinese have fired the first shots, at least here in New South Wales. We don't know how that fits in with the nuclear blasts, but I for one believe that the Chinese were behind those as well. And if so, they have already killed millions of our citizens. And these are crack troops. They took Port Macquarie in a matter of minutes. I saw it with my own eyes, me and Constable Buchanan over there," he indicated. "They moved with precision, and clearly knew their objectives. That can mean only one thing: they've planned this thing to the most minute detail," he paused, looking at his prisoner, on the ground.

The man was dead.

Ox rolled him over, and the crowd let out a collective gasp at the foam coming out of the man's mouth.

"This man was a spy. He and a bunch of others were trying to take over the Control Tower. They were there before the Chinese soldiers, in their Chinese 'unis, even got out of their aircraft. The soldiers arrived by an unscheduled landing, what they call an 'air-land assault', using a Boeing 737 if you can believe it. Then they raced to capture their objectives. They have already secured a beachhead in this region. I'm sure that they mean to use the airport to build up their forces in this area, and then move inland. That means your town is next."

The crowd began to argue, and shout questions.

Raising his voice, Ox continued.

"No. The Royal Australian Army won't be coming to our aid. We're on our own. You and I, we are the army; it's a come-as-you-are fight. Whatever's left of the army is likely doing everything they can to get this situation sussed, responding to the devastation in the cities that were nuked, and mobilizing and dispersing whatever forces they can. But even if we had not been caught by surprise – as we clearly were – our armed forces, God love them, would have been overwhelmed by the scale of this thing. So they need us to back them up, and fight alongside 'em.

"So we've got two choices. One, grab your loved ones and evacuate inland, as far as you can from wherever the Chinese are. And I recommend you get on with this right away. There's no shame in running for your lives – save your loved ones and live to fight another day. But you don't have much time. From what we saw in Port Macquarie, they are following a well-orchestrated plan, and moving like clockwork.

"The second choice, the one I have made, is to stand and fight. We have to move as fast we can, bugger them up, slow them down. Hit them hard now, before their reinforcements have a chance to deploy and lock this region down."

"How do we do that?" asked one man.

"Go home, pack up your hunting gear, camping gear, and as much food and water as you can, and mobilize your community.

Set up road blocks on all the roads. This one behind me would be my first priority," he said, pointing in the direction of the road behind him, and adding as he turned back to the crowd, "…and start killing any Chinese that come up the road."

Sergeant McCreary looked down the road, imagining a column of Chinese soldiers headed his way.

"What about attacking them in Port Macquarie?"

"Maybe, if you can get enough men together. But you are up against crack troops. These are their Special Forces, you understand? Not conscript soldiers like we faced with the Iraqis in the First Gulf War. These guys won't surrender, and they probably won't take prisoners, either."

Ox turned to face Sergeant McCreary. "If I were you, I would send a patrol car out to the intersection of Highway One and Thirty-Four. And send another farther up 34, to the outskirts of Port Macquarie, to get some eyes on the town. If the Chinese don't move out right away, then we could set up some sort of choke point, try to contain them. If we lose Highway One that will trap a lot of people who need to be evacuated. We should move everybody to the west, up Highway 34."

The crowd began chattering, discussing what Oxley had said. Then one spoke up, quieting the group again as reality began to sink in. "So we're all there is? A bunch of retirees and farmers?"

"Look, Mate, do you have a rifle? If you do, go now and get it, and come back here with your kit and some tuck. We'll tell you what to do. If not, bugger off and find some other way to be helpful – help with the evacuation or gather food and supplies that the evacuees will need when they get farther inland. Whatever you like, Mate, but just get on with it," Ox said, getting tense as the minutes ticked by.

Nobody moved for a few moments, and nobody spoke. It was as if they were transfixed, not by fear, but by the incomprehensible choice – engage in a life and death struggle or abandon their homes and flee to the west.

Oxley understood that the townsfolk needed to be told what to do, and decided that he would have to be the one.

"Alright then!" He shouted, with his old military voice. "I'll make it easy for you. Until I am relieved by proper military authority, on the authority of my former military service, I hereby declare martial law on this region and appoint myself as commander of the resistance in this sector. Sergeant McCreary, send a car out to the coast road and establish an Observation Post. Now!" He commanded. "You two!" he said, pointing at two men who had brought their rifles and looked ready for a fight, "You go with one of McCreary's lads and back him up until reinforcements arrive. Now MOVE!" he shouted, loud enough to get the men into high gear.

Without further delay, a corporal and constable from the NSW Police Force and the two civilians Ox had pressed into service and two others who had decided to go along to help, all headed out, the police interceptor leading and two pick-up trucks following.

The sudden activity broke the crowd up somewhat, with many people heading for their cars, either to evacuate their loved ones or to retrieve weapons and kit – or both.

Twenty four hours later, Oxley, McCreary, and two dozen men from Wauchope were dead; the town of Wauchope abandoned before a single Chinese soldier had set foot in it.

In his headquarters at Newman Senior Technical College, Colonel Ma swiftly typed his first day's Situation Report and passed it to General Leung for approval.

After reading the SitRep, the general smirked: "Why have you put in so much detail about the skirmish on the coastal road? Do you really think General Bing really cares how much resistance the local farmers were able to put up? All he will care about is that we achieved all of our Day One objectives. We captured the Aerial Port of Disembarkation without any losses, other than the seven Dragonflies who wound up dead at the Control Tower and that one Little Dragon who's gone missing. We seized the armory and captured assault rifles, handguns, ammunition and other equipment of their 41st Battalion; we captured Local Area Command for the state's police forces, and their firearm registry – that'll sure make it easy to track down and seize the firearms the locals have in this sector – and we have established bed-down facilities for my Brigade. All in all, I'd say we've accomplished our Day One tasks, wouldn't you? So why bother putting in all that crap about the spirited defense that some local cops and civilians threw together at the cross-roads?"

"Because, General, it was not according to plan," the Colonel responded. "Yes, we have seized the operational centers of gravity here, and we now dominate one important line of communication, the coastal road, but we lost eight men in that skirmish. They should not have been able to hold us off for the eighteen hours that they did, and we should have been able to push much farther inland, at least as far as the next town, Wauchope, with motorized patrols."

"But that was not our Day-One Objective, it was a Discretionary Objective – a 'would be nice' – not part of the overall timetable, and we were prepared to take far heavier losses, don't forget."

"True, General, but those estimates were for enemy defensive action, such as shooting down some of our civilian-pattern air transports, like what happened in some other sectors. But I'm telling you, from experience, those civilians fought like professionals there. I think we are in for a much tougher fight here than we expected."

"Well, you can leave it in if you like, but take out that part about the hostages. We don't need to advertise that their surrender was only after we started executing those children at the petrol station. No need to put that in the official record."

"But General, that was done on your orders, not mine." The Colonel had been disgusted by the General's order; he considered it beneath an honorable soldier.

"Colonel, do you want to join them? I think the mass grave is still open. The General's face was tight and his voice thick with anger. "I'm sure we can find some space for you in amongst the women and children, and those local heroes you are so impressed with."

Colonel Ma thought about it for a moment. *Would it be better to take a bullet in the back of the head now, or go along with this madness for even one more day?* But when he thought about his wife and son, who would be punished if he strayed from his duty, no matter how repugnant it now appeared, he knew what he had to do.

"Consider it deleted, General. And congratulations on your great victory today," Colonel Ma said, fawning humility in the required manner.

The general smiled, truly ignorant of the hollowness of the praise. He was that intoxicated with the power that had been placed in his hands.

8

ROPE-A-DOPE

At 3:10 AM on May 20th the heat and humidity in Darwin was still oppressive. However, Major Blakely did not even notice the relative coolness of the air-conditioned briefing theatre being used as the Command Post for EXERCISE ROPE-A-DOPE. He strode right past the outer ring of senior NCOs and junior officers, taking center stage and interrupting the presentation being made by the General from Land Combat Readiness Center, 1st Division Royal Australian Army, out of Brisbane.

Major Blakely's voice rang clearly throughout the room. "General Davis, I'm sorry, Sir, but I have to cut you off. We're at war," Major Blakely said simply.

The General was offended by the interruption. "Major Blakely, I don't know how you Yanks run things in your exercises, but here in Australian we preface our exercise inputs with 'Exercise, Exercise, Exercise.'"

To some of the men in the room it was their first major combined exercise, and to some extent at least, everybody in the collection of American, Indian and Australian units were still struggling to find their asses – even with both hands – so there were more than a few 'deer in the headlights' looks from the audience. For some of the junior officers from the MAGTFA, like the eager young platoon commander, Lieutenant Jarvis, the expression was quickly replaced by the "can do" expression they wore when concealing their confusion behind a warrior's mask.

Jarvis and the other young Marines ramped up their listening and watching, gathering in all the new information with a razor sharp focus which they had developed in the 'trial by fire' that was the life of a junior officer in the Marine Corps.

But Major Blakely was not concerned with their reaction, nor the Australian General's increasingly red face. He knew he had to treat the portly Australian with respect, but had absolutely no fear of the man.

"Sir, this is not an exercise inject. The exercise is over! We are at war! More importantly, we are all in a great deal of danger," Blakely said, taking up a firm stance in the middle of the stage and speaking loud enough for the entire audience to hear his every word. "Now you can go and check with your own military, or you can sit down and shut up, and let me tell you – all of you – what we know at this time. With your permission, General," he added, giving the general a chance to recover from the shock.

"This better not be some kind of crazy way to run an exercise, Major. But go ahead, you have the floor."

"Thank you, General," Pausing only for a moment, Major Blakely looked into the eyes of some of the more senior, command-grade officers from the Australian and Indian militaries, and his US Marine Corps peers from the MAGTFA.

"When you all left your cell-phones, Blackberries and other electronic devices at the entrance to this facility you entered a black hole. Right now, many of your commands, your staff, and so on are undoubtedly trying to reach you. So in a couple of minutes, when I am done, I suggest that go to the commissionaires at the entrance and retrieve your communications devices, or get to a work-station and contact your chain of command to verify what I am about to tell you. But for the next couple of minutes, nobody leaves this room," he said, ominously, just as a number of armed Marines took up positions at the exits from the theatre. Blakely had a captured audience.

Immediately there were sounds of zippers and snaps being undone as over sixty military professionals took out their field note pads, binders, or 'junior general' binders, to take notes.

"I've just received confirmation that the United States is at Defense Condition One. We are under nuclear attack by the Russian Federation. Anchorage and Honolulu were the first American targets hit, along with Inuvik, Frobisher Bay and Winnipeg in Canada. At this time a full retaliatory strike is underway, which President Parker ordered before evacuating from Washington DC." Blakely paused for a moment, but nobody interrupted. He thought momentarily of his brother, Matt, stationed at the Mount Weather bunker where President Parker would have evacuated to.

"Missiles are hitting targets throughout the United States, and our missiles will begin striking the Russian Federation within the next twenty minutes."

The general from the Land Combat Readiness Centre could not hold his tongue any longer. "Major, what is your source of information. I mean, how can I be sure you are not being spoofed or led down the garden path, and where is Colonel Ferebee, anyhow?"

Blakely turned to face him. "Sir. Colonel Ferebee will be joining us in a moment. I was with him in the Comms Center, on a direct line to the 3rd Marines, when the news broke." Turning back to the group at large, Blakely continued. "We were actually in a secure conference call with the Commanding Officers of the 3rd and 1st Marine Divisions when the first reports came in. I personally heard Colonel Wagstaff in Okinawa, Colonel O'Leary in Honolulu, and Lieutenant Colonel Crowe at Camp Lejeune confirm the reports of inbound missile tracks. The tracks were being reported by USSTRATCOM and passed to the component commands, so what we overheard in our teleconference was taking place live, and fully authenticated in the 3rd Marines Operations Center," Blakely explained. "Then we lost Honolulu. Colonel O'Leary's voice simply cut out, mid-sentence, but there was a lot of shouting in his Ops Centre just before we lost them. So we conferenced-in another Marine unit on Oahu, who reported visual sighting of a mushroom cloud over Honolulu. We then raised USPACOM on another secure line, and were given a very hasty, verbal, Fragmentary Mobilization and Dispersal Order directly from Admiral Gaines.

"At this time we have no indications as to why the Russian Federation would start a war with us. There were no indications of any tensions, however the war is real, and it's moving swiftly. While General Mobilization and Dispersal Order has been given to all US Military units throughout the globe, no specific orders have as yet made their way to us from USPACOM or any other higher headquarters, and our comms with them have since gone down – probably saturated.

"Colonel Ferebee is consulting with American and allied Marine, Naval and Air Force units in this region, to get a sense of our main weight of effort, but his preliminary orders to me, which I am to pass on to all of you, are as follows."

"SITUATION. The United States, and in all probability, our allies and friends throughout the world, are at war with the Russian Federation. Atomic weapons have been used against us, and a full retaliatory strike is in progress. Our initial assessment is that all military installations are potential targets of our enemies. Nuclear, Chemical and Biological attacks, as well as conventional warfare attacks, cyber-warfare, sabotage, espionage and other forms of warfare are either underway or considered imminent.

"MISSION. The mission of all American forces in Australia is three-fold: First, <u>Dispersal and Force Protection:</u> we are in Survive To Operate mode as of this minute. Second, <u>Assembly and Force Generation:</u> MAGTFA will mobilize and draw in additional American and allied units as available within the Australian AOR and operate within an ad-hoc Combined Joint Task Force structure of Brigade or greater strength, as able. Third, <u>Force Employment</u>: after liaising with American and allied forces in this AOR and on order from Higher Headquarters, MAGTFA will commence expeditionary or defensive combat operations.

"EXECUTION. With all haste, all units of MAGTFA and any Australian or allied units authorized by their command elements to do so, shall use EXERCISE ROPE-A-DOPE, hereby re-designated OPERATION ROPE-A-DOPE as a template around which PHASE ONE, Force Protection and Dispersal, will be carried out except that all timings shall be compressed such that H-Hour shall be 03:45hrs local time, or 1815hrs Zulu. All units must be Oscar Mike by 03:45 hours or earlier if able. That's less than thirty minutes from now. All personnel and units not already included in the original ROPE-A-DOPE Op Order shall grab your deuce gear, any additional kit, rations, ammunition or other combat stores that you can lay your hands on, and disperse using any vehicle you can get your hands on. We will be using the Robertson Barracks Parade Square as an ad-hoc assembly area and strive to be Oscar Mike immediately after the high-readiness units and other participants in ROPE A DOPE depart."

"Logistics and other support personnel, throw open the stores and abandon record keeping. Facilitate the issue of additional weapons and ammunition, MOPP gear, vests and so on for anybody, American or allied, who does not have all their kit, and then evacuate your post by 0430 hours at the latest.

"Rendezvous assembly area will be as per ROPE A DOPE or as directed by military police, Recon Platoon, Fox Company, in vicinity of Mount Bundy airstrip and the Bundy Creek maneuvering range, two kilometers west of the hamlet of Adelaide River. That's 113 km south of us here in Darwin."

Major Blakely eyeballed Lieutenant Jarvis from the Recon Platoon of Fox Company, 2nd Battalion, 3rd Marines, and got a silently mouthed 'HUA', embracing his specific task.

Blakely then looked at his watch. "Marines, you have now twenty five minutes to pass these orders down the chain of command, and have your men Oscar Mike ASAP.

"Anybody with questions, stay back," he said. The door opened and Colonel Ferebee stormed into the room. Commanding Officer MAGTFA, Colonel Ferebee joined Blakely at the front of the now highly tense group of men.

"Why are you all sitting there, Marines?" Ferebee barked at the men. "Major Blakely has given you my Orders. Use the exercise plan to fill in the holes. This is a Survive to Operate situation – perfect for the Marines! Now MOVE!" he commanded.

"HUA!" Chaos erupted as the MAGTFA officers and SNCOs swarmed out of the theatre to track down their subordinates and begin the urgent dispersal out of Robertson Barracks.

Some of the Australian and Indian officers headed out to grab their cell-phones and try to check in with their commands, but most stayed in the theatre to listen as the senior officers had an urgent pow-wow.

Colonel Ferebee looked around the room quickly, a man whose blood was up from making life-and-death decisions for the past half hour. He focused on a group of Indian men clustered together. "Group Captain Gahrwal, I don't know where you and your team fit in to all of this, but you are welcome to consider yourselves a lodger unit within MAGTFA, and ask for anything you need. We'll do what we can to help you once you know your own plans," Ferebee said to the Indian Air Force officer serving as Military Attaché to Australia. He and his contingent of officers from the Indian Air Force and Indian Army had been in Darwin to observe the exercise with the Marines.

"That's all I needed to hear," Gahrwal said. "There are nine of us and we've got our own gear and transportation. We should be able to take care of ourselves. We'll check in with your MPs at the rendezvous. Thank you, Colonel." He departed with the rest of his team on his heels jabbering away at each other in a language that sounded like English, but not exactly.

General Davis stepped over to Captain Thorne, the platoon commander from 1st Commando Regiment of the Australian Special Ops Command. "What about you, Captain? You going to throw in with the Americans, or operate independently?"

"If it's all the same to you, General, until I hear from Sydney or Perth, I think we'll make our own arrangements. We'll touch base with you lot at your rendezvous once we know our mission."

"Good on ya, Captain, carry on," said the General, who then seemed to have made up his mind and addressed the remaining personnel in the room, mostly from RAA's 1st Division.

"Until I get confirmation from 1st Division in Brisbane, or from 2nd Division in Sydney, I'm going to use my authority as Commander 1st Brigade, Darwin, to order the following: All 1st Brigade personnel scheduled to participate in EXERCISE ROPE-A-DOPE shall go along with the Marines, as per Colonel Ferebee's comments. That's mostly 1st Armored Regiment and elements of 5th Battalion. For everybody else, we'll carry out some combat operational planning on the fly and activate our Base Defense Forces here at Robertson Barracks for Chemical-Biological-Radiological-Nuclear attack. We will NOT disperse the entire base, however we will deploy advance parties of 1 Combat Engineering Regiment, the 8/12 Artillery Regiment, the 5th Battalion and the 2nd Cavalry Regiment as per STANDING CONPLAN ALBATROSS," he said, turning to Colonel Ferebee to add: "That's the Force Protection and Dispersal Plan we talked about a while back, Colonel Ferebee. We'll check with our G5 on this, but from my recollection, it's essentially a no-notice field deployment to our range in the Fly Creek area, here," he indicated on the map he had pulled from his well-worn, old-style leather map case.

Ferebee looked at the point on the map. "I've visited that range. You've got some good facilities there, if a bit austere for a command element. But that looks like a good spot for now. But just so I understand, your advance parties will be there with a view to potentially making that your mobilization area, if you disperse additional forces out of Darwin? And in the mean-time you are ramping up Force Protection measures, CBRN, and base defense forces, other than the units detached along with the MAGTFA?"

"Quite right, Colonel. We have to be here to defend Darwin and our critical infrastructure. And it will take a few days to mobilize our reserve units. I have to strike a balance. So that's the part that will be left behind. You've got our Colonel Harper with our units that are now, effectively, part of this Combined

Joint Task Force you are standing up. That'll have to do for now, we've got to see to our units now. We'll track you down on the radios, later this morning. Agreed?"

"Sir!"

"Ta," General Adams said, as he zipped up his own notepad and headed out of the room, moving with a sense of purpose that was in sharp contrast to the sloth-like manner he had shown less than thirty minutes earlier.

With that, the theatre emptied as the few remaining Marines and Australian Army personnel scattered.

Had it not been for the fact that EXERCISE ROPE-A-DOPE had originally been scheduled for an 0600 H-hour, the vehicles and kit for the core elements of MAGTFA would not have been sitting around in assembly areas, ready to go. The carefully planned seating assignments, order of march, vehicle spacing and interval timing planned for ROPE-A-DOPE was now completely out the window. The highly flexible Marines understood that dispersion meant *throw yourself up the road, impose order on chaos and don't stand around waiting to be told what to do.* The men and women of 3rd Marines were masters at choreographing the complex movements of a battalion on the fly.

As he watched the vehicles pulling into line with speed and efficiency, Colonel Ferebee was confident that his Marines would arrive at the Mount Bundy training area in good order, ready for anything.

After a few more words with Major Blakely, walking with him towards a line of Humvees outside the building loaned to the 3rd Marines to use as their Headquarters, he jumped into his command vehicle and sped off, leading a short convoy comprised of the headquarters element.

They were not the first Marines to depart the grounds of Robertson Barracks. Lead elements and security details had begun darting out in the preceding five to ten minutes. The remaining Light Armored Vehicles, trucks, fuel bowsers, water trucks, supply trucks, support vehicles, Humvees and other vehicles of the MAGTFA followed in convoy groups that stretched out for over a kilometer, their tail lights snaking up the highway like a coiled snake in the pre-dawn darkness.

As the Marines flowed smoothly out of Robertson Barracks in a precise, efficient manner, the Australian Army units beginning to disperse out of Robertson Barracks to their own dispersal site at Fly Creek were more of a disorderly exodus. The off-duty Australian personnel got their instructions by word of mouth or telephone, but it was the unexpected escalation of noise and rumbling activity of an army on the move that really woke everybody up, including the Australian civilians in Darwin.

Unlike the main force of the MAGTFA, which was to go to Mount Bundy for the initial mobilization, Colonel Ferebee and his Headquarters element headed to Fly Creek, where the lead element of the Headquarters Battalion were already setting up a brigade HQ by the time General Adams own staff showed up.

Some sixty six kilometers inland from Darwin, Fly Creek lay a dozen kilometers off the main highway, to the west, in a remote area. It would not have been Ferebee's first choice, as he would have preferred to set up much farther inland. However Fly Creek would put Colonel Ferebee within easy reach of his forces while also giving him good access to the Australian chain of command. It was not ideal, but would allow him to focus on the strategic situation sooner, with his CP set up faster than if he went farther inland. *In any case, we've got our USMC rotary wing resources dispersing from the airstrip in Darwin, so at least we have some air power to work with. But we need more, a heck of a lot more,* Ferebee thought, hoping to hear good news about the Royal Australian Air Force's fighter force.

Donning the headset that had been handed to him as soon as he had sat down in his command HMVW, Colonel Ferebee listened to the communications feed that his radio operator had piped in to the headset. They had tuned into a variety of UHF, VHF and HF frequencies assigned to the Australian Defense

Force, in order to build a picture of the battle space as it began to take shape. There were numerous confirmed reports of Chinese land forces deploying out of small port cities and aerodromes, immediately engaging in combat operations. Coming as a complete surprise, the attacks had the Australians reeling. They had nothing in place to stop the massive invasion and this terrible situation was in addition to the horrors faced by those affected by the nuclear attacks at Australia's largest cities.

What Ferebee heard shocked him, but also confirmed that dispersal had been the right decision. Sydney had been nuked, along with Brisbane, Canberra and a number of military installations in New South Wales and Queensland. There were reports of ambushes, sabotage and small skirmishes throughout the east coast of Australia, and the complete decapitation of the national civilian and military authorities with the destruction of the Australian Capital Territory and the capital, Canberra.

What was left of the two divisions of the Australian Army, perhaps a brigade or two, were scattered across the country and faced with what appeared to be an ever-growing enemy force, of at least Group Army size. *Likely multiple Group Armies organized into smaller Task Forces, following a well-rehearsed set of plans,* he estimated.

With the overwhelming size of the enemy force added to the shock of the destruction of the Australian military bases and most important cities, it was no surprise to hear the desperation and panic coming across the radio nets. Australia was utterly devastated, facing complete destruction. Much of the radio chatter was incomprehensible due to overlapping transmissions. However there was a gradual trend towards panic being replaced with grim determination, with units popping onto the net to report that they had been activated and were dispersing, or reporting having been rendered combat ineffective due to disastrous interference, pre-emption by the enemy, and sabotage. It now appeared that China, with boots on the ground engaged in combat in Australia, must somehow be behind the nuclear attacks. It was the only rational explanation, but identifying the scale of the Chinese gambit helped Ferebee come to grips with his task, and it was daunting to say the least.

But there was also some good news, beginning to form a picture in Colonel Ferebee's mind. Adelaide, Perth, and Darwin had been saved by the Air Warfare destroyers that somehow happened to be on alert in or near those port cities, providing a 200 nautical mile anti-missile umbrella and preserving Royal Australian Army, Navy and Air Force units and saving countless civilian lives in the process. These surviving units comprised no more than one-third of the original fighting power, perhaps 30,000 personnel all tolled. With just under 2,500 Marines under his command with the Marine Air Ground Task Force Australia, Colonel Ferebee considered his mission to hurt the Chinese anywhere he could, more than the defense and liberation of Australia. It just so happened that Australia was where his piece of the global war was to be fought. However, he knew that the enemy had the upper hand and were pouring in their follow-on forces through the airfields and ports they had already seized. But Australia was an immense country, a continent really, and with the enemy largely confined to the east coast, from Cairns to Melbourne, the rest of the Australian continent was still free.

The more damage we can inflict on the Chinese here in Australia, the better for the overall war effort, and for America, he thought, as he watched one of his planners annotate his map while their Humvee sped along the highway. Everybody listened to the chatter from the Australian Army radio nets, but the young Captain sitting next to Colonel Ferebee was marking his map with symbols to indicate friendly and enemy units, disposition and strength.

The battle-space was beginning to take shape.

Colonel Ferebee's mind had begun to drift to another battlefield, nearly two centuries before, where a man faced similarly overwhelming odds, with only 1,500 men to stand up to an entire army of ruthless invaders.

Thinking of the vastness of the Australian continent, the hostile terrain between the enemy and himself, and the extremely limited lines of communication in terms of rail and road, he saw himself in a similar context to the man who brought Texas into the United States. Colonel Ferebee imagined how it must have been for General Sam Houston back in 1836.

In just that moment of reflection, Colonel Ferebee became inspired. *That's our Centre of Gravity: Time and Space*, he realized, and then sprang into action with his staff, laying out how he intended that the Marines and Australians would use their one advantage to maximum effect.

While Colonel Ferebee and the other Marines and military personnel were putting distance between themselves and Darwin, the Duty Watch staff and dispatchers of the Northern Territory Police, Fire and Emergency Services finally understood why the Navy and Army bases were suddenly on full alert. The emergency response agencies in Darwin began to call in all of their off-duty personnel to fully activate the Northern Territorial Government's Emergency Operations Center, NTEOC.

They had already been active, dispatching police and ambulance crews to a reported shooting at a vehicle storage yard just outside of the city limits. The first officers to arrive had been gunned down in a hail of gunfire, with only one officer making it out of the ambush alive. The Staff Sergeant on duty was still piecing the details together as he scrambled to put together something of a plan to contain the situation at the Toyota vehicle storage facility when he learned that their homeland had been attacked. He was not certain that the two events were related; however he knew that he needed all hands on deck, and a fully ramped-up EOC.

While the police staff were busy force generating police and other emergency personnel, the other personnel of the NTEOC were busy ramping up, carrying out a snowball-style recall of key personnel. They were also firing up the computers, communications systems, and turning on as many different television channels as they could display on their 'Wall of Knowledge' to try to get some idea about what was going on.

After giving up on Channels 7, 9, and 10 from Sydney, and Channel ABC Brisbane, they found a few channels out of Adelaide and Perth that were on the air, along with BBC World News out of Kuala Lumpur. There was a great deal of confusion, with bewildered newscasters struggling to handle the avalanche of reports of nuclear attacks in countries throughout the world.

With images of mushroom clouds coming in from a variety of feeds, the morning news anchor from Adelaide had reached her wit's end and had some sort of nervous breakdown. She was quickly replaced by her producer, who took over the broadcast. However, he was barely able to keep it together himself when the sheer scale of the crisis became clear; untold millions of people were dying the world over.

At first there had been a few dozen channels on the air, coming from various satellite feeds. Every so often, one after another, major news channels suddenly went off the air. In the cases of BBC World News Asia in Kuala Lumpur going off the air it was soon evident from a report on another channel that the Malaysian capital had just been hit with an atomic weapon.

As operations staff of the territorial EOC continued to call in and wake up any of the police, fire and ambulance first responders who had not been woken up by the rumbling military mobilization, and more and more information came in, it suddenly dawned on them.

"Darwin could be next!" shouted a 911 dispatcher, who had left her desk in the communications cell and stuck her head into the EOC to see what was going on.

"Maybe we should evacuate the city, just in case," said one of the white-shirted officials from the Fire & Paramedic Service.

"There's not enough time for that. If we are going to be hit, it will be in the next few hours, I reckon," said one of the cops from the Northern Territory Police Force.

"So what should we do? We can't just sit here."

"Maybe we should do what the military are doing, and disperse some of our key personnel and equipment. Maybe we should send some fire-trucks, ambulances and police out of the city. That way, they could be intact, and operational at a safe distance, and return after the city is attacked," said the dispatcher.

"Good on ya', Sally! That's the best idea I've heard all morning. What do you think, gang? Let's do that. At least then we've got a plan," said the Senior Watch Officer.

"You're in charge, Robbie. At least until the Mayor gets here. I'm sure she will agree, so why don't you go ahead and give the order, and we'll all get behind it!" said the senior police officer.

"Bugger me!" the Staff Sergeant said, and then paused to collect himself. "Everybody, you hear that? We are going to order all emergency response resources, police, fire, ambulance – the crews and rigs out of the city. Sally, pass it on to the other dispatchers, and get them started."

"Roger, Sir," she said, happy to finally know what to do. She clicked the transmit button on the Wi-Fi transmitter clipped to her waist and spoke into her headset as she returned to her workstation in the adjacent room.

"What else can we do?" asked the Senior Watch Officer.

"What is the military term? For stuff like electrical power, water, engineering works and so on?" asked one of the paramedics.

"Critical Infrastructure," said the cop, surprised that she did not know even the most basic of terms. *She's probably never even read our Emergency Operations Plan, but she's the one who showed up to man her station, so she'll have to do,* he thought.

"Right, people! We've got this big brick of an EOP, and no time to read it. Why don't we simply use the recall contacts for *anything* that sounds like critical infrastructure, and try to alert them to send their vehicles, mobile equipment and technical types out of harm's way?"

"So we are evacuating the entire city, only just starting with essential personnel and equipment? How will that look for the citizens at large?" asked someone who had just arrived, a step ahead of the Mayor.

The Staff Sergeant recognized the Mayor as she strode through the door. "Oh, your honor, you're here! Good on ya.

We need you like you would not believe. Are you aware that we are at war?"

She quickly looked around the NTEOC and then at the Staff Sergeant. "Yes, I heard it on the radio and saw some of it on the tellie downstairs. I heard you've begun sending units out of town. Dispersion? Great idea. Where are we after that? Have we started the full evacuation?"

"No, not yet. We were discussing it, but right now we're thinking about the critical infrastructure. Shouldn't we try to send the engineers, line crews, and so on out first, before the public chokes up Highway One?"

"This is not New York City. There's only one hundred and thirty thousand citizens to move. We've got to save as many of them as we can. Order the full evacuation, don't waste time trying to reach infrastructure and utilities personnel. They'll understand what to do when they hear we are evacuating. Use the local radio stations, like it says in the EOP. Follow the plan," she ordered.

"Yes, your Honor," said the Watch Officer, when suddenly a bright flash lit up the skies over Darwin, followed by a sudden boom.

The windows of the Territorial Government building shook, but did not break.

As he dove for the floor and covered his face with his arms, expecting to be shredded by glass or burned to a crisp, the Staff Sergeant thought that the shock wave felt something like the mild earth-quakes that occasionally happened in the Darwin area.

Had it not been for the quick thinking Lieutenant Commander on night watch aboard DDG 116 *Thomas Hudner*, who had put the ship on high alert the moment he received the DEFCON ONE message from the communications cabin, the 550 kiloton warhead carried by the Russian R-29 *Vysota* Sea-Launched Ballistic Missile, SLBM, launched from a Delta-III Sub Surface Ballistic Nuclear, SSBN, submarine, would have obliterated everybody aboard the American warship, the ship itself, the dockyard, and most of the city of Darwin.

Intercepted in its terminal descent towards the target, the missile had been destroyed as it passed through 30,000 feet. But despite being over six miles away from Darwin, the bright flash and accompanying shock wave was powerful enough to set off car alarms throughout the city.

It was the first of three missiles to target Darwin over the next hour, which were tracked, identified, and intercepted by *Thomas Hudner's* Lockheed Martin SPY-1D passive RADAR, fire control system and SM-3-A Standard Missile.

The Captain had made his way to the command deck long before the first missile engagement and had quickly gotten himself up to speed on the message traffic, while his crew activated defensive systems and brought the warship to full operational status, but he was having great difficulty comprehending the data.

He simply could not believe his eyes.

"This can't be correct. Have you looked at this, XO?"

"Yes, Captain. I have. It doesn't make any sense to me either, but the tracks don't lie. The first one was one of ours."

"And the next two, those were Russian? Am I reading this correctly?"

"Yes, Sir. The best I can figure is that somehow, in our counter-strike, USSTRATCOM accidentally targeted Darwin, or perhaps us."

"That's impossible."

"I know. Why would we hit our allies, not to mention one of our own warships?"

"No. That's not what I mean. I mean, how could the first missile have been ours, if ours was a counterstrike? You would think that the Russian missiles would have come first."

"Shit! Here comes another missile."

The crew of *Thomas Hudner* carried out their antimissile procedure for the fourth time, which amounted to watching the SPY 1D weapons system carrying out lightning-fast calculations, and firing the SM-3-A missile for its two minute acceleration to meet the incoming target, the Russian missile closing with the warship at thirteen thousand miles per hour; the smaller missile from the air warfare destroyer closing at a more modest Mach 5. In the Combat Information Center, CIC, the violence of the explosion in the lower reaches of space was reduced to a few changes to the icons on the RADAR display, and the sudden termination of the two missile tracks at the point at which they had momentarily co-existed.

With the fourth missile destroyed over forty miles out, the crew let out a cheer and breathed a sigh of relief. Those who were focused on the strategic situation, such as the Captain, XO and senior officers also felt some relief that the missile had originated in Russia, and not from US forces.

After a tense few minutes watching the plot, waiting for any subsequent missiles, the Captain and XO resumed their discussion.

"I don't' know, Skipper. None of the message traffic fits either. There are reports that cities all over the world have been hit, that we are at war with Russia, *that we struck Europe*, that *France struck England*, and so on. It's a complete mess. Heck, it's as if someone got into the Joint Priority Integrated Target List and changed all the targets, so that we attacked everybody."

"And the Russians also attacked everybody?" asked the Captain, suddenly looking even more focused as he read another dispatch that he had just been handed.

"How many missiles do you suppose have hit China?"

"Hard to say. We've lost the uplinks to Honolulu and San Diego, but we've still got comms through the USPACOM net. Want me to find out?"

"Yes. Do it right now, while there's still time."

As the XO headed into the communications cabin, just off the CIC. The Captain and the Lieutenant-Commander on watch focused on the RADAR displays.

"So no more missile tracks? What are these air-breathing tracks?"

"That's a pair of RAAF F-18s that got off Tindal before it was hit. They're headed for Brisbane, for reconnaissance, to confirm how bad the city was hit."

"How bad was Tindal hit?"

After the XO gave some instructions to one of the systems operators, data appeared on a corner of one of the smaller screens. "Utterly destroyed, I am sure. It was hit four times."

"Us or them?"

"Both."

"Jesus," the captain said, thinking of the airmen and support personnel who had seemed so friendly when he had been through the RAAF air base on a familiarization tour just weeks before.

"Sir. There seems to be a bit of a pattern here."

"How so, Lieutenant?"

"Well, look. Here are the tracks we got off the Alligator, before we lost the link to Honolulu. See the way these tracks converged on their targets from two sides, here in Darwin, and Tindal; and here, where the Carrier Task Group MALACCA is – or was – and there, in Singapore. It's the same over there, in the Philippines. Everywhere in this region targets were hit by both us and the Russians."

As he spoke, data began flowing on another monitor, the image making an obvious, terrible statement.

"Holy shit. It's the Chinese! That explains everything!" said the XO.

On the monitor, pushed out on the secure Very Low Frequency secure feed from USPACOM, a global summary was depicted in 3D, with red, blue and white lines strung out all over a rotating globe. Launch areas in Russia, in red, were linked with gossamer-thin red lines to their targets in America, Europe, Asia – all over the world. Only slightly less numerous were the lines in blue, from the continental United States, to the same targets, the world over. There were also a considerable number of targets from other source areas, at sea in the North Atlantic and the Pacific Ocean.

There were white lines, from "all other" nuclear powers.

"Oh, My God! It's Armageddon. There must be thousands of tracks," observed the Lieutenant-Commander.

"And almost none of them are into China," observed the Captain, confirming the logic of the XO's conclusion.

Captivated by the tracks that were still making their way to targets, they watched in silence as missiles hit anonymous cities in the Asia Pacific region, and more well-known cities they recognized in Europe and North America. Watching it unfold on the high-resolution displays was hypnotic, and deeply disturbing.

Suddenly a yellow spark terminated one of the missile tracks in flight. And then another.

"Look! Something took out that missile. And there's another one! What is it, antimissile defenses?"

"I don't think so. If it is, it's too little, too late."

As they watched, the number of yellow sparks rapidly increased.

"Hey, it's the red ones. All the Russian missiles still in flight are being taken out."

"That's right. Maybe they're being aborted!"

Minutes later, yellow sparks began appearing at the lead of the blue tracks, rapidly accelerating until all the blue missiles in flight were aborted as well.

"Sir. We just got Mission Orders on the Secure VLF."

The captain took the sheet of paper, and then activated the ships intercom to pass it on to the crew.

The Captain was about to inform the crew of their situation when he noticed new tracks appearing on the plot.

"What are those tracks?"

"Air breathing, Sir, subsonic."

"Transponders?"

"None, Sir."

"Project them along their courses."

After the SPY 1D system operator typed in the commands, thin lines shot ahead of the airborne tracks.

"Could those be Cruise Missiles?"

"No, Sir, too big. That's why we can see them at all. Normally we would not see anything that far out, but look, this one will have Closest Point of Approach with us at four hundred miles."

"What's along their flight paths after the CPA? Any bases or military installations? Cities?"

As the display operator scrolled through his screens, examining one track after another, he suddenly leaned back and took a breath.

"They're aircraft from China, Sir. Some of them will pass pretty much on-top us, but at high altitude. These ones, ten or twelve, seem to be eventually converging on the Adelaide region. The rest of them seem to be headed to eastern Queensland and New South Wales."

"You sure they are from China?"

"Yes, Sir. Look, watch the regression and back-track."

He entered a series of commands and then rolled a track-ball on his console, flying the symbols backward on their flight-paths. This also sent the track-predicting lines on reverse course, each track making a bee-line for their places of origin, clearly inside China.

"Roll that forward again."

"Aye, Sir."

"Do the Australian F-18s have Link 16?"

The system operator smiled, understanding what his Skipper had in mind.

"Yes, Sir, they most certainly do!"

In the cockpit of a Xian JH-7 "Flying Leopard" Fighter-Bomber just approaching Adelaide, a highly skilled pilot was operating his weapons systems as he closed on the target area, adroitly defeating enemy radars and imagining himself like a pilot at Pearl Harbor. "Target visual," he reported over the secure UHF link back to an airborne platform that extended the eyes and ears of the fighter package comprised of his and eleven other customized variants of the JH-7.

Suddenly his Electronic Support Measures and other automated threat-detection systems lit up all at once. *Shit! Someone has me locked-up!* thought the pilot as he began evasive maneuvers. Suddenly he became free from the restraints of his ejection seat, enveloped inside a cauldron of searing heat. The last thing he was conscious of was the feeling that his arms and legs were simply gone. He was dead before any signals of pain, or of the flesh and bone being torn apart in the violence of the explosion, reached the boiling bucket of goo that had been the brain of one of China's most skilled fighter pilots, Commanding officer of one of 7th Fighter Division's JH-7 squadrons.

The strike package of twelve JH-7s had been configured for an Air-Ground strike on enemy air defenses in the Adelaide region. Their weapons systems, jammers, Electronic Counter Measures and other systems had been carefully tuned with the most up-to-date downloads extracted from the RAAF's own computers, so they were confident in their ability to evade and defeat enemy air defenses. What was supposed to be a complete surprise had turned out to be even more one-sided than any of the planners back in Jinan had even war-gamed. Unfortunately for Colonel Yip and the other Flying Leopard pilots, the Australians were the ones who had surprised the Chinese thanks to the Link-16 data passed to RAAF Adelaide Sector Air Defense from DDG 116 *Thomas Hudner* up in Darwin.

The first volley of SM-3A Standard Missiles had come up to greet the leading elements of the Chinese attack from the Royal Australian Navy's sole air warfare destroyer, RAN *Hobart*, still at anchor in Adelaide Bay. Those of Colonel Yip's formation that had survived the first wave of missiles, and had begun to turn their attention to the threat from their ten-o'clock low then had to deal with a sudden new threat only moments later, that of a dozen Australian F/A-18 Super Hornet fighters coming in on them from their three-o'clock, at the effective limit of their threat detector's range, the RAAF fighters closing at Mach 1.7.

One of the more mathematically gifted of the Chinese pilots struggled to calculated the closure rate as he turned to face the incoming Super-Hornets, his Wingman barely able to stay with him in the abrupt turn to starboard. Just as Major Duan concluded that the 40 nautical miles between them would be closed in just over two minutes, his mind was challenged again with a new rate of closure to apply to the quickly reducing standoff distance – that of the missile tracks that had suddenly detached from the Australian attackers.

The AIM-120 AMRAAM missiles tore into his and his wingman's JH-7 twenty seconds later. From the point of view of the active seeker in the Advanced Medium Range Air-to-Air Missile, the fact that the Chinese fighter pilot had pulled hard in an attempt to turn away from the missiles had made the microcomputer brain of the missile's vector geometry and probabilistic time-and-space projections that much easier as the JH-7 profile changed from head-on to an almost perfect 90-degrees, presenting the AMI-120 with the underbelly of Major Duan's aircraft, as if embracing the inevitability of the missile impact.

With dozens of other missiles soon flying in from the Australian F/A-18s, and a second wave of missiles coming up from RAN *Hobart*, not to mention a few other surface to air missiles coming up from other units on the ground in the Adelaide area, the entire PLAAF strike package was soon obliterated.

To residents on the ground, who had had no idea that war had broken out between Australia and China, the first few explosions in the sky over the Barossa Valley and the northern suburbs of Adelaide had looked to many as some terrible air disaster, perhaps a mid-air collision.

But when the sky filled with the razor sharp lines of the missile tracks from the north-west, and the rising plumes from the local air defenses on the ground and from the warship in Adelaide Bay, and the brilliant cacophony from the series of explosions that took place directly over Adelaide, the civilians simply stared up in open-mouthed astonishment.

To one old man, what was taking place was very familiar. It brought back memories of his youth in London, during the Battle of Britain.

9

FOG OF WAR

Colonel Ferebee was satisfied that his new Command Post was fully operational. With the Australian and Indian military personnel adequately integrated, the CJOC would truly be a Combined Joint Task Force Op Centre. There were problems that would still take considerable time and effort to resolve, such as comms back to the continental United States and some of the remaining elements of 3rd Marines across the Pacific. But Ferebee felt that he was getting enough information to form an accurate assessment of the strategic situation. And that assessment was that Ferebee and the MAGTFA were on their own. With the world still reeling from the devastation wrought by the Chinese - controlled nuclear war between the United States and the Russian Federation, and the rapid destruction of military facilities, warships and strategic sites across the globe, it was clear that the opening moves in this Nuclear Extinction War, NEW, this total war against the Chinese military, had been won hands down by the Chinese.

Some of the best information had come in from warships of the USN, much of it from the 5th and 7th Fleets. The naval forces had assembled a picture of all known warships into a global database termed "Recognized Maritime Picture", RMP, which was a snapshot of all known maritime activity, be it commercial, enemy, neutral or friendly, at any given time.

With America's naval forces now largely destroyed, entire Carrier Battle Groups obliterated by nuclear weapons, and smaller task-forces and individual warships taken out by anything from SLBMs, SLCMs, ALCMs, torpedoes, mines, port-side sabotage and in some cases ship-on-ship warfare with conventional guns, the revised RMP, some five days after the NEW commenced, was largely guess-work. Whether all the warships were sunk, or merely exercising extreme emission-control measures to disguise their locations, it seemed to the Naval LnO at the CJOC that the only known warships still operational in the South Asian AOR were a handful of Australian frigates, the 3 USN and sole RAN air warfare destroyers, and perhaps two dozen warships of the Indian Navy. On the enemy side, other than the scores of commercial ships that the Chinese were using to deploy follow-on forces into the port cities and towns under their control, largely along Australia's east coast from north of Sydney all the way up to Cairns, there did not seem to be any Chinese Naval presence anywhere near Australia. It was highly unconventional to land their forces from these commercial vessels without naval protection, however the gamble certainly had worked for the Chinese, with reportedly tens of thousands of Chinese forces staging through the captured port facilities and quickly pressing inland right through the thin lines of bewildered Australian soldiers.

There were some indications of a few Chinese warships. Of greatest concern were the Jin Class SSBNs and likely two or three SSKs that were lurking around in the littoral waters of the Indonesian Archipelago, north of Australia.

That the Chinese were operating in the Indonesian waters with impunity indicated to Colonel Ferebee and the Australian General Davis that Indonesia had fallen quickly to the Chinese. This fear was soon confirmed by one of the spooks up from Pine Gap who reported that the Indonesian military frequencies had made a smooth transition to operations in Chinese, rather than Indonesian – but that the vocal signatures of unit operators had not changed, meaning that some of the Indonesian comms techs were bilingual in Chinese. Ferebee had found this hard to believe at first, but had come to accept that the degree of influence that the Chinese had had over the Indonesians had been thoroughly planned, and to the most minute of details.

The initial radio intercepts monitored by Pine Gap were soon confirmed by CIA assets still operating inside Indonesia. The PLA units were operating shoulder to shoulder with the Indonesian military. There would be no pressure on the Chinese from the Indonesians, and that meant that Indonesia had been taken out of the equation, in terms of resistance. Had there been any at all, it would have been swiftly dealt with, they learned. The elite PLA Marine Force of specially trained sea-based assaulters from the 164th Marine Brigade of the 41st Group Army were being used to quell any anti-Chinese activity in the Indonesian Archipelago. The presence of the Chinese Marines in Indonesia convinced General Adams and the rest of the CJOC how successful the Chinese take-over of the Indonesian power structure had been.

"So from this point, with the East Coast under full invasion and our forces whipped out or in complete disarray, and with China now able to base out of Indonesia to the north, we can anticipate them to press in on Darwin from the sea and overland from Queensland," said General Davis, with a defeated look.

"That's my assessment, too, General. However I think that with the naval and aerial defenses we now have covering Darwin sector we should expect that their main axis of advance will be westward along Highway A6?"

"Quite Right, Colonel. Those roads all come together and form the single, solitary route from Queensland into Northern Territory, the A2, at Cloncurry."

Looking at the map on the table in the center of the CJOC, Colonel Ferebee and General Davis updated each other on the location of units under their command, with Ferebee providing Davis a print-out of the mostly USMC units, working with Australian attachments, that had deployed eastward towards the Mount Isa – to - Cloncurry sector as a follow-on from the urgent dispersal they had carried out with OPERATION ROPE-A-DOPE less than a week before.

For his part, General Davis did not have the superb situational awareness that the Colonel from MAGTFA had at his disposal, but he and his staff were working furiously to establish contact with surviving units from the 13 brigades that made up Australian Forces Command, reserve units of the 2nd Division, teams of 1 Command Regiment anywhere in the country, and with any dispatch center, outpost or other asset of local police units and Territorial Police Force.

The situation was desperate, with civilians evacuating westward in advance of the rapidly expanding Chinese occupation flowing inland from the port cities of the east coast. It now appeared that Chinese units had carried out daring air-land assaults farther inland, taking out operational level centers of gravity – key road intersections hundreds of kilometers inland – so as to pave the way for rapid westward movement of the Chinese formations that were staging along the coast.

"Colonel Ferebee, do you reckon that setting up here in Katherine is the right place?"

After the disorder of the initial evacuation of forces out of harm's way in Darwin in the morning hours of the first day, General Davis and Colonel Ferebee had found that the site at Fly Creek had been unsuitable. Not only were the last few kilometers of roadway leading to the site too narrow for the bustling traffic of military vehicles coming and going, but it was also too far off of the three key roads being used by the joint forces of the US Marines of MAGTFA and the Australian military units. Personnel and equipment were being shuttled in both directions as ad-hoc units were being formed and in many cases re-formed with a better balance of integral logistics and engineering units for more sustained operations. Having their command and control base so far off to the west, in the boonies, and in such confined terrain, turned out to be a bad idea.

After evaluating alternative sites, General Davies and Colonel Ferebee decided on relocating the CJOC some 300 km farther south of Darwin, to the community of Katherine. Just 20km from the obliterated RAAF base at Tindal. The community itself was still intact, and the prevailing winds had blown the fall-out farther south-east, away from Katherine. Even better, some off-duty RAAF personnel and a few who had been evacuated by the Wing Commander before the first missiles had struck were in control of arrangements in Katherine. These men had pulled themselves together and taken control of local facilities such as the high school and nearby community center, and advised the CJOC that these were available and ready for use by the military.

Within hours of the decision to relocate from Fly Creek to Katherine, a column of MAGTFA personnel from the CJOC's advance party, engineers and other support personnel had reached the small town and had put together the CJOC in short order. This ensured a seamless transition for the command element, who arrived by helicopter later in the day.

While the American personnel were focused on their many tasks, mobilizing the entire MAGTFA and CJTF force for deployment and combat, the mood was altogether different within the Australian forces and their civilian population.

They were devastated, and reeling from a seemingly unending series of body blows as it became clear how badly Australia had been mauled by the Russians and, incomprehensible as it was, also *American* missiles and the fact that the entire world was caught up in some insane war of annihilation fueled by the gargantuan missile arsenals of the two nuclear superpowers somehow having gone to total war against each other.

So when the word came that two of the Royal Australian Air Force's F/A-18 Super Hornets, which had been launched to investigate the first reports of a nuclear detonation at Brisbane, had shot down four commercial aircraft filled with Chinese Special Forces, the Australians had had something to cheer about. It was the first, and so far, only good news in the war. But it gave the Australians and their American friends a taste of victory.

The Chinese may have kicked the living shit of the rest of the world in the opening moves the war, but the fight had only just begun. Something like the World War Two battle of El Alamein, which Winston Churchill had said "...now this is not the end. It is not even the beginning of the end. But it is, perhaps, the end of the beginning."

From a military perspective, the situation was grim, and by no means clear.

What they did know was that the Darwin region was in good shape. Darwin, along with smaller communities in Northern Territory and cities as far south in Adelaide, South Australia, had been saved from airborne/air-land assault by the Australian and American SM-3A missiles from DDG 116 *Thomas Hudner* at Darwin.

In a two-hour period, *Thomas Hudner* and the RAAF F/A 18s working with them had shot down three successive waves of air assaulters, comprised of a total of sixty civilian-pattern aircraft in three waves of twenty. These waves had been converging on Darwin, Adelaide River, Katherine, Tennant Creek and Alice Springs in Northern Territory; several aircraft tracking towards the Adelaide area in South Australia, and a few that were headed for towns like Mount Isa, Cloncurry, Charter's Towers and Longreach in Queensland.

Before any of the airliners had been destroyed, the *Thomas Hudner* had first vectored the RAAF Super Hornets in on two of them for visual confirmation. The fighter pilots reported that the aircraft had all their windows drawn, and while they could clearly see the fighter pilots formed on them, they refused to respond on Guard and other well-known civilian air-traffic frequencies. And even after having had warning shots fired across their flight paths they had ignored the fighters instructions, and in one case they had even attempted to crash into the fighter.

After that the order had been given and all of the remaining airliners which had originated in China had been destroyed by missiles from *Thomas Hudner* and from the F/A-18 Super-Hornets.

Unfortunately, this had only covered the central sector. Some of the aircraft in the first two waves of aircraft bound for the West Coast, north of Perth, had made it through. The third wave, however, had been entirely destroyed, twenty four aircraft loaded with Special Forces soldiers intent on executing their air-landing mission had been eliminated. They must have known how dangerous their daring flight across Australia would be, and the risk of being shot down if the Australian air defenses proved effective. Those who made it, and landed at their objectives, breathed sighs of relief. Those who did not, died in terror as their aircraft were blown to pieces around them, the soldiers torn to shreds or suddenly free-falling to their deaths. General Bing's mission planners, in the bunker under his HQ in Jinan Military District, had determined that the mission risk of equipping the men with parachutes, and therefore less ammunition and rations, was not justified by the low probability that the Australian air defense network would react swiftly enough to pose a significant mission risk. This risk analysis had proven accurate in terms of the East Coast – the Gold Coast sector – where all of the aircraft had reached their destinations unscathed, with three waves fully disgorging their passengers safely at their APODs. The central sector, on the other hand, had been an unmitigated disaster, with sixty aircraft downed, with over twelve thousand men lost. Most of these men had been drawn from Chengdu Military Region Special Forces Unit, "Chengdu Falcon". Specialists at airborne insertion, sabotage and offensives strike, these men, had they reached their targets – the small towns along the remote highways of Western Australia, South Australia and Northern Territory – would have crippled the ability of Australian and American forces to move, so their destruction may have proven to be a game changer.

It all depended on the ability of the invaders to adjust their plan, for follow-on attacks to fill the gap, and for those units who had made it into the western region to pick up some of the slack. For the defenders in Adelaide, Perth, and Darwin, it meant that finding, fixing, and destroying these units was of the utmost importance. Due to the vast distance across the largely unpopulated north coast, over which the invaders' aircraft were passing, and the limited range of *Thomas Hudner's* eyes, which could cover only the central sector, the number of Chinese aircraft who had reached their destinations along the extreme west coast was unknown, and thought to be up to a dozen.

There had been some worry that commercial airliners could have been caught up in the battle, but the Navy took care to not shoot down any aircraft that was squawking legitimate transponder codes, or who responded to radio calls which identified them by latitude and longitude. In a dozen or more cases the terrified aircrew landed in small airports in the middle of the outback, their landing gears sheared off or mired in dirt as the aircraft over-run the ends of the short runways.

The unknowns, and how the battle space was shaping up, would take days, even weeks, to fully put together as the communication grid had been taken out with the destruction of Sydney, the hub of the national telecommunications grid. That meant that intelligence analysts and operational planners of the CJOC, and the capabilities of the NSA and CIA analysts in Pine Gap, had to use every means possible to gather reports of enemy incursions, attacks, and movement at every little town across the territory.

It had been one of the Australian civilians in Pine Gap who had realized that there was still one national communications grid that was likely still intact; the School of the Air network. With so many tiny communities spread across the immensity of the Australian outback, ever since the 1960's, the School of the Air program had outfitted these communities, in many cases even individual cattle stations, with HF transceivers which were used for school children to receive their school lessons and to send in their school work to regional 'Teaching Studios" at Darwin, Katherine, Alice Springs, Broken Hill, Dubbo, and Port Macquarie. The direct satellite transmission of video link from the teachers, operated from Sydney, was clearly inoperative; however it only took a few minutes to confirm that the radio network was still working on the HF frequencies. The military easily tuned into and began transmitting and receiving on these frequencies, activating the network of up to 50,000 stations.

Suddenly the CJOC had an effective telecommunications grid which the enemy had overlooked. What's more, they could use student numbers, class lists and even the School of the Air records as a means of verifying that any particular station was still in the hands of the families, communities and aboriginal native bands. The CJOC could simply ask them questions based on the School of the Air records in much the same manner as one's bank or credit card company would ask personal verification questions when a customer calls to do over-the-phone banking.

With the School of the Air, General Adams was able to pass critical information out swiftly to the Australian citizenry, to activate civil defense and to inform people, including those who would otherwise be entirely cut off from civilization at large, of what they could do to help force-generate ad-hoc militia units and to bring in supplies, arms, personnel and transportation resources in support of national mobilization.

After word had spread that communities up and down the east coast had been taken over by Chinese Special Forces from commercial aircraft, some of the innocent civilian airliners had been met with armed gangs of locals who had come out to defend their towns. But once they determined that they were indeed civilian passengers, they shouldered their rifles and welcomed the bewildered passengers, in some cases doubling or tripling the tiny outback town's populations. The displaced passengers were faced with finding a place in or a way out of the tiny community.

Perth had not been entirely destroyed, having been hit by only one of the four missiles that had been targeted against the Western Australian capital city. DDG 111 *Spruance* had closed to be within extreme range when the missiles had started coming in, and was just in time to save the Western Australian city from complete devastation, but one missile had been targeted to an industrial sector on the northern limits of the city and had been beyond the range of the *Spruance*'s missile defenses. DDG 111 *Spruance* had been close enough to completely save an RAAF base and a RAN dockyard just south of Perth. The bulk of the Australian continent was in Australian hands and generally unscathed - however, those hands were few in number and were a great distance from where the Chinese invaders and the bulk of the Australian population were, on the east coast.

So while the vast majority of the Australian continent was still in free Australian hands, over 80% of Australia's 60,000 military force had been destroyed or overrun in the first week, and over six million civilians had been killed in the blasts zones of Brisbane, Sydney, Melbourne and Canberra. A further fourteen million more Australians were already behind enemy lines, along the heavily populated east coast, the Chinese forces' Stage One objective now entirely in Chinese hands.

With all of the information now available to General Adams in the CJOC, thanks in large part to the School of the Air network, it became clear to General Adams that other than local militia and civil defense forces that had begun to mobilize there were only three viable military formations: The Combined Joint Task Force – North, CJTFN, was comprised of the Marines of MAGTFA, along with Australian Special Forces and Army units; the reserve units largely of the Australian 2nd Division and a trickle of Indian Army personnel, which had begun to flow in from India via Perth. The Indian force was joining with forces being stood up in Adelaide, South Australia, as Combined Joint Task Force Central. CJTFC would ultimately see a much larger force from India along with as many men as could be pressed into service from the Perth region in Western Australia.

On the Air Force side, once the Indian Air Force SU-27 and SU30 multirole fighters and Russian-Built IL-76M Air-to-Air Refuellers began to arrive there would be an Indian Air Force umbrella expanding eastwards from Perth.

But until then, with the Chinese Air Force units that had already arrived and were operating from captured airfields on the east coast, the enemy enjoyed regional air superiority over as much as one third of the Australian continent.

From the initial reports, it was clear that local Australians had commenced a heroic insurgency against the occupiers in Queensland, New South Wales and Victoria. These poorly coordinated efforts ended tragically, as did the feeble efforts of small, ill equipped Australian units. In many cases the dying started right at home as the men ran into Chinese spies who had seized armories and depots and fought desperately against the locals, trying to hold on long enough for follow-on Chinese forces to arrive to reinforce and relieve them. So the Australian soldiers could not even get to their arms.

Before the end of the first week, the J2 Intelligence staff of Americans and Australians working together in the CJOC in Katherine estimated that two full PLA divisions were fully operational in Queensland; three more in New South Wales; and vast numbers of additional personnel were arriving daily. Intelligence reports indicated that mounting bases in as many as three different PLA military districts were involved, and, according to Lieutenant Colonel Peter Weir, the US Army Ranger attached to the Australian 1 Cdo Regiment and something of a subject matter expert on the order of battle of the Chinese forces, there could be as many as five different Group Armies active in the Australia & New Zealand campaign.

While information coming out of New Zealand was still very sketchy, it appeared as though both the 112th and 114th Mechanized Infantry Division of the PLA's 38th Group Army were quickly tightening their grip on New Zealand, and the 113th Mechanized Infantry Division had seized all of Tazmania.

Along the Gold Coast of Australia, the 41st and 42nd Group Armies were active. Solid intelligence from the Port Macquarie area had established that the 121st Infantry Division and the 123rd Motorized Infantry Division, along with elements of engineering, communications and other formations of the 41st Group Army were controlling occupied areas in New South Wales, while the Brisbane to Cairns sector, the eastern coast of Queensland, was in the hands of 42nd Group Army, with units of 124th Amphibious Mechanized Infantry Division and the 163rd Mechanized Infantry Division having been identified.

What really worried Lieutenant Colonel Weir, however, was whether the 42dn Group Army's Special Operations Battalion, from Guangzhou, was also deploying. If confirmed, that would convince him that the Chinese were intent on deploying fully two distinct Group Armies, of up to 160,000 soldiers, to the Gold Coast alone.

The one bit of good news was the nearly complete devastation that American and Australian naval and air defenses had inflicted on the air assaulters and the follow-on sea-transported forces of the 13th and 14th Group Armies. Adams and Ferebee had known that three waves of air assaulters had been decimated before reaching their landing zones. But when the CJOC Naval LnO passed on reports of dozens of civilian ships loaded with Chinese military personnel heading for the Australian north and west coasts had been sunk by surviving US, Indian, and Australian naval units in the region, they grimly celebrated the terrible loss of life that had been delivered to the enemy soldiers who were just hours from reaching their sea-port destinations in Northern Territory and Western Australia, with tens of thousands of enemy combatants and their war-fighting material having been sent to the bottom of the eastern Indian Ocean and Timor Sea.

But the considerable success on the west was lost on General Adams, who was focused on the heavy losses his country had taken, and the disastrous situation unfolding in Queensland and New South Wales. What really got to General Adams was the speed at which the situation was changing. He had been optimistic when hearing reports of Australian units that had stood up and reported being in place in blocking positions, well entrenched and ready to thwart the enemy's advance. The battles had then taken place, fast and furious, and then all hope had been lost when it became clear, time after time, that the Australians had been destroyed. It was the speed with which the Chinese forces cut his boys to pieces that had destroyed all hope in General Adam's heart, and was behind his next comment to Colonel Ferebee.

"Maybe we should reconsider our setting up here in Katherine, and move farther south – maybe all the way down to Alice Springs and your Pine Gap facility?" General Adams asked. "I mean, if they hit Darwin, we're now just 300 kilometers from there. That does not buy us much time. We're facing total defeat here. I don't think we can last a second week. There are just too many of them coming, and they're moving so damned fast!"

Looking appraisingly at the General, Colonel Ferebee took the man's defeated look into consideration. *If the rest of his men are this beaten already, there's no hope. I've got to do something*, thought Ferebee, and then he drew on the inspiration of Sam Houston, that he had reflected upon during the opening hours of the war.

"General, I agree with your assessment that things are desperate. But this thing is not over, not by any means, General." Then in a quiet voice, which only the General could hear, Ferebee spoke to him: "Listen, Braeden, you've got to snap out of it. Your officers are watching you. How you act here and now will have an effect on your men. They, and a few of my Marines," Ferebee said, far more modestly than he felt of the contribution his men were going to make to the coming battles. "They are the only thing that can stop these invaders from achieving total victory, but you're getting them all killed, throwing them up in these little blocking actions of yours in Queensland. You've got to abandon most of that sector, and think on a longer time horizon. Your men want to fight, but you have to be their leader, and *you* have to hold them back from these pointless, suicidal skirmishes. You've got to tell them what to do, not just sit here and let them run the show, sitting here like this, listening to them die.

"You've got to grow a pair of balls, take charge and stop making defeatist comments. Maybe then you can lead your men to having something of a strategic plan, a plan for victory, rather than attempting to simply slow them down. God knows you have enough territory to work with. So pull your men back towards Cloncurry, have them cache any excess weapons and provisions laterally off the axis of advance for later use. Have them travel light, and fast, and disappear into those cattle stations and remote villages off-route. They've got to avoid engagement for a while.

"Let's suck the Chinese out to the west. Then, when we've got the right conditions – at a time and place of our choosing –

when the enemy has become over-confident and over-run their logistics, we'll cut their throats and turn them back." Ferebee said, with increasing energy.

Ferebee could see that he had gotten to the Australian General. The man's face had turned positively purple, first out of shame and anger, and ultimately out of the hot blood of combat. Even a General, thousands of kilometers from where the action is taking place, can be either in, or out, of the fight. And with the new energy that Colonel Ferebee had stimulated, the image of taking the fight to the enemy being so contagious, something had changed in the General's frame of mind.

Before Colonel Ferebee's eyes, the Australian General swung into action.

"Major Blakely, Captain Thorne, come over here and tell me again that idea of yours. I want Colonel Ferebee's take on it. It may be just the right idea, after all," commanded Adams, surprising the MAGTFA Liaison Officer and the intense Captain from 1 Cdo Regiment, who he had both been shut down hours before when they had first tried to run their audacious plan past the General.

15

RUN FLAT

Weeks after the war broke out, Wisconsin, USA

He knew it would not go as smoothly as planned, but when Owen MacInnes slammed on the brakes, with adrenalin suddenly rushing through his veins, a sudden wave of panic took hold of him. While his senses told him that he had put his group into a dangerous situation, his intuition told him *run!*

He was just about to throw his pick-up into reverse, and do a five-point turn to head back towards Ian and Beth in the Range Rover XL, some 500 yards behind, but something inside him told him to *calm down! Play the situation out like you and Ian agreed.*

It was the first time they had encountered a full-on road block, and they were still only a few hundred miles out of Madison, Wisconsin, USA.

The goal was to reach St Charles, Illinois, where Ian had coordinated safe lodgings with his cousin over the amateur radio network. Ian had used some of his precious silver coins to buy a hand-held UHF system from a disaster response coordinator they had met in Verona, Wisconsin. The man had not only coordinated their passage through the sector, but had also put them up for the night. He showed Ian his radio shack, and suggested that he use the amateur UHF radio network during their travels. He had a variety of fixed and portable UHF equipment in his radio shack, and showed Ian how to use, and he explained some of the basic Radio-Telephony, RT, procedures and call signs.

The portable UHF device came in handy from the start, allowing Ian to seek out safe harbor along the way as they picked their way around the devastation of the cities and military bases that had been nuked. Ian used the call sign: "W9XZ2/P", the WPXZ2 borrowed from the friendly disaster response coordinator in Verona, WI, and the "Slash-P" to indicate that he was using a portable transmitter. Ian quickly got more comfortable with the jargon and R/T protocols used by amateur radio operators, and Owen contributed the social connections and networking skills.

Once they reached St Charles, the plan had been to work with Ian's extended family to negotiate safe passage to Gary, Indiana, where Ian helped Owen make radio contact with people who knew some of his friends from his six year stint in the Army. The idea was that a contact in each successive community would help them parlay safe passage past the road-blocks and ambush sites. Then, once safe and sound for a night's rest, they could plan the next leg. Provided they were able to gather good intelligence at each safe haven along the way, and they had names of well-respected locals at their destinations, they would be able to leap-frog their two-vehicle convoy all the way to Altoona Pennsylvania, where Catherine's large extended family would have a place for them.

Owen did not really like his in-laws all that much, but he had no reason to dislike them. To Owen, the problem had always been one of insecurity, and he knew it. Catherine's father, the retired General Upton, had seemed dismissive of Owen's choices in life; that he had not continued his career in the army, nor even acquired a formal education for that matter. As the old General had put it once in a private conversation with his daughter, which Owen had surreptitiously overheard: "Catty, the man is *shiftless*. The best he's ever done for himself was to reach Master Corporal in the Army Reserves, and then take his release? For what, to be a construction laborer? Or what is it now, mechanic's apprentice? He'll never amount to anything, the man has no ambition. You would do far better with Gideon James, from your high school days. Why, I've heard –"

"Knock it off, Dad. Owen is my man. Period. You better treat him better, Pop, and stop your little comments all the time, making Owen feel unworthy of YOUR family. He has proven himself to me, time after time, and that's what counts. And I love him, Pop, just the way he is. So if you ever want to have grandchildren to play with, or have any sort of relationship with me for that matter, you better start treating him like a son. He's your only shot at it!"

Owen had withdrawn from his post by the barn window, and had made it to the far side of a line of hay-bales before Catherine had exited the barn, but he later admitted what he had overheard. From his point of view, hearing his lover tearing into her old man like that proved her love for him in a way that really mattered to the young man.

For the General, his daughter's comments had really hit hard. The old warrior had always wanted a son, and had just the four daughters to show for his efforts. Of his girls, only the eldest, Margaret, was married. Her husband, Matthew, was a Warrant Officer serving in a highly classified position at the Mount Weather Emergency Operations Centre, just over the state lines near Bluemont, Virgina, which the General knew to be the primary evacuation bunker for the President of the United States. But despite his best efforts, he had been unable to forge any close bonds with his son in law, other than the polite, respectful comments you would expect a retired General to receive from a professional, serving member of the Armed Forces. The General put it down to the gap that traditionally existed between senior enlisted men like Warrant Officer Blakely, and senior officers, even retired ones like the General..

Maggie and her husband were infertile, so the General's only other hope for a grandson, and for a son-in-law he could talk with at family dinners, now rested with his only other married daughter, Catherine, and her loser of a man, this MacInnes boy.

But despite his dashed hopes, upon the realization that his daughter had chosen her lover over her father, the old General began to feel better. The more he thought about it, the more he felt pride in his daughter's strength of character. *If she loves him that much, maybe there's more to the man than I realized.*

That had been two years ago. Since then, Owen and Catherine had been married, back in Richland Center, WI. It had been a simple ceremony, what with Owen not having any family. There had just been the couple's best friends, Ian and Mary, as best-man and maid of honor, and a small number of guests.

On the Upton side of the family, a full contingent had driven up from Altoona, and even Warrant Officer Blakely had taken some annual leave to be there with his wife, Maggie, for her little sister's wedding.

The old General had still not fully made up his mind about MacInnes. However, judging by the way his daughter behaved, it was clear that the young man was treating her fairly well. And the fact that Owen had completed two full years of apprentice training with Randy's Auto was a positive sign.

Unfortunately for everybody, the General did not show any signs of his softening stance on MacInnes, showing only his stony, cold, and unreadable face to the young man.

He had intended to open up to the young man the next time the MacInneses – and it was so hard to see his daughter as anything other than an Upton – showed up at the family farm in Altoona, PA.

And then the nuclear war had broken out. All forms of normal communication had rapidly ceased to work. Despite their best efforts, Owen and Ian had been unable to make UHF contact with anybody in the Altoona area, but they kept trying. And with each passing day as they progressed from Wisconsin to Pennsylvania, Owen's group found the atmosphere at each small town, roadblock or civil defense post to be more and more desperate. It was as if they were moving towards some ultimate doom, the way it got worse the farther east they travelled.

In the six months since Madison Wisconsin had gone up in smoke, along with pretty much every other major city, military base, international airport and major critical infrastructure or industrial installation, the world had gotten much smaller and meaner.

The effort to survive had become very personal. Each individual was out for themselves and their loved ones, often fleeing in panic as far as they could from the dangerous after-effects of the blasts and the radiation carried in fallout, in the furious first hours and days at the start of the war.

But when the missiles had stopped coming and the truth of the massive scale of destruction had become clear, individuals turned to their neighbors, friends, and local communities to seek and to offer help.

Where a community was strong, or had some degree of functioning, especially when outside of the danger zones, there were initial successes, where the entire population cooperated in a spirit of good-will, community service, and patriotism. However, as grocery and other supplies had dwindled, the attempts by civil defense authorities and FEMA to control the distribution of food, water and medical supplies had quickly become strained to the breaking point. Even the most well-managed communities soon began to fall apart.

It was in this context, in early June, less than two weeks after the war broke out, that the young newlyweds in Richland Center, Wisconsin, met with their close friends to discuss their options.

The MacInnes couple hosted what would be their last dinner in Richland. Their close friends, Beth and Ian Morgan, brought their last two bottles of wine to contribute to what they all knew would likely be their last 'normal' evening together. With the increasing violence, home invasions, and increasingly desperate situation in Richland, they all knew that they had to do something.

Thankfully the power was still on. The thirty megawatt coal-powered electrical power-plant that served Richland Centre and dozens of smaller communities in the area still operated as if nothing had happened, however with the arrival of coal supplies now permanently interrupted and with increasing demands on the power-plant, there were already rumors of systemic failure. With the influx of refugees from Madison and other cities into town, and with the increased electrical demands for the emergency hydroponics operations being set up by local officials, the rationing of electrical power and eventually total black-out was inevitable.

The lights were sure to be out before winter. On top of that, the rumor was that with all of the dust and debris thrown up into the atmosphere as a result of the nuclear war, the early onset of winter was a harbinger of not only an early chill, but of a much longer nuclear winter that was expected to plummet temperatures in the continental United States to colder than twenty below, and to last for years, perhaps a decade or longer. To the MacInneses and their friends, that meant that they would be faced with extreme cold in apartments with no electricity, no wood stove, trapped in the mountains of western Wisconsin with no way to escape the accumulating snow.

While the two couples made pleasant conversation about the meal, putting off the serious discussion to come, surprisingly it had been the most fragile of them who had broached the topic, and in such a forceful way.

"Listen," began Beth, "I overheard something at work, and you all have to hear it," she said, surprising even her husband, Ian.

It had long been her habit to never discuss what she overheard at the Armory, with her husband, or any other civilian, for that matter.

Beth Morgan worked as a civilian Administrative Assistant to Lieutenant Colonel Hurdman, Commanding Officer at the Detachment's headquarters at the armory just outside of Richland Center. She often overheard the military personnel of the First Detachment, 829th Engineering Company, 32nd Brigade, Wisconsin National Guard Richland Detachment, talking about things as if she weren't there. For the most part they seemed to be obsessed with personnel issues, their own careers, and other forms of military gossip that was of no interest to her.

But with the suddenness of the war breaking out, the military was the best source of information as to what the war was all about, what was going on in the world, and how bad things had become in the United States.

Since the war began, she had shared everything with her husband, and, more and more, even with their best friends. But she had avoided sharing any operational information, such as what the 829th Engineering Company was doing in terms of organizing for operations.

That is, until today.

"What is it, Beth?" her husband, asked, concerned by the fearful expression on her face.

"You can't tell anybody this. I'm sure I will be shot," she said, ominously.

The others looked shocked, but remained silent.

"They are talking about abandoning their post."

"Who are? The entire formation?"

"No, just the senior officers. The Lieutenant-Colonel and the Major, you know, the Operations Officer? I overheard him and Lieutenant Colonel Hurdman talking about how many of their personnel had gone AWOL or had not returned from their assignments recently. It's all confused, with Martial Law in effect. They just don't have enough resources to man all of the sites, and there have been more and more mutinies, like when the Reservists sent to guard some warehouse or other piece of critical infrastructure loaded up truckloads of supplies and took them away to who knows where."

"You mean the military is looting the food supplies they were supposed to be guarding for the town council?"

"Yes, Owen, but not looting for the 829th or the military at large. They're taking it to their families and organizing themselves into little bastions, to protect their own. There was nothing like that going on at first, but when the CO briefed everybody about how the local food supplies would run out within about six months, and that there was going to be mass starvation as the nuclear winter deepened, a lot of soldiers panicked, desperate to take care of their loved ones. That's why so many simply don't come back to report in on the next Monday's parade. And the unit lost even more personnel when they sent out squads to investigate. Some of them got ambushed by deserters, others just disappear without report. So now it is clear that the Wisconsin National Guard has lost control of the situation."

"So how many are still serving, staying under military control?" asked Ian.

"As of yesterday, the First Sergeant told the CO that they were effectively below Company size."

"What does that mean? Aren't they a battalion? How many men is that?"

"The 829th was officially an under-strength battalion, so 350 or so personnel. When the war broke out, they updated their so-called Parade State and found that they were down to 280 personnel, so that's two or three companies, maximum, well short of a battalion. Last Friday, when the CO gave that depressing briefing about the long-term food supply outlook, they still had almost two hundred men and women under effective command, but as of yesterday, the Monday report from the Master Sergeant was that they had eighty or less personnel who were still responsive."

"Responsive?"

"Answering their radio calls, sending in Situation Reports from their taskings – the warehouses and grocery stores."

"Shit," Ian said softly as he hunched over the table, listening intensely to his wife.

"I had no idea that they were falling apart," Owen said to Ian, then turning back to Beth: "I see them all the time, driving up and down Highway 14 in their Humvees. But it makes sense to me. What's the point in putting your life on the line to guard the town's food when it's obvious that there won't be enough for everybody. And from what I hear, the global nuclear war has completely destroyed the system that moves bulk freight across the planet. So no more food will be coming, other than what we've got here, now." Owen's gaze ominously scanned all the food now on the table. Everyone was silent for a moment. Then Owen looked up and spoke again.

"Did you hear what Wisconsin Public Radio said, in the morning update yesterday? The war is definitely China's fault, and the Chinese military forces have been taking over places like

Australia, New Zealand, places in South America and Africa – wherever there were good food-producing areas."

"Well, what does that matter to us, Owen? There's going to be a nuclear winter," Ian said. His voice was low and even, trying to be as unemotional as possible as he continued speaking. "By the time the radiation and dust-cloud finishes encircling the earth, the temps will fall, who knows how low. Nothing will grow, not even here. It'll be starvation, looting, and the complete breakdown of society," said Ian.

"That's what Colonel Hurdman and his Ops O were talking about," interjected Beth. "They were talking about grabbing as much of the weapons, ammo, IMPs, fuel and so on, and throwing in with some of the men who want to flee for the hills."

Catherine's voice joined in, soft but deliberate. "Did they say where to, exactly?"

"No, Catherine," Beth said, turning to her. "But I think it's up near Pier County Park, on Pine River, where the CO has a hobby farm or a cabin or something. He used to talk about it with some of the other officers, and the ones who he seems chummy with – out of those still around – some of them also have recreational property in that area.

Catherine leaned in closer to Beth. "So when were they going to do this, abandon their post?"

"Well, they heard someone coming and stopped talking about it. But I'm pretty sure it was going to happen tomorrow night because later in the day the Ops O was on the phone with the Transportation Officer and the Supply Officer, talking about details like they do just before a major operation or a training exercise. But by the hushed way he was speaking I think that the exercise is actually their own 'bug-out' operation. All of the details sounded like they were related to tomorrow."

"So what will happen tomorrow, when the townsfolk get wind of Lieutenant Colonel Hurdman abandoning his post?" asked Ian.

"All bets are off." Owen said. "All hell will break lose. It will be every man for himself, with no fear of the military stopping it.

I bet that any remaining military men left out of Hurdman's group will raid the armory and become armed gangs themselves."

Ian leaned forward, his elbow on the table. "Owen, if you're right, we should get the hell out of here *right now*. Tonight, before all of this happens."

"I agree, but we've got nothing. We don't have a plan. And where would we go?" asked Owen. "We don't even have any guns, do we, guys?"

"No," Beth said. But I know where we can get some."

"Where? The Army?"

"Yes, exactly."

"That sounds crazy, Beth. We'll get killed trying."

"No, Owen, hear her out. Go on, Beth, what's your idea?" her husband asked, encouragingly.

As she laid out her idea, it actually made a lot of sense. By the time the four of them had 'what if?'ed it to death, they all felt that it was their best option. At least, in terms of securing vehicles and fuel. But then they turned to the more important question.

"So where will we go?"

"Home," said Catherine, simply.

"She's right, said Owen. I hate to admit it, but her dad's farm in Altoona, Pennsylvania, would be our best bet. They've got tons of forest around their farm, so lots of firewood. The place is off the beaten track, so it won't be constantly attacked by looters, and the old bastard has guns. Lots of guns. I know that for a fact."

From the look on her man's face, Catherine knew that it pained him to have suggested that they go to her dad for help, but it really was their only good option.

"Owen, thanks. I just know that you and Daddy will get along better this time. You two really are very much alike. You just have to give him time to see you the way I see you – the way you are."

"So would you be welcome there?" Ian asked, not really understanding what the issue was.

"Of course we will. And so will you guys. I've talked about this sort of thing with dad. He's quite the survivalist, you know. And he always says that you need a strong community, and lots of people, to hold things together in a crises. That's also why he encourages Maggy to bring her brother in-law along to the family dinners – to expand the network of what Daddy calls 'good people'," Catherine said.

"Who's Maggy?" asked Ian.

"She's my sister. Her husband is a Warrant Officer in the army, and his brother is a Major in the Marines. Dad encourages Maggy's husband to invite his brother, Joe and his family to family dinners at Dad's ranch on account of the Blakely brothers' mom and dad being gone. He has sort of adopted the entire family," she said.

"Well, there's more to it than just that he likes having lots of people around his big empty ranch. It's also because he does not have any sons of his own. So yes, I agree with Catty. General Upton has adopted the Blakely boys into the extended family. What's really going on is that the General wants people to make use of his 100 acres. And he is always talking about how he has agreements with other ranchers about how they will cooperate wen the shit hits the fan."

"Well, the shit has hit the fan, so I sure hope they're cooperating well, 'cause they're in for some surprise guests!" said Ian, clearly having made up his mind about embracing Catherine and Owen's plan.

Ian and Beth returned to their flat to pack their Ford Explorer with food and water. They figured they were ready to go fully an hour before the planned rendezvous time at the garage, when Ian had a brainstorm. He did not even take the time to explain it to Beth, he just hurried her out the door of their apartment and into the secure parking lot in the basement, where their SUV was parked.

"What's gotten into you, Ian?" asked Beth.

"I'll explain later, if everything is as I hope when we get to Randy's.

She was impressed with the intent and focus in her husband, and did not mind waiting the few minutes it took for them to race down Orange Street to 'Randy's Automotive', the now all-but abandoned garage where Ian and Owen both worked.

The place had been raided more than once in the last week, and was nearly devoid of useful items, but Ian had come up with a brilliant idea which he shared with Owen when his buddy arrived, driving his old Honda Civic.

The two men looked around for "Run Flat Randy", their boss, but he was nowhere to be seen. The man had been through hell lately trying to protect his business from the looters and had been beaten senseless a few days ago. For all they knew, Randy was dead, or had fled to the hills where he used to go hunting.

Ian told Owen his plan.

"That is a fucking great idea, Ian. Let's go check," said Ian, and the two men rushed around to the back of the vandalized building.

Their eyes lit up when the saw that the broken down old F-250 was where it had always been. It had been overlooked by the looters as it was without tires, engine, and a few other parts that had been removed from the old truck over the years.

But there, securely bolted to the front end was an articulated snow plow, from when the truck had been used as a utility vehicle on a farm up in the hills. The plow had been reason enough to keep the run-down old truck running for years, simply to keep the half-mile driveway clear in the winter, but in the end the old truck had too many problems and had come to Randy's garage to rest and rust in peace.

The two men, one a master mechanic and the other his 3rd year apprentice, made quick work of removing the heavy blade assembly from the deceased pick-up. Rather than try to move the blade rig itself, they simply towed the corpse of the F250 out with the Ian's much heavier Ford Explore 4WD yanking hard at the chain rigging, leaving deep gouges in the tarmac as the old wreck was dragged away from the snow plow and the Explorer brought up to it.

After nosing the Explorer into position up against the blade, they spent a few hours rigging the lower mounts, hooking up the hydraulic lines and electrical controls, and finally rigging the manual controls through to the cab of Ian's Explorer.

After that, they looked around the welding shop and found that the oxy-acetylene rig and their welding tools were still where they kept them. They carried on with modifications to Ian's truck. They cut up and installed a few slabs of plate-steel on the interior sides of the doors, and improvised some fold-up hinged plates to provide additional side armor that could be swung up against the bottom half of the windows, if and when needed.

Next, they moved the Civic and the Explorer into the shop bays and hoisted the Explorer up to give it a thorough "peace of mind" inspection, and installed a large piece of sheet-metal under the body, extending from front to rear. They also beefed up the suspension with a few techniques that Ian had learned when he used to work on monster trucks. This gave the vehicle more road clearance and the room to install upgraded shocks to accommodate the increased weight from the snow plow assembly, steel plates, and other modifications.

They had just lowered the hoist and began to turn their attention to the collection of provisions and camping gear when they were surprised by a homeless man who had entered the shop through the rear door.

"Randy! It's you! You had us scared for a minute," Owen said to his boss. "You look terrible!"

"Thanks for the complement, Owen," said Run Flat Randy. "I feel even worse. I tried to drive out to my cabin up near Viola, and ran into a road-block just five miles from my road. I tried to back out of it, but they ran a school bus across my escape route. They took everything and beat the living crap out of me."

As the women came to Randy's assistance with the first aid kit, he told them more about his ordeal, and the long walk back to his shop.

Eventually Randy asked what they were up to. He was not upset at them at all, and was quite interested in the modifications they were making to Ian's Explorer.

"Wish I had this with me yesterday. I would have been better off to ram right through their road block. It was just two cars nose-to-nose. This rig could have blown them apart and not even slowed down in the process," Randy said, approvingly.

"That's what she's designed to do," said Ian.

"And you have enough provisions and fuel, to reach Altoona?"

"Not quite. We need more gasoline, but we have enough food and water, and tons of camping gear. We're also going to have a second vehicle, tomorrow morning, when we hit the road." Owen went on to detail Beth's plan.

"Wow. That's gutsy, little lady. Sure you can pull it off?"

"I have to. There's no other choice," she said, simply.

"So what do you think, Randy. Will this tank of ours work, if we encounter something like you did?"

After looking the Ford over, Randy got up from his hands and knees. "That belly plate could help, if you run over some wreckage or other obstacles, and those TNT Nitro Shocks really give you better ground clearance, but you have missed a few important things I might suggest. For a price that is…"

"A price? Randy, we've got nothing. What do you want?"

"Take me with you, for a start," he said, with a tone of desperation that surprised the men. Both of them took it as a sign that Randy's experience at the road block had really taken the wind out of him.

"Of course, Boss. We'll take you with us! No question. Besides, you're the only one with any military training." Owen said, referring to Randy's fifteen years in the Army, his two tours in Afghanistan.

"Thanks, Owen. But you've got a few years in as well. But thanks, I can offer my combat experience. But on this enterprise, you and Ian are the boss, Owen. I would much prefer just to be a henchman, and follow your lead. You've got women to protect and I'm all by myself. So use me as a soldier. I'll do my part. But in that line, there are some things you need to think about. When you – we – encounter a road-block, or other situations like I've seen in Afghanistan, you have to already know the SOP."

"SOP? asked Beth.

"Yes, the 'Standard Operating Procedure', what you will do, without having to talk about it. You have to act fast, to get ahead of the decision-making cycle of your enemy. And from what I saw up in Viola yesterday, they'll have nearly all of the advantages. But with this rig, and a few anti-ambush techniques I can teach you, we could turn the tables on whoever we come across."

Randy went on to discuss the sorts of things they could do when encountering an ambush.

"So as long as everybody does their job, in a predictable way, and everybody is on the same page without even having to communicate, then the advantage tilts back to us."

"Randy, that's a big if. And it seems that your 'Actions On' plan puts Beth in the greatest risk," said Ian.

"Yes, it all hinges on her performance. But as far as risk goes, we are all in the same boat. Cause once we are in it – find ourselves in such a situation – there's no going back. If we don't deploy and set up rapidly, in the way I have laid out, then we're all doomed. We won't even get out of the county, let alone across four state lines and all the way to Altoona."

"I'm not afraid, guys," said Beth, "Knowing you are out there, covering my back, will give me a boost. And I can be very convincing when I need to."

"She's right," said Ian. "Have you ever seen her work a room? I've seen my Beth take on some pretty aggressive, over-confident types at her Toastmasters events. She sets 'em up and then knocks them down. It's like that line from Star Wars: "Your overconfidence is your weakness.' When whoever she is working on finally realizes that he has under-estimated Beth, it's too late, she's already won the contest. That's why she makes friends so easily, too. People realize that she's this super-smart, secure, and thoughtful person and they want to do whatever they can to help her succeed."

"Yeah, and in that scene, doesn't the Emperor retort: 'Your faith in your friends is your weakness?'"

"Yeah, Owen, but just remember the moral point here: the good guys win, despite desperate odds, because of how they trust each other. And that's what we're going to do."

"OK, Randy, I agree. It's our best shot. And I know that I'll do my part," said Owen.

"And trust me, Owen, I won't let us down," said Beth.

Randy straightened up, painfully. "But that's not all. We also need to do a little more work on the Explorer."

"Like what?" asked Ian.

The veteran hitched a thumb in his belt and grinned. "Why do you think they call me 'Run Flat Randy?'"

After installing the Continental Self-Supporting Sidewall run-flat tires that Randy had been storing on the roof of his small garage, and strapping four extra SSR run-flats to the growing mass of supplies and equipment stowed on the roof of the Explorer, the three men worked together to jack-up the rear end of each of the two fuel tanks at the back of Randy's lot.

Looters had gravity-drained the fuel tanks almost completely dry, but by raising the rear end up by eighteen inches and drilling a hole in the bottom of the front end of the tanks, the three men were able to recover the final twenty gallons of diesel from one tank and close to thirty gallons of gasoline from the other, into a variety of jerry cans Randy produced from the crawl-space.

Randy surprised the others by revealing that he had some firearms.

"I left them here, buried in my stash, when I headed out to the cabin – just in case. I may have lost my Ruger and Glock, and all my gear, but at least I have my trusty old AR15, and the Colt-45, and about two hundred rounds," he said, much to the relief of the others, who were inexperienced with firearms.

"Will you show us how to use them?" asked Catherine.

"For sure. In fact, let's do a bit now. We've still got a few hours before Beth heads off on her mission. It won't take long, especially if you help me, Owen, by showing the ladies the basics with the Colt while I go over the AR15 with Ian." Randy said, showing Owen a bit of respect.

Hearing her plan talked of as a 'mission' made Beth see herself as if she were a spy, about to engage in a dangerous adventure – which was exactly the way that it was.

Over the next hour, Randy and Owen showed the others how to load, unload, make safe, and fire both the handgun and the semi-automatic military rifle.

"The procedure is pretty much the same with any firearm. You just have to spend a few minutes finding out where to press to release the magazine, how to load and chamber the ammunition, how to cock it – chamber a round – where the safety is, and so on. But the most important thing is to keep them clean. That takes more learning. You have to know how to break them down completely, to clean and oil the components, and to reassemble them with your eyes closed. Keep 'em ready for action. But Owen and I can show you all of that later."

The look on Ian's face when he dropped her off just outside the main gate at the Wisconsin National Guard base told Beth that her husband was extremely worried for her. But when he spoke to her he tried to sound relaxed and confident.

"Be careful, cupcake."

"I will. Just have everybody else ready to go 'cause I don't plan to hang around long when I get out," Beth said, with more confidence than she felt. But there was no going back. She was that committed.

The Corporal at the main gate was tense, but still friendly to her. The CO's secretary was one of the few civilians still coming to work. Everybody assumed that the CO was giving her boxes of Meals Ready To Eat, MRE's, which the small base had considerable stockpiles of in the Quartermaster building. In these days, food, fuel, cigarettes and alcohol were the only real money aside from silver and gold, of course, which few people had, and even fewer were willing to part with.

So despite her nervousness, Beth had no difficulty with the first part of her plan: *Go to work as usual.*

When the CO and Ops O walked past her desk, just outside the CO's office, they barely registered her at all. Once in the CO's office they quickly shut the door behind them.

Beth busied herself with administrative paperwork which she knew had no meaning whatsoever, hoping to appear absolutely normal and therefore, invisible.

About a half-hour later the CO and Ops O exited.

"Beth. If anybody is looking for me, I'll be at the QM for the next hour, then the Mess."

"OK. Thanks, Sir," she said, and then added: "Before you go, is there any chance I can have Friday off? I am thinking of moving in with some friends..." she lied, hoping to learn more about the CO's state of mind and his plans for the week.

From the expression that flashed on his face she knew that he was about to lie to her in return. She had seen this on his face whenever he had been in a situation where he had to pretend to be helping someone only to take some action behind their back; such as when the Lieutenant Colonel had promised a young Captain going through a custody battle that "I'l do all I can to help," in the context of helping the young officer get better access to his children. But the CO did nothing to help, and focused his efforts immediately on having the Captain posted to another unit, even farther from his kids, just to get rid of the 'administrative burden'. Through a number of such situations over the last four years, Beth had come to read Hurdman's face like an open book.

"Sure, Beth, you can have the entire day off on Friday. I don't have much on my plate that day, so I won't really need you."

She took this as absolute confirmation that the man would be nowhere near the base by then. That made what she was about to do that much easier.

The moment she saw the CO and Ops O walking quickly across the parade square she flew into action. First, she took a copy of the CO's office key from the key press and collected his car keys from the little wooden box he kept his keys in on a side table. On her first trip down the back stairs to the small garage bay the CO used in the old wooden building, the petite woman decided to carry the CO's combat jacket. She knew it contained ceramic plate and composite layered body amour, which she figured could be useful for her group.

Once in the garage, she unlocked the CO's brand new Range Rover XL. As she pushed the heavy combat jacket into the back seat she realized that the expensive SUV still had that new car smell.

Taking a quick look around in the garage, she saw a few things that she thought were worth taking, but decided to hold off until she was finished in the CO's office.

After four more round-trips between the office and the garage she had taken the man's duffel-bag full of combat gear, 'Chemical Biological Radiological Nuclear', CBRN, kit, and the man's personal cache of weapons. Despite the training the previous night with Randy, Beth had no idea which end was which, nor how to use them, but she had seen the CO personally field-stripping, cleaning, oiling and re-assembling them on many occasions and had overheard him brag about the amount of fire-power he always had close-to-hand. So she knew that the nicely packed bug-out bag of weapons and ammo represented considerable firepower. Ever since the war had started, the man had been somewhat obsessed by the risk that his base would be over-run by hordes of desperate civilians. It was as if he wanted to be taking them out from his office window, shooting civilians as if they were a horde of zombies. The guy was a jerk. How he made Colonel was a mystery to Beth – and to many of his men.

The reality of it was that the civilians had largely laid down and taken it, and certainly never mounted any protests or security threat to the base until recently. It started with a few of the smaller units, sent to guard larger grocery stores and gas stations in the community, where people expected to find what they needed, and had been forced to use live ammunition to put down protests by hungry locals. In a few cases, the soldiers had held back, unwilling to fire on their fellow Wisconsinites, and had paid the price when the mob got out of hand and overwhelmed the soldiers. Then the shooting had been fast and furious, but too little too late, with the eight or ten reservists from the 829th Engineering Company, the typical size of a section sent out to guard such a business, wound up dead, their weapons and ammo falling into the hands of the locals along with the goods from the store, warehouse or other facility that was then completely looted within a matter of hours.

By the time follow-on forces from the Quick Reaction Team arrived to investigate, all they found was their friends' bodies, minus kit, and a completely looted facility.

Once word of such outcomes made it around the unit, the soldiers were more willing to open fire on civilians, and had begun to see the citizens as the enemy. But it also led to more and more sections of men deciding on their own that looting the warehouse or facility in their care, quietly at first, while guarding it, and then stripping it out and making off with as much as they could haul in their military vehicles was the way to go.

These men had families and friends in the community, and figured that the situation was becoming so desperate that holding it together for what was left of the army, in such a global disaster, was pointless. In the end, everybody would starve. Far better to make sure your loved ones have a chance. 'Fuck the Government' was the sentiment of the day.

To his credit, Lieutenant Colonel Hurdman had held the 829th together far longer than a great many other reserve units. But Beth knew that the Hurdman did not do this out of love for the rule of law, nor for the oath he had taken as an officer. He had done it out of hate. Hate for civilians, the enemy, who he would fight to the death to stop from defeating him personally.

She thought of his mindset as that of a Nazi soldier in a bunker, knowing that his side was going to lose in the end, and yet was prepared to fight one final, desperate battle.

But then, in the last few days, the CO had become more hopeful, once he and his Ops O had come up with a plan to abandon their base and head for the forested areas up in Pier County. There would be far less of a threat from the urban refugees making their way from the devastation of Madison, seeking food and shelter in the smaller communities to the west, and, ultimately, overwhelming each small town in turn just as they were in the process of doing to Richland Centre. Farther north in the hills, Hurdman and his gang would have more defendable terrain, very little local population to worry about, and of course they would have a massive stockpile of ammunition to protect themselves and their horde of supplies.

As for the ammunition, the fully-loaded mags, and the Colonel's weapons themselves, Beth saw this as probably sufficient for the small group she was part of.

The two steel ammo boxes which she took from the bottom of the CO's weapons locker had been very heavy. But she was confident that the extra two trips it took to carry all of the ammo down to the Range Rover were worth the effort.

As she departed the second-floor office for the last time, she took one last look across the parade square to see if anybody was coming. What she saw surprised her a bit, but then again, not at all.

What was unusual was to see so many vehicles driving around on the far side of the square, in front of the QM building. During normal times it was absolutely against the Base Standing Orders for anybody to operate a vehicle on the parade square. So as she looked at the assembled trucks, HMVWs and a few armored reconnaissance vehicles, she thought that the Master Sergeant would be going absolutely ape. But then she saw Master Sergeant Sampson out there, directing traffic, as the convoy was assembled into line.

She knew that she still had a little time, but decided to get moving just in case. As she passed her desk, she looked at her workstation for the last time and smiled at the sense of freedom she felt.

After throwing a dozen boxes of MREs into the back of the Range Rover she suddenly thought about fuel.

Looking around the garage, she saw a few useful things, like cleaning supplies, quarts of oil, a large first aid kit and a few other things – these she threw into the vehicle. But no gas.

As Beth thought about it, she looked at the little door to the Rang Rover's fuel-filler cap. "DIESEL FUEL ONLY" she read, in small lettering on the portal.

"Diesel!" she said, out loud, and then rushed through a connecting corridor to the vestibule that connected the garage to a large steel shipping container that had been installed a few years before, as part of an upgrade to the facility which had been funded by FEMA.

The heavy steel door was unlocked, and the interior was lit with a deep red glow from the indicator lights that were always on in the back-up generator room.

On the floor next to the massive fuel tank, next to the control panel, were eight military-standard five gallon cans labeled "DIESEL FUEL".

She tried to lift one of them but found it too heavy. She looked around and found a two-wheel dolly. She had used a similar dolly a few times up in the office, and understood how to use it. She simply tipped the first fuel can over slightly, and slid the flat steel base of the dolly under the can, and then tipped the can back fully onto the dolly's rails. Then she wheeled the can down the hallway and into the garage. Once there, she lowered the dolly's handles onto the tailgate, and slid the jerry can along the rails and into the vehicle's trunk. *Who needs a man. OK, a man would really help about now!* she thought. As she strained to repeat the process two more times, her strength failed, and the third fuel-can fell off the dolly and onto the floor. She knew that she would not be able to pick it up, so she gave up. "Two cans will have to be enough!" she said out loud, and then slammed the tail-gate up.

Just before activating the garage door opener clipped to the vehicle's sun-visor, she had an inspiration.

After starting the vehicle and moving it as close to the automatic garage door as she could, she turned the engine off and got out and went back to the rear of the garage and the abandoned fuel can.

She opened the fuel can cap of the overturned fuel can, letting diesel fuel pour out onto the concrete. Then she headed to the side wall, where there were a few rolls of paper-towel. She feared that the increasing smell of fuel in the air meant that it would ignite the moment she lit the paper-towel, so she pressed the garage door opener and watched the door begin to rise.

Beth peeked under the door as it rose past eye-height, and saw nobody around at the back-side of the CO's office building, she felt relief and sucked in a breath of fresh outside air.

Using her cigarette lighter from her purse, she lit a roll of paper towel which she had first dipped into the growing pool of diesel. Once it was burning nicely, she dropped it onto the floor in the middle of the garage, a ways ahead of the growing pool, and then climbed into the vehicle and closed the door.

She half-expected a massive explosion, but she knew something about how much more difficult it was to ignite diesel fuel. So when there was no 'kaboom' behind her as she drove out of the garage she was not surprised. In fact, she worried that maybe it would not be hot enough to ignite the fuel, and stopped to look back.

The paper towel was still burning nicely, like a torch, with a few steady licks of flame. Then she saw that the expanding puddle of diesel fuel had almost reached the paper-towel, near the front of the garage. She decided to trust that it would eventually ignite, and continued to drive away without waiting any longer.

With no alarm sounding by the time she reached the main gates, she had largely forgotten about her attempt to start a fire and was more focused on the sentry who seemed to be preparing to seal off the exit side of the gate. When Beth approached, he paused, recognizing the CO's secretary driving the CO's car. He assumed that she was on an errand for him, and waived her through before returning to his task of sealing closed the main gate, as per the orders he had just received from Base Ops. *She'll just have to come in through the north gate when she gets back*, he thought.

It took another thirty seconds for the paper-towel roll to ignite the diesel pool on the floor. Having reached the flash-over temperature, flames accelerated across the floor and expanded hungrily throughout the garage, looking for more combustible material.

Beth had already turned onto Highway 14 and driven the half-mile to the edge of town before smoke became visible coming out of the old wooden headquarters building. By the time anybody from the base had actually reacted, and sounded the alarm, Beth was well on her way out of town, heading northeast on Ithaca Road for her rendezvous with her husband Ian and the others. *Take this job and shove it!* she sang softly to herself.

Colonel Hurdman saw the fire coming from his office, and immediately worried that his combat gear was still inside, and his expensive new vehicle was probably already on fire, but he did not even think about his civilian secretary who for all he knew could be in danger inside the building.

I guess I should have sent Corporal Porter to collect the Range Rover sooner, and not left it in the garage, he thought to himself, regretting that he would not have his brand new vehicle with him up at the bastion at Cunningham Lake. He'd have to settle for the HMVWs and other standard military pattern vehicles in the column of his now company-sized formation. But then he had a hopeful thought. *Soon enough, we'll have road-blocks across Highway 80, so we'll be seizing all sorts of fully-loaded SUVs. I may not get another Range Rover, but I'll probably have my choice of Suburbans and Escalades*, he thought hopefully to himself.

"Quartermaster!" he shouted at the Master Sergeant who was conferring with some supply techs as the last of the trucks was being loaded.

"Sir!"

"Get me a fresh set of kit – web-vest, rucksack, CBRN – the works. Looks like my kit's going up in smoke!"

"Yes, Sir. I'll have it here in ten minutes," replied the Master Sergeant.

"And draw me a new rifle and nine-mil, and a Kevlar helmet."

"Understood, Sir. We'll get you a full replacement of your combat kit. We know your size." The QM replied, nodding his orders to the supply techs who literally ran into the QM building to draw the replacement kit for the CO.

"Sir, what do you want to do about the fire?" asked the base Senior NCO.

"What can we do? The fire-fighters stopped coming to work weeks ago. Just let it burn."

"But sir, what about Mrs. Morgan? Shouldn't we try to see if she needs help?"

"She'll be fine. If not, then she's a casualty, and we're in a combat situation. We are no longer in the business of helping the civilians – that would put our mission in jeopardy. She'll have to fend for herself," the CO said, and then climbed into the lead HMVW, and looked across at his radio operator.

"I want the column ready to be Oscar Mike within fifteen minutes. Pass the word."

He did not look at the Master Sergeant again, and did not see the look of disgust on the soldier's face. The senior NCO knew full well that the only mission the CO was interested in was his own well-being. He no longer considered what they were doing to be military, ethical, nor in any way patriotic. But he went along with it, out of the hope that he would be able to collect his wife, son, and daughter-in law and bring them up to the CO's personal bastion up in Pier County in time for he and his family to hunker down for the coming cold of the nuclear winter. Then, maybe somewhere down the road if the opportunity presented itself, he could conveniently 'frag' that Colonel.

That it was human nature to abandon concepts of humanity, generosity and good-will in favor of personal survival was something the Master Sergeant well understood, but that did not make it easier on his conscience as he imagined the nice young lady, Beth Morgan, suffering with nobody coming to her rescue.

As the column of vehicles pulled out of the north exit of the base he was still troubled with his choice. Had he known that

Beth was safe and sound and at that precise moment embracing her husband at their rendezvous point, he would have been proud of what the young lady had done.

The four HMVWs, two LAV-3s and three M939 6x6 5-ton trucks vehicles in the convoy of traitors departed town heading north on Highway 80 for a very short drive to the Pier County area just as Owen MacInnes led his two-vehicle convoy to the north east. For the five friends, it would be a harrowing thousand mile journey to Altoona, Pennsylvania. A journey which only three of them would survive.

It took them six weeks to get to within striking range of the Pennsylvania state line. As food supplies ran out, and the situation became more and more desperate for survivors in the Ohio area, the situation on the roads became more and more desperate, particularly so in the area just south of Akron.

Their strategy of negotiating safe passage from one community to the next by finding out the names of the biggest players in each successive town. In many cases an invitation was coordinated over amateur radio networks, which made it possible to leap-frog from one town to the next without too much difficulty.

But in recent days the areas under control of one faction or another seemed to have become more unstable, and much smaller. It was as if the world was shrinking, to the point that people had given up on rebuilding their nation. Perhaps it was the plummeting temperature and the novel arrival of snow in August, but people suddenly had reached a new level of desperation; they had become totally consumed with the struggle to survive.

The toll the travelers had to pay, even when their arrival at each successive road-block had been coordinated in advance in some way, had depleted their supplies to the point that all they had left was a few MREs, barely enough fuel to reach Altoona, and because they had not had to fight their way through anything thus far, they still had most of their ammunition.

Then things began to change for the worse. They noticed it when they left a bad situation in Petersburg, Ohio, where they had overstayed their welcome and been told to leave or face total forfeiture. It had been something of an armed stand-off, and ended well only because Beth had appealed to the local ring-leader's reputation for being in solid control of his men, that they had been allowed to go on at all. It had also cost them their silver coins. At least the gang in control of Petersburg had told them where to expect to find the next roadblock, at the exit off the Pennsylvania Turnpike nearest Ellwood City.

"Let's face it, we're going to have to fight our way through the next few road-blocks," said Randy.

"Can't we just go around?" asked Catherine.

"If we had the time to scout, and the fuel, but we don't. We have just about enough to make it the fifty miles to Butler, but that's all."

"What if we abandon the Range Rover?"

"That won't help us. It's a diesel, and the 'plow' runs gasoline," said Ian.

"Then we are just going to have to ambush the next ambush. At least if we do that, and get the drop on them, we may be able to score enough fuel to carry on the rest of the way to Altoona," said Randy.

"I'm not sure that's such a good idea. Maybe we should try to sell the ammo, to buy our way through the next roadblock?"

"Beth, if we do that, we'll have nothing left, and we'll look weak. Nobody sells their ammo. It's like a shark sensing blood in the water, they'll eat us alive," said Owen.

"But we're still what, a hundred and fifty miles from Altoona? There's going to be dozens more road-blocks in that distance. We'll never be able to make it through so many with nothing to barter with," Catherine said. "Maybe we should approach one of those farms, offer him everything we've got for some time to lay low and keep trying to get in contact with my dad on the radio. Maybe Dad can send someone out from his end, and then we would not have so far to go. Or maybe we should get off the roads altogether, and hike through the farmland and forests, be really careful and travel light over land?"

"That would be as dangerous as the roads, Catty. At least with the vehicles we have some protection. Out in the open the first we would know of any danger would be one of us getting shot by a high-powered hunting rifle in the hands of some farmer. Besides, so much of the land is flooded, and what's not soggy wet is covered with six inches of snow. We just don't have the equipment to travel overland in this mess," said Ian, looking out at the dismal wet snow falling on the slushy highway.

After discussing it at the abandoned rest area they had pulled in to while they talked, their two vehicles facing in opposite direction for security, they agreed to continue along the highway until they reached the Pennsylvania Turnpike and try to negotiate their way through the expected road-block at the Ellwood City exit.

It had not gone well. The road-block was not locals at all, but a group of desperate refugees from the burned-out suburbs of Pittsburgh who had been halted in their own quest northwards into the countryside and out of the squalid conditions of the FEMA refugee camps around the radioactive wasteland Pittsburg had become. With no food supplies of their own, the group had most likely turned to cannibalism, or had sustained themselves by taking everything from any unfortunate travelers who had come upon their small territory on the freeway off-ramp.

When Randy saw the murderous look in the eyes of the men at the road-block, he had given the signal to open up on them. Randy and Owen began firing first, while Beth and Ian drove the vehicles and Catherine added some wildly inaccurate shots from her side of the second vehicle. Changing out the clips from her handgun one after another, Catherine was really pouring it on, putting rounds down-range like a soldier. Her father, General Upton, would have been proud.

In the end the gunfight tapered out as the people manning the ambush had taken heavy losses and took cover from the seemingly unending fire coming from the well-armed little group.

Once the firing from the road-block had ended, Randy put his foot down, accelerating the Ford to thirty miles per hour before lowering lowered the snow-plow to just a fraction of an inch above the road surface. It actually worked exactly as the manufacturer had intended, clearing a path of snow from the road and curling it aside like well-spread cake icing.

And then the impact. Randy, Ian and Beth were jolted by the impact as the Ford's snow plow blade tore through the much lighter vehicles and junk that made up the road block. Suddenly the way ahead was clear. The Ford continued down the off-ramp onto Ellwood City road. The ride had been much smoother for Owen and Catherine following in the Range Rover, but they had taken some parting shots from the ambush party, and Catherine had been hit in the neck.

A few miles farther along, when Randy found a safe area for the two vehicles to park, they did what they could to stop Beth's bleeding, but it was clear that she needed immediate medical attention.

And then they saw the damnedest thing. A police cruiser, with its lights flashing, approached from the north. Desperate to get help for his wife, Owen got out of the Rover with his hands raised, and approached the cruiser, ready to take a bullet in the off chance that the men in the police cruiser would help.

They did.

The men in the state police interceptor had been watching the cannibals at the road block for days, trying to determine whether or not today would be the right day to clear them out once and for all, when suddenly the battle between Owen's group and the cannibals at the Turnpike had taken place.

After verifying that Owen's group did indeed have enough food and supplies to prove that they themselves had not fallen into cannibalism, which appeared to be the greatest concern for the authorities in Ellwood City, the locals took the weary travelers into town and gave Catherine the medical treatment that she needed. While they did demand a modest payment – 500 rounds of 5.56mm ammunition – they gave Owen's group enough fuel for the Ford in exchange for the Range Rover.

Five days later, with Catherine in much better condition, the group resumed the trek, with safe passage provided by the Sheriff, at least as far as Butler, where safe passage had been arranged by the Ellwood City authorities. Butler was not quite as generous, taking the group's UHF radio and nearly all of the remaining ammunition – over 1,000 rounds of 5.56mm – leaving them with just six clips for the two AR15s and a few clips for the handguns. However, the militia in control of Butler helped Owen's group as far as the hamlet of Cadogen, and safe crossing of the Allegheny River into Ford City,

At this point, just seventy miles from Altoona, and safety, the group ran out of luck entirely. Hoping to make the final stretch to Altoona on the back-roads of the Crooked Creek area, they came across a well-entrenched group of locals in some place called Shelocta, and were hemmed in with a semi-trailer having been pulled across their exit.

Shit, here we go again, thought Randy, remembering a similar tactic when he had been ambushed on his own before linking up with Owen's group. They had tried to ram the road-block, but it had been too well fortified, with railway steel driving into the ground. The snow-plow had been torn off of the Ford, and the vehicle came to rest high-centered on the wreckage.

Owen and Randy got out to fight on foot, working well together as they advanced like two special forces soldiers moving in on the men manning the road-block. They would have made it, too, had it not been for a tangle of barbed wire that lay under the six inches of snow, tripping Randy. When Owen had tried to help Randy up, both men were shot, in rapid succession, by the locals. It all happened in a matter of a few intense seconds.

It was only when the women and Ian surrendered that the truth of the disaster had become known. Owen and Randy did not have to die at all. Had they tried to negotiate one more time, rather than try to push through with brute force, they would have learned that the locals had been pestered repeatedly by a group out of Altoona to keep an eye out for Catherine MacInnes and her group, which the General had heard was trying to each him through the amateur radio network. Safe passage had been agreed upon, for the rest of the way to Altoona.

Catherine was inconsolable with grief at the loss of her husband, as was General Upton at the loss of the son-in-law he truly only came to appreciate after his death.

That Catherine was pregnant with Owen's son was little compensation for the tragic, pointless loss. Safe within her father's well-organized group at the ranch in Altoona, Catherine got over her grief faster than her father, frequently thinking of Owen with pride: *he got me home; he saved baby and me*, while the old General could only think of Owen in terms of *the good son I could have had.*

11

ART OF TOTAL WAR

After Thorne and Blakely had presented General Adams and Colonel Ferebee with the concept of operations for the Mount Isa operation they turned their attention to more pressing matters. Whether the daring Mount Isa plan would ever be put into motion would be up to the J5 planning staff of the CJOC, and would take weeks, if not months, to put into place. It all depended on the speed of advance of the enemy and what could be learned of their operational practices. Having conceived the plan, and having put Adams and Ferebee onto some of the men to assist with the operational planning process, Captain Thorne and Major Blakely were free to carry on with their duties.

Without wasting any more time in the CJOC, Captain Thorne and a group of men from 1st Commando Company of the Australian Special Ops Command, 1st Cdo Coy, Australian Special Ops Comd, were about to set out on a more immediate mission. They were joined by Lieutenant Colonel Weir, the US Army Ranger on exchange with Australian Special Forces Command, Major Blakely, the USMC Liaison Officer along with and a fire team and some communications specialists from the MAGTFA, and a platoon-sized force of Australian soldiers from 1 Division who had volunteered to go along.

In the hours after the Marines and Australians had assembled at the rendezvous point not much information had come out of Sydney. But Captain Thorne had learned that his headquarters in the Randwick neighborhood was most certainly destroyed, being a mere two kilometers from downtown Sydney's ground zero. He had been given a direct order from the highest ranking officer he could track down in Special Ops Comd, a Major Smedley, in Adelaide. His orders were to gather any Special Ops personnel as they might encounter and operate independently or in cooperation with the Marines and with RAA's Forces Command at Captain Thorne's sole discretion.

They were to move with haste and operate within enemy occupied territories in Queensland, with a view toward gathering intelligence on the enemy command and control, rear elements, and communications capabilities. While they were directed to avoid becoming bogged down in risky engagements, they were also encouraged to neutralize, interdict, dislocate and otherwise take advantage of any serendipitous opportunity to degrade the enemy's strategic centres of gravity and operational decisive points. Skirmishes at the tactical level, even to save lives, were considered pointless and ultimately would expend what little capability Spec Ops Comd had left.

Thorne understood what this meant, and made sure that his men did as well. It meant that morality was out the window – as were the rules of war. Some of the nasty, insurgency warfare tactics he had discussed with the American Ranger, Lieutenant Colonel Weir, no longer seemed repugnant. *We'll have to be fast and light; cruel and creative*, Thorne thought, *and we will have to turn our backs on whatever horrible fate our citizens are experiencing - make ourselves into something fierce and terrible that will gradually get under the skins of the enemy soldiers. We'll become a nightmare to them, as long as we don't get sucked into becoming attritted and used up before this campaign of terror of ours begins to produce results.*

The task of slowing or turning back the PLA's inland advance, or of ultimately throwing them into the Coral Sea, was left to the US Marines of the MAGTFA, the Australian Army, and, God willing, the vast numbers of potential reinforcements promised by the Indian Army, *if they can get here before it's too late.*

As the men saw to filling their rucksacks with as much ammunition, rations, water and other essential gear as they could get their hands on, they looked rushed and perhaps overly eager to depart, to take the fight to the enemy. The only exceptions were Captain Thorne and the dozen or so men from 1 Cdo, and the Ranger, Lieutenant Colonel Weir, Major Blakely and most of the Marines, all of whom had recent combat experience in Syria. The difference between the Special Ops types and the regular Australian Army soldiers was stark, to say the least.

It was clear that the sixty men who had been thrown together for the mission did not have the comfortable camaraderie and fellowship that soldiers normally have when they live and fight together. The Australians were all from different units, and had reported in to whatever reserve armory, police detachment or military checkpoint they could find when they had realized that their nation was under attack. In many cases, they had turned up in civilian clothing because they had been on vacation or on leave of some sort. However, most of the men who were part of the Australian Army's Special Ops Command, SOCOMD, had their basic kit – less ammunition and special weapons – with them in the boot of their cars at all times.

Quick to find a way to seek each other out despite the decapitation of their command and control, many of them had used the School of the Air network to make contact with the CJOC in Katherine. Where their location was simply too far away for them to participate in the current mission, they had been encouraged to contribute to force generation in their local areas until called for by the CJOC. Others, who saw themselves as more fortunate, albeit more likely to die soon, had been handed off to Captain Thorne's group. So the mission assigned to him by Major Smedly out of Adelaide came with the implied task to gather these men, to force generate as many SOCOMD personnel as he could in the Northern Territory sector, and to get on the move before the front lines became more well defined and therefore less porous. Of the sixty men assembled so far, just under half were Special Ops trained. The rest were volunteers from the regular Army units of Formation Command, mostly drawn from 3rd Brigade, Darwin.

The resulting ad-hoc unit had considerable talent but was not operating with the quiet precision that special forces soldiers typically demonstrated, Thorne had observed. But that would disappear quick enough once the regular army soldiers from 3rd Brigade relaxed a bit and stopped looking at the Special Ops personnel and Marines as if they were mutants.

For their part, the commandos and Marines were happy to have some reinforcements, despite the regular soldiers' lack of special training. *Battle will sort them out*, thought the Captain, as one of his men spoke up.

"Oiy, Thornie, when are we going to get the fuck out of here? What are we waiting for?"

"Vehicles, Mate. We can't go in those big fat Loggie trucks. The Pandas will see us coming for several kilometers, or hear us, more likely."

As he spoke, he saw the dust being kicked up on the dirt road from the west.

"Great, here they come," Thorne said. "Oiy, one of you lot, go fetch Colonel Weir! Tell him we're leaving in ten minutes."

"I'm on it, Captain," said one of the soldiers, jumping up and rushing off to find the American Ranger, glad to finally be heading off.

Two years before, as an instructor at the Ranger Training Brigade at Fort Benning, Georgia, the then Major Weir was an expert in

Army and land forces doctrine in general, and had only recently cultivated an interest in the order of battle, tactics techniques and procedures of the People's Liberation Army. The growing military rivalry between the United States and China that had made him realize that it was his duty to get to know as much as possible about the Chinese military, to know the enemy as it were.

This view was reinforced when his commanding officer had shown him photographs taken of Weir himself, along with all of the senior officers of the Ranger Training Brigade, and the Brigade's facilities, depots, engineering works, warehouse, parade ground and the various support buildings associated with the RTB.

The photographs had been found in the hard drive of a laptop which the police had seized from a motorist they had detained one evening. A citizen had noticed the out-of-place vehicle at the end of a dead-end road that overlooked the main gate of RTB and had reported it to the police.

The police seized the man's laptop and handed it over the military officials after the man had tried desperately to activate some keys on his laptop. While they thought that they had had probable cause to search the man's computer, and would have been free to do so and hold him indefinitely without charge under the Defense Authorization Act of 2011; somehow the Chinese embassy had learned of the arrest, and had had some diplomats and high-powered lawyers appear at the Atlanta PD office before the man had even been photographed or identified.

The man had been permitted to leave the country without further interview, but had not been permitted to have his computer despite the furious protests of his embassy. The military promised to forward the computer to the embassy if they would confirm that it was the property of the Chinese government, which they refused to do. The Chinese did not press the issue, and claimed that the man had found the computer in the hotel room when he had checked in, and had no interest in the computer. Of course, they did not disclose that their spy had told his handlers that he had activated the file-destruct keystrokes, and that the data was destroyed. Or at least he had believed so. In his panic, as the police had approached his rented vehicle that night, their flashlights shining brightly in his eyes, he had been partly blinded and had hit the wrong combination of keys, merely shutting down the laptop and not activating the self-destruct mechanism. The information technologists of the RTB's G2 section were able to overcome the laptop's security features, and access the data.

There was nothing to clearly link the man to the laptop, nor the laptop to the Chinese. However, the large quantity images of defense-related personnel and establishments, and the careful records of date, time and geo-coordinates that the highly organized spy had on the laptop's hard drive were clearly the work of a foreign intelligence operative, and therefore an act of espionage.

For the US Army, it was yet another indication of the level of effort that PLA were placing on intelligence collection on the Americans. But for Major Weir, seeing his own face in the foreign intelligence operative's photos had put a chill down his spine. It had gotten personal.

Major Weir began to look at Chinese nationals visiting America as potential spies for the PLA. The more Weir looked into how deeply the PLA were spying on the American military, and how deeply they had penetrated the global internet, hacking into military and corporate computer systems alike, his distrust soon verged on paranoia. At one point he even considered getting psychological counseling, until he realized that the best thing he could do was to *learn as much about them as they wanted to know about us.*

That had been two years ago.

Since then, he had come to respect the PLA, the Chinese Army, along with the PLA-Navy and the PLA-Air Force, as a professional, highly disciplined military with an immense, if somewhat low-tech, arsenal of weapons systems to go along with their five million soldiers.

Feeling something like a fifth-wheel in the Katherine area as the Allied forces ramped up via the new CJOC construct,

Lieutenant Colonel Weir had decided to go along with Captain Thorne and Major Blakely on the dangerous mission so that he could observe the weapons systems, tactics, doctrine and general behavior of the Chinese units that were by now deeply entrenched in the east coast of Australia. His intent was to return to the CJOC with valuable insights into how to neutralize their numerical superiority through psychological warfare, special operations, decapitating strikes against their command elements, and any other dirty tricks that Australian insurgents could use in the occupied sectors against the overwhelmingly powerful Chinese occupation force.

He was certain that the PLA would have adapted their traditional tactical and operational doctrine to compensate for their presumed lack of heavy armor and logistical support at least in these early phases of their invasion. He thought that the allies needed to have a better picture of how they were making use of the Australian vehicles, equipment and infrastructure that they seemed to have put such a great emphasis on seizing in the opening hours of the invasion. And like the spy detained at the RTB in Georgia who had started him off as student of Chinese military doctrine, Lieutenant Colonel Weir took along a high-quality digital camera to capture the faces of whoever and whatever he saw, and a laptop into which to organize the data.

Looking more like a band of gypsies, with water cans, gas cans and some hastily roped-down tenting scrounged from some of the local sheep stations, the column of fifteen generally beat-up old vehicles did not look like the sharpened spear into the enemy's heart that the vehicles' occupants saw themselves as. And that was the point. They wanted to look like just another gang of locals, fool-hardily moving towards the front lines.

To even get to the area they had selected in their map recce, they would have to travel the 1,400 kilometers from Katherine, Northern Territory, to Cloncurry, Queensland, along Hwy A6. From there they would break into smaller teams and disperse into the communities from Charters Towers farther east along the A6 to the occupied sector in the north coast of Queensland, and down the A2 and A4 highways to the south-east to Longreach, Emerald and Charleville, ultimately leading to the central east coast.

With the enemy rolling over each and every effort of local militia to slow them down, the Special Ops force had departed Katherine with no clear idea of where the front lines would be by the time they reached the half-dozen communities they had selected as critical cross-road, tactical and operational level decisive points, where they knew that local militia would put up the most spirited defenses.

After discussing the intelligence the CJOC had received from Queensland via the School of the Air network, Lieutenant Colonel Weir and Captain Thorne had spent some time discussing their mission objectives with Major Blakely, the Marine Liaison between MAGTF and the Australian Army.

What they knew was that the general evacuation from the combat zone had largely stalled, at about 200 kilometers inland from the coast, when the evacuees had put some distance between themselves and the Chinese and had reached towns which appeared to have put together robust security forces, hastily organized by local militia units, police, or isolated pockets of soldiers.

From the reports they had received so far it sounded like the Chinese had captured the northerly port city of Cairns without much resistance. In much the same way as it had played out in cities and towns all along the east coast, it had started with Little Dragon agents and their local Dragonfly recruits interfering with police and military units in the critical minutes when a more coherent response could have made a difference, perhaps thwarting the sudden arrival of passenger aircraft and the rapid disgorging of highly trained Special Forces of the PLA.

In Cairns, the invaders had seized the Cairns International Airport and the docks along the east side of Trinity Inlet in a matter of minutes, their assaulters fanning out to lock down the area and set up road blocks with layered defenses on the three highways leading out of the small city.

In the first forty-eight hours after their arrival the Chinese had received numerous passenger aircraft, cargo aircraft, and even a squadron of Shenyang J-11's, the Chinese manufactured variant of the super-maneuverable fourth-generation Russian SU-27 fighters. The multi-role fighters had arrived in waves of six fighters each, accompanied by Russian-built IL-76-M air tankers that had sustained them in the four-hour flight across the Philippine Sea.

Commercial ships began arriving on the first night. According to the reports, which came from an observation post that had been set up on a ridge overlooking the city of Cairns from the west side of Trinity Inlet, in the Yarrabah Mountains, the build-up of forces had gone like clockwork.

The reports had detailed the sequence of events, which amounted to well-coordinated Aerial Port of Disembarkation, APOD, operations at Cairns international airport. The Sea Port of Disembarkation operation, SPOD, was at the Trinity wharves, where they rapidly off-loaded the equipment, vehicles and engineering support for what appeared to be a full armored Brigade along with what could best be described as a hornets' nest of highly mobile 'technical' squads of soldiers, darting about the city and pinning the civilians in their homes with sporadic gunfire.

Sitting in the back seat of a Toyota Camry, a Chinese officer calmly watched the unfamiliar features of Cairns speed past him while the accompanying soldiers in the car scanned the area for any potential opposition. Leading a platoon from the Special Operations Battalion from Guangzhou Military Region, the Lieutenant was expert in the spearhead tactics that had such great success on their initial air-land assault of the Cairns International Airport. His platoon had immediately commandeered local vehicles at the airport and then put them to use in racing past the bewildered civilians straight down Captain Cook Highway, passing the five kilometers through downtown Cairns on Sheridan Street to the wharf district, and seizing the small naval base, HMAS Cairns. The makeshift motorcade had blasted into the wharf area and captured the base with lightning speed and precision. The only resistance had been a handful of security personnel, lightly armed Royal Australian Navy Shore Police and some unarmed commissionaires at the main gate. The assaulters under the Lieutenant's command had overtaken the main gate and raised the barricade bar in under a minute; the entire base, and the three small *Armidale* class patrol boats of the Australian Patrol Boat Group were his in under ten minutes with no loss of life other than the two dozen Australian Navy and security personnel who had been gunned down in the fast-moving action. His men had then hung on to their objective for the next two hours until they were relieved by follow-on forces that had arrived in subsequent waves of the initial air-land assault.

In the relative peace of the next few hours, a Chinese Colonel made his way through the base on foot. He saw a fellow officer striding briskly his way from the opposite direction. He recognized the man, and although he out-ranked him, he immediately accorded him respect. "Lieutenant," the Colonel raised his arm in salute simultaneous to that of the Lieutenant, almost as if the Colonel had saluted the young Lieutenant. He was that impressed with what the Special Ops team had accomplished. For his part, the young officer casually acknowledged the Colonel before passing by on his way to the ward-room of the tiny RAN base, and the continuation of his important mission.

While the Lieutenant's men enjoyed a full day of rest in the ward-room, they had watched as specialists of the PLA Navy's logistics element had readied the RAN facility and Cairns port facilities in general for incoming vessels that arrived overnight and quickly began disembarking the men and equipment of the larger formation, the 42nd Group Army, Guangzhou Military District. The day of rest had been more of an annoyance to the highly motivated Special Ops personnel who wanted to get out on a reconnaissance or other task that put their skills and training to use.

So it was with great excitement that they scoured the small navy base and quickly located the inflatable boats required for their next assignment. The young Lieutenant kept a close eye on the dressing of his men as they crossed Trinity Inlet simultaneously, six men each in the five rubber boats they now used, courtesy of the Royal Australian Navy.

The Lieutenant observed his men with satisfaction; all of the intense training was now paying off. His eyes darted left and right; constantly checking for any potential problem. But so far, there was none. They stayed in line beautifully and made quick time crossing the broad inlet before dragging their zodiac-style assault boats up the narrow beach and into the mangrove forest on the east side of the estuary. They abandoned the rubber craft without pausing as they began to fight their way through a few hundred meters of muddy, thick mangrove swamp. They soon reached the gravel road atop the levee, where the men automatically spread out on both sides with ten-meter interval spacing and advanced at an alert, jogging pace along the series of dirt roads for a half dozen kilometers until they reached Pine Creek Road. The intersection of the dirt road and the paved road told the Lieutenant that they had followed the correct levee road, and were where he had planned during his map recce.

As briefed, the team at the front of his column darted off the road after just a few hundred meters, disappearing into the steeply rising jungle to the north-east. Staying back for a minute until the last of his platoon had left the paved road, the Lieutenant was pleased that they had not encountered anybody on the road, and that their insertion in the hills northeast of the Cairns had gone unobserved. He then raced to catch up to his men as they progressed up the hillside towards their objective.

They had reached about the half-way point, climbing 200 meters up the mountain before they paused to prepare for battle. He watched his men catch their breath for five minutes, check their weapons and gear, and hydrate.

On his signal, they then closed silently with the enemy, known to be at the clearing atop the 400 meter-elevation peak that overlooked Cairns, the port facility, and the airport.

In a brief yet fierce action his men overwhelmed the half-dozen soldiers who had been operating an observation post. They fatally shot the radio operator and executed wounded defenders, but they took the officer alive – a prize to take back to the Command Post of the 124th Amphibious Mechanized Infantry Division, to hand the prisoner over to 370th Military Police Brigade for interrogation.

The Lieutenant was proud of his men. They had carried out the action exactly as per their training and captured an enemy officer. Surely the intelligence value would bring his unit great credit. *Too bad he's not a US Marine*, thought the young officer, who knew as well as any man in the 42nd Group Army of the animosity that his unit, and the US Marines, had for each other dating back to the Korean War. *Of course, it'll be the 3rd Marines, not the 1st Marines, that we will ultimately come into contact with*, he thought, looking forward to the time in the coming weeks and months when the two divisions and four brigades of 42nd Group Army would gobble up the two thousand kilometers westward to reach Darwin and engage the Marines. He had been briefed that the 42nd Group Army now had a new culmination point objective for the campaign. It had been confirmed that the 13th and 14th Group Armies had been taken out of the equation and that the Generals had made drastic changes to the campaign plan.

Thinking of so many of his countrymen who had been so mercilessly murdered by the US Navy and the RAAF shooting down the air-assaulters and sinking the follow-on forces, *they're going to pay for this when we reach Darwin,* he thought, his blood boiling with hatred for the Americans in particular.

As his men led their prisoner down from the clearing and into the jungle below, he watched with pride as his men helped each other carry the litter onto which they had loaded the captured communications equipment, and enjoyed a moment of satisfaction for a job very well done.

Before getting up to his feet to begin his own descent he looked out across the captured city below, just a few kilometers from the captured OP. With his unaided eye he could easily make out the assembly areas, some of which he knew of; others he could only guess at. But he could clearly see that the small city was not fully under the control of PLA forces. With all the men and equipment mobilizing in Cairns, the Lieutenant felt the energy and power of the 42nd Group army, and strained his eyes to make out the lead elements of the 124th Division as it departed Cairns heading south into the farmland of Wright's Creek, and into battle. From the morning briefing he had attended before his mission, he knew that once the 124th had wiped out the Australian's 3rd Brigade that had deployed from Townsville, some two hundred kilometers to the south of Cairns, there would be nothing to stop the 42nd Group Army's 80,000 personnel from locking down the entire northern half of Queensland and then pressing on with vengeance towards their revised objective, crossing the 2400 kilometers of Queensland and Northern Territory to close with and defeat the hated 3rd Marines, who he knew would be moving towards them from Darwin.

We should be able to defeat the Americans within a month, well before the nuclear winter sets in, he thought, relishing the image in his mind's eye. *Glory is everything.*

The first organized resistance put up by the Australian Army had been put up by 3rd Brigade, Forces Command, who had set up a defensive line at Wright's Creek with a company of Light Armored Vehicles from 1st Armored Regiment, and a Battalion of well entrenched soldiers thrown together from 1st and 2nd Btn, Royal Australian Regiment. No. 4 Field Arty Rgmt's contribution of a mix of 155 mm towed howitzers and a few of the newer M777A2 lightweight towed howitzers and two Observation Posts feeding into the Regiment's Joint Fire and

Effects Coordination Centre, JFECC. Before the battle was joined the Australians felt that they had assembled some formidable firepower and had set up in favorable terrain, against an untested enemy that was unfamiliar with the local terrain and was in the throes of their initial mobilization ashore. The Australians were confident that their artillery alone would be devastating to the enemy, who would be forced to throw their units piece-meal up the highway into the Australians' kill zone.

The battle had been short and fierce, with well-placed artillery rounds raining down on the advancing column of Chinese tanks, infantry fighting vehicles and armored personnel carriers, which had been offloaded at the Cairns dockyards less than 48 hours before.

The defenders had enjoyed a moment of hope, after taking out a dozen targets at the head of the Chinese column, but the defenders had been over-run after being hit from the air by cluster-munitions and some form of agile projectile, perhaps optically guided smart-bombs, from a squadron of SU-27s that were already operating from Cairns International Airport.

The last report that the radio operator from 3 Combat Signals Regiment, 3rd Brigade, had been able to send to the CJOC was that Chinese were now moving out of Cairns with a variety of specialized units that amounted to the lead elements of a full division, possibly of the 38th Group Army. Based on unconfirmed reports, it even sounded as though two full divisions of the 38th Group Army had *passed through* the shock troops of the 42nd Group Army, taking up the lead without pause, however that assessment was met with skepticism.

In the CJOC in Katherine, over two thousand kilometers away, Colonel Ferebee and General Davis and the rest of the Ops Centre could hear gunfire, then some shouts in Chinese, then the transmission from the Cairns sector abruptly ended.

Another Alamo, Ferebee sighed grimly to himself.

12

MASSACRE AT CHARTERS TOWERS

She knew that Sunny was in trouble, ever since Sunny's father had translated an intercept for the Americans before they had abandoned Pine Creek and moved the CJOC down to Katherine. The news had been particularly devastating for Sunny's father, Stanley Yao, who could not even speak. He had just sat there, staring at his notes at the workstation, in shock.

Agness had been there with her boyfriend's father when he had finally made contact with a School of the Air station in the right area. Recognizing that something was wrong, she pressed Stanley for the information. Stanley struggled to speak, but eventually took of his head-phones and spoke five words:"Charters Towers has been over-run".

Everybody knew what that meant. Stanley's son was either dead or a captive of the 124th Division, which had been driving inland from Cairns and Townsville. Ever since, there had been no further news out of that sector and Stanley had become, to put it in her father's military jargon, *combat ineffective.*

And with the rumors of Chinese atrocities running rampant, there was good reason to fear the worst. But Agness Blakely was in love, and could not sit still and wait for the dreaded news. She had to know. She had to try to do something to save her Sunshine, as she thought of Sunny Yao.

For the first time since she had arrived in Australia only four months before, Agness Blakely was glad that she was part of the home-school program in Darwin, or at least, had been, while school was still being delivered through the School of the Air network. She had originally been opposed to her parents' decision to keep her out of the local Australian public school system and to register her for what she thought of as a supremely boring form of home schooling. Perhaps intuiting that the technology could give her some additional ways to contact her lover at his dormitory at a boarding school in Charters Towers, Agness applied herself to learning the technology and radio protocols and to ingratiating herself with the regional School of the Air administration in Darwin.

So it was Agness who solved the mystery of what was going on in Charters Towers. She had been persistent in her efforts to contact someone in the area, anyone who could report on what was happening in Charter Towers. But in order to do so, she had had to be a little bit sneaky about it.

The School of the Air radio network had become militarized, and was being used by the Australians to coordinate their militia and self-defense forces to piece together which communities had scraped together enough men and weapons to put up a fight and to coordinate the evacuation of civilians to more defensible communities.

As a result, it was next to impossible for Agness to get any help from the radio operators, who had shooed her away from their consoles whenever she had tried to get them to help her call stations in the Charters Towers area. So she had taken another approach, and began to make herself useful to the radio operators in other ways.

And she had help.

When her father noticed how she was always hanging around the console, listening for reports and pestering the radio operators, he had taken the CJOC's J6 Communications Officer aside and explained the situation. Once the man understood that the Major's daughter was worried about her young man, who was among the missing children that the J6's own daughter was counted among, the officer had agreed to Major Blakely's request to find her a role in the listening watch. He did not have to tell the man that Agness would also be trying to keep tabs on her father, who was headed east on a mission deep into enemy territory.

At first, Agness had been employed as a scribe, taking notes and messages for the radio operators. But when they got to know her better and found how responsible and mature she was, they gave her more and more responsibilities. Within a week she had been given her own two-hour shift, albeit in the overnight watch when radio traffic was at a minimum.

But that was all she needed. Once she was established and had mastered her duties, cycling through her radio calls, the station-identity and duress verifications, and sending out the seemingly endless list of messages in the order that they were provided to her, she found that there was always a good ten to twenty minutes before the end of her shift when, as long as her work was done, nobody objected to her project of going through the list of cattle-stations and other call-signs in the area around Charter Towers seeking any remote family farm, hamlet or other radio station that could help in her search.

Her efforts at first had seemed futile, as she soon learned that most of the families west of Charters Towers – in the Free Sector – had long since evacuated farther west, fleeing as fast and as far as they could from the advancing Chinese forces.

But once in a while she got word from the occasional farmer who passed on bits of rumor or observations that helped build up the picture of what was going on in Charters Towers.

She recorded the information and passed it on to the intelligence section, who closely monitored the information produced through the School of the Air network, plotting the reported enemy units on their tactical maps.

It had become clear that the Chinese had seized Charters Towers. It was an operational center of gravity, where five major roads intersected. By controlling the town they controlled the crossroads and could send out patrols and reconnaissance in force throughout the region, and deny the same flexibility to the Australians and Americans. However it appeared that the Chinese forces in Charters Towers were still too few in number to send their patrols out much farther than a few dozen kilometers in any direction. It seemed that they were holding fast until larger forces arrived to reinforce them before expanding farther to the west.

This fact gave Agness some hope. If the Chinese forces at Charters Towers were weak enough, perhaps the Australians or the Marines could organize a raid, or maybe even liberate the town. Or maybe the town could rise up and overwhelm the invaders, as was taking place with mixed success throughout the Chinese-controlled areas up and down the Gold Coast and in other areas that she had heard about in the course of her duties.

But when she finally got in contact with a cattle station just a few kilometers southwest of Charters Towers she was shocked by what she heard. She hoped that she had misunderstood, and called for an Australian to come over and listen, to translate the outback slang into more a more comprehensible form of Australian – English.

"Cattle Station Blackjack - Four, this is CJOC North, please repeat your last, Over," the Australian officer transmitted, Agness having given up her seat at the console for him.

"What are you, a cut lunch commando? I told your lady friend clear as daylight, so why do you keep on me with your earbashing?"

"Roger, Blackjack. Relax, Mate. We just needed to verify that we had gotten you right. I'll read back your last." The Lieutenant referred to the notes that Agness had made in the communications log, and read out: "Brigade Group of 124th Division Red Pandas has moved in and are applying force indiscriminately and without quarter', over"

"You've got it, Mate. Get some help here, fast. I've got to shut down now, some sort of disturbance taking place on my property. Blackjack – Four, out."

Agness still did not understand what it all meant, but by the ashen face on the RAAF intelligence officer who had taken over the radios, she knew that the news was terrible.

Almost two weeks earlier, when the war first began, Sunny and his two mates had been arguing about whether to go out to find out what was happening, or to hunker down in their dorm rooms at Lord Byng Academy until they had a better understanding of what was going on outside. They had been woken up in the middle of the night by a series of popping sounds.

"Fireworks?" asked Jeff.

"Get real," answered Sunny, as he peered out the window, "Those are all kinds of small arms being fired."

"Guns? Maybe it's terrorists," David offered. "A few terrorists going nuts on the north side of town?"

"Or just gun nuts," Jeff added.

The three had developed a close friendship in their time at the Academy. Sunny had lucked in with these two fellows. David was a senior from Sydney, one of the first boys to have befriended the new student from America. He soon became Sunny's 'best mate', the son of a British mining engineer working in one of the gold exploration companies in the region.

Jeff was the third in the group; a boy from a rich family in Sydney, he had endured Sunny and David's teasing about being a "rich folks' kid" with his easy charm and warmed his way into their friendship. In a short time, most of the other kids at the school knew that you did not pick a fight with any one of these boys, or you'd also have his other two friends to contend with, too.

It did not take them long to realize that the popping sounds were actually gunfire. It was coming from the north, near the airport, it sounded like there was a battle going on. But it did not sound right. There were lots of gunshots, and a few small explosions, but none of the louder noises you would expect to hear; there were no sounds from tanks, artillery or bombs.

"Sounds like a gangsta rumble," David said, hoping that was all it would amount to. "They've got access to unreal types of guns, I reckon."

Sunny snapped his head around and faced David. "What gangsters would be crazy enough to take on an airport?"

"Plenty," Jeff said. "Maybe they've got a real big drug shipment they're protecting."

Sunny turned back to scan the horizon. "You've been watching too many bad movies."

"Bad movies, oh get out…" Jeff sniffed at Sunny.

"Quiet!" Sunny snapped back, as a plea for silence. As they listened, and peered over the rooftops to look at the occasional plume of smoke, they continued their endless argument.

The gunfire thinned out. "It's getting quiet. Maybe it's over."

"No, it's not."

"Screw you."

Then the gunfire started up again in earnest.

"No, screw *you*."

When the sounds of the running gun-battle started coming closer to their location, and were accompanied by sirens and the occasional screams piercing the normally silent night air of the little town, they became increasingly afraid.

"What the hell is going on?"

"I don't know. I can't see for shit."

"Well, let's not just sit here like a bunch of stunned asses. Let's get a better look. Come on."

The three boys decided to head outside to try to get a look at the airport from the grasslands on the north west side of town, which overlooked the runway from a safe distance, and was not that far from Lord Byng Academy. They headed out on foot, intermittently running and walking, north on Dalrymple Road. They quickly turned back when they saw what happened to a motorist who had screamed past them, heading out of town on Dalrymple. The sporty Mazda screeched to a halt, near where Dalrymple intersected with Read Road, which came in from the north side of the Airport. The red tail lights of the vehicle illuminated as the driver stopped. The white reversing lights then came on as he tried to back away from whatever he had encountered. Suddenly the small car exploded in a ball of orange flame and a surprisingly large plume of black smoke.

"Holy shit! Let's get back to the Academy!" said one of the boys.

They three of them ran back towards the center of town.

Just before they reached Hackett Terrace they saw a couple of pick-up trucks whizzing by, with Asian-looking soldiers kneeling in the vehicles' boxes, their weapons aimed out to the sides, firing periodically as if to herd people back into their homes.

Unsure of what to do and afraid to cross Hackett Terrace, which was being patrolled by the Asian soldiers, they took cover in the tree-line and bushes in Centenary Park. It gave them a good view of Hackett Terrace, Gordon Street, and the main intersection at Bridge Street.

"Let's cross. The Academy is just two more blocks from here," said David

"Hold on. Let's just sit and watch for a few minutes," said Jeff. "Shh! Listen!" he added, hearing the sound of an accelerating vehicle.

Moments later, they saw an interceptor from Queensland Police Service. The vehicle's lights were flashing; however, the siren was off. The boys realized that they were in great danger when they saw that the QLD Police Services cruiser was running away, with two of those 'technical' pick-up trucks in hot pursuit. One of the soldiers firing at the police car must have hit one of the wheels, as the interceptor suddenly swerved and lost control, flipping over and then rolling end-over-end down Hackett terrace right in front of the boys.

They watched in horror as the two trucks pulled up, spilling out a handful of soldiers. The men fanned out, establishing a secure perimeter while others pulled the two police officers out of their inverted vehicle.

Clearly alive, albeit stunned and bloodied from the crash, the cops were no threat to anybody. Yet one of the soldiers walked up, aimed a pistol at each officer in turn, and put a bullet into each man's brain.

Of the three young men hiding in the bushes a hundred meters away, Sunny Yao was the most frightened. The other two were terrified, to be sure, but it was Sunny Yao who had the deep, personal, stomach-turning fear that one has when they know that they are personally in peril. *They're speaking Chinese. Shit,* Sunny thought to himself.

He watched the soldiers strutting confidently around, and tried to piece it all together. He'd remembered the talk back home, about who would want to put America – and Australia – down and out. Yet as he watched the soldiers, it was in disbelief that he tried to discount all the alternatives one by one – Japanese? Vietnamese? Commie guerrillas? Terrorists? – until he came to the one obvious, unavoidable answer – China. *That must be the Chinese Army, the People's Liberation Army*, Sunny realized. *I am completely fucked!*

The boys did not say a word to each other. They just waited in silence until the soldiers dragged the cops' bodies to the side of the road, rifled through their pockets to retrieve their wallets, and removed their weapons. Others cleaned out the wrecked police car, removing a shot-gun from the cab and some duffle-bags from the boot of the car.

After a few minutes, with the sound of the soldier's vehicles having completely receded, the boys darted across the road and hopped over the picket fence of one of the well-landscaped old houses on the other side, cutting through a series of other yards until they reached Lissner Park. Darting from tree to tree until they got to the south end of the park, they did not stop, nor talk, until they reached Lord Byng Academy.

Once inside, they found other students gathered together in the main floor hallway of LBA, talking in hushed voices about what they had seen in their own forays out into town. Others had seen the bodies of civilians lying here and there on the roads, and in some cases had witnessed Chinese soldiers killing civilians indiscriminately. The others had turned off the lights and hoped that the soldiers would not have any reason to enter the LBA.

Some of the children, who ranged in age from thirteen to eighteen, continued to try to raise their parents on cellular phones; others tried to tune in a television station or radio station, or to get on to the internet, but nothing seemed to work. What the boys did not know was that the local internet, phone, and cable service in Charters Towers was based on land-line cables, and that the entire network was operated by one single company. In military terms, it was a 'single point of failure', the lines having been cut by a team of Dragonflies who had been assigned to cut off all communications into and out of the sleepy little town at the precise moment that the first air-land assaulters touched down at Charters Towers Regional Airport.

With no news coming in from the outside world, the kids were on their own, at least for the time being.

They all agreed that it was too dangerous to head outside again, for the moment at least, but argued about what it all meant and what they should do about it. So they hid in their dorm rooms and in other places within the boarding school, in small groups. In some cases their grouping was based on shared point of view about what to do next, or simply a circle of friends out of the diverse group of students who had been dumped in the boarding school by their wealthy, expatriate parents. Already strangers in a strange land, and without parents or other family to turn to, they turned to each other for support. But they did not see themselves as the terrified children that they truly were.

A range of their young voices could be heard throughout LB A, expressing different feelings: "Oh, God. We're all going to die."… "Maybe we should just surrender." … "They wouldn't shoot us if we had our hands up, would they?" …"Let's go out there and kick some ass!" …"With what, fuckhead? Your football?"

In David's room at the far end of the second floor, the same three boys had stuck together, not wanting to go along with the daring talk of other groups who were working up the courage to go out and 'get into the fight'.

"Sunny, we can't go back out there, we'll get killed," said David

"But David, if we can just get out of town, we'll be free and clear. Things are happening so fast and if we don't get out of here soon we may end up prisoners of war," said Sunny, unsure of how to bring up what he really feared.

"We won't be prisoners of war. Come off it. We're not soldiers. We'll just be captives, or detainees, or whatever they call it when a whole town is occupied. We could be forced to work, like the French and other Europeans were made to work by the Germans in World War Two, but at least we'll be safe."

"I think we should just sit and wait it out," said Jeff. "Once things settle down, we can figure out what to do. Besides, our side might win. The Chinks – Sorry, Sunny – the Chinese don't seem to have a lot of men here, yet. Maybe if we go outside, we can find help to fight them off."

"With what? Our bare hands?" said David. "Besides, Jeff, one of the local boys might mistake Sunny for a Chinese guy, and shoot him. It looked to me like some of those Chinese men shooting at us were in civilian clothes."

Slightly relieved that someone else had broached the topic, Sunny opened up.

"Look, Guys, David is right. I can't do anything about the color of my skin; I'm scared shitless. I don't want to be here when the sun comes up and we find ourselves in Chinese-occupied territory. There must be Australian military coming to fight them, and then I'll be in danger from both sides. I have to get the hell out of here, tonight.

David and Jeff did not reply. They just looked at Sunny, trying to absorb what he was saying. Everything had been coming at them so fast.

Sunny knew he had to go; he had no other choice. He took a slight breath in and said what had to be said. "You guys may have more options than I do, so if you don't want to go along with me, I understand," he said. There. He'd laid the cards on the table. David and Jeff still did not answer, but they looked at each other, as if one was asking the other for an answer.

Sunny hesitated in the silence. He started to turn and head out the door.

David was the first to speak. "What am I, King of the Dipshits?" Sunny turned back. David was not smiling; nevertheless, Sunny was glad. "I'm not taking off on you," David continued.

"We're sticking together, Sunny," Jeff said. "After all, what the fuck else are we going to do?"

While the boys talked about their options for a few more minutes and the darkness began to fade into pre-dawn, the town became much more quiet. From what they boys could tell, the Chinese had won the battle for the town. They could hear people shouting orders in Chinese. David and Jeff kept asking Sunny to translate, but he could not hear the shouts well enough to catch very much of what they were saying.

And then suddenly the boys heard Chinese shouting *inside* their building. The sounds came up clear as a bell from the entry hall below. They were terrified, as were other kids who had poked their heads out of their rooms to listen to the alien language and peer up and down the hall to see what other kids were doing; the more timid ones ever so gently closed their doors and looked for places to hide in their dorm rooms. But the three boys crept down the darkened hall together, to the top of the stairs, crouching down as if that would make a difference.

When they got close to the top landing they got down on their hands and knees and peered through the gaps between the ornate woodwork of the handrail.

There were about a half-dozen soldiers below.

One of them brushed the flowers and other ornaments off the table in the foyer to clear the surface for whatever he had in the leather satchel on his hip. The noise of the decorations crashing to the floor carried along the main floor corridor, drawing out some other students from their dorm rooms on that level, eliciting a quick burst of gunfire from one of the soldiers.

Judging by the screams and muted anguish coming from the kids' rooms at least one of the students must have been hit.

Strangely, the soldiers did not even care to investigate. It seemed as if they were not the slightest bit afraid of the children. The Chinese soldiers just wanted the civilians to stay back, to hide in their rooms, while the soldiers did whatever they were doing.

Sunny could hear the men clearly now. He understood what they were saying. He listened carefully, absorbing everything he heard.

"Get the map out,," ordered one soldier.

"Captain!" replied a very tall, skinny soldier, who whipped out a leather map-case and unrolled it on the table.

"Show me where we are?"

"We are here, at Lord Byng Academy," another man jabbed his finger on the map, "It is to be the Officer's quarters. There are fifty rooms on each level, with two beds per room. There is a kitchen, normally served by a staff of seven, a dining hall, an exercise room and other comforts. All in all, it is quite suitable for our Officers."

Smiling in agreement, one of the young Captain's closest friends seemed to find something amusing.

"What is it, Lieutenant?" asked the Captain.

"Did you not hear the name of this establishment? 'Lord Byng'," he said, now smiling broadly.

"Yes, I know the name. I have read it a hundred times in my mission planning. So what?"

"Maybe that's why we missed it, because we read it first, and did not simply hear it spoken."

Mouthing it to himself a couple of times, the Captain finally got it. "Oh yeah. Well, I don't think that General Bing will ever come here, but yeah, it is an interesting coincidence. Of course, the General Byng that this place is named after was a British hero in the First World War. He commanded Australians at Gallipoli and the Canadians at Vimy Ridge, so there are lots of schools and such named after him. He was part of the British nobility, hence the 'Lord'. Whereas in the case of General Bing, he will be made Lord, or Emperor, or whatever noble term he chooses, only after winning the war. Then there will be lots of schools and hospitals named after our General Bing," the Captain lectured, to the smiling agreement of the junior officers and senior NCOs assembled in the foyer.

"No reason we can't carve off one of the sides of the 'Y'", so it would read BING instead of BYNG, offered one of the Sergeants.

Hearing the overly casual manner the Sergeant spoke to himself and the other officers, the Captain snapped back into the task at hand, and the requirement to remain aloof. He sneered at the Sergeant for his impertinence.

"Get rid of the students and establish a security perimeter. I want this facility transformed to an Officer's barracks in time for Colonel Yip's arrival tonight," ordered the Captain.

"What do we do with the children?" asked the Sergeant.

"Kill them, of course."

"No. I mean, what do we do with their bodies?"

"Oh. I see your point. We don't want a stinking mess here. Okay. Don't kill them here. Take them out to that racetrack, where the other civilians are being herded to. All except the kitchen staff. Keep them and a few boys here as servants. Keep a few of the prettier girls too, for Colonel Yip and his staff to play with."

"Yes, Sir."

"And get that English speaking corporal in here. May as well have him tell some sort of story to the students in English, so they are easier to manage."

"Yes, Sir." The skinny soldier headed outside, presumably looking for the English speaking corporal.

Turning his attention back to the map, the officer turned his attention to a Chinese man in civilian clothes.

"So how many Dragonflies do you have in town?"

"Originally I had six men here in Charters Towers. One you met at the airport. He did a great job of taking out the airport security when you and the first wave landed. Two others died at the Queensland Police Service's Police Detachment. They failed to take out all of the police officers there, I'm afraid. But some of the soldiers on patrol hunted the last of the cops down on the streets soon after. The police have all been accounted for, by the way. The three other Dragonflies are still at the telecommunications hub, setting it up for local control, for when we begin transmitting instructions to the local population at large, they'll be working with Corporal Tang."

"That's it? You only had six? Pretty risky, wasn't it, trying to cover all three objectives with so few?" asked the Captain.

"Well, all of the other Chinese residents of this town were unsuitable, and I thought it too risky bringing in a fresh face from my base of operations. The Chinese in this town see themselves as Australians first, and could not be trusted. I did better in Townsville, here, on the coast," he pointed out a small port city on the northeast coast, "I got two dozen Dragonflies in place there. They did a great job during the initial assault, if I may say so myself."

"Yeah, I heard that we got the that port facility without too much trouble. Is it true, your Dragonflies were able wipe out an entire Company of Australian soldiers?"

"Not the entire company, but we certainly made them combat ineffective. My boys broke into the armory and armed themselves to the teeth. They got a 50-calibre and a bunch of FN-Mag-58s set up right on top of the Australian's assembly area, waited until a good number of men had responded to their general mobilization call, and then opened up on the reservists as they stood around on the parade square waiting for instructions. The poor bastards never stood a chance. That, and with the Intel and transport my Dragonflies in Townsville provided the follow-on force that came off the bulk cargo ship, and we got control of the entire dockside area before the Australians even knew who they were at war with!"

"Fantastic. Too bad we did not do as well in Perth or in Darwin. Fucking Americans. They really screwed up our operations there."

"I heard it was the Indians."

"No. Well, Yes. The Indians did sink a couple of ships in the Indian Ocean, but it was the American warship in Darwin, and a couple of Australian fighter jets, that shot down most of the airliners headed for the central and western targets. I heard they also got pretty much all of Group Army 13's follow-on forces in the Indian Ocean, and totally destroyed the 14th's ships in the East Timor sea,"

"They did all of that with just one warship and a couple of fighter jets?"

"Something like that, who knows, really? The real failure here – or success on their part - was due to their CIA people at some communications facility in the middle of Australia. They somehow figured out what was going on and got some of the Australians organized very rapidly, at least in the Central Sector, anyhow."

"Does that put our operation in jeopardy?"

"Far from it. We may have lost two Group Armies, but we still have three that landed essentially unopposed along the east coast. All it means is that we have to press hard through this town, towards Darwin ultimately, to make up for our losses. Maybe the units that reached the extreme north west will keep them busy long enough for the 124th Division to pass through here, and move on into Northern Territory," said the Captain, confidently.

"So at least some of the air-land units made it safely to the west coast? Did we at least get a foothold there?"

"Yes, we got a foothold. But not much more than that. We have inserted some very talented units, and they have control of the north-coastal highway – at least in a few spots – so they can cut off any organized response out of Perth and hold on for a month or so, buy us time for tertiary units to arrive once the sea lanes are cleared of enemy warships."

"Tertiary? What about the second wave?"

"Fucking Americans sunk them too. Gone. But we got their Carrier Task Force in the Malacca Straights soon after. Nuked 'em good."

"Holy shit! Will that be enough? I mean, after the third wave, from what I understand, and that's it for six months."

"Yes, but we've got enough of an advantage on the northeast, thanks in large part to some of the other Little Dragons who paved the way, that once we get across this Highway A2 and capture Darwin we'll own the top half of this continent. Then all we do is push down to Alice Springs and Adelaide in the center, link up with our Special Forces holding along the west coast, and we'll have a lock on this continent no matter how many men the Indians get ashore in Perth."

"You make it sound so easy, Captain. But there's still a lot of towns and cities to capture, and a few thousand kilometers to cross. I'll tell you one thing, this Australian continent is *massive*."

"Yeah," replied the soldier, thoughtfully. "But we have the advantage. They have no idea what's going on. Their air force, navy and army are mostly whipped, and we have the weight of numbers. Once we snuff out the threat of counter-attack and clamp down hard on their civilians to stifle any ideas of insurgency, we'll be in good position to hang on for six months. After that, there will be so many of us here, and we'll be so well entrenched, there will be nothing the Australians, Americans, or Indians can do."

"So the push to Darwin is the key?"

"Yup. But enough of that. We've got a town to exterminate. Well, almost exterminate, that is. We want a few survivors to get out, to tell the Australians just how ruthless we are. Then we will have less trouble pacifying the more important towns, down in Queensland."

"More important? I thought that Charters Towers was important, strategically," replied the spy.

"Oh, don't get me wrong. This place is crucial on the operational level. It'll be the headquarters for the 41st Group Army, and our logistics base for pushing two divisions westward. But in the longer term, it's not going to be important, because it's not a food producing region, and when the nuclear winter sets in and people begin to starve to death all over the world, it's going to be all about the food."

The Captain was interrupted by the tall skinny soldier, who had returned with the Corporal Tang.

"There you are," said the Captain. "Get on with it. Tell the students here that nothing bad will happen as long as they are not resisting. As long as they cooperate with our forces, nobody will hurt them. Tell them that we just need to process them with the Red Cross officials who are at the racetrack on the west side of town, and that they will be free to go once that's done," said the Captain.

"I know the drill, Sir. I've repeated it about a dozen times already tonight," said the Corporal.

"Don't take that tone with me, Corporal. Just get them out of my barracks, or you'll be thrown in with them at the racetrack when we open up on them!" shouted the Captain.

The Corporal shut his mouth, headed off down the hallway with the tall skinny sergeant and a few privates, and began calling out to the students in English.

Sunny had understood it all, but his two friends did not. They were listening to what Corporal Tang was shouting in English down on the first floor. The promise of Red Cross officials and safe passage made the boys hopeful. But when they saw the expression on Sunny's face, and the urgent way he gestured at them to follow him away from the stairs, they knew that something was seriously wrong. They followed Sunny back down the second floor hallway.

He led them quickly to the stairwell at the far end of the hallway without stopping at his dorm room, walking tiptoed on carpeted hallway. The other two boys followed suit, instinctively trusting Sunny.

Hesitating for an instant at the top of the rear staircase, Sunny thought about the other children, and thought of warning them. Safely out of sight for the moment, Sunny and his two friends crouched down together.

"They're lying. I understood them in Chinese, and what they are saying in English is not true. They're going to herd them into the stadium, where they have already herded others, and then they're going to slaughter them all," Sunny said.

"No way," Jeff whispered in disbelief. "Soldiers don't do that kind of thing."

"Shut up, and listen! We have to get out of here. We can try to warn the others, and get killed, or we can sneak out and save our asses. What do you guys think?"

"Shit. That's heavy. Those kids have no idea. They'll go along with that Red Cross bullshit – I would. We have to warn them," said David.

"I agree," said Jeff, but I don't want to get killed doing it. What should we do?"

Looking at the fire alarm, Sunny got an idea. "Come on, follow me!"

Sunny led them down the stairs, right past the main floor, and into the basement. He hoped that the soldiers would focus on the first two floors, looking for kids in their bedrooms, and not explore the mechanical spaces in the basement right away.

Feeling safe once they were in the mechanical room at the extreme end of the complex of historical original buildings, more additions and the maze of connecting passages that made up Lord Byng Academy, Sunny told the boys his idea. They nodded their heads in silent, albeit vigorous, agreement. Then the boys proceeded up the narrow stairs from the electrical room up into the back end of the administrative offices, which were thankfully unlocked. They felt safer there than any time since the crises had begun because they knew that the soldiers would have to break in through the locked front door of the academy's offices and work through the confusing series of interconnected old rooms before they would be anywhere near the back office. That is, unless they came through the basement as the boys had done, but that seemed unlikely. Even some of the students did not know about the back way into – and out of – the office.

After discussing his plan in hushed tones for less than a minute, they were ready. Each boy had a task, and took up positions. David stood on top of a chair, holding a cigarette lighter. Jeff held three lengths of pipe he had scrounged when passing through the mechanical room. With the weapons tucked under his arm, he stood ready by the fire alarm pull-handle. Sunny was seated at the desk normally occupied by the Vice Principal each morning, facing the microphone that sat on the desk.

All three boys knew that they would not have much time, and were primed and ready to put their plan in motion.

The ear-splitting squeal shocked the soldiers, who looked around at each other in near panic. The children, on the other hand, welcomed the horrible sound. It was the first bit of normalcy in an altogether abnormal night. They listened intently as the Public Address system came to life, the unpleasant noise fading away once the circuits had warmed up.

What they heard, however, surprised them, because it was in Chinese.

Over the intercom, they heard an unintelligible stream of sounds, which only the soldiers understood, and reacted to.

Had the students spoken Chinese, they would have understood the following:

"Attention! This is Colonel Yip. The enemy is about to attack. We do not have sufficient forces in place to hold this town, and we must immediately withdraw to the east. Take whatever transport you can get your hands on and run for your lives. We will regroup fifty kilometers to the east. Do not harm any more civilians. This is a direct order from General Bing!"

And then Sunny added in English: "Run for your lives, kids! They are going to kill you all when you get to the racetrack!"

He then switched the PA system off and headed to the exit.

Without missing a beat, David had already flicked on the lighter and held it under the heat sensor of the fire sprinkler; Jeff pulled the fire alarm.

As soon as the heat-strip softened and crumpled, setting off the sprinklers throughout Lord Byng Academy, Sunny and David each grabbed a length of pipe from Jeff. The three boys burst out the fire exit at the west end of the complex and ran for their lives.

Inside the Academy there was pandemonium in two languages. In Chinese, soldiers were arguing with each other about the order to retreat. Many believed that it was a real order, somehow broadcast from Colonel Yip directly. However, a few, including the Captain, believed that they were being tricked.

With the alarm bells ringing and soldiers rushing about and looking out the windows for signs of the enemy, the students were forgotten for the moment and began to slip out through the exits and main floor windows.

Most of the students got out of the building and ran away in all directions, quickly disappearing in the pre-dawn darkness. But around forty still remained, believing that they would find answers with the promised Red Cross. Even knowing that a number of students had already been shot they clung to the hope that if they co-operated with the soldiers then they would get through this.

The Captain motioned to all the remaining students gathered in the hallway to come forward. Cautiously, a few moved forward. They saw the Captain bark an order to a soldier standing beside him. The soldier looked to the left and to the right, obviously confused. He answered the Captain, in a panicked tone of voice. The students couldn't understand Chinese, but they could see that the soldier was having a disagreement with the Captain.

The argument ended as fast as it had begun. The Captain pulled a revolver out of his holster and in a brisk, business-like manner, he aimed at the soldier and shot him in the head. As the soldier's knees buckled under him and he crumpled to the floor, the students understood what they were dealing with. They turned and ran in all directions, disappearing like ants under a lifted rock.

The Captain was only able to shoot a handful of them before they were all gone.

Sunny and his mates were a dozen or so meters in front of the group of students that were fleeing in the same general direction, and wanted to stay ahead. They all had an extra spring in their stride with the knowledge that they had saved most of their school mates. But then David pulled at Sunny and Jeff to follow him, and take cover behind a wood-pile after they had clambered over somebody's fence.

In the safety of the back yard, they caught their breath, and assessed the situation. There were shouts in Chinese, all about.

But none were close. The boys could see a few groups of students passing their area, some walking along the sidewalk, looking back nervously to see if they were being hunted.

They were not.

Suddenly, a single, loud, CRACK broke the silence, followed by the fire-cracker popping sound of automatic gunfire. Then there were screams of "Don't' shoot! We surrender!" followed a few seconds later by more shooting, and then silence.

"Shit. This is real, guys," said Jeff. "They really were going to kill us all. What else did they say in Chinese back there, Sunny?"

"The guy in charge told someone to tell everybody that they would not be harmed. You heard that bit about the Red Cross, right? Well, just before that, the guy in charge, a Captain, I think, told his men to kill everyone. But then he changed his mind, and said to take them to the Racetrack, where the other civilians are being taken, and then all of them will be killed there."

"Oh my God! They're rounding everybody up and then they're going to kill them? That's insane. Why would they do that?"

"Because they want to make an example of this town, so that other towns will hear about it and not make any trouble."

"Sounds like something the Germans would have done in the Second World War," said Jeff.

"Yeah, it's brutal. But it means that we are in some kind of really big war, where the Geneva Convention or whatever the rules of war are – is completely off the table," said David.

"So what should we do? Try to get a car?"

"No way, Jeff. You saw what happened to that red car earlier. And by now they'll have road blocks set up all around town. No, we should stay on foot for now, and stay away from the main roads. Let's just cut through the back-yards, stay out of sight, and make our way out of town. That way is west, right?" Sunny said, pointing west. Then he turned his head in the opposite direction, towards the glowing horizon to the east. "Yeah, look, the sun's coming up so that is definitely east, where their forces are coming from."

"Coming? They're already here, mate!" said Jeff.

"No. This is a small number that came in through the airport. I heard them talking about it. No, they have a much larger group, something called a Group Army, that's landed in Cairns. They talked about something called the "124th Division" coming to base out of Charters Towers before pushing west to Darwin, and that Charters Towers will be the base of their supporting logistics."

"Wow, Sunny, you really got a lot of information out of that conversation we overheard. Good thing you speak Chinese."

"I heard more," Sunny said. "A lot more."

"Can you remember it?" David asked.

"I think so."

"I bet it's important stuff," said Jeff. "We should get you to the good guys, in Darwin."

David gave Jeff an 'are you an idiot' look. "Sure, no problem, dude. That's just a tad over two thousand kilometers from here. And we're on foot!"

Sunny's face remained set. "Doesn't matter. We have to get this information passed on somehow. I know who we need to get it to. My girlfriend's Dad. He's a Major with the U.S. Marines, That's where I'm going. You want to come?"

"Yeah," said David.

"Yup," said Jeff. Just one-word answers, but the way they both said it was with resolve. It would be all the way.

With that the boys began moving westward, picking their way through back-yards and watching for soldiers before dashing across the streets. They continued south-west for about two kilometers until they reached the outskirts of town, south of Rainbow Road.

There had been a few close calls as there were numerous groups of soldiers going house-to-house, ferreting out the citizens and loading them onto buses. On a few occasions the man of the house struggled and was beaten savagely, or his loved ones were threatened until he complied with their instructions. More often than not, the boys observed, people went along with the soldiers, no doubt believing the Red Cross story or simply too afraid to do anything else.

From time to time they saw people running off into the bush, as they themselves were doing, making their way out of town on foot. Those that tried to drive generally ended up dead, with more and more motorized patrols zipping around the streets. It seemed that the longer the Chinese had been on the ground the more organized and spread out they were. The boys looked at the way that the invaders were quickly locking up the town and herding the population into detention at the racetrack. It terrified them and made them sick. It was a horrible, unspeakable nightmare that they could not do anything about.

But their fear helped to drive them on. There was no disagreement between them about what was to be done. They had already seen enough evidence; and with Sunny's information, they now had a mission. They stayed away from the houses, which became easier as they passed the larger houses on larger plots of land at the end of town. Soon they were into the sparsely treed scrub land. The going was rough as they approached the rolling hills, but less dangerous with fewer roads to worry about.

They were drawn to the large water tanks atop the hills beyond, by the prospect of water, but when they reached the graffiti-covered blue tanks they were disappointed to find that there were no faucets, no way to get water from the town's water supply.

Exhausted and bewildered, they plunked themselves down with their backs to the one of the tanks and looked over the townsite below. The twenty meter hilltop they were sitting on gave them a commanding view of the area. They could see all the way to the racetrack, at the far side of town.

"Hey, there's smoke rising from the racetrack! Do you think the Army has come, and rescued the town?" asked Jeff.

"No way," Sunny said, "We would have heard some tanks or heavy weapons."

"All we heard was gunfire," David said in between heavy breaths.

"When?" asked Jeff, "Just now? I haven't heard any gunfire."

"A few minutes ago," David answered. "Back when we crossed Mossman Street! There was a whole whack of shooting."

The three boys looked over towards the Racetrack in silence. Then Jeff turned to Sunny. "Those Chinese guys in the school, they said they were going to take everybody to the Racetrack and kill them?"

Sunny's response was soft but grim. "That's what they said."

Three boys stared down at the burning pyre at the Racetrack. Boys who were sick and stunned at the evil in front of them.

They continued on. When they had gone at least a dozen kilometers from town, and had not seen any Chinese soldiers for a while, they decided to take a risk and try to find someone at a cattle ranch they came to.

They approached with great care, keeping the white-skinned boys in front so that Sunny would not be the first person the rancher saw.

Just as they paused at the front gate, and read the sign: "Blackjack-4" at the rural-style mailbox, the ranchers' dogs heard them, and came yelping at them.

Then a big man came out, shotgun in hand. But he soon determined that the boys were harmless, and invited them in. The boys were relieved to be in a safe place, with a man armed with a gun. But it was the connections that the rancher had – to the School of the Air radio network – that really got them excited. Sunny nearly leapt out of his shoes in excitement. But his hopes were soon dashed, as the rancher informed him that his radio set was unserviceable, as he had not had to use it since his son had grown up. But he said that he could probably fix it if it was that important to send a message.

He asked Sunny what he knew of what was happening in Charters Towers. The rancher listened in disbelief. But he must have had some military training, as he suddenly snapped to a more serious bearing, got out a notepad, and had Sunny go over it all gain, in careful detail, as the former soldier-turned-rancher took notes.

"When I get my set working I'll transmit this information along the line to the military. That I promise you," he said, and then sat back and exhaled, shaking his head. "God Almighty," the rancher said, "It's more than a soul can believe!"

They stayed at the ranch for three days. Three days! It was a miracle. The boys had been convinced that the Chinese were only minutes away. But the rancher was a good guy, offering them food, drink, and a place to rest. After their terrible ordeal, they were glad for the chance to eat and get their strength back.

Their stay was not a pleasant one. Sleep came fitfully to the boys. Each would wake in the night, startled by a nightmare, or convinced that any creak in the house was the Chinese coming for them. The following day, the rancher offered the boys a beat-up old vehicle so that they could make their way to Darwin. They accepted; and for the rest of the day they gathered fuel and supplies for their journey while the rancher serviced the vehicle.

As the boys got into the four-wheeler, Sunny turned back to the rancher. "I don't know how we can repay you. I don't even know if we can get there, let alone bring your vehicle back."

"Hell, boys," the rancher said with a glint in his eyes, "I don't know if any of us, me or my mates, will be here in another day or two anyway. Just get there, for us all, will you?"

The boys were escorted to a road-block about one kilometer west of the cattle station. The road-block seemed like it was well defended, with wrecked vehicles and other junk piled up on either side of the road and a large truck used as a moveable gate. The checkpoint was operated by a well-armed group of cattle-ranchers, calling themselves militia, some ten kilometers west of town where the two roads leading out of Charters Towers intersected with Highway A6 to Cloncurry, and from there as the A2 to Darwin.

Leaving the "Blackjack" checkpoint, the boys drove through the day and into the next night. Sunny was driving while the other boys slept when they drove over the Queensland – Northern Territory border. They had not seen another eastbound vehicle for hours and had been overtaken a number of times by faster-moving westbound vehicles.

On the local radio, they heard that night driving was forbidden as the roads were required by the military, and that martial law was in effect. They had debated pulling over, to wait for daylight, but Sunny wanted to press on through the night.

Nearly asleep at the wheel, he drove headlong into a column of armed civilians driving east, with their headlights off. Sunny slammed on the breaks and jumped out, waved his hands. "Don't shoot," he shouted. He had left the headlights on, and saw that the driver of the lead vehicle was wearing something strange on his face. *Are those night vision goggles?* thought Sunny, his hands still high in the air.

Sunny saw the man raise his weapon, focus his eye on the target, and squeeze the trigger.

The driver of the lead vehicle had been intent on taking action to interrupt the massacre taking place at Charters Towers; the RAA Sergeant-Major from 1st Bde was on a personal mission. His daughter was among those trapped in the enemy occupied town and something in his heart told him that she was already dead.

He was in a rage and desperate to find her, so when he had been forced to halt his vehicle and deal with the approaching vehicle he had become infuriated. When he saw the Chinese man get out of the vehicle, waving madly at them as if to surrender, he lost all composure. *I'm not taking any Chinese prisoners today,* he thought, as he took careful aim and squeezed the trigger.

The sound of the round glancing off of the Chinese man's vehicle told the Sergeant Major that he had missed, even before his trained eye re-focused on the target for a follow-on round. But before he could pull the trigger again, and even as his aim-point followed the man in his desperate leap towards the relative safety of the ground, he sensed something solid coming into contact with his F88 Austeyr assault rifle.

The second round disappeared into the darkness without making contact with anything other than dirt, some three hundred meters beyond where his aim-point had been. "What the fuck!" he shouted, as he shifted his weight and turned to face the source of the unexpected interference.

"Stand down, RSM!" commanded the officer.

"What the hell are you talking about? No more than two hours ago you told me that we would not be taking prisoners," complained the Sergeant-Major, struggling to free his weapon from the steady pressure being applied by the Marine's weapon pressing up against his own.

"Prisoners, no. But we had agreed to rescue as many civilians as we could, if the opportunity arose during the raid."

"The raid hasn't even begun, and you're jeopardizing our mission by letting that yellow bastard live another minute!" the Regimental Sergeant-Major spat in disgust. "How do you know he hasn't found a way to alert his kind?"

"His kind?"

Looking at the officer as if he were a lunatic, the RSM sneered: "The *Chinese*, Mate. His people!"

"Because, RSM, I am *his people*."

"What the fuck are you talking about?"

"That's my future son-in-law, and he is an American citizen. Now stand down and let me introduce you to the man you were about to murder," said Major Blakely.

13

ROAD TO CLONCURRY

Master Sergeant Rideout scanned the outback landscape as his vehicle sped along the trail. He was looking for any familiar feature that might jog his memory – anything to ensure that he and everyone else would find their appointed destination.

It had been a while since that magic time there with Guay and Hayman. So much frenzied preparation, and then everything else since. He was hoping that this Task Force would be able to make a difference — but in the present situation, was that hope just a forlorn luxury?

His driver broke his concentration.

"Top! How much longer before we get to the TP? Isn't it somewhere along this stretch, where we're no longer right next to the railroad?"

Looking at the topographic map on his knee, and then at his watch, he replied: "That's right, Corporal Roebuck; we're coming up on the Turning Point in a few more minutes. So you *were* listening this time! It should be in visual range within the next couple of minutes."

"Too bad the GPS don't work no more."

A soldier called out from behind in the vehicle. "Yeah. We've got to rely on basic map reading. But don't worry," he continued with a smirk, "Top's got some *topless* local knowledge."

"She had a *bra* on, Lance Corporal. When telling stories about me, make sure to keep your facts straight," said Rideout.

Dumbass, Rideout thought to himself. His focus suddenly shifted back to the landscape as he noticed an outstanding detail. "Okay, Corporal," he said to the driver.

"What?"

"There it is. You see that culvert?"

"What, that boxy concrete thing?"

"Yeah, that's our visual feature. Look for a track to the north."

"Roger that," the corporal answered. He eased up on the gas pedal ever so slightly.

"Coming up pretty quick," said the Top Sergeant. He squinted in an attempt to see fine features more clearly. Then the track appeared. "

"There it is. Turn left, there," said the Top Sergeant.

As the procession of vehicles pulled off the A6 Highway, the radio in the Top Sergeant's helmet crackled.

"You sure about this, Ride? Don't look like a road at all," transmitted Master Gunnery Sergeant Gannon, from a few vehicles behind the Top Sergeant's SUV. The long–standing friend of Rideout was along for the mission as Ops Sergeant for the specialized Task Force.

"That's the idea, Master Guns. No – I'm sure of it; this is the way to the billabong. You and the engineers pull off and get that drag thing going. Let's do this disappearing act quickly." He was slightly relieved at having found the way again; it took the edge off of his excitement at the prospect of playing a major role in an important mission. On another level he was energized at being able to return to a place that had become so personally meaningful.

Gannon responded to his transmission. "WILCO. All units Tango Fox Bravo, BEARS DEN," he said , his long training and well working relationship with Rideout coming into play like a well-oiled machine.

As briefed, and on Master Guns Gannon's code-word, BEARS DEN, the communications gear was shut off in the two LAVs and eight civilian pattern SUVs followed Top Sergeant Rideout over the sand and patches of bare rock, heading north.

Master Gunnery Sergeant Gannon's little 'Japanoid' utility truck stopped. Master Guns and the three engineers riding with him immediately got busy hauling out a rolled up section of chain link fence, and some cables.

Within three minutes they had unraveled the fencing and hooked it up to the bumper and were on the move again, dragging the carpet of chain-link fence over the tracks made by the rest of Task Force Billabong. Every little trick to make sure their tire tracks wouldn't be seen by the Chinese.

It only took them five minutes to get lost.

They had had no problem following the tracks at first, but after just a few hundred yards they had encountered an expansive dome of rock, easy enough to drive over but with no tracks to lead them. They stopped at the top the large dome and scanned the perimeter, seeing only rock, sand and parched grassland all around, other than what looked like impassable, rocky terrain to the north-east.

Suddenly a man appeared at the edge of the dome, having materialized out of the rocky terrain to the north-east.

"What the hell's the matter with you guys? It's this way!" yelled the Marine, who then turned his back and disappeared back into the rocks.

"Drive on, Marine!" Gannon said, shaking his head in disbelief.

"Master Gunns!" replied the engineer, his burly arms wrapped around the tiny steering wheel. He looked a bit ridiculous, but seemed comfortable enough in the tiny utility vehicle they had been provided for their dangerous mission.

As the Japanoid vehicle reached the far end of the dome, the impossible became possible. They drove over the edge of the rock and into the gulley that the rest of their formation had disappeared into.

After another two hundred meters, the track curved and descended sharply, and leveled off at the long, grassy shoreline of the billabong.

All along the line, Marines were rigging camouflage nets to the trees that lined the edge of the billabong, having already tossed their tents and other camping gear out onto the grass.

"Your spot is over here, Master Guns!"

"Thanks, Lance Corporal," said Gannon, stepping out of his vehicle. After motioning for the engineers to carry on re-packing the chain-link fence and putting the Japanoid to bed between two thick bushes, he headed down the line to inspect the camouflage and see how the troops were doing. He knew in advance that Top Sergeant Rideout would have things well in hand.

By the time he got to the LAVs at the far end, deeper in the line of trees where the dried ox-bow lake ran into a bone-dry waterfall, he was satisfied that the place was the perfect hideout for Task Force Billabong. He looked down to the gully below, where an inviting green pool of water lay hidden, and exhaled at the beautiful sight.

The beautiful Australian Military Police Sergeant Hayman, that Master Guns Gannon had assigned Top Sergeant Rideout to accompany on that 'acclimatization tasking' was there, with a few civilians dressed like Crocodile Dundee.

"How Ya Going, Mate?" a beefy, wide-shouldered civilian grinned widely. "You my long lost cousin?"

"Hi! What do you mean?"

"I mean, your man here says your name is Gannon. That right?"

"Sure is. Master Gunnery Sergeant Gannon, United States Marine Corps at your service. Why do you ask?"

"Cause, mate, you two might be kin," said another civilian. "This here is Liam Gannon, mayor of Julia Creek," said a third civilian, this one in some sort of uniform, who introduced the first civilian.

Then it all made sense to the Master Gunnery Sergeant.

"So you're the one. I spoke with some of your staff, when I…" he stopped mid-sentence to look back up at the Marines still busy setting up their campsite, their vehicles now completely invisible under the trees and well-matched camouflage nets.

He looked back at Master Sergeant Rideout, "Is now a good time, Top Sergeant?" he asked.

"Go for it, Master Gunns!" Rideout said, smiling.

The Australians must have known what was coming, as a couple of them headed to two quad vehicles they had ridden in on and began undoing the tarps, revealing a range of coolers, BBQ and other gear.

"Lance Corporal, go and tell the three engineers at the far end of the line to bring the 'package' here, and pass word along the line that there will be an inspection here, by the water, in five minutes."

"Master Guns!," the Marine replied, but then stopped, and asked: "What's the order of dress for the inspection? Dress of the day?" asked the Lance Corporal.

"Guns and gonch!" laughed the Top Sergeant, unable to help himself.

The Lance Corporal did not understand at first, but as he watched the impossible sight of both his Master Sergeant and his Master Gunnery Sergeant strip out of their clothes, right down to their underwear, and then proceed to leap into the billabong, he clued in. It was to be one of those rare, legendary moments when the normally strict, rigid discipline was to be relaxed and the men would be allowed to have some good clean fun.

He rushed off to pass the word.

By the time he made it back, in his underpants and bare feet, there was not even the slightest pretense of an inspection. The fifty two men of Task Force Billabong were there at various stages of undress – many of them completely nude – leaping into the cool water of the billabong.

This time around, Sergeant Hayman did not partake, but she was not the least bit uncomfortable to see the extremely fit, and in some cases very well endowed Marines frolicking in the billabong, just as when she had first introduced the Top Sergeant to it, less than two weeks ago – just before the war had started.

"These Yanks sure are enthusiastic! It's like they've got a lot of steam to blow off!" said one men from Julia Creek.

"Too right," replied Sergeant Hayman, "I reckon it's hard for them, being so far from America, with no news on their loved ones, and now fighting for a country they don't even know."

"Damned right, Windy. But they don't seem the slightest bit afraid of what's coming our way."

"You mean the Chinese?"

"No, crackers, I mean the nuclear winter."

"I'm not sure they're looking that far ahead. That's months away. No, these men know that they're not likely to live much longer. All the Marines – and our boys – won't have much of a life expectancy when the PLA's 124th Division and the rest of 42nd Army Group get here."

"I don't know, I wonder if that plan cooked up by our Thorney and that American major has any chance of success."

"Sure. As long as the Pandas motor on past here and don't find this hiding place. As long as they pass through Julia Creek without looking too closely in the barns and abandoned buildings your lot will be holed up in. As long as the deception at Cloncurry works, and as long as…"

"Shut your gap, woman, that's enough 'as long as's!" You'll have me ready to die, leaping into the billabong, abandoning all constraints like our American cousins over there if you don't sew up your defeatist prattle!" said the town's only policeman, with a wink.

"Now let's get this kangaroo meat on the barbie!' said the other local, "These lads are in for a treat!"

Two hours later, after the Marines had enjoyed 3 or 4 beers from Liam Gannon's bottle shop, and Master Gunnery Sergeant Gannon had convinced himself that he was indeed related to the burly Australian, the Marines of Task Force Billabong had made the hidden oasis their home. The next few days of preparation were sure to be uneventful, as the Yanks and the Aussies looked like they were going to get along fine.

Four hundred kilometers to the east, on a rock-strewn expanses of outback, a man stared glumly ahead. He was the cattle farmer who'd put up the three boys from Charters Towers, and had just seen them ride off into the distance.

He turned back to his mates minding Blackjack checkpoint with him, just ten kilometers west of Charters Towers. *Soon the Chinese will be coming,* he thought to himself. *How long will we be able to hold them off?*

He saw Emil, ten feet away, checking his rifle one more time. *Bloody good bloke,* he thought, looking at Emil. They'd delivered calves together, pounded fence posts, dug ditches and built barns and sheds together over the years. Great years, but would they now end here?

The rancher saw others spread around the checkpoint. Raymond, nervously looking in the direction of Charters Towers. Young Art, too young to have even had a girlfriend yet, and now it would all be decided for him here. Not far away, his one-time worst enemy Royce O'Callan puffed out his chest in a phony-brave, cocksure fashion as he vigorously sucked on a smoke. *Just like Royce, the bugger,* he sighed, *But I don't know how far your tough-guy attitude will carry you this time, mate.*

The rancher turned in the direction of Charters Towers. *Will they come in tanks? In jeeps? Or will they fly over in helicopters or napalm us from airplanes? Sooner or later, it'll be over,* he thought.

He thought that now he knew how the ANZACs must have felt before they went over the top at Gallipoli. He'd seen it dozens of times in the movies, how the doomed soldiers wrote farewell messages to their loved ones and pinned them to the side of the trench as they waited for the British Officer to give the order for them to climb the ladder, up out of the safety of the trenches and into a hellish rainstorm of bullets – not that he'd do that here. Warfare may have changed since then, but what he felt in common with the ANZACS was the certain knowledge that there was no hope of coming out of this alive. *Would it help at all?* he asked himself, *Will we make any difference? Guess we'll never know.*

He looked back at his mates and thought of a poem he'd had to learn back in his school days. It was a poem about World War One, and sometimes he'd heard it at war memorial services. He didn't remember much of it, but one part of it sung in his head right now: *We are the dead.*

Myself and Emil and Raymond and Art and Royce and all my mates over the years who are standing up here and now to fight - we are the dead. Our lives, our work, our land – all our hopes and fears, our joy and our tears have been spent here in our land. Now it will end here. And all on account of those damn Chinese in town there.

He felt a surge of anger at the whole thing. He'd make as many of those bastards pay as he could; he'd make some of them cry and wish they'd never come here. Then he sighed and looked at the ground. He gazed at the dry rock and sand at his feet, the ground he'd stood on for all these years. He felt a twinge of sadness. He remembered marrying his wife all those years ago when she was but a slip of a girl, and now she'd been in this ground for the last five years. He thought about how he'd surely be joining her soon in Heaven, then he heard a faint sound in the distance. He looked up. The hum of motors coming from the town. He straightened up and looked ahead, his grip firm on his rifle.

"They're on their way, boys," he called out with steel in his voice. "Let's give 'em hell."

We are the dead.

Away in the distance, far from the gunfire and sounds of desperate, doomed battle, the Task Force continued digging in at the Billabong. Over the next week, as they settled into a relaxed routine of camping out, waiting for the war to pass them by, the men found themselves looking forward to the visits of men from the nearby town, who were coming out every night to personally get to know the brave Americans who had come to help fight for Australia.

In many cases, the men had prior military service, and war stories of their own experiences with American soldiers in Afghanistan, Iraq and Syria. In other cases, they had never met an American, and were curious. They always brought along some good tuck, drinks, and others special things to share, and to help keep the Marines from becoming frustrated and bored with the long period of idleness.

By the time Captain Thorne arrived with fresh intelligence on the Chinese preparations for their advance from Charters Towers, the men knew that their short holiday was coming to an end.

The men gathered around as Thorne read what he had. The spirited defense put up by the local militia at the Blackjack crossroads just west of Charters Towers, with numerous snipers distributed along the many hills and rocky features, proved to be a great annoyance to the Chinese. It may have ended quickly; however, when word had gotten out about the fifteen hundred civilians murdered at the Racetrack, farmers and former soldiers were drawn to the area like fireflies, looking to find a way to kill at least one invader each.

Eventually the stream of fresh militiamen was cut off by the increased strength of the 124th Mechanized Division, which began to push farther and farther out with patrols in force, clearing the area of harassment out to a two hundred kilometer range, paving the way for their next advance westward, towards Julia Creek and the Billabong.

The younger soldiers and the more office-bound officers just took these last words at face value – "clearing the area of harassment". But the more experienced men, like Rideout and Gannon and the other vets had the imagination to know what bravery and fear and courage and blood had been expended by the men at Blackjack crossroads. Many of the Billabong men looked down in contemplation.

"That's all for now, boys," Thorne concluded his briefing, and then turned around and walked away.

From the intelligence that had been collected by the Special Forces men with Maj Blakely and Captain Thorne, it was clear that the 124th Division, PLA, was now fully deployed into Charters Towers and being rapidly re-supplied, making ready to continue their advance. All that seemed to hold them back were delays in building up additional stockpiles of the fuel, oil, water, spares and other war-fighting materials that would be required for the second-line and third-line logistical support for the 124th.

However, by the end of the third week after the massacre, the 124th Division was ready to advance. What surprised Lieutenant Colonel Weir, now back at the CJOC directing the intelligence gathering operation from Katherine, was that the logistical supplies being stockpiled in Charters Towers seemed to be far more than was necessary for a single division. There also seemed to be an over-emphasis on mobile air defenses. These included the Hangqi-17, the Chinese version of the Soviet-era designed Buk/SA11 Gadfly, a medium ranged self-propelled Surface to Air Missile, SAM, with a 200nm range against cruise missiles, smart bombs, unmanned aerial vehicles, fixed and rotary wing aircraft. And there was also the Chinese developed QianWei-2 "Vanguard-2" man-portable, shoulder launched, all-aspect infrared RADAR-guided, fire-and-forget missile. Perhaps more of a concern than the HQ-17s, which could be unreliable and easily jammed, the QW-2 was a newer missile, produced in massive numbers by China since 2001, and equipped with a dual-band passive IR seeker. To make matters worse, the QW-2 had also been given upgraded resistance to flares, chaff and other countermeasures. In the hands of well-trained personnel, it would provide a very effective air defense canopy out to a range of 3 miles and up to 10,000 feet. It seemed as though the Chinese were setting up an entire Anti-Air Brigade, deploying something of an over-capacity in terms of highly mobile and very sophisticated air defense weapons systems.

One of the Priority Intelligence Requests, PIR, pushed forward by Lieutenant Colonel Weir back in the CJOC was to determine whether the enemy was deploying variants of the PL-9-D. The PL9 was a concern not only because of its ten mile lateral and 24,000 foot vertical range, but also because of its 95% single-shot kill probability. If there were many PL-9-Ds in the area then it would be clear that the Chinese intended to protect more than a single division along the Charters – to – Cloncurry line of advance. That could spell disaster for the Allies, as such an extensive and integrated SAM umbrella would give the Chinese forces regional air superiority and the ability to conduct air operations with impunity while denying any use of the same airspace to the Allies.

If the PLA also got their hands on a larger runway and found a way to deploy high-readiness fighter aircraft and perhaps some type of airborne early warning aircraft farther to the west, then they would actually have regional *air supremacy*.

Soon enough, the reason for the long pause and over-the-top buildup was explained by the earth-shaking arrival of heavy armor, artillery, and unending convoys of an entirely unexpected unit at Charters Towers.

With everything riding on the disposition of the Chinese units when the expected advance commences, Lieutenant Colonel Weir ordered Major Becker to send out one of his teams in the Charters Towers area to capture, *at any cost*, a few prisoners from the newly arrived unit which was setting up a bed-down area just north of the water-tower, on the west side of town.

Without giving a great deal of detail on how they accomplished their mission, the two surviving members of the eight man team who had set out on the mission were able to hand-off the captured PLA Communications Specialist, for interrogation by a uniquely talented team that Major Becker had sent forward and had waiting for the fresh prisoner at a remote cattle station south of the A6 highway, thirty kilometers west of Charters Towers.

It had only taken the Becker's torture team four hours to break the young conscript before he sung like a bird for Yao Ming, Major Weir's ace in the hole.

Sunny Yao, after being intercepted on the highway by Major Becker on his tour of the front line communities in Queensland and New South Wales, had accompanied the team as they linked up with small units of the Royal Australian Army's 2nd Division, local militia units, and some of the more well-managed militia groups that were harassing the advancing units of the People's Liberation Army. Sunny quickly proved to be indispensable, not only for his perfect command of Chinese languages and accent-free English, but also for the close bond of trust that Major Becker had for the young man, making Sunny's translations of the radio intercepts and verbal interviews of Chinese subjects tortured by the Australian Special Forces and Marines of the MAGTFA to be without the uncertainty that normally comes when third parties are used for translation services.

Both the Australian Army and the Americans had had negative experiences related to bad intelligence generated by locally employed persons used as translators in Afghanistan and Syria, so the demand for Sunny's skills was high. For his contribution to the Allied Cause, Major Becker gave Sunny a field – designation as a member of his personal staff, and put him on the payroll of the MAGTFA as a civilian contractor reporting directly to the CJOC J2 Intelligence Section via Major Becker or Captain Thorne in his absence.

According to Sunny Yao, what the conscript gave up provided the CJOC with an entirely new picture of the enemy's plans for the sector.

Despite the trust given to Sunny, the information still had to be verified. However, that could be done by collecting long-range digital images of the insignia, markings, recognition features and observations of the standard pattern of vehicles of the new unit deploying into the area, and, if lucky, a few more prisoners. *However, they come at such a high cost*, thought Major Blakely. So while he continued his due diligence to validate the Intel, he had Captain Thorne brief it to Task Force Billabong with his own personal assessment of its reliability.

The was detailed, accurate, and timely and had an immediate impact on the personnel, particularly the Marines. The tone at the Billabong camp tightened up, with the men sharpening their bayonets, preparing their weapons, and redoubling their already strenuous fitness routines.

They were getting ready to go to war.

At about the same time, *Zhong Jiang* ranked Lieutenant-General Leung was in his Command Post set up in the auditorium at Lord Byng Academy in Charters Towers, receiving the latest intelligence reports from the Army Group North's Battle Staff.

"Before we move on to our own forces, show me those aerial photographs again, from Hughenden all the way to Cloncurry."

"General!" replied the Intelligence officer.

As he clicked through the slides, displayed on one of the 56-inch plasma screens that they had inherited courtesy of the boarding school, at the front of the horse-shoe of folding tables that made up General Leung's Command Post, he looked to the Lieutenant General for a nod to move on to each successive slide. From time to time the General would ask questions about the occasional cattle station, farm, cross-roads or other location on the 400 kilometer route from the Forward Edge of the Battle Area, FEBA, to the final objective in the Queensland Sector, the town of Cloncurry, which had been assessed as the Operational Center of Gravity for the Allies.

The final cross-roads town before the long, solitary highway through Northern Territory to their ultimate objective of Darwin, the capture of Cloncurry would give the Chinese absolute control of all ground-based movement in the region.

Based on the intelligence, it was clear that the enemy's main effort would be a defensive line comprised of the Australian Army's 1st Brigade and a Battalion of US Marines from the MAGTFA who were busily preparing entrenched positions and engineering improvements at Cloncurry, where the Allies were expected to put up one final, desperate attempt to stop the juggernaut that Lieutenant General Leung now commanded.

With elements of both the 41st and 42nd Group Armies now fully deployed in Queensland, General Leung enjoyed the two stars now on his shoulder – the NATO equivalent of a three-star General. *Once I have Queensland sewn up, General Hengyan has to give me the 20th "All Brigade" Group Army to serve as my strategic reserve in Queensland while I alternate fully five Regiments in turn as we leap-frog our way through to Darwin and onwards to Perth in the west, and south through Alice Springs to Adelaide,* he thought, relishing the prestige of having an entire Field Army Group under his command, with five Regiments forming the two Divisions pressing westward and the remaining three Divisions of his two Group Armies, 41st and 42nd Gas, deployed mostly in the vital coastal areas of Queensland.

The 20th Group Army is one of General Bing's own units. He'll have to promote me to Er-Chi Shang Chiang grade! He thought to himself, visualizing the *I-Chi Shang Chiang*, General Byng – future Emperor Byng – putting the three-star epaulet on his shoulder, making Leung the western equivalent of a four-star General, a Chinese General Eisenhower.

He brought his attention back to the pictures.

"So there has been no activity in the Richmond to Julia Creek sector?"

"None, General. Since they completed the evacuation there's been nothing but the occasional dingo there. It's deserted. Scorched earth. You see here? They set their petrol tanks off, and the engineers from 3 Combat Engineering Regiment brought down the water tower. 'No worries', as the Australians say." He smiled at his little joke, but the General continued staring coldly. The officer got back to business. "We'll just bring along more of those captured Reverse Osmosis Water Purification Units and a few extra water bowsers to make up for the loss. Once we capture Julia Creek we'll be able to move our logistics base of operations forward, get the ROWPUs operational, and begin stockpiling for the next push with the 370th Regiment rotating into the breach first."

"But won't that clog up the highway? I mean, it's already a traffic jam, what with moving both the 124th and 163rd Divisions along with the Air Defense Brigade from the 41st Group Army up from Charters Towers. We have to put the follow-on Regiments of the 163rd Division up the road first and then follow up with their log trains...and the front line units, the 370th, 371st and 372nd Regiments of the 124thth Division last."

At risk of interrupting the General, Colonel Wu interjected: "General, we've gone over this carefully with your staff, and they agree that we have the right balance here. We're moving the two divisions up in six waves of a Brigade each with a log train interspersed between each Regiment. Except for the first of the 372nd, Colonel Yip's Regiment, who we are now holding at Emerald until they are full-strength. They have fallen out of the order of march - some delay with their Combat Engineering Battalion stuck up in Cairns. Anyhow, as long as we can leap-frog one Regiment through the lines at a time, at the towns designated as re-assembly areas, and replenish them in place as they sort themselves out in individual Regiments before the major engagements. Our sequence will work better that way and we can stick to your original timetable."

Not convinced, the General pressed: "But what if we do not encounter as much resistance as our Intelligence Directorate expects? Won't we run the risk of seeing our tanks and APCs sit idle, with an open road in front of them and no more gas in the tank, like the Germans in '41?"

"General, this won't be another 'Operation Barbarossa'. We have enough air power to cover our logistics lines of communications. The enemy has less than a full squadron of F/A-18s still operational at Katherine and Darwin, with the destruction of their base at Tindal, so they won't be able to penetrate our air defense umbrella to interdict our supplies. So what we send up the road at this end will make it through all the way to the front like xiangqui marbles down a pipe. All we have to do is schedule the log trains in the same sequence as we rotate our front-line units in before the next phase of advance, as per the timetable."

"No."

"General?"

"No. I do not accept your recommended Course of Action."

"But General, you want us to begin the advance on Thursday, don't you? If you make any drastic changes to the plan at this late stage we will have to re-write the orders altogether, and there isn't sufficient time. You..."

"Shut up and listen, Colonel Wu." said the General, in a voice so quiet that the entire Battle Staff stopped breathing in order to hear him. There could be an opportunity for promotion for some unlucky Lieutenant-Colonel, if General Leung were to execute his chief of staff for his insolence.

"No. You invoked Barbarossa. So let's discuss it in those terms. I want you to make your 'assumption critical for planning' as the enemy puts it in their operational planning process, that the enemy *will* fold like the Russians did at Smolensk. As you say, they won't have enough air power to make a dent in ours – we have regional air superiority. And the Air Force assures me that we'll have air supremacy when their additional tankers arrive. So I accept your assessment of our air defenses as a fact. But you are not thinking strategically over the long term here. Unlike General von Brock, we *will not* over-run our logistics and face a terrible, Napoleonic disaster in the coming winter."

"Winter, General? But General, you've just heard the meteorologists tell us that the nuclear winter won't affect us here in the southern hemisphere for another six months. Plenty of time to wipe out those Marines and take Darwin."

"That's what the Germans thought about what was left of the Russians at Klin. I've been there myself, you know, and seen the Panzer that the Russians put on a pedestal in Solnechnogorsk to mark the farthest the Germans got into Moscow. To this day it marks the offensive culmination of Operation Typhoon, when they ran out of gas and were hit by a brutally cold winter and the tide was turned.

"Well that's not going to happen to me. No, Colonel Wu, I want you to *completely invert the orders.* Lead off with a logistics train for the 3 Regiments from the 163rd Division, then their 3 Regiments themselves. Send a Battalion ahead to seize Julia Creek until the first log train arrives. Have the engineers follow, to begin putting together the fuel farms, and then have the 370th, 371st and 372nd Regiments from 124th Division pass through the 163rd Division at Julia Creek and advance in convoy rather than combat formation until their leading patrols come into contact with the Marines at Cloncurry, at which time the Regiments of the 124th switch into combat formations and press on into engagement with the defenders at Cloncurry. On their heels, have the second log train, for the 163rd Division ahead of the 163rd itself. Have this log train push through to be as near to the Cloncurry front as possible, and have them improvise an assembly area in that flat terrain about 30 kilometers west of Cloncurry."

Following the General's extremely aggressive line of thought, the Colonel wrapped his mind around the new concept of ops.

"You mean here, just west of where the A3 comes up?"

"Yes. That will be the logistics base for the two divisions from the 42nd Group Army, ready to resupply them after they wipe out the defenders at Cloncurry."

"So with them we fortify Cloncurry and replenish the 42nd for what, two weeks instead of the 30 days the schedule lays out, and we have the 163rd pass through Cloncurry, and take the lead, to press on right away? How far, Mount Isa?" asked the Colonel, now fully grasping the audacity of his general.

"Exactly. By that time, the 20th Division from 41st Group Army will be moving up to join us, and we will have already moved our logistics support over what, 500 kilometers west of here. That will have us in Darwin and Katherine fully two months ahead of schedule and long before the winter sets in. The enemy will not be able to reconstitute their defenses that fast – we'll be inside their OODA loop.

"So those are your orders? I understand the directed COA. Your innovative plan to completely invert the orders will simplify matters greatly for us, as it does not require a complete re-planning of the entire campaign. It really is a stroke of genius, General." The Colonel knew how to kiss ass, and pull his own out of the fire in the process.

Three days later, Highway A6 rumbled with two full Divisions on the road or moving into line behind those that had already departed. There was a continuous stream of tanks, infantry fighting vehicles, light armored vehicles, reconnaissance vehicles, water trucks, fuel bowsers and an astonishing variety of engineering support, air defense, transport support and command vehicles stretching from Hughenden for two hundred kilometers to the west.

If the enemy had been able to penetrate some strike aircraft into the sector it would have been a killing spree like the Americans had in the First Iraq war, making the long lines of Iraqi soldiers flowing out of Kuwait into a macabre highway of death. As it was, the worst thing about the unending columns of the 42nd Group Army was the constant annoyance of bumper-to-bumper driving, their normally much more disciplined vehicle spacing now totally out the window thanks to General Leung's audacious plan.

As a Regiment from the 163rd Division passed just a few hundred meters south of the Billabong camp, the fifty men of Task Force Billabong hunkered down to hug the shaking earth.

With Chinese fighter jets, helicopters and a variety of unmanned aerial vehicles patrolling the skies and providing top cover for the seemingly endless series of convoys, and highly mobile reconnaissance squads probing every dirt-path and animal track as far as twenty kilometers either side of the narrow highway, the Marines' very lives depended on the accident of geology that had created the illusion at the rock dome, making the entrance to their billabong invisible.

"Top, they're going to see us!" said one Lance Corporal, who was becoming shell-shocked after the excruciating hours of constant rumbling.

"Relax, Justin. I've felt this sort of shaking before," Top lied, "It's not as close as it feels. They can't see us, and if they do, we'll open up on them and then flee to the north, to those mountains the Aussies told us about," Top reassured the terrified young man.

It had been a mistake to mention their contingency plan, the one place they could run to if they were discovered. With all the air power buzzing in the skies the Marines would be quickly spotted and wiped out in a matter of minutes if they abandoned their camouflaged sanctuary and tried to run.

"Let's go there, Top! There's just too many of them. They'll come in here for water or something, and find us." Justin said, as he started to get up out his fox-hole as though he was going to run.

The lights went out for Justin as his Corporal butt-stroked him. He fell into his trench, unconscious but not permanently damaged.

He was the lucky one. The other Marines had to endure four more hours of rumbling before the entire Chinese Army – so it seemed – had passed by their position.

They were not detected.

On several occasions, Master Gunnery Sergeant Gannon, watching the images being transmitted from an optical system that had been set up near the dome and was being displayed on the monitor in his LAV deeper in the billabong. He saw a series of Chinese reconnaissance patrols, each in turn had driven right over the dome and then carried on farther north, each time coming with a few tens of meters of the hidden track leading to their sanctuary.

Each time the patrols must have assessed the terrain as impassable, and carried on with their patrol, keeping station with the massive force that was flowing west along the narrow highway.

By the end of the day of thunder, surprised to be alive, the Marines began to believe that the Chinese had all passed. They began making preparations for the next phase of the operation.

And then the next wave of Chinese units began to pass.

There were three more days of nearly continuous rumbling before it was all over and they received the signal to mount up.

"How sure are you about this, Jock?" asked Major Blakely.

"No doubt about it, Major. They've taken the bait. Looks like they have pushed their log trains ahead of their formation, other than this pesky Brigade that came in to 'sus' the town," said the intelligence Warrant Officer from the Australian Army.

"Any word from the townsfolk?"

"Yes. The recon teams reports that Pandas are going for the schools, the warehouses, and the other facilities, as per Lieutenant Colonel Weir's Combat Estimate. Other than that, Combat Engineer Brigade of the 124rd Division, which entrenched a defensive perimeter it's a whole lot of engineers and supply types transforming the town into one massive logistics supply base of operations. Similar logistics facilities have been set up another 30 kilometers to the east, and of course there's their massive fuel dump and logistics traffic jam in Julia Creek, as we discussed earlier."

"And your observation teams in the outback, they can be relied upon for these numbers, they are accurate?"

"Dogs balls, mate, they're absolutely solid. They have those PLA recce booklets Lieutenant Colonel Weir provided, and at some of the cattle stations we have our own people – trained Int Ops to guide the locals – so yes, Major, this is good data."

"So they've sent two divisions up, with enough supplies to take them how far, Mount Isa?"

"Not just that, mate. Their logistics and air defense units are way out of proportion, as are all those fuel farms. We assess this as being sufficient to put a Corps sized formation up the road all the way to Darwin, provided they don't peel off more than a regiment or two in the Cloncurry-to-Mount Isa sector. More likely they'll begin to move up another division into reserves, once they finish emptying the first two Divisions out of Charters Towers.

"Look here, Major," the Australian Warrant Officer brought up a new schematic on his computer. "This is the ORBAT you had prepared as of yesterday." The image showed a broad red arrow sweeping west from Charters Towers, with a diamond shaped box around the number 42, with a large "XX" under the diamond, indicating Enemy unit of Division size. Beside the diamond was "163rd", representing the 163rd Armored Regiment of the 42nd Group Army, People's Liberation Army. A similar division, the 124th, was shown at Charters Towers. Farther to the east, along the gold coast, were four or five other divisions, of the 42nd, 41st, and 38th Group Armies, along with a variety of other units ranging in size from Regiment to Battalion, distributed across the occupied zone.

"Yes, that's what we had before your latest inputs. Based on what we now have out of Charters Towers, go on, Warrant."

After a couple of clicks, the sweeping black arrows thickened, and an additional number, 124th stacked on top of the 163rd, along with a symbol for air defenses, and another for command and control.

"Major, I think we agree, this is now a more accurate representation of the ORBAT of the enemy forces deploying towards Mount Isa. We have the full weight of the 42nd Group Army, two divisions, and they are augmented with an Air Defense Brigade, robust Engineering attachments and a follow-on force comprised of the 20th Division from the 41st Group Army. Therefore we upgrade this to an Armored Corps," he said, clicking the computer and making "XXX" under the "42" diamond. It went without saying that the "XXX" would be upgraded to "XXXX" if the 20th Division were moved farther to the west, as that would make the enemy formation a full "Army" size designation, with well over 120,000 soldiers.

It also went without saying that the massive, reckless commitment the enemy was making at Cloncurry, and the speed with which they were moving their logistics and Anti-Air defenses forward, the enemy advance was unfolding pretty much exactly as Colonel Ferebee had briefed the operational planners of the CJOC. It had been left to Major Becker and the Australian Special Forces teams to collect the intelligence necessary to confirm the accuracy of Ferebee's forecast.

"So it's all over, then. Phase Three, I mean. They'll be closing with our defenders at Cloncurry by what, 0600 hrs?"

"Actually, it appears that lead elements of their 370th Regiment will be moving into line by 0200hrs. But nothing we can't shove back when they make first contact. The real trick will be the timing with Thornie's team inside the town and your lot at the billabong near Julia Creek."

"Too right," said Major Blakely, in his best imitation of the Australian slang. "OK. Give Captain Thornie the revised timings and mission go-code, and I'll activate the team at the Billabong. Colonel O'Neil, just west of Cloncurry has already been cleared weapons hot by Colonel Ferebee in the CJOC. O'Neil's battalion will engage the enemy upon first contact at his discretion."

"Well, seem to engage them, anyhow," said the Warrant Officer, sharing a conspiratorial smile with Major Becker.

Wan Shanyu had a dark, dirty secret that he had to keep from his fellow soldiers in 4th Battalion, 370th Regiment, 124th Division, 42nd Group Army. At the bottom of the food chain, the simple infantry soldier knew that he was among the least well supported soldier in the campaign. Wan was a conscript, and as an infanteer he knew that he was highly expendable. He always had been, even when he was a simple farm boy. Wan was originally from the remote village of Hanwuyi, in what had once been rich grasslands of the Tarin Basin in the western-most part of the region his people called Shinjang. The Chinese called it Xinjiang.

It had been six years since he abandoned the fantasy of restoring any productivity out of the small patch of land that his forefathers had worked for generations. By abandoning his homeland he was in good company, as many of his ancestors had been among the 200,000 people of Yueshi, or 'yue-shi' –'Moon Clan' - origins. In ancient times the Moon Clan had had been pushed out of their homeland by the expanding Qin state, who would ultimately go on to become the founders of the Chinese Empire.

One aspect of his secret was that he was Muslim – but that was not the worst of it. As a Yuezhi, part of an ethnic group that was more Indo-European than it was Chinese, he was dually cursed. Of course Wan had suppressed these facts, first from his employers in the wild west of the Xinjiang oilfields, and more recently from his fellow soldiers in the lowly 4th infantry Battalion.

Being a Chinese Muslim was the least of his worries. He knew that there was an unspoken degree of tolerance for spiritual views as long as they were not expressed openly or promoted. Besides, with his homeland sharing borders with the Islamist state of Pakistan, and just about as far as one could get from the vast majority of China's population in the east of China, people from his region truly were foreigners in their own country.

But for Wan, his religion was not the issue. The true terror in his heart and worry constantly on his mind came from the new wave of ethnic purism among the 'real Chinese'.

He had barely even heard of the issue before, but in the last few months there had been something of a hysteria working its way through the ranks of the People's Liberation Army, with everybody seemingly trying to prove that they were direct descendants of "Beijing Man", once termed "Peking Man."

Wan did not understand much of the debate, something about there being archeological evidence that proved that while the Yangshao culture had reached western China from Indo-

European origins, there was an older, indigenous Chinese culture that had already arisen in Eastern China ages before. Contrary to western beliefs of the origins of the Chinese, the new theory was that these Lonshan Chinese diffused *east to west*.

That fit with Wan's simple understanding that his people had been all but pushed out of China to the west, by the more dominant and ancient Chinese culture. But what was new to the long-established story was the notion that these Chinese, the 'real Chinese' according to the current wave of cultural nationalism, had evolved from *Homo erectus* in China. That they did not evolve from *Homo sapiens* who spread out of Africa about 100,000 years ago, as western archeologists have determined that the rest of the world's population had originated from.

What this meant was that those whose blood went all the way back to the *Homo erectus* Beijing Man, the 750,000 year old fossil unearthed near Beijing in the 20th Century, were essentially a *different race from everybody else in the world*.

Soldiers wanting to fit in to this new hysteria, and not to be seen as sub-humans in contrast to the more ancient people that the *real Chinese* had evolved from, went so far as to sharpen their back teeth, apply make-up to their cheeks and even to constantly hold their facial expressions in such a way as to emphasize the broad check bones and facial structure of the Chinese *Homo erectus pekinensis* ancestor – and to distance themselves from the 'lesser breed', the African-originated *Homo sapiens*.

The importance of demonstrating that one was from the *Homo erectus* branch of the Human genus was particularly important in the military operation in Australia, of course, as the theory also supported the view that because Australian aborigines shared a great many of the traits of *Homo erectus*, along with the Chinese. Therefore the Chinese invasion of Australia was more of a home-coming than an invasion by a foreign culture.

What's more important, and what had caused Wan some long, sweaty nights, was the rumor that once the conquest of Australia was complete, and perhaps of the world at large, only Chinese of *erectus* origins would have any rights at all. Everybody else, the conquered peoples of the world, those of uncertain or mixed origins, and even loyal soldiers of the PLA who lacked enough of the distinctive *erectus* traits would be treated as sub-human.

To Wan, it brought to mind images of the ethnic nationalism, eugenics and extermination camps of the Nazi era, and chilled the large-headed man with the thin-walled cranium. He was sure that his *sapiens* ancestry stood out like a giraffe amongst a herd of zebras.

As for the herd itself, Wan knew that the majority of soldiers stayed out of the debate. Men like Colonel Pan and other senior officers had spoken out against such nonsense. These men had given Wan hope that it would all go away like so many other fads. But the number of men who were actively promoting the idea, while still relatively few, seemed to be gaining traction. Like the brown-shirts of the 1930's, these zealous supporters of the Beijing Man ideology were so aggressive and ruthless that their impact was gaining a life of its own within the PLA.

He did not know it at the time, but it must have been working on him at a sub-conscious level as he waited in his trench for the battle to begin. He sat alone thinking as the two other men assigned to his Observation Post were catching a few minutes of sleep after a long night of digging into the hard terrain.

The internal stresses battling within him must have come to some determination because the moment that Wan heard the air-raid alarm, and saw the men and women of the air defense regiment rushing to activate their weapons systems, his decision had bridged the gap from subconscious to conscious.

I'm on the wrong side! Wan thought as he looked westward, expecting to see the SU-30 Mark I, Flanker-H long-range fighters of his Indian cousins approaching.

The aircraft of the Indian Air Force were well beyond Wan's visual range. When they were detected by the HT-233 passive threat detection system they were still over five hundred nautical miles away. There he was, sitting in his fox-hole in the hills above 'Chinaman Creek' Dam, on the west side of the Cloncurry River. He knew that the other side was on its way. And he knew that he was supposed to be alert, scanning the area assigned to his Observation Post. But he was not himself any more…

The OP was a good three kilometers from the safety of the town. A town that was now thick with military vehicles and men getting ready for the push to the west. Exposed on the west flank, overlooking the town's fresh-water reservoir with a name that was surely offensive to any Chinese, Wan knew that until the lead elements of the 370th Regiment began to push out towards Mount Isa, some 120 kilometers farther to the west, his and the dozen other OPs scattered across the west side of the Cloncurry river represented the front lines.

He was at the point in time and space where the Allies could crash into the PLA, in the perfect spot to bear witness to the war. A war that had finally come to Wan Shanyu, after so many months of training and secrecy. After a complex series of train, sea, truck and foot travels that took him and so many other bewildered soldiers from China to the most remote place he had ever seen.

All fear had somehow left him. He felt himself in a surreal situation. No longer having any personal connection to the outcome of the battle. He would either wind up dead, an enemy POW, or be doomed to the ultimate fate of suffering and pain that sub-humans like himself will ultimately receive if the General Bing and his *pure Chinese race* come to rule the world. Wan felt that he was merely an observer of the historical clash between two ancient human races. He would not lift a finger to help decide the battle in either direction, he knew.

So when a small group of men moved past his arc of fire, darting from one gully to another just below the railway bridge between Chinaman Creek Dam and his OP, he did not fire. Nor did he take any action to wake up the two others in his OP. He simply watched to see what the small group of men would do next.

The enemy must not have seen that the dark spot between two boulders hid the sharp eyes of Wan Shanyu, nestled into position as he was for his thirty minute watch.

Had Wan taken a shot at them, or raised the alarm, perhaps the four-man team made up of two Marines and two Australian Special Forces personnel would not have been able to set themselves up on the hill opposite town. They would not have had such a clear view of the Chinese units marshaling in the town of Cloncurry. Had the Marines and Australians been taken out, certainly other such teams would have tried to pick up the slack. But they would not have been in as good a position as this particular team had been in, able to activate their LASER target designator at the appointed time; able to illuminate their primary target.

The laser-guided missiles were all for show, in fact. The two dozen medium- range missiles would be fired just over two hundred kilometers from Cloncurry. They were supersonic cruise missiles, which accelerated to Mach 2.8 as they closed with initial target coordinates before picking up the pre-programmed signature of the LASER-illuminated targets.

But the real devastation about to be inflicted on the Chinese was not going to come exclusively from the 200kg warheads of the cruise missiles. Those would be just the opening move in complex game that Major Becker and Captain Thorne had conceived of several weeks before; one that relied heavily on the predicted behavior of the Chinese commander, Lieutenant-General Leung back in his Command Post in Charters Towers.

In that regard, the expensive and impossible-to-replace missiles fired from the dozen SU-30s would have been almost as effective had they been assigned in to strike warehouses or random targets in the crowded staging area that Cloncurry had become. The effect would have been the same.

"Incoming aircraft! Range: three hundred twenty kilometers!" reported the weapons system operator reported from his cramped console in the WZ551 Armored Command Vehicle. Calling out the data displayed on his console, from the array of passive and active threat-detection systems of the Air Defense Battalion protecting the two fully divisions assembled at Cloncurry for the coming battle.

In General Leung's Command Post, the report of inbound enemy aircraft was soon reinforced by the tactical plot which had been relayed from the Air Defense Regiment's central command and control trailer in Cloncurry, which gathered the data from the WZ551's and other air defense detection systems and missile batteries.

The batteries were autonomous, able to operate independently. However, the onward transmission of data to higher headquarters first passed through the C4I trailer, for integration and encryption. The few seconds lost to processing were insignificant in the big picture, because when General Leung saw the rapidly increasing number of icons, each signifying an air-breathing threat confirmed through electronic sensory measures as having the emitter characteristics of enemy SU30 and SU27 fighter-bomber aircraft, he was thrilled.

"Just as expected, the enemy is making their last stand in the Cloncurry to Mount Isa sector. Send the CAP from Charters Towers to reinforce the Cloncurry sector," he ordered.

"But Sir, if we send the Combat Air Patrol away, we'll be vulnerable here. We've stripped out our own air defenses to throw everything up the road. We have no eyes to the north or east," replied the Air Defense subject matter expert.

"We have long-range passive and active detection towards the west and south, do we not?" demanded Leung.

"Yes, sir, fully operational."

"And if an attack came from the west, it would have to pass the Cloncurry sector first. If from the south-west, out of Adelaide, we would pick them up in plenty of time to re-task assets back to cover, is that not correct, Major?" Without waiting for a reply, General Leung went on. "And do we not have total control of Indonesia to the north, and Cairns to the east?"

Looking exceedingly uncomfortable, the Air Weapons expert knew that it was pointless. "Yes, Sir. We can adjust. However I still believe that sending the CAP away leaves us vulnerable."

"Noted, Major. Now send the CAP along with all available interceptors from Weipa and Cairns," the General added.

This time the major did not bother to raise his objections that deploying strike aircraft from the dry-bones base at Weipa, and the main base for the PLA Air Force in Cairns, would strip the entire north-east sector of strike aircraft. But he also understood what the General was thinking. It was an audacious gamble, to concentrate all of both patrols and strike aircraft, perhaps thirty fighters in all, with everything committed to responding to the inbound Indian Air Force jets.

He passed on the orders and watched as the Interceptor Squadron in Weipa and the Air Wing in Cairns acknowledged the orders, and announced the estimated launch times.

"Good. But that ETA puts them on top of Cloncurry about 15 minutes after the enemy attack begins. Tell them to go full-throttle, after-burners, to get there as fast as possible."

"Sir! You are aware that they will be bingo fuel when they arrive? They would not have sufficient reserves to make it back to base."

"That's your problem, Major, not mine. Get a couple of IL76's up to tank them on the way back, or divert them to land wherever you have to – in Longreach, Hughendon, Winton or on a stretch of highway for all I care. We have this one opportunity to smash the enemy's few remaining strike aircraft – and take them out of this war altogether," General Leung said, excitedly.

In his mind, the Air Defense expert went over the risk management equations, calculating that the probability of enemy air attack on the soon-to-be undefended areas was "remote"; that the impact of such a strike would be "severe"; and concluded with an operational risk assessment of "medium". It fell well within the Lieutenant General's level of operational risk management authority. For anything higher, of course, it would have required a command risk assessment from General Bing himself – with all of the personal risk associated with attempting to pin such a dangerous gamble on the supreme military commander. Having satisfied himself that the risk management decision had been taken at the appropriate level, and that he was not personally responsible for the outcome, he then set himself to the task.

After giving the orders, the Air Defense major in General Leung's command staff had completed his role. All that was left was for the sequence of events to unfold, choreographed as much by the hopes of the allied planners at the CJOC in Katherine as by the ego and aggressiveness of Lieutenant-General Leung in the Command Post of the 42nd Group Army in Charters Towers, Queensland.

From his vantage point five kilometers outside of town, on the extreme west flank of the security perimeter, the ambivalent young soldier from the Tarin Basin kicked his two sleeping comrades into startled alertness and passed on the general alert that had been radioed across the comm net to all units in the Cloncurry area. He did not mention the four-man team that he had seen a few minutes before.

The three men watched the skies, two of them nervously, and one with aplomb. Wan felt by this point entirely detached from any personal stake in the outcome of the battle. He felt no particular stake in which way it went; only a strange, detached curiosity at the events unfolding around him. The other two men were terrified, as if the enemy would expend valuable missiles, bombs, or 50-calibre rounds against their fox-hole.

Wan turned to the east and looked back at the small town. He could make out the few remaining infantry fighting vehicles and transport trucks rolling westward, out of town. It amazed him how many had passed through in just a 24-hour period. He had observed a half-dozen regiments, which he knew were from both the 163rd Division and his own 124th Division.

Wan had seen the 370th Regiment leading the column westward towards Mount Isa. Obviously, even to Wan, the task for the 370th was to advance as recon in force. *They must have reached Mount Isa by now,* he thought, *it's only 120 kilometers from here, and they left what, eight hours ago?*

Wan was interrupted from his idle calculations when he saw men running around at a number of locations in town. He quickly realized that it was not the men of the two mechanized infantry divisions that were swarming to their equipment, but rather, the men of the Air Defense Regiment, removing covers from their batteries and bringing their SAM sites into full readiness. *Here we go*, he thought.

In his WZ551 Command vehicle, the weapons system operator was highly confident that his battery would make a few kills. Not only were there so many juicy targets appearing on the western extreme of the long-range plot, pushed to his own system from the HT 233 passive array serving his battery, but the Air Defense Battery and PLA in general also had the advantage. The enemy air attack had been predicted, and was expected to be comprised of up to two squadrons variants of the Russian designed SU27's and SU30's of the Indian Air Force, and possibly a squadron of American built F/A 18 Super Hornets of the Royal Australian Air Force.

The system operator had been provided with the full range of jamming frequencies, threat-detection wavelengths, electronic counter-measure signatures and other technical data to be loaded in the battery's computers in preparation for the expected attack.

As he watched the men of his battery remove the arming pins and dust covers from the self-propelled missile trailers that made up his SAM site, he was as confident as his superiors that the Air Defense Regiment would not only fend off at least 95% of the incoming missiles, but that the integrated, layered air defense canopy that they had assembled at Cloncurry would withstand subsequent waves of the air attack, culminating in the destruction of much, if not all, of the enemy's offensive aircraft.

As the first volley of missiles began to fly out of his SAM battery he looked at the display to follow their progress. His mind was focused on the display, doing mental gymnastics as he calculated closing velocities in his mind. So when he sensed that the floor of his command vehicle began to raise, along with half an acre of perfectly flat, well-graded parking area, his mind had just enough time to register an instant of surprise.

There was not enough time for his synapses to communicate any complex analysis of the sensation, as his brain was instantly overwhelmed with the sensation of his body being smashed to pulp by the shock wave. He was dead; pulverized by the shock wave of the massive explosion before he had any conscious warning that he would die in a plume of rock and dust that had been thrown thirty meters into the air.

A ton of buried high explosives, in the form of a massive improvised explosive devices comprised of a dozen artillery shells, some C4 and a hard-wired detonation circuit will do that to you. That is, if you happen to park your Air Defense Battalion assets right on top of the pre-positioned explosives.

If he been in a position to look back on the sequence of events that had taken him to his end, the young technician might have traced it back to the "all clear" report that had been given by the sappers from the Engineering Battalion of the 124th Division, who had cleared away a few hastily implanted, easily discovered, Improvised Explosive Devices left by the enemy.

Had he asked himself why such a small town as Cloncurry would have had so many nicely graded, abandoned parking lots distributed around the periphery of their small town, he might have doubted the conclusion made by others that they were simply parking areas for the ubiquitous cattle-trains and agricultural equipment that passed through the cross-roads town.

But even if he had gotten that far, and suspected that the IEDs found by the engineers were simply diversions, he would never have expected that his own passing of the report of incoming waves of enemy aircraft, and Higher Headquarters' eagerness to wipe out the Indian and Australian fighters, would have caused them to launch their precious few squadrons of SU-27s, SU-30s, and J-11 fighters from Charters Towers, Weipa, Cairns, and Townsville.

"THREAT DETECTED!" commented the Electronic Support Measures warning system, as Squadron Leader Tanta closed to within two hundred and fifty nautical miles from the target area. Tanta read the emitter types, which matched with the data provided to him in the pre-mission intelligence briefing.

The Indian Air Force's fleet of Russian manufactured Sukhoi Su-30MKI Flanker long range fighters had the benefit if advanced avionics upgrades done by the Indian Air Force, making Squadron Leader Tanta's aircraft the most advanced strike aircraft in the region.

Tanta knew that the PLA Air Force had their own fleet of SU27s and SU30's and had most likely hacked the Indian Air Force enough to take away much of the IAF's technical advantages over their Chinese rivals.

But the BrahMos supersonic Air Launched Cruise missiles his aircraft carried, along with the eleven carried by the remainder of the dozen Su30's in the strike package, would be difficult for the enemy air defenders to shoot down. Tanta knew that with their high speed – four times that of the American made Tomahawk cruise missile – and with over thirty times as much kinetic energy, the 200 kilograms ALCM BrahMos was the most advanced weapon in the IAF's arsenal.

Too bad we have so few BrahMos left, he thought, as he watched the time-to-target numbers reduce rapidly on his Heads-Up-Display. Had they had even one single nuclear-tipped BrahMos left, the battle would have been over before it had begun. However, the IAF had not resolved the technical problems of mounting a nuclear warhead on the BrahMos when the war with China had begun, and was left with just a few dozen operational BrahMos missiles with conventional high explosive warheads after the devastation of the first few days of the war.

As it was, the dozen assigned to the Cloncurry strike, and the half-dozen for the northerly strike package committed to Weipa as part of the Cairns strike package, would just about expend their irreplaceable stockpile of cruise missiles.

Hope they take the bait, he thought, before giving the order.

"All Lancer units, GOOGLY," he said, invoking the code-word derived from the sport of cricket, giving the order for the

Su-30's to each fire their sole BrahMos missile at the designated target.

The targets themselves had been automatically assigned to each aircraft by the computer program in Tanta's aircraft, which was in communication with the other Lancers' computers in the strike package. The LASER designated targets were to be illuminated by Allied Special Forces personnel on the ground in the Cloncurry area. The targets were key elements of the very robust integrated air defense system which the PLA's Air Defense Regiment had established at Cloncurry, and had to go.

Despite his own Top Secret security clearance, Squadron Leader Tanta had no need to know the planning or intelligence that went into the target selection matrix. He had not been told that the Australian Special Forces and US Marines had come up with a carefully planned series of events which required a cruise missile strike against the enemy formation at Cloncurry.

He did not know that the dozen targets assigned to his strike mission were not the SAM missiles around the periphery; he did not know that the planners at the CJOC has assigned other resources to those peripheral batteries.

Despite the fact that Wan was looking directly at one of the air defense SAM batteries, he was startled when missiles began flying out of the rail launchers on the self-propelled vehicles. But no sooner had a half-dozen SAMs tore off westward towards the enemy aircraft that were closing in on Cloncurry, when suddenly a series of enormous explosions shook the earth below him and massive plumes of orange flame and grey smoke erupted one after another in the town.

Wan did not dive to the ground like his terrified compatriots. He stared in astonishment as perhaps twenty massive explosions tore the town apart.

The grey strange crackling smell and perfectly spaced pillars of smoke reminded him of videos he had seen of the carefully prepared blasts in the rock cuts of open pit mines, where massive chunks of hard rock are blasted into rubble for the mining trucks to haul away for processing.

And that was exactly what he was witnessing. Only in this case, while it was true that the sites of the blasts were carefully chosen by mining engineers, and the blast detonating sticks and additional nitrogen-based explosive grains were carefully placed under the supervision of qualified mining engineers, in this case the objective was not to uncover valuable mineral ore.

Rather, the mining engineers had actually covered the prepared blast sites with crushed rock, and then graded the areas to look like large, well-used parking areas. They had even gone so far as to park a few truck-trailers and vehicles on the sites to make them appear to be staging areas for the transport rigs and other vehicles that once plied the busy A6 highway from Charters Towers to Cloncurry, and beyond.

The work had been completed nearly a week before the enemy had begun to pay close attention to the area, with air surveillance from manned and unmanned aircraft.

Of course, the planners at General Leung's command post in Charters Towers had suspected dirty tricks, and had tasked sappers from the Engineering Battalion of the 370th Regiment, 124th Division, to look for IEDs and other dangers. And the sappers had done their job, finding and destroying two dozen IEDs which the Australian Army had constructed from artillery shells, packets of C4 and other military munitions.

However, the PLA's sappers had not considered looking deeper, and had not detected the ten-centimeter diameter holes drilled into the bedrock under the nicely graded parking lots. They had not discovered that these drill-holes went down a good ten meters each. They had not discovered that they were packed with enough mining explosives to convert the bedrock into pop-corn sized gravel – and to convert the Air Defense Batteries which were so conveniently placed on these parking areas scattered around the periphery of the town into shards of shrapnel, scraps of flesh, and unrecognized bits of bone.

Even with the hypervelocity of the BrahMos missiles and their 200 kilogram high explosive warheads, those air defense assets struck within the confines of Cloncurry by the Indian Air Force's cruise missiles, demolished as they were, were at least recognizable as having once been vehicles of some sort. The air defense assets destroyed by the Australian mining engineers' blasts, in contrast, had been utterly destroyed beyond all recognition.

When word reached the CJOC in Katherine from several of the Allied Special Forces teams, there was jubilation.

"Sir. We have another confirmation from Cloncurry. The cruise missiles cleaned up! All but two of the parking lots occupied by SAM sites went up on schedule. The two sites that failed were illuminated in time, and taken out by the BrahMos's. We got *all* the core C4ISR and Air Defense assets within town!"

The tone in the Command Post of the 42n Group Army was decidedly less cheerful.

"General, we are getting conflicting reports out of Cloncurry," said the Air Defense major, clearly distressed by what he was reading on his computer screens.

"Out with it, Major!" demanded a senior staff officer, voicing the General's thoughts at the major's hesitation.

"Sir, we have lost contact with the Air Defense Regiment."

"What do you mean? We lost their feed? Get a verbal report. How many enemy aircraft have they shot down?" demanded General Leung.

"That's just it, sir. *They are entirely off the net.* I don't know what happened. One minute we were getting reports of missiles launched from our SAM batteries, the next, we lost all sources of data," said the major, deeply distressed.

"Er, General. I can explain," said a Colonel from the 124th Division.

"Go ahead, Chang,"

"General. I'm getting reports from my Engineering Battalion – the one we held back to provide security to the logistics units –

anyhow, they report that enemy missiles struck the town. It appears that ten or twelve missiles struck."

"Ten? But there were no more than that reported inbound! We should have been able to shoot down most of those. What went wrong, Major?"

"I can't explain it, General. Unless they upgraded the propulsion system with those hypersonic motors, but the Indians were still years away from accomplishing that according to the intelligence reports. Perhaps the Indians found a way to interfere with our detection systems," the major offered.

"Bullshit. How could they interfere with the passive systems?"

"Sir. I have more coming in now," interjected the Colonel from the 124th. "There are reports that many of the explosions, which took out the Air Defense units, *preceded* the incoming missiles by as much as five to ten seconds."

There was silence in the CP.

"Are you telling me that they just blew up? Colonel, how could that happen?"

This time it was the ground forces Colonel's time to be uncomfortable and confused. "We may have missed something when we cleared those areas. Our sappers… They may have missed some IEDs," he began, trying to piece together everything that he was seeing on his own secure chats and other data. "From what I am seeing here, many of the explosions were unusual in appearance, extremely large, throwing up enormous amounts of debris. That's it, Sir!" he said, excitedly. "Drill rigs! I should have thought of this before. We had reports of some drill rigs having been left abandoned in the town. We assumed that they were just mining equipment for those big gold mines in the area. But they could have been used to set explosives deep under the town, beyond the depth that our sappers could detect," the Colonel concluded, feeling as if he had dodged a bullet.

"So you are telling me we have lost our Air Defense umbrella? All of it? And that the Australians used their mining technology to blow up the entire town? Is that what you are telling me, Colonel?"

"No, Sir! Yes, Sir. Well, yes and no," he finally settled his mind. "Yes, we have probably lost most if not all of the SAM batteries, but no, they did not blow up the entire town. They just blew up the areas where we located our SAM sites. The logistics supply areas, the fuel farms, the staging areas for the container-trucks, and the warehouses – those are all intact. We still hold the town. Even the bridge out of town is un-touched, so we are not cut off from the 163rd and the 124th Divisions. All we have lost is the Air Defense Regiment.

Partly relieved, the General turned his attention to the updated plot of the Mount Isa sector.

"So what's happening there now? Give me the air picture first."

"Sir. Our fighters closed with the enemy aircraft, but the SU-30's pulled back after they fired their cruise missiles. We did shoot down several aircraft. A handful of F/A 18s and a number of unidentified aircraft, perhaps thirty."

"Thirty? That's good, right? But why 'unidentified'?"

"We did not have enough signature or ECM data to verify what they were before our medium-range missiles shot them down, other than the Super-Hornets. The other aircraft could have been anything. Most likely they were SU27's that had stayed emissions-dark, and got caught with their pants down."

"Well, I hope you are right, that they are Su27's. Better keep a solid CAP over the area until we sort out how few fighters they have left. And move as many air defense assets as you can from here in Charters Towers – get them on the road ASAP – we need air defense to replace what we have lost in Cloncurry."

"But sir…" the major began, only to shut up when he saw the look in Leung's eyes. "Yes, Sir, we'll have the two batteries rolling within the hour. It will take them about a day and a half to reach Mont Isa."

"Very well. Keep the tankers up, 24/7 if you have to, and keep as many aircraft over that sector as you can muster," the General concluded and then turned his attention back to the Colonel. "Now, what's going on on the ground?"

"A bit of a disappointment, General. 2nd Batallion, 370th Regiment of the 124th entered Mount Isa unopposed. The Marines there pulled out across the bridge to the west side of the river. You can see where they entrenched," he showed the General on a map. "-on this ridge line to the north west, here, where the highway climbs up out of town on the west side of the river."

"And the Australians?"

"Very little resistance. Just enough to slow us down a bit coming into town. Looks like they were trying to buy time for the Marines to cut and run."

"Colonel, that does not sound right. The Marines don't have a reputation for fleeing from a fight, now do they?" the general asked, suspiciously.

"My thoughts exactly, Sir. I think they had deployed into town originally as a show of force, perhaps hoping we would pause until all three regiments of the 124th Division could be in position before moving in on the town. But as we moved so much faster than they expected – thanks to your brilliant plan – they must have fallen back to more defendable terrain on the rise out of town."

"When will the 370th be ready to attack?"

"I've given the order to commence immediately. We should have word soon, Sir."

"Excellent," Leung said, looking at some of the tactical data on the big screen TV's. "Don't give the enemy any time to prepare; just keep moving forward as fast as possible. Come to think of it, this puts some pressure on our timetable. We are moving faster than expected there. Better have the 163rd push their logistics dump from here," Leung said, indicating the massive fuel dump just east of Cloncurry, "to mount up and move through Cloncurry, and begin to establish a refueling base at Mount Isa by tomorrow."

"But sir, we don't have engineering support there anymore. We would have to pull the Combat Engineers of the 370th back from Cloncurry to do that, and they're busy with the wounded and fire-fighting at Cloncurry," said the colonel.

Not missing a beat, the detail-oriented General searched the tactical display for alternatives.

"What about this unit, at Julia Creek?"

"That's 2nd Battalion, Combat Engineers, from the 163rd. Yes, we could have them deploy to the dump this side of Cloncurry. It's only about eighty kilometers. But then once they pack up the bladders and get the fuel farm moving, we'll have to pull them back to Julia Creek. We need them there for security, and to help with the scheduled move of the 20th Division when we get into the next phase."

"Agreed. Now, I've got to go for a conference call with General Ma. When I get back in about two hours I want to hear that the 124th has cleared the west side of Mount Isa, and broken through the Marines line there on that rise," General Leung commanded as he got up and left the Command Post.

"Yes, General," bounced off of his back.

Four hours later, General Leung finally returned to the Command Post. He was pleased as punch to hear that the enemy lines had folded, that the 124th Division had pressed on two hundred kilometers farther west from Mount Isa, and were closing in on the Allies' hastily prepared position at Camooweal, right at the Queensland – Northern Territory border. The 163rd Division had driven right through Mount Isa and was arriving at an assembly area named 'Inca Creek'.

"So what's the problem?" asked General Leung, excitedly.

"Fuel, sir." Colonel Pan, the senior PLA Ground Forces member of the battle staff, spoke up. "We have outpaced even your aggressive timelines, and really have to pause the 163rd. As you recall, they were supposed to hold back at Mount Isa, to resupply, before leap-frogging through what was supposed to be a tired and battle-weary 124th. But as the enemy keeps falling back, the 124th just kept pressing ahead – those were your orders, after all – so it's not surprising that they have pressed ahead so far along the open road.

Enjoying the good mood that the General was in, PLA Air Force Colonel Song joined in. "General, we have some great footage to show you."

With a nod from Leung, Colonel Song signaled a major, who nodded to a sergeant. Suddenly one of the big screen TVs came to life with high qualify visuals looking down on a column of vehicles snaking along a narrow road.

"This is courtesy of the Foreign Intelligence Directorate. You may recall, Sir, in 2013, they obtained the complete package of the Sniper Advanced Targeting Pod from the computers of Lockheed Martin corporation? Anyhow, the fitment of the American system into our SU-30s went very well. We have a couple of Sniper-AT-Pod-equipped aircraft in theatre. This footage was taken less than an hour ago, about 100 kilometers west of Mount Isa."

"Impressive, Colonel Song. I have been briefed on this, but have never seen it before. What am I looking at?"

"You see these vehicles? Here, and here?" the Colonel gestured to the display, where a line of small vehicles could be seen moving west along the highway, and then to a few other lines vehicles moving to the south, away from the highway.

"These are civilian vehicles that are fleeing just ahead of the Australian and Marine rear guard. We are moving in on them so fast that they can't even run away fast enough! Many of them seem to be headed into this Camooweal Caves National Park, but they seem to be trying to get as far from the A2..."

"Don't you mean the 'A6?'" interrupted General Leung.

"No, sir. The name changes from A6 to A2 once you pass Cloncurry," Colonel Song paused until the general nodded. "Anyhow, they seem to be doing whatever they can to get off of the A2, the Barker Highway, so as to avoid being run over by our armored infantry regiments bearing down on them. I can only imagine how terrified they must be."

The image shifted to heavy, dark vehicles.

"And these are a few Australian or USMC infantry fighting vehicles – their rear guard. By now they will have reached the tiny town, hamlet really, called Camooweal and will undoubtedly be setting up some sort of defenses. After our fuel bowsers reach the 372nd, they will simply move in and clear the town, later tomorrow at the latest. Then we'll have the 163rd Division leap-frog through the 124th and take the lead as we move into Northern Territory."

"Colonel Song, we should expect the enemy to consider the defense of this border town to be an important psychological event. They will throw everything they have at us, particularly in terms of aircraft. Do we have any air defense units there, or just the CAP?"

"Nothing on the ground, Sir. Just the CAP. We've got both serviceable air tankers over Cloncurry now, keeping a six-pack of SU-27s up twenty-four-seven over the highway, all the way to the border. We can handle anything they throw at us," the Air Force colonel said with confidence.

"Very good. Now, Colonel Pan, go on about the fuel issue."

"General. Because of the excessive speed of advance, the 372nd Regiment, at the Forward Edge of the Battle Area, just east of Camooweal, and the rest of the 124th Division coming into line behind the FEBA, have robbed too much fuel from the 163rd Division. Now both Divisions are running extremely low. We need to take a 48-hour pause to stage fuel to all six regiments that are involved.

"Approved. We could use a good rest here as well, Colonel Pan. Let's have everybody go to ground for the night. It's been a busy two days without much rest for anybody. Of course, Colonel Song, that does not apply to your CAP. With all of our losses in the Air Defense Regiment, your fighters better stay right on top of the 124th."

"Understood, General. We're keeping a six-pack of SU-27s stacked in pairs for three levels of CAP over the FEBA, and a four-pack of SU230's on station with the tankers, a few hundred miles to the east, making ten fighters in total. That is our max effort for continuous operations, but we can sustain that for up to five days. Beyond that, we'll have to scale back the CAP. It's already robbed too much from our reserves – we've got basically nothing up here or in Cairns, other than transiting aircraft rotating into or out of the Camooweal CAP," said Song.

"Very well, we'll look at scaling it back after we see if there's any fight left in the enemy."

With that, the 42nd Group Army ground to a halt, with the forward Battalion of the 372nd Regiment having closed to within fifteen kilometers of the border town of Camooweal. They could see the soft lights of the small community illuminating the cloudy skies, but were more than pleased with what they had accomplished, gobbling up so many hundreds of kilometers and reaching the western extreme of Queensland so far ahead of even the most optimistic of schedules.

It would be the farthest west that any unit of the PLA would reach in the campaign.

14

BILLABANG

Both ambush teams had deployed without incident; one to take up a position twenty kilometers to the east of the Billabong; the other five kilometers to the west. On cue, top Sergeant Rideout and the rest of Task Force Billabong started up their engines and climbed their vehicles out of the Billabong hideaway. As they pulled onto the A6 Highway, turning right and accelerating towards Julia Creek, the men became tense.

Rideout could sense it. No longer hidden by the terrain and camouflage of their sanctuary, the three Light Armored Vehicles and dozen civilian pattern vehicles were fully exposed on the open expanse of the highway which had seen so much heavy traffic from the People's Liberation Army over the last two weeks.

Things had really begun to settle down three days before, however, when the two Chinese divisions had completed their crossing of western Queensland from Charters Towers to Cloncurry. From what Top Sergeant Rideout understood form the intelligence SitRep, the mining engineer's booby-trap at Cloncurry had been devastating for the enemy's Air Defense Regiment. With plenty of air power available to compensate, however, the enemy had continued to advance the six regiments of their now Armored Corps formation, and had already made contact with the security forces first at Mount Isa, where the Marines of the MAGTFA had immediately withdrawn as if afraid to be overrun by the fast-moving Chinese divisions pouring into the Camooweal area.

But this time, when a lightly armored and fast-moving reconnaissance team from the PLA's 372nd Regiment ran into a company of US Marines at a check-point just ten kilometers east of Camooweal, the Marines did not budge. From the vigorous way that the Marines pursued the surviving members of the Chinese recce platoon, hunting them down in a high-speed chase as the PLA soldiers retreated to the safety of their advancing formation, it was clear to all involved that the Marines were going to stand and fight. That battle lines had been drawn.

Having made contact with the Marines with only the loss of a few dozen men from the 372nd Regiment, and with the rest of the 124th Division settling in to the line, the PLA seemed content to establish a five kilometer wide front, and halt offensive operations for the moment. In the tense quiet that ensued, the front was patrolled on one side by the Allies to the west and by recce teams from the rapidly-entrenching battalions of the 372nd Regiment to the east.

Unlike past encounters, it seemed, the Chinese were ready for an operational pause. It did not take long for the CJOC to determine, through intercepted radio transmission and other 'leakage' from Chinese military communications that they were monitoring with the aid of the CIA facility at Pine Gap, that the entire 42nd Group Army was being given a 48-hour operational pause for logistical resupply and a well-earned bit of rest for the weary soldiers. They were weary from travel, not from war-fighting, as there had not been any meaningful engagements other than the mines and missiles that had affected the engineering battalion and the Air Defense Regiment that had been hurt so badly in Cloncurry.

Once the CJOC had sufficient confirmation from Special Forces units and the network of civilians monitoring the A2 highway, the disposition of Enemy units became clearly understood.

The arrival of the third and final Regiment of the 163rd Division, taking up a position just twenty kilometers behind those of the 124th Division, meant that the Chinese had taken the bait. Intoxicated by the speed of their advance they had over-run even General Leung's aggressive timetable, and had unwittingly raced directly into Colonel Ferebee's trap. The collision of PLA forces with the Allies at Camooweal was the signal for Task Force Billabong to commence operations. Being such a tiny force and with such a highest risk mission to carry out, the men following the lead of Top Sergeant Rideout and Master Sergeant Gannon were now required to operate more like Special Forces operatives then any of them had ever been trained for, and they knew it. So their tension as they sped west towards Julia Creek was understandable.

All thoughts of *What if they attack from the air?* and *What if their security forces are more substantial than we think?* were quickly dispelled the moment the small band of Marines blew past the Chinese military police checkpoint at the Y intersection on the east side of Julia Creek town-site.

In his side-view mirror, Top Sergeant Rideout watched as the dazed sentries were taken out by the Australian Special Forces and civilian militia who literally appeared out of no-where.

Rick recognized a few of their faces, from the many visits that the Australians had made with the Marines at the billabong. The close coordination between the Marines and Australians over the past ten days in the Billabong was beginning to pay off as the two hundred or so Australians who had snuck up to their start positions around the outskirts of the remote hamlet now swung into action in perfect unison with the shock-and-awe of the Marines rapid thrust into the town's center. As planned, the cue had been the sudden arrival of the Marines' convoy arriving from the east, which, as intended, had caught the security forces of the engineering and logistics battalion of the 370th Regiment - perhaps two companies in total strength – completely off guard.

For all they knew the convoy that suddenly appeared from the east was a strange PLA Ground Force unit making its way up the line to the west, as had dozens of convoys over the past two weeks. The presence of American standard military pattern vehicles and Australian civilian SUVs was not unusual, as all Chinese forces had been using a mix of seized western equipment along with the armor and specialized equipment that had been deployed from China by sea.

But when the shooting started, with a few quick-to-react soldiers at some of the entrenched positions around town firing upon the Australian soldiers militiamen, it quickly became clear to the security forces in Julia Creek that their boring little logistics supply base was under attack.

Fortunately for the Marines in the fast-moving convoy led by Top Sergeant Rideout, the troops guarding the Julia Creek Railway Station were not so quick to react. The defenders, all six of them, had come out of the one story railway station to look across the gravel parking lot to see what was going on in town when an American infantry fighting vehicle suddenly appeared in front of them, lurching to a stop no more than five meters in front of the terrified traffic techs.

The men did not react. They did not fight, run, nor raise their hands in surrender. They simply stared at the strange vehicle, hoping that it would not start firing at them. They were so stunned that they were unable to budge.

Sergeant Rideout's SUV crossed the large gravel parking area without stopping. Clearly that area was under control, at least for the moment. Feeling a profound sense of relief that they had caught the enemy by surprise, Rideout and his team continued their task, screaming around the townsite looking for any form of organized resistance, ready to take up a position from which they could coordinate the actions of immediate response teams from both the Australians and the Marines. The trouble was, there was almost nothing to deal with.

After racing around the rail yards and seeing a few small groups of Australians bearing arms and clearly in control, they turned north and headed deeper into town. They came across a fire-fight centered on the Shire Office, but quickly determined that the skirmish was all but over before it had begun, based on the bodies of Chinese soldiers that could be seen on the street, and a surprising number of Australian militiamen firing at the small stone building from positions on all sides. Nothing for Rideout to do there either.

"Let's head for the fuel farm," barked Rideout.

"Roger, Top," said his driver as he gunned the accelerator and sped up Julia Street towards the next block.

"There it is, see the skate park?" Top said, approaching a strange set of concrete ramps just to the right of the road.

"Oh, I see it." The driver pulled the vehicle over beside a typically Australian metal-clad box of a building. There were Marines moving about on the other side of the building, and the occasional burst of gunfire.

After stepping out of his SUV, Sergeant Rideout paused to look, listen, and sense. *All quiet*, he thought. *What the hell, there should have been more of a firefight.*

"Top! There you are!" said a Lance Corporal, who had just come out of another SUV that had pulled into the driveway of the town's only large sports field.

"What it is it, Conway?"

"Captain Thorne is looking for you. He's over at the warehouse on Coyne Street. Just turn right when you get to the end of this block, and look for the smoking Light Armored Vehicle."

"We lost an LAV? I didn't hear a thing. What happened?"

"Yeah, really crappy, that one. But there's good news there too. Better go look for yourself, Top," said the Lance Corporal, seemingly unwilling to go into the details of what had transpired.

"Thanks. I'll go see for myself." Top said, mounting up in his SUV and speeding away.

Two minutes later he had seen enough to piece together what had happened. As one of the three most important targets inside the town, the large warehouse had been the scene of a short, desperate battle. The Marines that had moved in on the warehouse in their eight-wheeled LAV-A2 had engaged and defeated the Chinese ZBD-97 infantry fighting vehicle that was known to be protecting the high value target, but there had not been enough Australian militia personnel in support of the sole LAV-A2, and it had been taken out with a well-aimed 120 mm High Explosive Anti-Tank Missile fired from a shoulder-launched Type 98 tube in the hands of a well-trained PLA soldier. That he and a dozen or more of his fellows had been dispatched shortly thereafter was small consolation to Top Sergeant Rideout.

The three dead Marines crewing the LAV had achieved their mission, taking out the 100mm armed ZDB-90, basically a Chinese-licensed knock-off of the Russian 100mm gun equipped BMP-3, but had paid for it with their lives. Thankfully, the six Marines riding in the back of the LAV had just deployed out the rear hatch when the HEAT round from the ZBD-97 had struck. The dismounted Marines completed the mission of clearing the warehouse of enemy defenders, with particular vengeance for their friends. The smell of death and toxic smoke still lingered in the air as Rideout pieced it all together.

Had the LAV failed to defeat the ZBD, there would have been an even chance that the entire operation could have gone the other way. As it was, most of the dedicated assault missions and Australian insurgency at large had gone the allies' way in Julia Creek; as much due to the shock and awe produced by the sudden appearance of US Marines moving swiftly and with deadly purpose within the very lightly defended town-turned-supply depot as to the careful planning and outstanding effort of the Australian army and civilian militia.

Seeing that the area was secure; and that the wounded men and prisoners were being taken care of, Rideout sought out Captain Thorne inside the warehouse.

"Captain Thorne, there you are," said Ride, simply, as he approached the Australian officer.

"Top. Good to see you. I'm sorry about your men. My guys feel terrible they got here too late to back them up. They just couldn't penetrate this deep into town as fast as things moved when your teams rolled into town."

"Fog of war. They accomplished their mission, and if it has gone as well as it looks, they've probably saved the lives of a great many more Marines and Australians. They're heroes."

"Quite right."

"So what's the good news, Sir?" Top asked.

"Look around you."

As Rideout squinted his eyes to look beyond the Captain into the darkness of the warehouse beyond, he made out some of the lettering on the boxes.

"Combat Rations? Those the same as our MREs?"

"Yup," replied Thorne, "We call them CR1M – 'Combat Ration – 1 Man'. The best that the Australian Army Catering Corps has to offer, but not quite so many menu options as your brown bags."

"How many of them are there here?"

"From what your Lieutenant Lion has tallied from this warehouse and the other caches and truckloads we've looked into so far in the rest of town, there's nearly one million cases. Eight 24-hour meal bags per case. That's enough to feed a Division for six months."

"Or to starve a division that the food was intended to feed in what, two or three weeks?" Sergeant Rideout said, to an enthusiastic grin from Captain Thorne.

Fuel, Food, Fight. Three things that the Colonel Ferebee and the CJOC staff had designed this operation around. To take away the enemy's fuel and food, and trap him thousands of kilometers from his mounting base at Cairns by cutting the strategic lines of communication at each and every fuel dump, log support stockpile, rail yard and rest area from Mount Isa to this side of Charters Towers. Julia Creek was just one of many pieces in the campaign plan. It was the one that Top Sergeant Rideout felt that he was personally responsible for achieving.

It took over an hour for Rideout to visit all of the key objectives in town before he was satisfied that the town had been completely cleared. He could not get over the fact that it had gone so well, with just six Marines killed, seven wounded. On the Australian side, they had lost four Special Forces team leaders and a score of untrained militiamen, but in comparison to the hundred and twenty PLA soldiers killed, eighty wounded and hundred fifty taken prisoner, the operation was a resounding success.

The same could not be said for a similar raid attempted at Cloncurry. There, whether *because of* or *in spite of* the devastating blow that the PLA Air Defense Regiment and engineering support battalion had experienced some two weeks earlier, the enemy had responded quickly to the attack by Australian insurgents and US Marines.

The attack had floundered from the beginning, with a few alert sentries opening up on the Australian militia that had attempted to swarm the town on foot from the bush land outside of town. But the Aussies had made good progress at the south-west corner, where an entire sentry post had laid down their arms and surrendered to the allies without firing a shot. However, lacking the speed, maneuverability and firepower that a couple of LAVs would have provided, the Marines could not take out the enemy's Command Post and other key coordination centers in the heart of Cloncurry. The Marines and Australians had taken heavy losses, perhaps as many as fifty Marines and triple that on the Australian side before the assault had been called off.

The probability that the Cloncurry Task Force would failure to capture the fuel farm and log support base previously been analyzed by the Operational Risk Assessment team at the CJOC in Katherine. Lacking the X-factor that Task Force Billabong had, in having a place to hide the LAVs, the Cloncurry force was handicapped, lacking the speed, maneuverability and firepower of the LAVs, therefore the Cloncurry assault had been considered to have a Medium probability of failure and a High degree of impact on the campaign plan. As a result, they had mitigated the identified High Risk by laying on a contingency plan.

It had taken less than an hour to put the backup plan into execution once the CJOC had learned that the town could not be captured. A singled coded message had been sent to the Australian P3 Orion aircraft orbiting over Groote Island in the Australian Gulf of Carpentaria. The Australian P3C crew then relayed the message onward to an IL76M air tanker of the Indian Air Force, orbiting two hundred miles farther to the east. Onboard the IL76M, Group Captain Singh changed the mission orders for two of his SU27 strike aircraft, and communicated these to the fighter pilots who had just completed tanking from the very same Russian manufactured air-to-air refueller that Singh was using as his airborne tactical control platform.

The re-tasking of two of the strike aircraft meant that there would be only two instead of four SU27s to be sent on the raid to Charters Towers, with the first two being re-tasked to hit Cloncurry. Four others assigned for an attack at the PLAAF operations at Cairns and only one, the ninth in the overall wave, assigned to attack the Chinese-controlled RAAF dry-bones air base at Weipa.

Group Captain Singh knew of the plan to capture or destroy all fuel supplies from Charters Towers all the way along the one thousand kilometers to Camooweal. He had allocated fully half of the Indian Air Forces' remaining stock of serviceable fighters for an anti-air battle over Camooweal, hoping to draw all of the estimated eight to ten Chinese Su27's and Su30s to the extreme west of their Queensland sector. That would leave the back door open to his two, now three-pronged strike package that had been holding out of range over the Gulf of Carpentaria, just north of Queensland.

Sitting on the ground with his wrists zip-strapped behind his back, his hands numb from the hours since he had surrendered, Wan Shanyu, formerly of 4th Battalion, 370th Regiment, 124th Division PLA, was now a relatively happy Prisoner of War.

Aware that he could be executed at any minute by one of the very angry looking Australians that he encountered, he was glad to be in the hands of the somewhat more disciplined, or perhaps simply more well restrained US Marines who had shepherded him and the other prisoners captured in the failed attempt to seize Cloncurry.

When he saw the Marines passing the word about something and then all of them looking to the skies to the North, Wan immediately understood.

If they can't capture it, they're going to bomb it.

Sure enough, a few moments later the quiet evening twilight was interrupted first by the sound of an approaching jet engine, and then the sky was filled with bright lights as some of the few remaining SAM batteries lit off missiles after the incoming jets.

From the massive explosion in the sky moments later, Wan surmised that at least one of the enemy, no, *allied* jets, he corrected himself, had been shot down. The lead Su27 had indeed been hit by a missile fired by an HQ-12 SAM battery.

The crew of the HQ-12 had been quick to reposition, in a 'shoot and scoot' operation meant to make it more difficult for a Suppression of Enemy Air Defense, SEAD, tasked aircraft. However, the two Su27s launched against Cloncurry were not on a SEAD mission.

They were each equipped with a pair of American manufactured CBU 105 Cluster Bombs. The cluster bombs had only begun to be used by the Indian Air Force since 2010, however the CBU 105 munitions held by the Australians were compatible with the launch mounts which some of the IAF fighters were equipped with, so they could make use of the Australian cluster bombs on the Indian fighter-bombers.

With ten sub-munitions per cluster bomb and four components per sub-munition, a total of 160 bomblets were deployed by the pair of Su27s before they attempted to evade the SAMs rising up at them from Cloncurry.

Programmed to explode fifteen meters above the surface if they do not find their pre-designated target, over 95% of the bomblets detonated in a three second timeframe.

From Wan's point of view, as his eyes tried to regain night vision after the brightness of the SAMs that had just scorched into the darkening sky, the sudden pop-corn sounds and accompanying flashes of light and smoke reminded him of the grand finale of a fireworks display. However, the beautiful impression only lasted a moment. Seconds later, fuelled by the millions of liters of gasoline and diesel fuel from the thin-skinned bladders of the massive fuel farm, and punctuated by the powerful secondary explosions from ZDB-90s and other Chinese armor hit by the carpet of exploding bomblets, the entire town went up in a hellish conflagration.

Wan felt for his countrymen who died in the inferno, despite the fact that he understood the military necessity of their death. Being a POW now, after convincing the two other men from his fox hole OP to surrender alongside him when the ground assault had begun, Wan was now hoping that the ultimate victory, an allied victory, would now come that much sooner.

It did not take a military genius to understand how serious the situation had now become for the 42nd Group Army.

From the reports coming into the CJOC in Katherine, the successes and failures of a large number of small operations was being plotted on a ten meter long stretch of wall that had been converted into a detailed map of the 1000 kilometers of the A6/A2 highway from Charters Towers to Camooweal.

The location of each and every ambush, where Marines and local Australian militia had captured or destroyed convoys of various sizes was detailed. In about half of the cases, the ambush teams had been able to capture truckloads of food, ammunition and supplies, commandeer the bowsers of fuel or water.

The captured war booty was quickly moved away from the A2 highway, along dirt roads north or south, off the main axis of advance. This was done to make it impossible for the PLA to send out forces to recapture the supplies, fuel and equipment.

After the initial setback of the failed assault on Cloncurry, the mood in the CJOC quickly changed to that of elation, as in the majority of cases, the ambush operations and depot-raids had been highly successful.

"Ok, now, simmer down, gents! The night is not over yet. We've still got those downed pilots to find with Combat Search and Rescue in the Camooweal area. Those guys don't know our CSAR procedures, and have no ISOPREPS - the list of personal questions the CSAR teams can ask them to verify their identities - so stay on top of that. We need each and every one of those IAF pilots," Colonel Ferebee said, reigning in the staff from what had become a bit overly-celebratory.

"Sir, what about the interpreters?" asked a Major from the 3rd Brigade. "Task Force Billabong is asking for interpreters to help figure out how to get the captured SAM battery up and running. They're also asking for some mechanics and engineers to help unload the train they captured."

"Train? I did not hear that one. Fill me in," said Ferebee.

"There were a number of tanks and infantry fighting vehicles low-beds in Julia Creek when they took the town. Looks like at least two Russian-built Type 99s."

"Wow, if we can get those up and running, along with some air defenses, we can build up a sizeable force at Julia Creek. Have Major Blakely send that kid he uses, what's his name?"

"Yao Ming," said a staffer, "Sunny Yao. But he does not know much about military stuff. We better send that Chinese Captain from 1st Battalion. We should also send Lieutenant Jarvis from the Third Marines along for good measure – he can provide us with a more detailed After Action Report and Combat Assessment – up the MAGTFA chain of command."

"Good idea, Captain. We may as well adapt our Branch Plans: Have everything that was going to go into Cloncurry shift over to Julia Creek instead. Cloncurry is of no use to anybody now. No, we'll make Julia Creek the area for Australian force generation, agreed, General?"

"Quite," said General Davies. "I reckon we can get a few thousand militia men into that area over the next few days. Many of them are familiar with heavy equipment, from the gold mines and such. Should be easy enough for them to learn how to operate some of that Chinese armor, at least as drivers. We'll get proper soldiers into the mix and train them up in no time," the Australian General said excitedly.

"Colonel Pan, are you telling me that it's gone? Completely gone?" General Leung asked the senior Army officer in the alternate Command Post. They had returned from the air-raid bunker to find their CP in flames from the cluster bomb attack, and had re-assembled the staff in another boarding school a few blocks away. However it was taking a long time to get the new CP fully up and running. Something seemed to be wrong with the communications gear, as connectivity with units all the way from their new CP in Charters Towers to the Mount Isa were down. They had great comms with the two divisions sitting idle near Camooweal, but they had little to report other than their urgent requirement for resupply of fuel, water and rations.

"It appears that the entire facility there was destroyed by enemy air attack," said Colonel Song, the Air Force staffer.

"The entire facility? What about the roads? Are they still open, or did they cut some bridges or crater the highway? What the fuck? Where was the CAP?" The General was losing his cool.

"The CAP shot down six of their fighters over Camooweal, with the loss of only two of ours. At this rate, along with the two the SAMs got here and the one shot down at Cloncurry, the Indians are quickly running out of fighters."

"Well, Colonel Song, they sure kicked the shit out of us in Cloncurry, and with the raid on the air bases at Weipa and Cairns it sounds like you've got some real problems of your own, so I wouldn't get too cocky if I were you," the General warned, seemingly looking for someone to direct his frustration at. "Pan, go over it again, what do we know of the lines of communication," the general commanded, more calmly now.

"Sir. We may have lost a few convoys. We definitely have lost the railhead at Julia Creek and an unknown number of rail-cars. May have arrived before the enemy captured Julia Creek. Until I get confirmation, I can only assume that the enemy has mounted some sort of large scale sabotage operation at a number of locations between here and Camooweal."

"Colonel, you get those assumptions turned into facts. I want to know where they struck, what they got, and what we still have. How long will it take for fuel to reach to the 124th?"

Looking very uncomfortable, the army Colonel struggled to find the words. "Never, sir. I think they got all of it."

Fuming mad, the General undid the clasp of his service pistol, as if he was going to execute the man. "What the fuck do you mean, 'never'? We must have fifty separate convoys along that thousand kilometers of highway. Are you telling me that it is all in enemy hands, the entire highway?"

Something snapped inside the Colonel at that moment. Suddenly he'd crossed a line: no more coddling this incompetent General. No more finding excuses for the loss of good men all because of the pathetic little ego of this worm with stars on his chest. The Colonel wanted, at this moment, if nothing else, his dignity back. Damn his career and his life if this was all it was going to amount to.

The Colonel turned to the General and looked at him with utter calm and disdain. "No, sir, but going by how many units we have lost contact with, and what the drones can see through these damned low clouds tonight, they must have put up a well-coordinated series of ambushes or road-blocks, probably using civilians, and captured or destroyed most, if not all, of the convoys." Looking straight into the General's eyes, with mounting hatred, he continued. "They had no security, sir, as you know. You gave the orders to push the Regiments up so fast, after all." With that comment, he had sealed his fate.

General Leung pulled out his pistol and aimed it at the officer. What he saw on the Colonel's face at that last moment was a sneer of contempt. The General shot him in the face without another word.

It would take another twenty four hours before the scale of the disaster was confirmed, but the late Colonel Pan had been correct, no more fuel would ever reach the 124th and 163rd Divisions, now trapped a thousand kilometers behind enemy lines. Two full mechanized infantry divisions, an air defense regiment, and a large portion of the available fuel and transportation resources in the Queensland sector had been lost – an entire armored corps!

On General Bing's orders, Colonel Song arrested General Leung, and assumed control of the Command Post. Having the 42nd Group Army commanded by a PLA Air Force colonel was highly unusual. However, Colonel Song understood that it would not last long. He would do what he could to establish a more defensible front line, not so far inland, and then beg for support from General Ma's 41st Group Army.

With no fuel, water, or rations, the two divisions of the 42nd would not hold out for long with Marines plunking rounds off of their armor all night long. As it was, talk of mass surrender had already begun. *Hopefully they will hold out until they starve to death, as the Russians did in Finland in the Second World War,* Song thought to himself, *and not surrender at the first sight of a Marine.*

15

INDIAN OCEAN

THREE YEARS INTO THE WAR

As General Patel looked upwind at the rising sun he knew that the breeze he felt was due more to the eighteen knots that the warship he was travelling on was making than any actual wind.

For all he knew there could be a quartering tailwind disguised by the ship's speed. As he thought about it his eyes picked up a white speck on the horizon. He had not been the first to detect the object, and a flurry of activity on the quarterdeck confirmed that something was out there as the sailors sprang to their combat stations.

General Singh, with no role while at sea, simply watched as the ship's crew made ready a 50 caliber machine gun equipped with a long-range optical system. Judging by the wires leading from the base of the monstrous lens, he assumed that the telescope had been modified with some sort of digital-optical components. He recalled Commander Malhotra, the ship's Captain, saying something of the sort.

That's right, recalled General Singh, *the telescopes on both flying bridges have been rigged to give a digital feed to monitors on the bridge, as was the 360-degree system mounted atop the ship's very cluttered mast.*

"Great for zooming in on Pirates to see what the buggers are on about," the ship's Captain, Commander Malhotra, had said.

Curious about what the ship's crew was getting so excited about, the Commander of the Indian Army's II Corps made his way up the to the Bridge deck to see what was going on. He had to step aside as a pair of helmeted, heavily armed crewmen rushed past, departing the Bridge on some urgent task.

"Beg' your pardon, Sardar," said one of the men to the General as he jostled past the landlubber. The tone of respect in the Master Seaman's use of the common tribal word for 'chief', *Sardar*, was not lost on Singh, who had found the ship's crew to be highly proficient and professional. Somehow, the encounter made him feel a bit less awkward aboard the ship, as if the navy personnel truly were behind him and his men, supporting them in their upcoming clash with the Chinese in Australia – more than simply transporting them across the Indian Ocean.

General Patel found an empty corner on the bridge, and made eye-contact with Commander Malhotra.

The relaxed nod from the ship's Captain seemed strange to the General. All around the bridge, men were rushing about as if they were about to go into battle, yet Commander Malhotra sat atop his stool in the center of the bridge as if he were not the least bit interested. But then it all made sense, as a Lieutenant drew the Captain's attention to one of the monitors, and said something inaudible to the Captain.

"All quiet on the bridge!" shouted the XO. The Captain leaned forward, finally revealing his level of interest.

The image on the screen jumped around a bit as the Lieutenant adjusted the controls, and then suddenly a green box flashed on the screen, indicating that the subject now centered in the picture had been locked into focus. From that moment on, the picture remained clear and steady; the camera's servos made tiny adjustments to compensate for the gyrations caused by wind and wave.

"Ascharga!" commented one of the naval officers in an expression of surprise that was understood by all, despite its Bengali origins.

The bridge fell silent as everybody looked at the monitor.

The speck on the horizon had swelled as the camera had focused in on it. It was a small sailboat, perhaps fifteen meters in length. At first glance it appeared like any other sailboat, but then a few unusual features began to stand out. Even the Army General, a landlubber for all intents and purposes, could see that there was something unusual about the vessel. It seemed to be much wider than a normal sailboat, and the mast had a very strange, stocky appearance.

"Lieutenant Verma, what flag is that?"

"Which one, Skipper? The blue one or the red one?"

"Obviously the blue one, below the Maple Leaf."

"I…" the junior officer hesitated, but then remembered the advice he had been given so many times before. *If you don't know, don't bullshit the skipper. He'll tear you apart if you pull that crap on him.* The XO had said. "I don't know, Sir."

The Captain pursed his mouth. "XO?"

"I haven't the foggiest. Looks allied, but not nautical. Could be a vanity flag, or something else that means something only to the ships' crew. It's certainly not a known flag of convenience."

"Looks a bit like something from the UK, doesn't it?"

"Quite, old man. I was just going to say, it looks almost…"

"Almost what, Parmeet? |

"Almost *Air Force*," the XO said, almost mockingly of the sister service. It was a long established tradition to treat the Air Force – of any nation – as a very junior service in comparison to the many centuries of warfare that the Navy, and the Army for that matter, had in their history before the upstart Indian Aerial Corps had been created just before the First World War.

"Helm, thirty degrees to port, get us a bit more broadside and bring her down the Starboard side," Commander Malhotra ordered, seemingly triggered by his XO's intuition.

"Aye, Sir, thirty degrees to port."

"And the convoy?" asked the XO.

"They're still well back. I just want to keep her wide while we assess. No point throwing the convoy into a tizzy."

"Aye, Sir." Replied the XO, not entirely sure about this.

"Boarding party ready to go, Sir!" Shouted Lieutenant Verma.

"Deploy the boarding party. No change to task," ordered the skipper.

On another monitor, the six-man boarding party could be seen settling into their Rigid Hull Inflatable Boat as it was lowered into the sea. No sooner had it contacted the water, and the boarding party settled near the center of the RHIB and the Master Seaman at the controls accelerated the craft briskly over the rolling waves; the experienced sailors hung on and leaned into the swell instinctively.

As they neared the smaller craft, their weapons trained and ready to fire, they saw the unusual sight of a big bald man standing on the deck of the craft smiling and waving wildly, like he was happy to see the Indian Navy. There was at least one woman with him on deck, and what appeared to be others visible through the small vessel's portals.

Back on the bridge of the warship, Commander Malhotra was discussing the 'Vessel of Interest' with his most senior passenger when he was interrupted suddenly.

"Signal from Keeling Island, Sir!" shouted the communications Leading Seaman, handing the printout to the Skipper, the XO reading over his shoulder.

After a few seconds the skipper handed the transcript to his XO and ordered: "Recall the boarding party, resume course and speed. Signal starboard elements of the convoy to keep an eye out for the vessel. Change contact from Uniform-23 to Foxtrot-14, *confirmed friendly.*"

"Aye Aye, Sir. Recall the boarding party. Resume course and speed, Signal convoy to watch for now confirmed friendly, Foxtrot 14." Repeated Lieutenant Verma.

With calm returning to the bridge, the General approached the Captain. "Commander Malhotra, how do you know that sailboat is a friendly? Aren't you going to at least make contact?"

Smiling, Commander Malhotra looked up from the small swing-out table fitted to his command chair, where he had been making notes into his personal logbook. "XO, give our 'brother from another element' the traffic!

Without a word, the XO handed the transcript to the General, who struggled at first with what seemed a ridiculously complex series of codes until he found the subject line and numbered paragraphs of the decoded message.

It was from the Detachment Commander of some sort of outpost of the Royal Australian Air Force, at some place called Keeling Island. The transmission told the General everything he needed to know about the small, unusual vessel with the Canadian flag and Royal Canadian Air Force colors. The information was intriguing, but he soon put it out of his mind as he read on. The message went on to describe a drastic drop in sea level, some seven meters lower since the war started three years before. It speculated that this was due to the drastic drop in temperatures caused by the nuclear winter and the associated deposition of massive quantities of snow in continental areas, particularly of Eurasia and North America, but also southern Africa and the southernmost areas of Australia.

For the first time in a generation, the sea level, which had been rising and threatening to inundate so many island communities, had retreated rapidly; the tiny atolls becoming much larger islands. The report went on to describe how the collection of islands that made up the Keeling Islands, by the end of the third year after the Nuclear Extinction War, had become a single formation of over 200 square kilometers. Despite the reduced sunlight of the nuclear winter, the tiny atoll had been transformed into a large island with a massive new area of fertile grassland where the inter-island lagoon had previously been.

Change had come rapidly to the Australian outpost, which had always been a strategic toehold in the eastern Indian Ocean. But now, with the world at war and so many starving throughout the world, any place where any form of agriculture was viable, had a taken on a new strategic importance, in addition to its location on the strategic lines of communication across the Indian Ocean.

The operational planners who had put together the resources for the deployment of another Army Corps to add to the expeditionary forces India had already sent to Australia had been excited to learn that evacuees from New Zealanders had brought with a number of sheep with them. They had built up a thriving herd of over two thousand sheep. The report went on to detail dried fish and other agricultural products that the outpost could contribute to the war effort.

And then the crux of the matter. The outpost needed some technical support, medicine, and the evacuation of a few personnel who needed medical treatment.

"XO, with that nasty weather coming through Perth starting tomorrow, what do you think about holding back in the Keeling Island area for 48 hours? We could throw together much of what they are asking for, give them some support, and rotate those sea-sick soldiers onto the land for some R &R. We'll put the convoy at anchor, and patrol the outer perimeter to cover the ASW threat," Commander Malhotra said.

The XO smiled, enjoying the potential adventure of exploring the transformed island as much as the idea of getting the poor soldiers a break.

"Certainly would avoid the low-pressure wave. Maybe we could load up on mutton in the process. I'm sure chef would love the chance to put a few new menu items on in the wardroom."

"Make it so," ordered the Captain.

While the soldiers of II Corps had enjoyed the R&R and the outpost was provided the required assistance, a few of the slower ships in the convoy had elected to carry on without resting at Keeling Island, out of courtesy for the time it would save the faster ships when they resumed the crossing. It was a risky choice given the possibility of Chines submarines, but the merchantmen were willing to take the risk if it would help speed the convoy to Perth. As it was, it took the warship and the bulk of the convoy several days to retake the slower ships after the respite at the Australian outpost, but the entire convoy was whole again before they were within 1200 kilometers of Perth, much to the relief of the merchant ships' crews.

But when the warship's crew detected inbound military aircraft closing on the convoy, the tension level rose again while they waited for the international friend-or-foe, IFF, transponder to confirm whether the rapidly approaching aircraft was friend or foe. Minutes later, many of the ship's company made their way to the upper decks of the ship to wave to their countrymen, the aircrews of the Indian Air Force Su-27 multirole fighters who had flown out from the new air base near Perth.

The jets had been sent out to protect and to welcome the convoy transporting the premier elements of the Indian Army's strike force, such as the six remaining battalions of the Mechanized Infantry Regiment, the Sikh Light Infantry Regiment, and the 1st and 8th Gorkha Rifles first to the Australian shore at Perth and ultimately into the war. India was sending the II Corps from the Indian Western Command to reinforce what was left of XII Corps of India's Southern Command which had been the first unit to deploy to Australia when the war had begun. In the actions with the PLA's 38th Group Army, the XII

Corps, particularly the 4th Armored and the 12th Rapid Mechanized Infantry Brigade had been badly mauled and were reportedly barely hanging on, despite the heroic efforts of the Australians to keep throwing new Battalions into the line. What they needed, and what was in critically short supply, was the speed, maneuverability and punch-power of Main Battle Tanks, such as the 58 ton Arjun with its rifled 120mm gun and fully integrated suite of sensors and communications equipment.

The war for India had started nearly a year before the war with China had broken out around the world. India, with surreptitious support from the United States, had launched a pre-emptive nuclear and conventional missile strike against the radical Islamic forces that had seized control of Pakistan's nuclear arsenal. The losses on both sides had been staggering, however, the failed Pakistani State had been much worse off than India, as the missile strikes and ultimate invasion and subjugation of Pakistan was militarily successful. It had also put India on a national mobilization for war, which had resulted in sufficient dispersion and military control of national resources such that when the global war with China broke out, India was perhaps the most well-prepared allied nation. They had been devastated by the Russian and American missiles, and had lost hundreds of millions of their population from the blasts, and the starvation and suffering in the years after. However, India had continued to fight on.

In Australia, the first contingent of the Indian Army, XII Corps, along with a sizeable force of fighter jets and air tankers, had been dispatched immediately into the Australian theatre of war. The IAF fighters and tankers had played a pivotal role in the early battles in western Queensland, where the US Marines out of Darwin and the Australians had achieved a major victory over the 42nd Group Army. However, in New South Wales, where the Indian Army had run headlong into the 38th Group Army, the Chinese had regional air superiority and much more carefully deployed anti-air defenses, and the Indians had sustained staggering losses. But the Indian military were undaunted, and sent replacements of aircraft, warships, and personnel across the Indian Ocean over the past three years to essentially maintain just over a single division to add to the two divisions that the Australians had to put together in the South Australia – to – Victoria sector. This had resulted in a fairly stable contest, with neither side having sufficient resources to lay on a major offensive. Certainly neither side had the three-to-one numerical superiority called for in conventional land forces doctrine.

Three years ago, in the first few weeks of the war, it had been all about sea and air power, at least in terms of force projection. The life expectancy of a pilot, or a sailor for that matter, was counted in days; all of the larger formations at sea having been destroyed by nuclear detonations from American and Russian Inter-Continental Ballistic Missiles.

The Chinese had orchestrated the American and Russian nuclear war to commence, and had in some cases subtly adjusted the target lists and warhead assignments to achieve specific results that had been years in the planning. Allied military resources still intact after the missiles attacks abated were hunted down in the days and weeks that followed, taking millions of personnel and vital war-fighting equipment out of the equation worldwide. The losses were particularly harsh for the navies of the world, proving the vulnerability of surface combatants to arsenal ships and other 21st century warfare techniques which largely overwhelmed the superior but ultimately more vulnerable defensive systems of the American Carrier Strike Forces and other naval armadas.

With several hundred Sea-Launched Cruise Missiles like the 3M-80E SS-N-22's Sunburst at their disposal, Chinese forces assigned to clear the Malacca Strait of American warships that comprised the *CVN78 Gerald R. Ford Carrier Strike Group* were able to lay something of a creeping barrage of 30-kiloton detonations, burning out the Carrier Strike Groups defensive systems. They first set off warheads two hundred miles from the Strike Group, and then with moving progressively closer Electro-Magnetic Pulse bursts, until the Guided Missiles Cruisers and organic defense systems of the *Gerald R Ford CSG* were rendered blind and defenseless. The CSG was converted to vapor, smoke and slag by several detonations right in the center of the formation. Over sixteen thousand personnel and one sixth of the United States sea power in the western Pacific had gone to the bottom of the Straits of Malacca on the first day of the war.

Whether by nuclear sea mines, torpedoes, or Air Launched Cruise Missiles, the weapon of choice for the Chinese was clearly nuclear, which they seemed to have in abundance.

In contrast to the unrelenting destruction faced by the USN, the highest value units of the Indian Navy had escaped destruction in the Bengal Sea, as the Chinese had focused more on destroying the CVN-69 *Dwight D. Eisenhower Carrier Strike Group, operating just north of the Indian Navy's* Naval Task Force.

The *Arleigh Bourke* class destroyer from the *Eisenhower CSG* had done a valiant job in protecting the aircraft carrier *Dwight D. Eisenhower*, and had saved the Indians in the process, but had then run into the same problems as the *Gerald R. Ford*, as the Chinese nuclear ALCM attacks continued until the American carrier was destroyed.

At the extreme end of the *Eisenhower CSG's* defensive umbrella, the Indian Carrier Battle Group had been damaged but not destroyed. The Indian warships escaped to the Indian Ocean where they would be out of range from the arsenal of cruise missiles the Chinese had at their disposal in Myanmar.

Throughout this phase, the Chinese forces were also being destroyed, as the Allies, having caught on to the Chinese deception at the start of the war, had then hit all Chinese assets with everything they had left. By the end of the first week, the Chinese forces had either been destroyed by American and Russian counter-attacks, or had exhausted their arsenals, or had run out of targets. At this point the war moved into a longer, more desperate phase where the few remaining warships worldwide played cat-and-mouse with each other, attempting to destroy the enemy while not being destroyed themselves.

For the Indian Navy, this was accomplished by sending long range maritime patrol aircraft into the Bay of Bengal, to watch for shipping or aircraft from China. But ever since the extreme violence of the Su-27/SU-30 on Su-27/Su-30, India v. China, air war over Nepal, in which hundreds of the most sophisticated fighter aircraft in their arsenals had been destroyed in an air-war of attrition, the sophisticated airframes littering the Himalayas with wreckage, there had been few to no air battles.

Based on what the Indians had learned from the Australians, about the Chinese air assaulters being reinforced by massive numbers of ground forces transported by all manner of commercial shipping, the Indians had watched for any opportunity to interdict the Chinese ships which had flooded into the Indian Ocean with their cargoes of soldiers and war-fighting material bound for SPODs the world over. Expecting to have freedom of the seas once the American warships had been removed from the equation, these follow-on forces, once identified thanks to the intelligence that came out of Darwin and Pine Gap, were highly vulnerable targets.

At first it had been difficult to determine which of the ships were Chinese controlled, but by carefully monitoring the signals from the Automated Information System of transponders that the commercial ships were equipped with, the Indian forces had been able to back-track the data and identify which ships had loitered at Chinese ports in the weeks before the war, and identified them as potentially hostile.

This helped reduce the number of suspect vessels from many thousands to several hundreds, which were then investigated.

In an ironic twist of fate, the very Indian Navy crews that had been working for years to quell the scourge of Somali piracy in the western Indian Ocean for decades now themselves turned to using the same pirate-like tactics. They found that using small, high speed boats was the most effective way to insert their boarding crews onto the suspect commercial ships which were, in many cases, not prepared to repel assaulters.

When the ships were crewed with terrified, innocent seafarers, the ships were seized by the Indian government and either sent to port in India, or held in a growing flotilla of commodities-reserves at sea in the south Indian Ocean. If they were defended or too distant to be seized, they were taken out by any means available so as to deny the Chinese expeditionary forces the much needed reinforcements and war carried by sea.

This practice had been hastily agreed upon with the Americans and other allies, as the world powers all understood the realities of nuclear winter, as food supplies, energy resources and other commodities would no longer be produced in abundance. The 50,000 commercial ships at sea or in port when the war had started now represented much of what would be produced or distributed for many years to come.

It had been part of the Chinese strategy to hijack as many bulk carriers and commercial shipping as they could. In many cases, they had inserted spies into the crews of the largest, most prized bulk carriers, tankers, container ships and general cargo ships with orders to take over the ships and have them loiter at designated locations on the high seas, from which they would be shepherded to Chinese controlled ports in the coming months and years. This reprehensible strategy, of using food and other vital supplies as yet another weapon in their nuclear extinction war proved that for the Chinese generals who had concocted this ruthless strategy, who now appeared to be winning the global war, the rules of warfare and any semblance of humanity had been cast completely aside.

So it was with a clear conscience that the Indian Naval Service, sank passenger ships found to be transporting Chinese soldiers, to execute and throw overboard any Chinese agents captured on the hostage-ships, and to capture for themselves any Chinese flagged vessels they found on the high seas.

But even with their dominance over the Indian Ocean, the INS simply did not have enough warships left to cover the massive expanse of the Indian Ocean, nor the fighting power to find, fix and destroy all of the Chinese submarines and smaller warships that had been dispersed before the war had begun.

Scores of ships made it through, allowing tens of thousands of Chinese conscripts to reinforce the ports which had been captured by the air assaulters, their gear in many cases having been secured by Chinese Little Dragon agents and their Dragonfly recruits from the local Chinese community from the depots and warehouses and facilities that these fifth-column agents had seized in the opening hours of the war.

But the Navy and the Air force were not India's only contribution to the global struggle to stop the Chinese onslaught. The Indian Army or what was left of it after the war with Pakistan and the destruction of most of the army's bases in India, was still a force to be reckoned with.

By ordering the dispersion of their units the moment that the nuclear attacks between Russian and America had first begun, India had saved much of its war-fighting capabilities. The problem was, there was no way to bring their thousands of Indian-modified, Russian built T-90 main battle tanks, infantry fighting vehicles, armored reconnaissance vehicles or massive horde of engineering and support vehicles to bear on the Chinese. The land between India and China is an impassible range of the world's largest mountains. The few roads that penetrate through the passes would take months of dedicated engineering effort to make passable for an army Hundreds of miles of Himalayas kept the two enemies apart.

So while the Indians did send some troops into Nepal to target specific Chinese units, and ultimately to begin the perilous job of working their way towards Tibet and China, this was not a sufficient pathway for their rage.

But Australia, their colonial cousin, was a different matter.

The close ties between the Indian and Australian military, the common rank structure, and the British military history and tradition they held in common, meant that the Indian Army was the perfect cavalry to help the Australians fight off their invaders, and plans were immediately set in motion to do exactly that.

And now, three years into the war, with the final of three convoys to transport the last big contingent of the Indian Army's Australian Expeditionary Force now successfully arriving in

Perth, it would be no more than a few weeks before General Singh's II Corps would begin the arduous journey across the thousands of kilometers of frozen, snow-covered wasteland that the new climate had transformed the Australian continent.

Two dozen transport ships of all kinds, from bulk carrier to roll-on roll-off ships had been used to transport the Indian Army. Normally, one would expect the ships to carry on to their next task, plying their transport trade from port to port, but there simply were no tasks for the behemoths. To make matters worse, the fuel shortages were now so severe that there simply was not enough fuel to send the ships back to India for subsequent loads. Rather, other ships still sitting idle in the intact ports of the Indian subcontinent would be used for follow-on forces, saving millions of liters of marine diesel fuel.

For the harbormaster at Perth, the problem of ships cluttering up his limited anchorage space was resolved by having the ships relocate to sheltered coves a few hundred miles farther down the coast to the south-east. Those that could not comply with the relocation order were unceremoniously scuttled at sea.

Along the Nularboor, the isolated highway from Perth to Adelaide, the transit would be fraught with danger, particularly with the air war over southern Australia being in such a state of flux.

For every Chinese jet that the allies downed it seemed that the PLAAF had another two to replace it. They seemed to be willing to take heavy losses if it helped wear down the squadrons of fighters from the Indian Air Force and the few remaining Australian F/A 18 Super Hornets. Attrition was a strategy for conscript armies, not front-line fighter jets. Yet the Chinese strategy was clearly based on a willingness to accept extremely heavy losses if it meant that the allies would eventually exhaust their meager aviation resources.

The two sides fought it out in the skies over central and eastern Australia, with both able to penetrate deep into the other's side on any given day, none achieving any form of stability in terms of regional air superiority over South Australia. The Indian Army would have to cover the nearly three thousand kilometers under the constant threat of long-range air interdiction by Chinese SU-27s. After three years of war, the Chinese had utterly destroyed the once robust road and rail links across the west, making the transfer of men and war-fighting equipment itself a major engineering and human challenge. Mother nature, with her newfound love for snow and intense winds, added a heartless bitterness to the challenge.

And if the Chinese agents that had pre-deployed into Australia remained as effective as they had been over the first three years of the war, then the Indian's progress across the Nullarbor could be made that much more difficult with simple acts of sabotage and interference. That, in addition to what Mother Nature had been throwing at them with the temperatures having plummeted to a steady minus fifteen centigrade over the southern interior areas of the Australian continent. The terrain had not seen sustained temperatures below freezing in over a hundred thousand years. It went without saying that the Australians and even the Aborigines had no experience in dealing with such extreme cold, and had all but consumed the meager supply of firewood and food supplies in the Nullarbor region as the nuclear winter set in during the first year of the war. Those who had not found a way to flee to the relatively milder climate to the north, in the Northern Territory, west to Perth, or south to Adelaide had begun to die off in accelerating numbers.

And even for a well-equipped and well led Army, experienced in mountain and winter warfare, fighting across the thousands of kilometers from Perth to the front during the nuclear winter was no small feat.

Just getting there, to the Adelaide-Melbourne sector where the land-war was being fought, could take upwards of six months, General Singh knew. It had taken earlier task forces at least as long, and that was when the roads were in much better shape, and flat-car train cars could be used to transport the T-90 and Arjun Main Battle Tanks and engineering support equipment.

Wish we had more fighters, thought Singh. Climbing into the lead vehicle in the line of big SUVs that had come to collect General

Singh and his staff from the dockyard in Perth, the general had a grim realization: *We're going to lose a lot of men before we even get to the Melbourne sector and link up with XII Corps. We are a long way from being able to finally start bringing the fight to the enemy. But if we can get the II Corps there in one piece, before the XII Corps collapses, we may be able to turn the tide, and push the Chinese back into the sea!*

16

TERRIBLE MISTAKE

Lieutenant Colonel Peter Weir had never been more proud of his son, Jake, than he was when Jake had completed the gruelling three weeks of "intake training" down at the Campbell Barracks, just south of Perth.

At first he had been uncertain if pulling strings to have Jake receive his military training directly from the newly formed SOCOMD training outfit had been wise. His other option was to send Jake down to Adelaide, where the Australian Army had built up a number of training brigades to pump new recruits through to build up the Australian Army.

With the Chinese invasion having been halted in the north with the help of the US Marines, and in the south with the help of the Indian Army's Australian Expeditionary Corps, the battle for Australia had stabilized somewhat, as both sides brought up re-enforcements and consolidated their defensive positions.

For the Chinese, this meant moving tens of thousands of men and equipment from the sea ports they had captured up and down Australia's east cost to the front lines farther inland. This presented a major problem for the PLA, as these convoys faced the ever present risk of insurgent activity. From the PLA point of view, the Australian citizens, militia, and scattered pockets of military units operating within the Chinese-occupied eastern half of Queensland and New South Wales were not an organized force. They were seen as insurgents, just as the Americans had seen opposing forces in Iraq and Afghanistan.

The insurgents were using improvised explosive devices – roadside bombs – as well as man-portable anti-armour weapons and small arms fire to harass the convoys. As a result, despite having full control of the coast highway, the A1, which ran north and south along Australia's east coast, the PLA forces were unable to move swiftly. They were forced to establish a strong presence at each and every small town, to protect the lines of communication, the roads and rail networks necessary to move such large military formations.

In most cases, this amounted to basing a Battalion or a Brigade in towns, where thousand or more PLA soldiers now outnumbered the remaining civilians, taking the homes of evacuated residences as their bed-down billets and pillaging the neighborhood as they saw fit..

As for the civilians, those who had not been deemed useful to the commander of the Regiment or Division given administrative control of the region, or by the 'Occupation Authority' that had been established using civilian officials organized in the Chinese community that were loyal to China, they had been eliminated – collected up, herded together, and then brutally mass-murdered as though their lives were of no account.

Some commanders had been unwilling to carry out the order to kill the civilian captives, and had permitted them to flee. However, the PLA chain of command had come down harshly on this sort of disobedience, executing a few PLA officers, mostly from the 41st Group Army in New South Wales, to make an example of them.

After that, the 'leakage' of civilians had been reduced to only those who had been smart enough to flee when the invasion had first began. However, within the first six months of the war, as much as 60% of the civilians originally living in the occupied areas had fled to the safety of the Free Australian Territory to the west. This left the coastal and nearby inland towns up and down the Gold Coast largely uninhabited, with most of the civilian hold-outs established in the cattle-stations, farms, and other large agricultural enterprises.

These small bastions of opposition each required considerable effort to neutralize, however this was acceptable to the PLA because each of these pockets of resistance would be useful in the long term campaign, and the defenders of these sites could be converted into slaves of a sort, forced to slaughter their animals or to harvest the agricultural commodities and to prepare these precious food resources for ultra long term food storage. The food was needed to support the needs of the occupying forces, and to a lesser extent their civilian captives, through what was expected to be a very long nuclear winter.

It was the same in almost every town, with the downtown areas having become ghost towns reminiscent of post-apocalyptic movies of the past. The quiet broken only by the occasional report of small-arms fire as a PLA unit dealt with some intransigent farmer outside of town.

As a result of the abandonment of the towns, the PLA forces were able to make use of a great many abandoned homes, facilities and other infrastructure. In military terms, each small town was seen as a "well-found improvised military base". On the Australian side, civilians fleeing the war were welcomed as heroes and the first veterans of the war. In many cases, the first question the refugees asked was "Where do I go to sign on with the Army?"

The mobilization of the new army was an emergency, as the war was a classical 'war of national survival'. Every possible resource was being brought to bear on the crisis. The first priority was the care and management of the women, children, elderly and infirm among the refugees. This also included an effort to help those who had fled the radiation and fallout from the nuclear bombs that had destroyed the major cities of Sydney, Brisbane, Melbourne and Canberra. The injuries and suffering had been of a scale that was so massive that it was simply unmanageable. Of those who survived the shock and blast effects, and had been able to begin the long trek to safety, most had succumbed to their injuries within weeks, there being no medical aid available. Others, who had ingested radioactive fallout, had taken longer to die, and had suffered far longer.

Taking stock of the staggering losses, Australian civil defense and military officials were faced with a national war effort to throw off an estimated eight hundred thousand invading soldiers from China with less than forty thousand Australian soldiers, twenty five hundred US Marines of the MAGTFA in Darwin, and a pool of perhaps a million civilian candidates suitable for military training. The rest, less than six million citizens in free Australia out of what had been a population of nearly thirty million, were applied to the efforts to prepare long term food supplies, to improvise hydroponic and other forms of food production in the face of the coming nuclear winter, and to support the surviving population. Even with the extraordinary degree of cooperation and the best efforts of what was left of the nation, it was clear that there would not be enough food, energy and other supplies to support the surviving population for the anticipated ten-year length of the nuclear winter – let alone support the rapidly expanding military effort.

Terrible decisions had to be made, regarding where the balance lay. How much should go into the war effort, and how much into saving the people? This question tortured decision makers at night. In the end, the decision had been made for them by the Chinese.

With the 38th and 41st Group Armies now moving across northern Victoria and eastern New South Wales, punching through each and every defensive line that the Australians had thrown together, it had become clear that Adelaide would fall in a matter of months.

All resources then went into the war effort. Saving the citizenry would have to take a back seat to national survival.

Without a large standing army to deploy, and with the bulk of Australia's military equipment, infrastructure and leadership having been taken out by the atomic warheads that had targeted the major cities and military installations of Victoria, New South Wales, and Queensland, it fell on local community leaders, police chiefs, and small military units to organize themselves.

In some cases, the innovative actions taken by a single person had made all the difference.

In the tiny town of Beachport, South Australia, with just a population of only eight hundred people, one man had had enough of the inactivity and gloom as the townsfolk debated about what to do. Without any authority other than what he knew to be right, down-on-his luck fisherman Mike Carleton had an inspiration. He and his son gathered together a few men and convinced them to help. They headed west along the coast highway to the site of the Woakwine Cutting. There, using earth moving equipment and the man's own expertise with explosives, they installed a rather unorthodox piece of engineering which, if things were as bad as they seemed with the Chinese advancing westward along each and every highway, could come in handy should the PLA send a force westward into South Australia along the Great Coastal Highway.

With the surprise at the Woakwine Cutting having been prepared, the men then set about to organize defenses further west, in the more defensible terrain between Lake Eliza and Lake Hawdon South.

It was the same across the nation. Locals took it upon themselves to destroy bridges, erect barricades, evacuate livestock, poison water supplies and create all sorts of innovative surprises for the advancing formations. Where they were given guidance from those with military training, or specific direction from the quickly mobilizing new Australian Army, larger scale efforts were organized.

Many of these were amateur, and quickly defeated by the aggressive actions of the reconnaissance-in-force tactics used by the PLA. Where the militia were able to stall the advance, the PLA would call in air support or bring down a well-coordinated bombardment from artillery formations which the PLA Ground Forces moved from place to place in support of the battalion or brigade charging along a particular highway.

And where the defenses seemed formidable, or where destroyed bridges or other obstacles required excessive resources, they attempted to bypass these using secondary roads. Knowing full well that they could be being funneled into an enemy "kill zone", the PLA were cautious enough to send out numerous reconnaissance parties to determine where the enemy would attempt ambushes or other confrontations.

In the case of the advance through southern Victoria into South Australia, for example, a regiment of General Sheung's Army Group South, the prestigious 1st Armoured Division, 65th Group Army, out of Beijing Military District, was defeated by one just one man.

General Sheung still could not believe it, however after putting the pieces together, the facts ultimately told the story.

Colonel Baoshu Jing had encountered so little resistance in the shell-shocked population of Portland, Victoria, which had been seized by air assaulters and then reinforced with shiploads of armor, men, and supplies for the 65th Group Army's 1st Armoured Division that within a month of his arrival in Portland he had sent his best regiment westward, up the Great Coastal Highway, with the instructions "not to stop until Adelaide". Jing's vision was that the 180 T-99 tanks and 98 infantry fighting vehicles of his 1st Armored Division would reach the highlands above and to the east of Adelaide before the Australians could put up any sort of defense.

Jing sent out smaller units in a spoke-and-wheel operation based at his headquarters in Portland, placing no more than a Battalion in each of the larger towns. His main effort was to push as much of the 1st Armoured and the 14th Artillery Brigade up the coastal highway as fast as possible, and quell any local resistance as it came. With no more than cops and farmers to deal with, there was no risk of a major military engagement. Therefore, according to Jing's risk analysis, the course of action that held the greatest operational risk was being *too slow*, giving the Australians time to build up defenses in Adelaide – his objective.

And then his men had fallen prey to the wildly creative imagination of the unemployed fisherman from Beachport.

Recon parties from the 1st Armored Division had determined that with several bridges having been destroyed along the main route through Milicent, and the Princess Highway, weeks of engineering support would be required to re-open the route. But much of the 65th's Group Army's engineering support equipment had been lost when one of his supply ships had been destroyed by the Australians. Lacking the bridge-building equipment required, Colonel Jing sent his force up the narrow but well maintained Southern Ports Highway, which hugged the coast.

Moving such a large formation on a single-lane highway was a difficult task, even without the risk of enemy action, but they made good time at first. Within another two weeks the formation had passed the tiny seaside town of Beachport, just inside South Australia, when they had learned of a sizeable force of militia and Australian Army that had entrenched in the narrow terrain between two large lakes, some 40 kilometers farther west.

With his planners urging caution, Jing ordered his armor to hold in a flat area at "Magery's Lane", just 30 kilometers from the expected battle area near Lake Eliza and 10 kilometers past Southport. Meanwhile, Jing's planners organized the deployment of artillery and infantry support another five kilometers ahead, so that a well-coordinated assault could be orchestrated.

The plan, classic land forces doctrine, was to clobber the defenders with artillery and any air support that could be mustered – almost none in this case – and then to move forward with sufficient infantry to support and protect the armor, and have the armor provide the fire power, manoeuverability and speed that only armor can deliver, and punch through the enemy formation and carry on to exploit the break-out. Jing imagined his beloved ZTZ-99 tanks rolling over the Australian rear element and driving over their reserves, clearing the road to Adelaide.

But just hours before the order to commence would be given, his tanks were removed from the equation.

Hiding in the bush just 500 metres from the densely packed formation of tanks and infantry fighting vehicles of the PLA's 1st Armored division, Mike Carleton nodded his head, giving the order for Rick Glass to connect the lead to the battery.

Rick was a retired miner, and had been among the first to go along with Carleton's idea. He had convinced others to help him gather the required blasting non-polar, 2-wire connecting wire; the fuses; several 25 kilogram sacks of "ANFO" ammonium nitrate prills; cap-sensitive high explosives and the blasting cap itself.

Like he had so many times before in the open pit mines he had worked during his 30-years career as a miner, Rick confirmed the circuit integrity, lifted the safety catch on the detonator, and pressed the button.

The earth shook and then erupted several hundred yards away, a giant grey plume rising out of the Woakwine cutting.

Originally carved from the limestone ridge in 1967, the Waokwine Cutting was a simple, kilometer-long thirty meter deep gouge carved through the rock to drain ten thousand hectares of swampland and the entirety of Lake George. The project took five years to complete, with over twenty thousand hectares of fertile farmland liberated from the soggy wetlands above Woakwine Ridge.

The reverse of this feat had been Mike Carleton's ingenious concept. He had long believed that if McCourt's Woakwine Cutting became plugged, the farmland above would be inundated with a massive quantity of water having nowhere to go.

He and the other men from Beachport had set up a wooden plug across the three-meter width of the deepest part of the cutting, to hold the drain waters back for the twelve hours it took to place the high explosives and sacks of ANFO, to bury them with packing pit-run fill, and then to bulldoze another ten meters of fill on top of their explosives-laden plug.

In the ensuing weeks the vast and highly productive farmland above the plug was flooded, with waters backing up for several kilometers inland. So when the shock of the explosion subsided, the plug in the Woakwine Cutting having been blown sky high, there was suddenly nothing holding back hundreds of millions of litres from flooding through. A deluge surged through the narrow cutting like the burst dam that it was.

The men loitering around their tanks and infantry fighting vehicles in the flat land below had felt the nearby explosion and had believed that they were under attack from their flank in the hills, and had scrambled into their tanks and infantry fighting vehicles.

That had been their death warrant.

Within minutes of the explosion, the land under 1st Division's 180 tanks and 98 infantry fighting vehicles was transformed into a shallow lake. As the water swiftly rose, the tanks were first completely bogged and then, as the water found its way into the portals and other openings, became watery coffins. Those men who escaped their tanks were washed away with the dirt, trees and other debris carried over the escarpment and into the ocean.

Half an hour later, when the water had completely drained from the flooded lowland next to the sea, the half-dozen men who had stayed with Carleton and Glass came down from the hills above to assess the damage.

The damage report they sent to their Australian countrymen farther up the road, and the damage report sent by the few Chinese soldiers back to General Jing in Portland, were pretty much the same: The 1st Armored Division was completely destroyed. The tanks and infantry fighting vehicles that littered the fied were full of mud and corpses, completely wrecked.

The news of the disaster had stirred the soldiers into action. On the Chinese side, the infantry and artillery units that had been deploying ahead of the armor were now cut off, and terrified by the news. They attempted to flee to the north, but ran into trouble on Claywells Road, where the small bridges over the agricultural canal had been destroyed. They were trapped by an obstacle that any army could easily overcome – had they the time to bring forward their engineering support.

On the Australian side, news of the destruction of the 1st Armored Division and the subsequent withdrawal of the infantry and artillery units in disarray spurred the Australians on to close with the fleeing enemy.

With the Australians bearing down on them, many soldiers abandoned their equipment and waded across the canal and tried to flee on foot to the east along Claywells Road.

Those who turned and tried to put up a defense were quickly killed by the advancing Australians, who had no more than a handful of Light Armored Vehicles and a few dozen civilian trucks full of lightly armed militia. The Australians killed or captured several hundred soldiers and harried onward thousands more fleeing personnel, who had abandoned their transports and crossed the canal on foot.

Of the five thousand PLA personnel of the infantry and artillery units who had attempted to flee the Lake St. Clair battle area, only a few dozen made it back to Portland and the headquarters of the 65th Group Army. The remainder had been mercilessly hunted down and killed by the militia, local farmers, and Australian special forces. It had been the first major victory on the southern front, and had not only turned back the Chinese offensive in the sector but had also yielded valuable artillery and other weapons systems, truckloads of munitions, and more than a few T99 tanks that had been placed on flat-beds and trucked back to Adelaide to be repaired and put into service with the Australian Army.

All across the area between South Australia and western Victoria, there had been other clashes. In many cases, great numbers of militia and Australian soldiers had been killed, up against well equipped, professional soldiers of the 38th and 65th Group Armies, but taken as a whole, these efforts had soon stalled the westward advance of General Sheung's Army Group South. Certainly the loss of the 1st Armored Division and the need to base large numbers of troops in each of the many crossroad and towns had left the PLA with insufficient troops to mount further offenses towards Adelaide without major re-allocation of forces in the region.

The Australians had bought themselves time, and used it to their advantage.

In the months after, the arrival of the Indian Army's 75th Regiment and 10th Mountain Division to the frontal areas provided a much more powerful Corps sized blocking force to reinforce the beleaguered Australian defenders of the border between Victoria/New South Wales and South Australia. The Chinese advance in the south was now stalled as well.

With the front largely stabilized, the race was on. As the Chinese worked to complete the pacification of the occupied areas and the deployment of two campaign sized formations for the next wave of assaults to come, the Australians frantically stood up additional divisions of poorly equipped infantry in Adelaide and brought in other units that had been created in Perth and other force-generation areas in the western half of the country.

For Lieutenant Colonel Weir, the speed at which these newly trained Australian solders were being thrown into the war and the short life expectancy of these inexperienced soldiers had caused him to decide to get Jake assigned to 1 Commando Regiment and the Australian SOCOMD organization based in Perth. So, strangely, by making Jake into a Special Forces soldier, he was protecting him from danger – at least for the time being.

Jake had done well in his training. He had the physical fitness and stamina to endure the strenuous training at Campbell Barracks, just south of Perth. What Jake lacked was the mindset of a soldier. The way Jake made his decisions was just too slow, and thought process was simply too complex to be an effective killer, Weir reflected of his son. *I'll have to take him along on a mission and find a way to teach him the art.*

It would be almost two years before the opportunity presented itself to Weir. In that time, Jake had been relegated to low-profile tasks, largely in the Perth region, where now Colonel Weir could keep tabs on his son, keep him out of danger. But he still wanted to spend some time with Jake in the field, to hone his son's skill as a soldier and, ultimately, to make a true Special Forces operative out of him.

And Jake showed promise. He had built a reputation of his own as a reliable and capable soldier who worked well with the Australian Special Forces personnel he had been mixed in with.

So when Colonel Weir had been approached by the CIA man, Rylan O'Connor, to put together a team to link up with O'Connor's contact in Indonesia, Colonel Weir had decided that not only would he personally lead the mission, but that he would also bring his son along.

It was a dangerous and important assignment, but one which Weir believed provided the right balance between the dangerous unknowns of a true Special Ops mission and the relative safety of an in-an-out of the task. If successful, and Weir was confident that he would be, having the mission under his belt would give Jake the confidence – and the credibility – that he would need if he were to advance beyond his current rank of Corporal in 1 Commando Regiment.

After a solid week of map study, cultural and language overview, intelligence briefings and war-gaming their upcoming mission, they were ready.

The team was comprised of four men trained in four completely different worlds: Colonel Weir – a product of 75th Ranger Training Battalion; Captain Thorne, Australian Special Forces; Corporal Jake Weir of the short course into the Australian Army's SOCOMD, and Sergeant Rick Rideout from the 3rd Marines. Despite their differences, the four men were operating as a Special Forces team, with the full support and assistance of the MAGTFA and the Australian Navy for their preparation, infiltration, ex-filtration and, if need be, Combat Search and Rescue or, in the worst case, the recovery operation to destroy their intelligence value and obtain their bodies for formal identification and burial.

The mission plan was to a quick "in and out" to meet with CIA contacts in Indonesia to discuss coordination and mutual support in a coordinated offensive against the Chinese in the Australian-Indonesian theatre of war.

CIA Station Chief, Rylan O'Connor, had put it all together but did not have the resources to carry out the mission, and had asked General Adams and Colonel Ferebee for support.

The team put together by the CJOC brought with them some secure communications equipment and code books for Rylan's Indonesians contact to be able to be in better contact with the CIA thourgh the Pine Gap facility. After providing the comms equipment, Colonel Weir was then to conduct the sensitive negotiations in person. He had been thoroughly briefed by O'Connor and understood the full range of implications that the proposed agreement would have on the Allied war effort.

As Special Forces missions go it was actually very routine. Capt Thorne had made up the plan, and had identified that the greatest period of vulnerability – once they were on dry land – would be presented by the two kilometer wide stretch of flat terrain which they had to cross on their exfiltration route to the coast. It could lead to their being exposed, and therefore it was given the most attention in their planning.

The Intel provided by the Indonesians was that the Chinese rotated their foot patrols on a randomly timed overnight shift change, between 0200 and 0400 hours each night, and similar timing during daytime. After rotation, the off-duty squad carries on in an anti-clockwise patrol down through the nearby village and returns to their support base through a valley to the east. With good intel on the enemy patrols, the team set off from Darwin in a small high-speed patrol boat operated by the Royal Australian Navy, and the final two kilometers to the shore by way of a Rigid Hull Inflatable Boat, RHIB, the larger, faster cousin of the ubiquitous Zodiak.

As they traveled the six hundred nautical miles from Broome in a straight shot north to the Indonesian island of Sumba, the men thought through the next stage of their mission. Colonel Weir and Top Sergeant Rideout would meet with the Indonesian nationalists in a safe house outside of Manoekangga. The site had been chosen for its remoteness, lack of population centers, and reasonable access from Australia. It was part of the 9th military district, Kodam IX Udayana, considered to be the least prestigious off all. But for the contact O'Connor had set up, getting in and out of Sumba, for their Indonesian contact code-named "Pebbles", it came with the plausible explanation that he had journeyed from Jakarta, the Indonesian capital and power centre, to visit his family on the remote island.

With over 230,000 active duty soldiers across the twelve military command areas, and an additional 180,000 Chinese soldiers operating in Indonesia, there would have been zero chance of a successful infiltration of even such a remote area as the Manoekanga delta. However, with careful selection of on-duty Indonesian soldiers who could be trusted to turn a blind eye in a particular direction when instructed to do so by their most trusted superiors, O'Conner and his Indonesian contgacts had engineered a gap in coverage of the approaches to one of the larger of the 18,000 islands in the Indonesian archipelago.

That left just the Chinese-operated post, established on the headlands that looked over the delta, as much to keep watch over the coastline as to serve as a constant reminder to the Indonesians that the Chinese now called the shots throughout the archipelago.

After a very rough ride in the Royal Australian Navy's fast-boat the team was relieved to be have a gentle mist and relatively calm seas just off of the island of Sumba for the final sea leg of their voyage. They were confident that nobody holding watch on such a dreary night would be able to see more than a few hundred yards out to sea, let alone the two kilometers farther west along the shoreline form the observation post where the team came ashore with their RHIB.

After a quick huddle under a poncho to confer with each other regarding timings and map recce, they all understood that they were exactly where they were supposed to be, and essentially on time.

They secured the RHIB to some rocks just inland from the shore, and covered them with bush and logs on the uninhabited stretch of beach.

Then, without a word, the men set off in three different directions. With the coast of Sumba Island free of snow, with Indonesia that much closer to the equator, the team would have no need of the snowshoes and other winter kit they had been using in the much colder climate that now gripped Australia.

Colonel Weir and Sergeant Rideout headed due north, up the steep terrain for a five kilometer trek through the sparsely treed terrain to the small hill where they would link up with "Pebbles". His actual name was "Major Bambang", one of the growing number of Indonesian soldiers who were part of the nationalist movement, who wanted to get rid of the Chinese who had taken over their country at the outset of the war.

When the war broke out, Indonesia's political elites had been given a harsh choice: peacefully embrace Chinese military control – even contribute forces to the Chinese effort in Australia – or face the utter destruction of their major cities, the annihilation of their people, and still face Chinese occupation. With so much to lose, and after recent years of steadily increasing influence from Chinese infrastructure projects, mutually beneficial trade and military cooperation, the Indonesian elites had chosen to take sides with China.

But no sooner had the Chinese moved their 16th and 23rd Group Armies, all the way from Shenyang Military Region, as the occupying force, but the true nature of Chinese military cooperation became evident.

The Chinese were terrible. From the lowliest civil servant all the way up to the President of the Republic of Indonesia, the Chinese officials treated the host nation officials as trash. Within a week, complaints of brutality, even rape and murder, began to circulate.

At first the elites put it down to the tensions that were natural when two great powers blend their forces. But when the President's own daughter was raped by a particularly brutal PLA officer from the joint Indonesian – Chinese military headquarters, even the pro-China elites recognized that they had chosen poorly.

However, with the Chinese now firmly in control of the organs of power, key military installations and having their own soldiers guarding the armories and depots, the Indonesians had played it cool. To throw off upwards of 200,000 Chinese soldiers was a massive undertaking, and one which required secrecy, discipline, and most importantly, *timing*.

And the opportune timing had been presented to the Indonesian nationalists. After the Chinese had run into some problems in Australia, and their commander, General Bing, had ordered the 16th Group Army to prepare for embarkation to Australia, the Indonesians saw an opportunity.

Their initial plans to stir up a rebellion after as much as one half of the occupation force were redeployed out of Indonesia had run into some snags, as the Chinese had ordered the Indonesians to provide two Indonesians divisions of mechanized infantry along with three engineering support regiments and other customized water-borne capabilities which the Indonesian Navy possessed, to roll up with the 16th Group Army for deployment to Australia.

With a large portion of their army now required to mobilize under the careful watch of the Chinese, and with the Tentara Nasional Indones, TNI, the Indonesian National Armed Forces so full of Chinese spies, the conspiring leaders had chosen to quell any talk of rebellion and to foster a mild increase in cooperative spirit between their men and the Chinese.

The Chinese had taken it as a sign that the Indonesian elites wanted to ingratiate themselves with the Chinese, for personal gain or in a misguided attempt to serve the interests of the Indonesian people. Whichever, it pleased the Chinese to no end.

Pulling this off had been a delicate task, as so many Indonesian soldiers, sailors, and airmen had come to despise taking orders from the crude and pushy Chinese. They resented being forced by their leaders to go along. Those who stirred up trouble with the Chinese had been taken out, one way or another, by the Indonesians themselves. In some cases, this was achieved by applying pressure to the man's family, by re-assigning him to some godforsaken outpost where he could be kept quiet, or in a rare few cases, assassinated by their own leaders. Keeping face with the Chinese, even if just for the few months needed to get through the mobilization phase, was that crucial for the plan.

And the plan was known to the Americans, who had their own agents within the TNI. Very few knew the full extent of cooperation between the TNI and the Americans, understandably, because if the Chinese ever caught on to the deception they would have slaughtered the Indonesian elites without compunction.

All that was needed was final coordinating information and to conclude the negotiations with the Americans. Obviously the Australians could not be part of this final phase, given that the price that the Indonesians wanted to extract from the Allies was partition of much of Northern Territory and Queensland, to become Indonesian territory after the war.

The Indonesians knew that any such barter with the Americans would be of almost zero value, other than to provide them with a pretext for their own invasion of Australia once the Chinese were defeated.

And defeated the Chinese would be, the Indonesian elites were confident, as their rebellion would be timed to inflict the greatest harm to the PLA forces. To snatch defeat out of the hands of victory, as the saying goes. But for the plan to work, it had to be carried out in such a way as to be a well-coordinated double-shock to the Chinese, with the allied offensives in the northern and southern fronts in Australia. That required the allies to provide the Indonesians with details of the Allied offensives in Australia, and for them to time these with the Indonesian operations.

The actual timing was dictated by the planned departure of the Chinese convoy of ships being loaded with the men and equipment of the 16th Group Army and the Indonesian divisions that General Sheung was expecting to receive as reinforcements for his Group Army South. With the complex task of coordination, scheduling and pre-positioning now in its final stages, the Indonesian spies had sent the coded message out on HF radio, the signal for the Americans to send their official representative, Colonel Weir, for a final rendezvous where operational details, ship's names, coordinates, manifests and most important, timetables would be handed over.

Colonel Weir's meeting with the TNI spy was a quick in-and-out, requiring no more than five hours to complete, from 'feet dry' upon insertion on the beaches north-east of the Manoekanga delta to 'feet wet' again when the team dragged their RHIB back into the water, and headed out to sea to rendezvous with the RAN vessel.

While Colonel Weir and Sergeant Rideout were moving swiftly through the light brush towards their rendezvous, Jake's task was to watch the path that led from the Chinese garrison farther up river to the sentry post on the headlands overlooking Manoekanga. From 500 meters away, hidden in an improvised OP, Jake was to observe and transmit the time and size of the expected Chinese patrol when it passed.

Using his training as a member of the Australian SOCOMD, Jake had no difficulty locating the trail, and selected a suitable location for his OP. After laying silent for a good ten minutes to ensure that there was no movement in the area, he quietly shifted a few bits of wood to improve his line of sight over the trail, and to make his own presence even more invisible than his brown-on grey ghost ghillie suit provided. Meanwhile, farther to the east, Captain Thorne moved up on his objective, the Chinese OP itself. His task was to watch the patrol arrive there, after having passed by Jake's OP. The plan was to then spend one hour in their OP before moving on to the east, and down into

Manoekanga, before turning to the north and following the Manoekanga river inland.

Captain Thorne's task was to visually confirm that the Chinese patrol had left their OP overlooking the coast, at which time he would inform the three other team members that there would be no eyes on them as they made their departure. But to get into position near the Chinese OP, Captain Thorne had to cross the exposed terrain between the forest and the OP at the headland. Jake's task was to watch the trail and to warn Captain Thorne when the Chinese patrol was approaching, so that Thorne would not be caught out in the open.

The entire plan was designed for the team to complete their mission without firing a shot, so that their arrival and departure would go unnoticed, always the best way to operate.

When Thorne transmitted his guttural throat-clearing noise over the tactical UHF frequency with the microphone strapped to his throat, Jake recognized it immediately and gave the 'all-clear' whistle sound. Hearing this, Thorne understood that Jake had still not seen the Chinese patrol passing his OP, and that it was safe to leave the tree-line and make his way across the open terrain towards the Chinese OP at the end of the headland.

What Thorne did not know was that Jake had fallen into a bad habit in the two hours he had been sitting in his OP. Rather than to keep his eyes constantly on the path, Jake had taken out his field note-pad and composed a short letter to Melody, his girlfriend. He wanted to capture the excitement and thrills he was experiencing on his first real SOCOMD mission, and felt that looking at the path every few seconds, and listening constantly for the sound of the patrol, was adequate. Besides, *this won't take long,* Jake he thought.

What Jake did not realize, but what a true Special Forces operator would know instinctively, was that the enemy was well trained, and moved swiftly and silently as they made their way along their patrol route. The highly disciplined soldiers from the 13th Group Army made no more sound than a gentle breeze as they walked along the hard-packed ground of the trail. They did not see Jake, who had his head down in his hiding place, and Jake did not see them either. So when Jake responded with the 'all clear' to Thorne's signal, his reply was based on incomplete coverage of the last half-hour. Jake's short note to Melody had grown into several pages of deep thoughts, Jake reflecting on how short and precious life was and that they should get married as soon as possible.

He had put far more attention into his letter to Melody than he had into his overwatch task. And now Captain Thorne was going to suffer the consequences.

Taking the Chinese patrol's trail from the north-west, that Jake had given the all-clear about, Colonel Weir and Top Sergeant Rideout arrived at Jake's OP after a successful exchange of secret documents.

"Has the patrol passed?" asked Colonel Weir, already confident that it had passed two hours before, based on his son Jake's signal.

"Yes, at about 3:20," Jake lied. He had never seen the patrol at all, and suspected deep in his heart that they must have passed when he had been writing to Melody. He had been worrying about it for the past two hours, ever since he had heard something, possibly gunshots, from the direction of the headland OP and Thorne, but he said nothing out of fear of being held accountable. He had not felt this badly since being caught lying to his father when he had stolen money from his dad during his high-school days.

"Well, we have not heard from Thorne yet, so he's late. The Pandas must be staying in their OP longer than expected," Rideout said, looking strangely at Jake.

"Let's get moving," ordered Weir, helping his son extract himself from his improvised OP. "We'll have to move carefully as we get near the clearing and the headland OP, unless Thorne comes back on-net with the 'all-clear'," said Colonel Weir.

After moving with care and haste the two kilometers to the clearing, they arrive to an unexpected scene. The corpses of two Chinese soldiers lay on the ground at the far end of the open field. *They should not have been there*, thought Weir, rapidly going through the possible explanations in his mind.

He looked at Jake and saw the shameful way that Jake was avoiding his eyes. *Shit*. Weir realized, *he screwed up*.

Without a word, Colonel Weir and Sergeant Rideout advanced as a pair, their suppressor-fitted EF88 assault rifles raised, their aim-points swivelling left and right as they moved in on the small structure.

Inside they found Thorne, alive, sitting in a plastic lawn chair by the window that overlooked the coast. The grey light of dawn made the coastline dimly visible in the distance, where their RHIB lay waiting.

By the thick red blood that made a stark contrast to the white plastic, it was clear that Thorne had lost a lot of blood. "What happened, Thorney?" Rideout asked, as he examined the three dead pandas that littered the floor of the small, concrete shack.

"They must have really been moving fast after they passed Jake's position," Thorne began, "cause they came up on me just minutes after I set out across the open ground."

Everybody knew that it was impossible for the patrol to have covered so much ground in such a short time. Jake avoided their accusing eyes as Thorne continued.

"I got two of them before they even started firing at me, and I almost made it to cover, but they got me in the leg. They dragged me in here, the three of them, and went to work on me. But I got a hand loose and got hold of one of them and got him to the floor. His mates thought it was good fun to watch him and I fight. So I made it look like he was kicking my arse, and over-acted a bit," Thorne said with great humour, pausing only to cough up some dark red blood.

"Take it easy, Thorney, let me look at you," said Colonel Weir.

"No point, Mate. I'm done for. I got my hands on another of them, used him as a blunt object on the third, and got his weapon. Got more rounds into them then they got into me. But I'm goners. I know it. My liver is perforated, I've got several rounds in my chest and guts..." Thorne trailed off, looking distant. His life was leaving him. Then suddenly he came alert again, just as Colonel Weir eased him to the floor and began opening his clothing to examine his wounds. He whispered in Weir's ear: "Don't' blame the boy," Thorney's last words.

While the team made their way to the RHIB, Jake refused any help as he carried Thorney's body over his shoulder for the final kilometer down to the beach. Nobody said a word. It was clear to all three that Jake's terrible mistake, diverting his attention from the task, had led to Captain Thorne's death. It could have other knock-on effects as well, with the Chinese now being alerted to the fact that forces unknown had taken out one of their patrols in Indonesia.

As Colonel Weir thought about it, he concluded that the mishap was not fatal for the operation at large, but his son's incompetence disturbed him deeply. *I'll have get Jake out of SOCOMD, and into something much less critical. Perhaps the Military Police, some place far removed from any danger, somewhere he can't screw things up too badly. Poor Jake, he'll have to live with this for the rest of his life,* thought Weir.

Meanwhile, several thousand kilometers away and deep in the frozen interior of Queensland, another mission was going horribly wrong.

Master Sergeant Gannon and the rest of his recon Platoon were in a world of hurt. They had been sucked into a trap, and cut off from the rest of the force. The platoon of Marines from the MAGTF had been scouting the Chinese defenses at Barcaldine, a tiny hamlet that was considered to be a tactical center of gravity for its cross-roads and airfield. It had been defended by 1st Brigade, 372nd Division, 42nd Group Army. The same Group Army that the Allies had decimated over two years before at the Battle of Cloncurry, where two entire divisions of the 42nd Group Army had been wiped out.

But this time it was the Marines who had over-extended themselves. Finding the town unoccupied, with the 1st of the 372nd having withdrawn to the east, the recon platoon and the supporting company of Marines had moved into the town to clear the buildings ahead of the Australians, who were a bit late to arrive with two companies of their own who were supposed to link up with the company of Marine led by Lieutenant Jarvis and Master Sergeant Gannon's recon platoon.

The trouble was, Recon Platoon was supposed to scout out the enemy positions in the town, and hold until the Australian force arrived before all three companies were to clear the town. With the Panda's unexpected withdrawal towards Emerald, some three hundred kilometers to the east, Lieutenant Jarvis had to make a judgment call. With the concurrence of MGySgt Gannon, he chose to send a three-man team one kilometer east on the A4 highway to cover the enemy's likely axis of approach, and use his remaining force of eighty men to sweep the town.

No sooner had he informed Colonel Ferebee in the CJOC in Katherine that the town was secure and the sweep nearly completed when the situation had been turned upside down.

It was a trap.

Colonel Yip, commander of the 372nd, had pulled his 1st Brigade out of Barcaldine, with a highly visible line of vehicles snaking out of town to the east, for the Marines to observe. But he had left three companies of his best men inside a half-dozen houses, waiting for the Marines to take the bait.

As the Marines became confident that the enemy had withdrawn, they became more and more dispersed across the small town, with four-man teams clearing individual houses and patrolling the streets.

Colonel Yip's men had chosen their hiding places well, typically at the end of cul-de-sacs and off of the main streets, so as not to be among the first to be encountered by the Marines. And when the time came, they poured out of their hiding places in sections of ten or twelve, quickly overpowering the first widely dispersed teams of Marines they encountered.

In his temporary CP set up at the town's hospital on the east side of town, Lieutenant Jarvis was immediately overwhelmed with radio reports and audible bursts of gunfire. His teams were under attack at a handful of locations, and his Observation Post on the highway reported a large enemy force approaching rapidly from the east.

Despite the best efforts of the Lieutenant to improvise a suitable rally point, the chaos that his men were facing, with large numbers of enemy soldiers cutting his teams off from one another, gathering his men together in one place proved impossible.

Within minutes, his men had taken cover wherever they were, and tried to hold on until a clear picture – and orders – were in hand.

It was a race, between the relieving Australian force and the much larger enemy force, and the enemy won.

Soon Jarvis's OP was off the net and the town of Barcaldine was literally swarmed with enemy soldiers, with dozens of Chinese soldiers jumping out of trucks and moving with purpose to secure intersections, larger buildings and other key positions.

For a moment, Jarvis considered surrender, to save the lives of his men, but he knew that in this war the enemy would give no quarter. Especially after what his men had done to the 42nd Group Army at Cloncurry.

The Marines all knew it, and fought heroically. They conserved their ammunition, and acquitted themselves well against the superior force, but ultimately ran out of ammunition before they ran out of enemy targets.

For some of the Marines it was the first time they had seen the true effect of PLA urban warfare doctrine, that of a fast-moving swarm of infantry locking down the entire town, unconcerned that they were losing a great many of their men in the process. They had numbers on their side, and knew that the Marines would run out of ammunition. Their greatest concern was to deny the Marines the time to call in air support – had there been any available – or to buy time for the Australians to come to their aid. The PLA were willing to take very heavy losses if it meant handing the Marines a defeat and taking out a one of the MAGTFA's limited number of irreplaceable recon platoons.

And that had been Colonel Yip's objective. The town of Barcaldine itself was important, but of far greater importance was attacking the high morale and confidence caused by the nearly unbroken string of victories the Marines had brought the Australians in Queensland. By wiping out the more than an entire company of Marines from the MAGTFA, and taking a few surviving Marines to be tortured and paraded before his men, Colonel Yip was poking a hot stick into the American eye.

By the end of the battle, Lieutenant Jarvis had been killed, along with Master Gunnery Sergeant Gannon. Only eight Marines had been taken alive. The prisoners were immediately transported to Emerald, where Colonel Yip and the rest of the 372nd Division anticipated having a few Marines to look at in the flesh, and take out their anger upon.

By the time the Australians arrived on the western approaches to Barcaldine, the 1st of the 372nd was once again entrenched in the town, making any attempt for the Australians to try to re-take the town completely futile.

The cavalry had arrived too late. Eighty Marines lay dead in Barcaldine. Eight would die in Emerald in the days to follow.

When word of the battle had spread across Australia it had bolstered the confidence of the Chinese forces, as per Colonel Yip's intention. However, on the Allied side, the mistreatment of the captured Marines, and the offense of the defeat, had failed to harm the morale of the MAGTFA. Plans were immediately drawn up to respond to Colonel Yip's actions.

For Colonel Ferebee back in the CJOC in Katherine, Colonel Yip had made it personal. *Colonel Yip, you are going to pay for this.*

17

OSAKA TO OTTAWA

It had been three days since the convoy of ships had passed them. With almost zero wind and only the gentle rolling of the calm seas, the sixty foot long *Grumpy Tortoise* was making less than two knots on her own, even with her high clue aspect ratio sail. But it was westbound progress nonetheless, gradually making its way across the solitary expanse of the Indian Ocean.

Colonel Mike Latimer and his wife, Sarah, liked it that way. It was a hell of a lot better than the constant wariness and lack of sleep they had gone through in their journey from Osaka to Adelaide.

Things had been cramped enough when there were eleven of them, on the journey from Japan to Australia. But now, after having bid farewell to one crew member who had chosen to stay in Australia, their number had been increased to twelve with the addition of their prisoner and the specialist provided by the Americans. And with the safety of South Australia well behind them and the unimaginably long voyage to North America still ahead, the mood on the *Tortoise* was subdued to say the least.

"Any luck with the charts?" asked Sarah, drying her hair with a small towel after her latest swim. A strong swimmer, Sarah had kept pace with their unusual sailboat while Mike kept watch for sharks, jelly-fish and any other threat to his wife of thirty years.

Zipping up his data-disk case, Mike smiled and flicked on the navigation system. It took only a few seconds for it to be up and running, and for the main page to be displayed on the monitor which Mike had set up on the small table in the after-deck near the tiller, it's umbilical tether snaking back into the main cabin to the navigation/communications panel.

Stepping down into the seating area to join her husband, Sarah recognized the turtle-icon at the center of the screen, representing their boat. The inch-wide swath of bathymetric data began to build out to the east on the computer screen as the *Grumpy Tortoise* plodded along to the west. Sarah knew that the gray-on-gray shades of the sea-floor data meant that the system still had not found itself; she also knew that it took hundreds of yards of data before tie-in could be achieved by the computer.

"Did you find a good chart?" she asked.

"Yup, but not a LIDAR one. Just one of the older deep-water series from NOAA."

"How far does it go?"

"It'll take us close enough to the Maldives and onward to the Seychelles, where we can use the next DTM card."

Sarah let out a breath of relief. She knew that once their nav system tied in with one of the super-accurate Digital Terrain Model cards – a topographical map of the sea floor – they would know exactly where they were. As she recalled how Mike had explained it to her in Tokyo, when he had shown her his design for the navigation system he and Tony had come up with, she had been sceptical. How do you *visually* navigate a sail-boat, in the middle of the ocean? But after thinking about it, and Mike's explanation that it was exactly the same as visual navigation that recreational pilots used, locating their position on a Visual Navigation Chart simply by finding an odd-shaped lake, an intersection of rail and road, distinctive topographic features or anything else that could be seen from an aircraft and found on the VNC, the underwater equivalent of map-reading made sense.

Of course, it all hinged on having a good sonar system that could bounce sound-waves off the sea floor and precisely measure the depth. You also needed a digital map of the sea floor and a computer program that could compare the tiny swath of data from the ship's sonar against the sea-floor map. The data requirement was enormous, but the job was made easier by Mike's ability to apply some of his skills as an Air Force navigator, using 'dead reckoning', combining what they knew of course and speed, sea current, drift, effects of wind and so on, which Mike plotted on a conventional sea chart. This helped him to narrow down the likely position of the *Grumpy Tortoise*, and reduce the amount of data that the nav system had to analyze.

When they were in coastal areas, or on the former shipping lanes, they could simply stick in a DTM card, set the scale to minimum, and input Mike's estimate of their current position and the nav computer would 'tie-in' their position, automatically finding a match between the sonar strip and the DTM data – a positional fix.

The problem was that for the vast, deep areas of the Indian Ocean, there were large areas where no Digital Terrain Model had been created – or if it existed it had not been acquired and added to Mike's library of digital charts. In these cases, with no nav data, they risked going hundreds of miles off course.

Such an error could prove fatal if it took them into populated areas where they would encounter desperate people, or to destinations which they knew nothing about. Their practice of staying as far from populated areas as possible, despite the added weeks at sea for each leg of their voyage, had proven to be wise. Even so, they had still had several scrapes, with several attacks and a great many stand-offs.

A few rounds from Mike's .50 calibre, splashing as warning shots ahead of the attacking craft, had discouraged many of the predators they had encountered, but in the relatively crowded waters off the Philippines and again passing the Indonesian archipelago, resulted in pitched battles.

Sarah's part in the battles had always been the same: call out the radar contacts on the 360-degree plot in the relative safety of the ship's main cabin, and keep an eye on the couple's teenaged daughter, Julia. For her part, Julia kept an eye on the two younger children, one from the Porter family and one from the Nelsons. With the children safe in the most well-protected part of the boat, their parents could focus on their role in the collective defense.

Barbara Nielson's task was to steer the ship, pull-in or extend the automated, telescopic mast or use the diesel motor to get the

Grumpy Tortoise moving in whatever direction Mike called out during an encounter with hostiles.

Being a Naval Lieutenant with command experience on one of Canada's smaller Marine Coastal Defense Vessels, MCVD, Lieutenant Nielson's skills at the helm, and the rugged vessel's surprising manoeuvrability at slow speeds, had made it very difficult for raiders to stay alongside long enough to board.

This allowed Colonel Mike Latimer and the four other men in the crew to pour on heavy fire from their firing points. Two of them men, while military, were not experienced soldiers. They could be relied upon to follow orders, and were trained in small arms, but were not marksmen. However, the other two, Roary and Clay, were from the Embassy's security detachment and had served together before as members from Canada's Joint Task Force Two, the elite Canadian special forces unit based in Ottawa.

They had also trained with the US Army Rangers at Ranger Training Brigade, and had deployed together with SOCOM units on joint operations which Canadian, British, American and other allied media would never hear of. Simply put, they were world-class veterans of the Special Forces world. That was why they had been selected for embassy security, where the enormous responsibility of providing security to diplomats and their families typically fell on the shoulders of just a small number of highly lethal professionals. They were not only experts with their weapons but also had a loose, confident way about them, seeming to anticipate each other's actions as only men who had been in firefights together on numerous occasions, in their case in Afghanistan, had in common. Their aggressive and highly effective warrior talents had come in handy when it came time to clear an enemy vessel, or to repel boarders that had made it onto the deck of the *Tortoise*.

Typically, Mike would fire the first shots at extreme range with the .50 calibre rifle. The sudden splash ahead of the aggressor's bow as they closed in on the unusual Canadian vessel had caused more than a few attackers to turn away and seek less well-armed prey. But for those who persisted, and closed in on the *Tortoise*, Mike would place at least one or two massive holes in their hulls at about the three hundred yard range.

The first few hits were part of the cost of doing business for some raiders, who were adept at repairing their vessels after a skirmish and had their crew ready to go with cloths and various sized wooden pegs to make temporary repairs to the inevitable bullet-holes they received when attacking their prey. It seemed that many attackers thought that once you engage in battle you are better off if you press the attack all the way until you capture the target, because it may end up being your only seaworthy transportation when all is said and done.

And with the high speed of the attacking vessels, Mike and the other men knew that the usefulness of the AR 50 was limited. Once the attackers closed to within a few hundred yards, the heavy weapon was no longer practical.

At this stage, they would open up with the Fabrique Nationale FNC1 assault rifles. These very old weapons taken from the armoury of the Canadian Embassy, along with several cases of 7.62mm rounds, gave the crew as much firepower as their attackers' typical AK47's, if not more.

With the advantage of good communications, a stable firing platform on the much heavier *Grumpy Tortoise*, and their military training meant that their attackers could rarely get within the five to ten yard range – where the attackers would normally be in a position to throw grappling hooks over the rails and board their victims ships.

With several pirates having been taken out by Mike and his men on the way in, the attacks had generally ended with the hostiles fleeing in disarray if not killed outright.

The few attackers who ever got aboard were momentarily thwarted by the triple line of razor-sharp concertina wire that paralleled the gangway that ran up and down the port and starboard of the ship. The few seconds it took to climb over the concertina wire kept them in the killing sights of the crew.

On one rare occasion, two raiders that had made it on board soon realized that the firing that was taking out so many of their men was coming from steel pill-boxes on the Port and Starboard wings of the ship. But when they closed in on the boxes they suddenly found themselves no-longer invisible. Small slits in the pill-boxes allowed the defenders to notice their approach. Suddenly orifices opened in the side panels, like the peep-and-shoot holes fitted to the door of Brinks armoured cars, and rounds erupted out of these holes.

The men went down to a few quick 9mm rounds fired by Clay and Roary inside two of the steel pill-boxes.

Other than that one very close call, the *Grumpy Tortoise* had easily thwarted the fast-boat equipped raiders.

The one time they had come up against a much larger vessel was an encounter with some sort of coastal defense vessel that had fallen into the hands of raiders. Facing vastly superior firepower of the armoured Naval vessel, Mike and his crew had reverted to a different tactic: that of holding off from firing, and attempting to communicate with the much larger vessel.

They never learned if the ship was indeed a warship of the Indonesian Navy, or a pirate ship, as they had used their one, terrible, weapon of last resort.

Mike called it their Armageddon weapon, as it was that terrible in effect.

When training the crew on what to do when facing imminent capture in a hopeless situation, Mike had gone to great depths to have them understand the moral implications of what they were being asked to do.

"You must understand, we are in a state of total war. We have been ordered to return to Canada by any means, and to take any measures necessary to avoid capture. Any means. And as you know, capture means torture and death – regardless of whether they are another nation or merely pretending to be officials. We are to treat all who come near as probable enemy. Our allies will have to prove themselves to be friendly, or have access to wartime codes to prove such. Therefore, if I ever give the order "Puff", you will not hesitate. You will act as if your life depends upon it, because at that point, it will." Mike had said, before showing the crew how Puff worked.

To the men operating the Indonesian warship, men who had for the most part at least some connection to their former role in defending their nation with the very same vessel, life had become a routine of targeting and boarding any promising ship that entered their region and then enjoying the bounty of goods looted from the unfortunate travellers.

In most cases, the rations and other supplies they looted from the smaller vessel would last no more than a week for the twenty two men aboard *KRI Sibarau.*

But in the case of the unusual, fat boat they were coming alongside on this night, and going by the number of fat western-looking people visible on the boat's deck, they were sure to find some goodies aboard.

"Heave to! Shut down your engines, and prepare to be boarded," the Indonesian Captain ordered.

Mike and the others aboard the *Tortoise* had watched the old warship approaching, first with binoculars and ultimately with the naked eye. From their point of view, the ship was massive, with a beam of 20 feet, length of 107 feet, and about 120 tons displacement. But in reality it was just an old 1960's era patrol boat. It had been sold to the Indonesian Navy by the Australians in the 1970s. Despite its age, the patrol boat was still capable of speeds up to 24 knots – much faster than the *Tortoise* could make under sail or engine power. But what really tipped the equation in favor of the Indonesians was the bow-mounted Bofors 40mm gun and the .50-calibre M2 Browning machine guns mounted on the deck. With heavy steel construction, even the AR50 was no match for the attack class patrol boat.

As the warship moved in on the Tortoise, Mike had given the order: "Prepare to Puff", and the crew had each done their part.

So when Lieutenant Nielson finally cut the *Tortoise*'s diesel engine and luffed and then retracted the ships automated sails, the *Tortoise* was coasting along at four knots, just upwind of the *Sibarau.*

The hatches were all closed, save for the main mid-ships fore and aft hatches, near each of which a few of the ship's crew stood on the deck waving at the Indonesian men in a friendly, compliant and decidedly non-threatening manner.

As trained, Nielson waited until crewmen from *Sibarau* had thrown grappling lines over the Turtle's rails, and were pulling the two ships close together.

It looked to Mike as though there were twenty or more men, all standing on the decks of the Indonesian ship, watching them with hungry intent.

Looking at them carefully, Mike made a few observations that confirmed his assessment of them as hostiles.

That made what he was about to do that much easier.

"PUFF," Mike commanded.

On the word of command the two men and one woman at the after mid-ships hatch literally dove through the hole, landing in a heap on the sail-bags and cushions that had been placed to soften their landing. At the foredeck, Mike was the last to disappear into the *Tortoise*, rolling over to look up in time to see Clay pull shut and dog the sturdy overhead hatch.

With their attention transfixed on the disappearing quarry on the deck of the small vessel, the Indonesians did not at first notice the odour, nor the fine spray that was emanating from the small boat.

In a few moments the spray had increased to a mist, and then a veritable cloud of vapour.

Then they noticed. *Shit!* Many of the men thought, when they realized what was going on.

The *Sibarau's* crew suddenly began to look about in horror, unsure of what to do, but the danger was clear.

With a cloud of droplets now wafting across their ship, the mist drifting over from the mast and other parts of the smaller vessel. The Indonesian men had become wet, and the air was filled with the unmistakable smells of diesel fuel and gasoline.

A few men chose to run towards the nearest portal, hoping to get a door between themselves and the fuel-air mixture.

A few other men stared at the cigarettes in their hands, and threw them into the air with horror.

The act was useless, of course, as a few errant cigarettes was not enough of a source of flame to ignite the cloud of fuel vapour that had engulfed *Sibarau*.

However, the sudden firing of maritime distress signal flares, with their incandescent and super-hot magnesium charges burning brightly as they flew from portals at the fore and aft of the *Tortoise* directly into the cloud and then smashing into the superstructure of the warship in a massive flurry of sparks, was more than enough to ignite the cloud.

The fuel-air explosion was visible from over eighty kilometres away. Its concussion cracked the deck of the Tortoise in several places, and tilted the two ships away from each other, snapping the heavy ropes that the Indonesian sailors had just completed making fast to the grommets on the *Sibarau's* deck.

Those men who had been caught in the open, with fuel-air in their lungs and their coveralls soaked in diesel, were burned alive – inside and out – in the massive fireball.

By the time the fireball plume had generated its own rising column of air, making the distinctive mushroom-cloud as it expended its fury and rose towards the sky, fifteen Indonesians were already dead.

It took several seconds for those inside to die, as the fire raced through the interior of the warship like so many angry dragons scouring the corridors and interior spaces of the ship in search of prey.

After the initial explosion waned, a new wave of explosions began within the ship as the fuel, oil and other combustible materials of the small warship went off in secondary explosions.

None survived more than a few minutes.

In the aftermath, as the two ships drifted apart and the all-clear was given, the crew of the *Tortoise* emerged from safety, opening the hatches and climbed up onto the blackened deck.

In the distance, the Indonesian warship was still ablaze, with the occasional pop and crack as various explosive and flammable materials cooked off.

Reading the strained expressions on the faces of his crew, Mike understood. It was one thing to kill in self defense, as a fast-boat of pirates closes in. It's altogether a different story when you pretend to be friendly and then suddenly burn everybody alive on the other ship.

"Mike. How do we know if we did the right thing?" asked Brenda, clearly troubled.

"You're alive, aren't you!" said Clay, with a tinge of anger in his voice. It was not that he was upset at the young naval officer, but rather, that he was still feeling the effects of the adrenalin and fury that accompanied battle, and had not calmed down yet.

"I understand your concern, Barb. But did you see the rank of the officer with the loud-hailer?" Mike asked.

"Yes. He was a Lieutenant-Commander."

"And what rank would normally command such a vessel?"

"Well, certainly not higher than a Lieutenant-Commander, but it could just as well be a senior Naval-Lieutenant. A ship like that would probably have no more than three officers, perhaps twenty men."

"My thoughts exactly. And what rank was the man standing on the foredeck, portside?"

"You mean the guy who kept waiving at us?"

"Yeah, the short guy."

"Come to think of it, he was also a Lieutenant-Commander."

"Exactly. And how did his uniform fit?"

"I didn't notice."

"It fit like a burlap sack. It was all ruffled up on his sneakers," said Roary, dismissively.

"I didn't see that. You sure he had sneakers on?" asked Barbara, starting to see where Colonel Latimer was going.

"And when you commanded your MCVD, if you were conducting a boarding, would you be at the loud-hailer, or in the bridge?"

"I'd be in the CIC, of course – on the bridge. OK, Sir, I get it. There's no way that was a professional naval crew. It was something else, something ad-hoc."

"Exactly. And we were well outside of Indonesian waters. Besides, from what I've heard on the UHF, Indonesia is completely under Chinese control now, so their navy would not be operating as if it was Indonesian. These guys were pirates. They must have been out here looking for prey. Who knows how many victims there have been. We are not in the business of being victims. So we had no choice. We did the right thing."

Sighing, Barbara was not completely ready to accept that burning them all alive like that had been the right thing to do.

"OK, Sir, I accept that we did what we had to. We had no other way to get out of that. But it still bothers me. I mean, just how far would you go to survive?"

"Just watch me, Mike said, stonily, before getting moving on to inspect the damage to his ship.

The crew of the *Grumpy Tortoise* had ultimately reached Adelaide, after giving the Chinese-occupied east coast of Australia a wide berth. Once in Adelaide, they had enjoyed a few weeks of R&R at a busy naval facility in the inner harbor. But soon Colonel Latimer had gathered everybody together, and informed them of their new mission. It was really the same as the one they had set out from Osaka with – to sail around the world to reach North America, and home. Only now they had an additional purpose, and two new passengers. Partly to make room, and partly for his own reasons, Clay had elected to stay in Australia. He wanted to link up with an old buddy, a former Special Forces instructor he had met in a joint training exercise at the Ranger Training Brigade a few years before the war had started. And in a meaningful coincidence, his old buddy Peter Weir, now Colonel Weir, had been the one who had given Colonel Latimer the new mission – that of transporting a captured Chinese Colonel to America.

The man could have been held in Australia until the war ended, however the Americans wanted to have someone from as high as possible in the PLA chain of command who they could interrogate and, ultimately, hold accountable.

Colonel Yip had been one of the PLA commanders on Colonel Weir's "Kill or capture" list. The man personally responsible for the atrocities in Charters Towers, Yip was one of General Bing's most zealous men in Australia; he had been instrumental in inflicting heavy losses on the Marines of the MAGTFA. After the defeat of the 42nd Group Army in the Cloncurry sector, Colonel Yip had been one of the few officers from the 42nd to survive General Leung's purge of his officers.

He had been given command of a Special Purpose Regiment tasked with harassing the Marines in western Queensland with Special Forces tactics. He had outsmarted the Marines on a couple of occasions, setting them up with planted intel and deceptive movement of his own forces in the Barcaldine-to-Longreach sector, drawing the Marines into a brutal ambush. Over eighty men out of a strike force of three hundred had been killed or captured by Colonel Yip's men. Of these, many had been tortured while others had been executed in a very open and brutal manner – as if to try to terrorize the Marines. Of course, it had the opposite effect. The Marines have a long memory, and do not forgive such inhumane treatment of their men.

Within two weeks of their defeat at the battle of Barcaldine, the Marines of MAGTFA had recovered. Hell bent on vengeance, they had sent a company deep inside PLA territory, travelling overland across the soggy, often snow-covered terrain of the Narrien Range, avoiding detection and engagement with Colonel Yip's patrols all the way to the outskirts of Emerald. The once sleepy outback town now housed Colonel Yip and the CP for 1st Brigade, 372nd Regiment, 42nd Group Army.

Supported with excellent intel from Australian Special Forces and a few local Chinese-Australians who had infiltrated Yip's headquarters as 'locally employed persons", Marine Corps Captain Scott and Top Sergeant Rideout had proven that Marines are indeed Special Forces in their own right. With just twenty six men they had taken out the sentries and penetrated Colonel Yip's compound, set up near the Botanic Gardens, moved into the house occupied by Colonel Yip and his staff, and quickly secured the dwelling. Using silencers and knives, they were nearly silent. Colonel Yip had been deep in sleep after a long day of planning for a raid on the Marines' encampment north of Longreach, when he had been rudely awaken by a Marine shining a flashlight into his face to confirm his identity.

"That's him. Bag him and tag him." Capt Scott said. All the while, as the take down had been carried out and during the exfiltration, Scott kept a close eye on Rideout. He was concerned that the Top Sergeant would let his personal feelings interfere with the mission, and take it out on the man responsible for

Master Gunnery Sergeant Gannon's death at the battle of Barcaldine. But the Top Sergeant did not stray from the mission plan. Rideout seemed to have taken his warrior skills up a notch, as though the seriousness and focus of his deceased comrade had rubbed off on him, altogether replacing his once cavalier manner.

Moments after his identity had been visually confirmed, Colonel Yip was unceremoniously rendered unconscious and then carried out like a sack of potatoes over Top Sergeant Rideout's powerful shoulder.

The team's exfiltration from Emerald had been difficult, as the alarm had been raised before they had reached the Zodiacs and Lieutenant Lion, waiting for them at Lake Maraboon. But with a well-timed series of explosions in town, some sniping and other diversions arranged by Captain Scott and some Australians, the Marines were able to get away with their prisoner.

Months later, once Colonel Yip had been transported all the way to Adelaide and the Allied high command, it had been quite a political battle between the Australians and the Americans. The Australians wanted to execute Yip for the war crimes he was responsible for at Charters Towers, and the Marines wanted to kill him for what he had done to Marines at Barcaldine. In the end the Americans had won out, and were about to convene Colonel Yips trial – likely leading to his execution – when orders had arrived from the United States that Yip was to be transported to the United States.

Despite the anger and rage that this order generated, the Marines had been forced to pass off their prized prisoner, and transfer him to the Australians from 1 Commando Regiment, who were to arrange the transfer of the prisoner. Colonel Weir himself, still seen as an American despite his new role with the Australian Army, had done his best to find an aircraft or other suitable means to transport Yip to the east coast of the United States. However there simply was no reliable way to get the man from Australia to America. But when the Canadian Colonel Latimer had shown up in Adelaide with the unusual vessel bound for Ontario, and word had gotten out of how well they had performed in the at-sea skirmishes they had faced along the way,

Colonel Weir decided to have the Canadians take the prisoner with them to North America.

Along with Colonel Yip, Weir decided to send along a Chinese-speaking Marine as the sole American member of Colonel Latimer's crew, both as translator to help with the supervision of the prisoner and to be something of a guarantee that Yip would ultimately reach the authorities in the US – or be killed if that proved to be impossible. He was Weir's ace in the hole.

Over the weeks since their departure from Adelaide, the Chinese speaking Marine had fit in very well with Latimer's crew, and had begun the long process of getting inside Colonel Yip's head. He was confident that by the time they reached America, he would have Yip ready to sing like a bird, perhaps even to reveal the location of General Bing's underground bunker in China, perhaps the most important bit of intelligence that the Allies were working on solving.

Sitting back on the vinyl of the afterdeck bench, watching the black-and white display of their navigation display change to an all-color display that suddenly showed all of the topographical features of the sea floor under and around their position to a radius of 100 nautical miles, Sarah Latimer smiled with pride in her husband's genius.

"We've got tie-in!" she said, with satisfaction.

Mike said nothing in reply, as he had picked up one of his well-worn old novels, and was engrossed in his book.

Watching her Air Force Colonel of a husband looking quite at home as Captain of his vessel, Sarah recalled the first time Mike had told her his plans.

They had been staying at Yumiko's apartment in the Kansai plain, on a weekend away from their post in Tokyo.

"So what's the big surprise, Mike?" Sarah had asked that Saturday morning, after taking a few sips of the chai that Mike had brewed for her, their morning ritual.

"We're going to visit a friend, and buy a boat!"

"What for? After all your talk about getting the hell out of Japan if things get much worse? Why would we buy a boat? And what, here in Osaka? That'll tie us down."

"Wait till you see her. She's a very unique little pig." Mike said, with a wry smile.

"A pig? What are you talking about, Mike?"

It was not until after taking the train to the dockyards on the south-east side of Osaka, and entering the small shipbuilding company's works that she understood why Mike had described the boat as a pig.

She was the ugliest boat Sarah had ever seen.

At first glance, Sarah had thought the twenty metre long vessel looked like any other mid-sized ketch-type of sailboat, but something looked wrong.

"It's aluminum?" Sarah was surprised to see the shiny silver, where the aluminum welds had been grinded smooth. But what really stood out was the ship's beam. She seemed incredibly fat.

It was not until they had been led up a gantry to a position high above the nearly completed hull that she really understood the shape of the vessel. She was not the long, sleek type of sailboat like the one they had used while posted at North Bay, where the couple had enjoyed free access to a friend's yawl, and honed their skills sailing the occasionally rough waters of Lake Nipissing.

"Why is she so fat?" Sarah asked, as she looked down into the open compartments of the ship, the deck not yet installed over the networks of aluminum bulkheads and interior walls.

The construction seemed overly heavy.

She tried to come to terms with what she was looking at.

"What the hell is this, a tug boat?"

"Nope. A sailboat. A sailboat designed with a purpose." Mike replied with excitement.

Sarah looked at her husband, turning to face him in full. "Mike, what sort of Mosquito Coast madness are you into now? This is not a sail-boat. She's so fat, and built like a brick-shithouse. She won't be able to move. And what is that, a swimming pool or something?" Sarah asked, looking at the large oval structure near the aft of the ship, about the size of a large hot-tub. There were other cylindrical shapes in other parts of the ship, and a great deal of complicated looking plumbing interconnecting the cylinders.

"Don't' jump to judgement so fast. Let me tell you about her, ok?" Mike asked, with that look that told Sarah that he had a great deal of emotional investment in the strange vessel.

"Ok, tell me about this pig."

"Yes, she does look like a pig, but we'll have to come up with a better name. Let me introduce you to her. She's a custom-made vessel, originally designed as a pleasure-craft for the Northern Passage, up in the arctic. You remember Tatsuo Yamamoto? That guy with the tall wife who looked like Olive Oyl?" Mike asked, referring to a wealthy Japanese he had gotten to know in the course of his duties as Canada's military attaché to Japan.

Colonel Mike Latimer had been tasked with assisting the man in negotiating with the Canadian government, territorial governments and other stakeholders in Canada for Mr. Yamamoto to obtain permits to build a network of resorts across Canada's arctic.

With the Northwest Passage having become ice-free for over two months each summer, there had been a flurry of international attention on shipping and tourism opportunities, and the Canadian Prime Minister had directed that all levels of government lean forward to help speed investment in the region, to help with the struggling economy.

The task had fallen to the Military Attaché to assist with the negotiations, as the Prime Minister's office had identified several former radar stations and other defunct military properties in the arctic as potentially suitable for the Japanese investor's ambitions. Using federal property, moreover, could allow the project to be advanced more swiftly, as it bypassed many of the local and territorial red-tape.

With the economic collapse in Japan, however, Mr. Yamamoto had cancelled the project after throwing tens of millions of dollars into research and design of the prototype sail craft.

As part of the liquidation of the Yamamoto Corporation, he had been forced to sell off everything, at whatever price, to stave off bankruptcy.

He had contacted the Canadian Military Attaché in Tokyo, the man who he thought of as a friend, as his personal and corporate world was falling apart around him.

"Mike, I can't pretend any longer. My Northern Lights program is cancelled, and we will not be moving forward with any of the projects in Nunavut and the Northwest Territories,"

"Wakarimasu, Yamamoto-San" Mike had replied with a smile, trying out his Japanese. "We knew this time would come, and I've already been given direction in this regard, from Ottawa." Mike replied, attempting to put the proud Japanese tycoon at ease.

"Direction?" Tatsuo Yamamoto asked.

"Let's face it, Japan's economy is in full collapse. The only people who think the yen still has any value are the poor old pensioners your government encourages to keep using the fiat currency. The rest of the world knows the yen is worthless. And with the US currency about to be replaced with those new G-Dollars, alongside our own gold-backed Canadian dollars, the whole world knows that gold is king again." Mike began.

"Sure. Gold is the only true money. But the problem is, until the new gold-backed dollar, or some other world reserve currency emerges, global trade is dead," the industrialist observed.

"Exactly. But in the meantime, the yen and the old dollars are still in circulation, even as the new currencies are being printed and distributed. So my instructions, or rather, those of my Ambassador, are to expend all of our Embassy's accounts denominated in Yen, US Dollar and Canadian Dollar by the end of the month, and to begin – and this is absolutely confidential Tatsuo – to begin using the G-Dollars on the first of next month."

Captivated by the inside information he was receiving, the industrialist's mind was moving a mile-a-minute. It suddenly seemed to him that there could be a way out of his troubles, perhaps even to stave off bankruptcy for his companies.

Mike went on. "So in regard to your commitments, especially the deposits and clean-up fees you've made for the Northern Lights enterprise – those we are going to convert to G-Dollars and keep on the books. You'll be one of the few Japanese with any of the new hard currency. But as for everything else, we recognize that the program is dead on arrival, and you'll be faced with the orderly wrapping up of the project. To help with that, I have been authorized to buy your prototype vessel, that fat pig you showed me in Osaka."

"Buy it? We've invested over a hundred million yen in that." Tatsuo began, but then faded, knowing full well that there was no point continuing the development of the prototype vessel if the program was already as dead as the global economy.

"What terms, or basis for valuation does Canada have in mind?"

"Well, here's the strange thing. I'm to offer you two choices. First, we'll pay you twenty million Japanese yen for it, if you can deliver it to the Port of Esquimalt, to our naval base there, in whatever condition the hull is in now." Mike began, clearly putting out the 'throw-way' option first.

"And the second approach?"

"You finish it, but not for the original purpose."

"And?"

"And we'll pay you twenty-million in gold-backed Canadian G-Dollars, and we'll accept it at your Osaka dockyards.

For Tatsuo, the prospect of getting hard currency and even keeping some of his employees working on completing the vessel, in this case for the Canadian military, opened up so many new possibilities. "Go on, Mike."

"We want the vessel to be completed, with some of the features as per the designs you showed me, but with a few other features added. And we want it completed by the end of the fiscal year – that's in just three months. Can you have her sea-worth by then?"

Feeling a bit ungracious for saying so, Tatsuo had to ask. "Will you advance funds now, to give me something to work with?"

"Yes. We can advance the nominal sum of ten million in the new currency right now, but you can't use it until the official launch of the currency at the end of the month. This is to fund the alterations – mostly cosmetic, add-ons to the fitment of the interior spaces and the deck, nothing major."

"So this ten million in new Gold Dollars, this is above and beyond the twenty million Canada is paying for the vessel?" Tatsuo asked, incredulously.

What Mike did not have the heart to tell him was that Ottawa had directed Canada's embassies, trade missions, and military attachés to throw around as much of the old money as possible and a massive surge of the new currency, upon its official release, so that the new Canadian G-Dollar comes out of the gates ahead of the new Euro and is competitive with the anticipated US gold-backed dollar, so that the Canadian economy will benefit from the restoration of the gold standard on equal if not superior footing to her rivals. Despite being a major producer of gold, Canada was still dependant on global trade, and the sale of her commodities. So if Japan, China, Korea and other manufacturing centres could not revive their failed economies, the economic stagnation affecting Canada would never end. As the ambassador hat put it to the trade and military staffs at the embassy in Tokyo: *'We're going to throw the new money around like a drunken sailor on shore leave!'*

From that moment, Mike had worked closely with Tatsuo, in an undocumented manner, on a military procurement project that entirely bypassed the complex web of red tape that was normally required of all military procurement. The project was entirely off the books, and if it were ever looked at in detail, would have been seen to violate all manner of actuarial controls, government regulations, security regulations and laws.

For his part in it, Colonel Mike Latimer had his own focus. The relatively small project he was overseeing with Mr. Yamamoto was just one of many ways the Canadian embassy was attempting to pour Canadian money into the Japanese tentacle of the global economy. But it was the one project that had a truly military purpose – that of serving as one of the contingency plans for the evacuation of Canadian Embassy staff.

Many of the staff, including the Ambassador, were from Japanese-Canadian families and had family in Japan. For some of them, should the Embassy be evacuated for any reason, they would have the option of remaining in Japan and taking leave from the Embassy during the emergency, or to return to Canada by the safest expedient means.

Some of the war plans and emergency scenarios – whether based on regional war or a cataclysmic earthquake and tsunami – called for sheltering in place, while others called for evacuation through any means possible. When the Embassy staff discussed the various scenarios, it became clear that in some cases, evacuation by sea would be more viable than an air-based evacuation plan. The trouble was that the Canadian Government did not have control of any sea-worthy vessels in Japan; and with the pressures on the Canadian Navy, it was rare for a Canadian warship to be on a port call to Japan.

So when the cable to the Embassy arrived detailing the guidance relating to the financial crisis; the direction to spend money on all variety of 'programs'; and the key signal that 'due regard for value for money, substantiation, and other normal best practices are hereby suspended', the Ambassador telephoned the Prime Minister to get voice confirmation that he had understood Prime Minister Currothers' intent.

After an unprecedented half-hour discussion with the Prime Minister, Ambassador Kirkwood put the phone down with a perplexed look on his face, and informed his senior staff of the situation in Ottawa and the new crisis in Washington.

"Shit is about to hit the fan when the Americans default on their debt. We are directed to repatriate non-essential staff and to close down most embassy services. That will leave no more than a dozen here. Mike, that means you and your military staff, but cut that back to less than a half-dozen. I'm sending everybody else home, and giving paid leave to the locally employed personnel," the Ambassador said.

That was when Mike had first gotten the idea of asking permission for Canada to "invest" in the vessel he had seen in Osaka. He knew that the ship's unusual design, and highly automated systems were right-sized for a dozen or so from the embassy, with lots of room for supplies. From that moment on, as Yamamoto's men completed the fitment of the ship, the remaining embassy personnel thought of the vessel as their ace in the hole. It allowed them to remain focussed on their efforts to shore up the economy of Japan and continue to serve Canada during this turbulent period.

Two months later, when Mike was showing the vessel to his wife, the ship still had not been given a name. Knowing that the Military Attaché and his wife were avid sailors, despite the man's Air Force pedigree, Colonel Latimer had been given the honour of being the ship's first Captain. The ambassador had insisted that Mike have his wife name the ship.

So even if the first visit to the shipyard in Osaka had been a shock to Sarah Latimer, she embraced the fact that her husband already decided that she would name the ship. When Mike showed her the ship for the first time, explaining the strange telescopic mast and boom and all of its intricacies, Sarah put her scientific brain to use in asking detailed questions, and had entirely put aside any reservation that the ugliness of the vessel had made on her. For her, "pig" was no longer a word that came to mind.

By the end of the tour, after satisfying herself that she understood the algae-diesel plant, unusual high-clue aspect sail design and the highly sophisticated navigation system, she hit Mike with the one questions he was uncomfortable about addressing.

"Mike, I get how this is supposed to be a 'green' design. That bio-fuel diesel engine, really makes sense. And I can accept that the sonar system has a benefit in collecting precise sea-floor data, and could even have other research uses when the guys at the naval yards in Esquimalt get their hands on it. But these other structures you've had them add, like those boxes on either side, and all those key-hole thingies all over the place. This thing looks like it's being retrofitted for some sort of combat. What gives?" she demanded.

"I can't lie to you, Sarah. Those are security features."

"Do you really think we'd need those? Just to sail across the Pacific, to the West Coast?"

"Well, suppose we had to go somewhere else?"

A look of shock took over her face as she finally understood. "You mean we might have to sail southwest? – like toward the Philippines and Indonesia?"

The stern, silent look on Mike's face was her answer. And she knew what that meant. It meant that for some reason, which his military code would not allow him to explain, Mike was preparing the ugly boat for the possibility of being sailed through the pirate-infested waters of southeast Asia.

From that moment on, she understood that the ugly ship was to be retrofitted to combat pirates and be self-sufficient. The image of a turtle came to mind, with some animal attacking the slow-moving creature as it withdrew its hands, head and feet inside the protection of its hard shell.

When the ship was complete and ready to be launched, the worsening economic situation made Sarah see the ugly boat as their only way to escape the coming chaos in Asia.

At a quiet ceremony, with the core embassy personnel, their spouses and children on hand, along with the Yamamoto family and several of the engineers, craftsmen and welders who completed the fitment of the fat boat, no more than fifty or so people, she swung the Champagne bottle with gusto, smashing it into the keel of the boat she had come to have a close connection to. Her words still hung in the air as the Champagne dripped off of the hull, and the blocking and rigging was removed, allowing the fat boat to slide into the dark waters of Osaka Bay.

She had kept the name secret until the final moment, just before flinging the tethered bottle at her:

"On behalf of Canada and the Yamamoto Corporation, I christen thee Her Majesty's Canadian Ship – Utility Hull number 4138, to be registered as a research vessel and known by her crew as the *Grumpy Tortoise*, may you protect all who travel in you!"

18

COMBAT INEFEFECTIVE

[Three and a half years into the war]

It frustrated Colonel Weir to be so far from the action. Ever since his promotion to full Colonel and secondment to the Australian Army's Special Operations Command he had been so wrapped up in the paperwork and endless rounds of meetings and briefings that he seldom had contact with the men of the Australian SOCOMD – his men – let alone with his American countrymen with the MAGTFA up in the Darwin sector.

Largely relegated to spending half of his time with the S5 planning cell of SOCOMD and the other half of his time reviewing the Special Forces Training Centre's latest version of the condensed "reinforcement training curriculum" that would turn regular soldiers of the Australian Army into lethal Special Forces soldiers, Colonel Weir knew that he was best used where he was. But despite that, he chafed at being relegated to staff work.

In the off chance that some turn of events could take him back into combat operations, he maintained his physical fitness regime. Perhaps not quite as rigorously as he had back at Ranger Training Brigade, but he could still hold his own when he ran with the younger soldiers.

He was as comfortable with the Australian Special Forces men of 1 Cdo Regt as he was with other Australians from Special Air Service Regiment. To him, the men of SASR were interchangeable with those of Special Ops Command, SOCOMD and on par with Rangers and Marines.

Ever since the war had started, and the Special Forces Training Center near Sydney had been taken out, along with the lion's share of Australian military and civilian power centers in New South Wales, Victoria, Australian Capital Territory, and Queensland, any surviving military installation safely located far to the west of the Chinese controlled areas had been quickly expanded to replace the lost capabilities.

In the context of Australian Special Operations, that meant Perth. More specifically, Campbell Barracks, just south of Perth. Home to the Australian Special Air Service Regiment, SASR, Campbell Barracks was the logical place to focus the entire Special Forces force generation effort. So while the newly formed units ostensibly were broken down into SASR units, 1 Cdo Regt, 2 Cdo Regt, Special Ops Engineering Regt, Special Ops Logistics Squadron, Military Working Dogs unit, Parachute School and Special Operations Training Centre, they were all Special Forces units under Australian SOCOMD. Unified by their cause, they were a very close, largely interchangeable, and highly motivated pool of Special Forces operators. They were just the type of men and women that Colonel Weir needed.

His mission, other than to ensure that SOCOMD personnel were properly trained, was to orchestrate a wide range of carefully designed missions. Some of his operations were focused on cultivating intelligence sources in enemy occupied areas, within the Chinese communities, through decrypted intercepts of enemy radio and other communications systems, and more conventional field work. For the first role, he had an entire organization of Australian civilian and military personnel ranging from former teachers from the School of the Air organization to academics and lay persons of Chinese origins. For the second, largely leveraging off of the capabilities of the first, he had a steady feed of information from the American facility at Pine Gap, with some first rate Intelligence Branch analysts at the Intelligence Fusion Centre that had been set up at *HMAS Stirling*, the Royal Australian Navy's major base on the West Coast.

However, all of this was insufficient. What Colonel Weir really needed was field work, the highly granular, specific information such as time-and-place, personalities and other information that fed into predictive behavior estimates. This was at the center of his close relationships with the personnel of SOCOMD. After getting to know them in his capacity as subject matter expert supporting their training, giving lectures on psychological warfare, insurgency operations, counter-intelligence and a myriad of other competencies, he would then change hats and be the man who sent them into high-intensity operations, extremely dangerous missions, and not uncommonly, low-return-probability, "LRP", missions.

The degree to which it affected him, sending his courageous young prodigies out on LRP missions, was a burden that he kept to himself. In his outward appearance, Colonel Weir was tough as nails. To him, it was pure military necessity. He had to send them out, put them in place to do their task despite the odds. And he had to ensure that they had every skill, every bit of technical knowledge, and as much support as possible for them to convert the LRP mission into a successful outcome. Not only out of caring for his men, but also so they could be used again for the next task.

Special Forces operatives, like the thousand or so US Marines still operational up in Darwin, were a rare commodity and had to be conserved.

With this philosophy at the core of the operational planning that he engaged the S5 staff with, Colonel Weir wanted to achieve the greatest effect with the least risk and resources applied.

This did not mean killing the enemy outright, nor sapping his will to fight. In some cases, such as USMC Colonel Ferebee's highly successful series of operations that defeated the 42nd Group Army two years prior, Colonel Weir's Special Operations in support of the larger mission were crafted to assist in drawing the enemy down the garden path, to play on their hubris and over-confidence until they had so far outstripped their logistical support lines of communication that they could be cut off from re-supply and ultimately forced to surrender or die in their vehicles.

That strategy had worked once.

Despite losing a Corps sized formation, the Chinese had made rapid adjustments to their operations, and ensured that they did not over-extend themselves like that again. They focused on tightening their grip on the local population. Not only to entrench militarily, but also to hunker down in preparation for the harsh conditions of the nuclear winter – and to have in place sufficient stockpiles of food, water, energy and other resources to survive.

But surviving the nuclear winter was only one aspect of the war. Conquest of the Australian continent was still the overall strategic goal, and one which the PLA had a fair chance of succeeding at.

In the first few years of the war, as the environmental conditions worsened and starvation became a problem, the Allies had put an enormous effort into relocating displaced civilians from the east coast, distributing them in an organized manner to the hamlets and towns in Western Australia, as far as possible from the frigid interior and from the combat areas to the east.

At the same time, they had begun their insurgency campaign against the invaders, doing everything they could to slow them down and interfere with their operations. This was intended to buy time until they could force generate enough organically Australian-produced divisions, and partly to buy time for larger formations of the Indian Army to be deployed, first arriving in Perth and then being transported across the frozen wasteland of the Nullarbor to Adelaide and then on to the front lines closer to where Melbourne had been.

And it was in this context that Colonel Weir had struggled to have the Australian High Command understand the long view. Not only was it essential to use Special Forces on the tactical and operational level to help win the skirmishes and battles of the war, but there was a more important ultimate objective of ultimately defeating the enemy. The way Colonel Weir had put it to General Adams and the others in the High Command: "We can win as many battles as you like and still lose the war, if we do not defeat the enemy's strategic center of gravity – their sheer numbers. At best, we will soon have six operational divisions, even counting the militia. That's no more than two hundred thousand men. And we face a technologically advanced, well-equipped and well trained Field Army Group, over twenty divisions, a stronger Air Force than we have even with the help of the Indians, over a million enemy soldiers now landed in Australia, and perhaps two hundred thousand Chinese Australians actively supporting them. They are destined to win this war. That is, unless they lose the will to fight; unless they come to the conclusion that they have lost."

"And how do we give them that perspective?" asked an Admiral, who had come to the opposite conclusion. From his point of view, the Chinese would win by attrition alone, even if it took them ten years.

"We need to work on specific individuals. We need to take the time to get to know them – build up detailed profiles and dossiers on their leaders here in Australia, from lowly Major on up all the way to General Ma. Then we need to deep-select the ones with certain attributes, the men who can ultimately be worn down, shaped by what they hear and see, ultimately rendered fatigued by their own consciences," Weir said.

"Fatigued? Those men are soul-less zealots. They thrive on suffering, murder, and destruction," Adams interjected. "Just how do you propose we tire them out? By dying for them?"

"That's just it. What I meant by 'deep select', we identify the most dangerous types, the General Bing zealots, the sort of men who will never stop. Men with no conscience. Those men, we will assassinate. They will be replaced by others, and with care, we can wind up having the right sort of men in the right place at the right time, and have them grapple with internal demons, morality, perhaps even nostalgic homesickness. In each case a carefully tailored series of pressures and inputs could be orchestrated. And for their men as well, in addition to using their fear of spiders, snakes, crocodiles and other uniquely venomous nasties to make them less effective soldiers – as we have been doing – we have to work on their personal understanding of what lies beyond the war, what their lives will be like if China wins, and how much better it could be for them if China actually loses and peace is achieved. And if we can combine the effects on the soldiers with the effects on their leaders we could put entire divisions into existential crisis at some critical juncture."

The moment of comprehension had been stark, but en masse the Australian High Command had finally understood Colonel Weir's strategic vision.

"So you are saying that you want to become the career manager for the PLA? Expend large resources to study them. Eliminate certain men. Move other men along into key positions. How? – by protecting them? Putting them on a 'no sniping list'? and then to go to work on their heads, have them conclude that the war, or their participation in it at any rate, is pointless?" asked the Admiral.

"Yes, Sir, that's about the size of it. At some critical moment, not now, but down the road when the stakes are at their highest, we render them combat ineffective."

"Colonel Weir, I gather you have read a little too much Sun Tsu," started General Adams, "And I am all for defeating the enemy with psychological warfare, but do you have any idea how much of an effort that would take? Not only on the analysis side, but in terms of field work, espionage, and the development of human intelligence resources?"

"Yes, General, as a matter of fact, I do have some idea," Colonel Weir began, his mood lifted now that he had the Australian High Command in a more receptive mood, "Here is what I have in mind…"

That had been three years ago, just six months into the war. Since then, the High Command had given him free reign to build up the required organizations, with increasing enthusiasm as they came to see that the cultivation of a deep understanding of the enemy, down to the sexual appetites, philosophical leanings, biases, habits of individual officers and the mountains of good intelligence that came as a by-product of Weir's massive project paid enormous dividends to the war effort at large.

Colonel Weir never told them that his inspiration had been the day back at Ranger Training Brigade, when his Commanding Officer had shown him the dossier that the Chinese spy had been building up on himself and other key staff at Ranger Training Brigade. He had no doubt that the PLA had a very thick file on him now, and that all of the attention he had paid to counter intelligence and loyalty-testing had more than likely kept him alive. *There's someone like me out there in the PLA, working on the time and place of my death.*

19

UNMISTAKEN IDENTITY

Even after so many positive interactions with Australians, and what he had to acknowledge as fair treatment by the Australian military despite the fact that the enemy was Chinese, he still felt hatred from Occidentals in general. It made him tense. He only truly relaxed when in the company of other Asians, despite the high risk nature of his work.

Thankfully, the military powers-that-be had given him assignments deep within the Australian-Chinese community, where he was basically autonomous, doing whatever he considered necessary as he moved around a particular community of interest.

By now he was very experienced in such missions, so it did not take him long to figure out who the players were in any given community. He had taken to looking at them in terms of several categories, only the last of which was of any great interest. He was not all that interested in the vast majority of Chinese-Australians, the so-called 'Brown Pandas', who were attempting in one way or another to stay out of the conflict. These were largely second and third generation Chinese-Australians, born and raised in Australia and for one reason or another they were unwilling to take up arms against the Chinese invaders. They would contribute to the war effort as required by the military, but not enthusiastically. They did everything they could to keep a low profile, hoping to come out of the war without having done anything that the ultimate victors would come after them for. It was the closest a Chinese could come to being neutral.

Then there were the Chinese nationals caught up in the war simply by virtue of having been in Australia – in the wrong place at the wrong time – when the war started. These 'Orange Pandas' were unfortunate souls who bore the brunt of the hostile anti-China response which the Chinese-Australians were largely exempt from by virtue of their Australian accents, citizenship, and the protection and safety of the extremely close-knit local Chinese communities. As it was, Orange Pandas, who had been mostly visiting students from mainland China, had already been a largely distrusted, perhaps even despised, group of outsiders even before the war started. These Chinese stood out like a sore thumb, with their heavy Chinese accents and lack of roots or contacts in Australia. Many simply turned up dead, or were locked up as suspected enemy agents in the many internment camps set up to isolate alien Chinese in the free-Australia side.

The spy knew that most of these unfortunates were simply students or tourists who were not part of the war; their ordeals a terrible consequence of the retributive justice the world at large sought to deliver against the Chinese state. Therefore, simply by virtue of their passports, any Chinese nationals found in the Free Australian territory had an extraordinarily rough ride. They got no support from the Brown Pandas, the ethnically Chinese Australians who may have spoken Chinese in their day-to-day lives, but did so with an Australian twang.

Of course, he knew that on the flip-side the Chinese nationals found things much easier within the Chinese-occupied sector, where they were quickly caught-up in the Chinese military administration of the occupied territories – sometimes with great enthusiasm. Not surprising, considering that they stood to gain great personal advantage by being of service to whichever Group Army controlled a particular sector.

These Chinese nationals within the occupied areas occasionally turned up dead, having been assassinated by 'Green Pandas' or other loyal Australians, as they were universally despised by those loyal to Australia. So they were of little interest to the spy.

Also of no interest were the 'Red Pandas', the Chinese Agents who had been sent ahead of the air-assaulters and follow-on waves of People's Liberation Army units several weeks before the war had started.

Originally termed 'Little Dragons' during the early phases of the operation, their role after the invasion had morphed into attempts at penetrating the Chinese community on the Free Australia side of the front, often by trying to pass themselves off as Australian-Chinese evacuees who had fled the Chinese sector.

If any of these were caught by the Allies they were invariably tortured for operational information – if they failed to clamp down on their strychnine-tooth before the suicide-tooth was removed.

And then there were the 'Green Pandas', the Chinese Australians who were actively loyal to Australia. These could be Australian-born, immigrant, or even Chinese nationals who were willing to fight side-by side with the Allies in the attempt to liberate Australia from the occupying Chinese forces.

These Chinese faced the ever-present oversight of counter-espionage experts coordinated by the notorious Colonel Weir, the American Army Ranger who had been so effective in advising the Australian Army's 2 Cdo Reg't in developing a series of loyalty tests, screening techniques and counter-surveillance routines to discover Red Pandas posing as Green Pandas.

Now operating as a full bull Colonel within the Australian Defense Force, not merely as a Liaison Officer from the US Army as he had been before the war started, Colonel Weir, RAA, had been put under the command of General McCullough, Commander of the rapidly-expanding Australian 1st SAS Regiment, Perth. The minute General McCullough got his hands on the then Lieutenant Colonel Weir, he had field-promoted him immediately to full Colonel in the Australian Army, in an unprecedented form of 'Acting While So Employed' designation – with the full concurrence of the US Army's 75th Ranger Regiment, who had only agreed to the General's demands with the understanding that they could have Weir back, at his former rank, when the war was over. Colonel Weir's new status, as an Australian, was considered to be the last favor that the US military could grant the Australians, with so much to deal with at home in the United States. So in a sense, the Australians had used up the last of the good will available from the United States, and would soon be expected to ante-up some meaningful contribution in the larger allied effort against General Bing's forces worldwide.

Wasting no time after he had been given a wide range of authority over both 1 Cdo and 2 Cdo assaulter training and their ultimate force employment in eastern Australia, and with his role as deputy commander of 2 SAS itself, Colonel Weir had developed dozens of Chinese speaking deep-penetration agents who operated within the Chinese-Australian communities. These agents would be gathering intelligence on the Red Pandas and Little Dragons who were subtly pulling the strings in the Chinese communities, or who continued to command ever-expanding networks of Dragonflies – Chinese loyal to the occupying forces. Hunting down the enemy agents, therefore, was essentially Colonel Weir's war. He considered his agents, and the elimination of Chinese agents, to be crucial.

These were the men the spy hunted, as the long term plan for Australia required the successful conversion of Australian-Chinese into the begrudging service, but service nonetheless, of the Chinese forces. And Colonel Weir's adept use of his own highly successful Chinese agents had been taking a toll on Major Fang's fellow Red Pandas – so he was always on the look-out for Weir's agents, who were extraordinarily difficult to identify.

They could be the old woman working in the Chinese restaurant, the young boy toiling as a laborer in the underground hydroponics farm; or the young woman performing as domestic help, doing laundry and other chores in the many barracks and other military facilities set up in every crappy little town within the Chinese Occupied sector.

In fact, Fang thought with disgust, *they could even be among those Australian whores we use as sex-surrogates – like that blond-tinted bitch we captured, raped, interrogated and then sliced to ribbons back in Broken Hill, before we withdrew to the east.* Fang's momentary pleasure at the memory of her screams was soon replaced by the reality of how poorly things were going on the south-western front.

Fucking Indians and their Arjun Main Battle Tanks and upgraded T-90s. If we don't get more air power in New South Wales, they'll push us all the way back to the coast, he thought, grimacing at the pounding the 41st Group Army had been taking ever since the Indian Army's 75th Armored Regiment and 10th Mechanized Infantry Division had broken through the Chinese lines north of where Melbourne had once been.

For a moment he succumbed to pessimism, thinking of the debacle at Cloncurry, where the Marines and Australians had wiped out two entire divisions. The bulk of the 42nd Group Army and more than half of the north-east sector's strike aircraft had been destroyed, putting the entire invasion into jeopardy. What made it even more catastrophic was that the enemy had stood up at least four new mechanized infantry regiments, thanks to the war booty captured at Cloncurry. Even now, three years later, the PLA had barely been able to hold the line at Charters Towers. The presence of so much armor in the hands of the Australians, the constant threat of smash-and-run attacks by the Marines, the constant threat of sniping of officers by the Australian Special Forces, and the occasional assassination of pro-Chinese leaders in the civilian communities had begun to take their toll.

Now, with so few PLAAF SU-27s and SU30's still operational to hold off the Indian Air Force's more advanced and upgraded SU-27s and SU30's, and the seemingly unending supply of fresh Indian troops having crossed all the way from Perth in the west to the front lines in New South Wales, it seemed to Major Fang that the Indians were willing to pay a heavy price to defeat the Chinese in Australia. *If only we had a few nukes left, we could have taken out their Sea-Port of disembarkation in Perth,* he thought wistfully. *If only my stepmother had been my grandmother,* he chided himself, with the Chinese version of 'would-have-could-have-should-have.'

Fang thought about the difficulties that the PLA had run into after the initial success of the invasion. Within months the Chinese expansion towards Darwin in the north and Adelaide in the south had been halted in its tracks, what with the surprisingly effective operations that the US Marines out of Darwin had thrown at the 42nd Group Army back at Camooweal, just at the border between Queensland and Northern Territories. After the catastrophic failure of the 42nd Group Army's first attempt to drive through Queensland, the PLA adjusted their tactics in favor of smaller, more defendable gains in an attempt to reduce risk. This put off any talk of complete victory, and seemed to be a turning point in the campaign. It also emboldened the enemy, who then adjusted their tactics in favor of ambushes and guerilla tactics while Australia focused on large scale mobilization and force generation.

Here in the south, Fang knew that the newly formed 14th Brigade that had been thrown together by the Australians in Adelaide, South Australia, was preparing for an offensive. With Chinese forces now facing a two-front campaign in Australia, Major Fang had long since come to the conclusion that the subjugation of Australia would probably take five or more years to accomplish – far longer than the twelve month's called for by General Bing's original timetable.

It was, to Fang, similar to what the Germans faced with OPERATION BARBAROSSA, the Nazi invasion of Russia. The similarities were significant: Germany had succeeded in launching the massive operation with complete surprise, and had achieved extraordinarily great success in the late summer and fall of 1941; then the extremely cold winter had set in. With the supply lines of communication having been extended so far into Russia, shortages of food, fuel and critical spares began to affect operations. The enemy had begun to recover from the shock of their early defeats and were mounting stronger defenses. So far, Fang reflected, the Chinese invasion of Australia had gone very much the same. *The difference*, he thought with pride, *is that we have done a far better job of organizing ourselves for a long, cold winter.*

And he felt personal satisfaction at having played a considerable role in it, what with his counter-counter intelligence work in New South Wales. He had personally eliminated a dozen otherwise highly effective enemy agents and had identified several good prospects, what the enemy called "Orange Pandas", Chinese Australians who helped convert the angry and uncooperative civilians into productive labourers in support of the Chinese forces.

The entire New South Wales sector was, or at least had been, the bread-basket of Asia with over 50,000 productive farms producing shiploads of everything from rice and oranges in the southwest of NSW – the Riverina Sector – to the grain and fruit of the central west slopes & planes – the Dubbo Sector, his current assignment, and the sugar, bananas, diary and livestock of the mid and north coast – the Newcastle-to-Grafton Sector.

Now, with food production having had the same catastrophic collapse as in all other food-producing regions of the world, with the onset of the nuclear winter, it was still seen as a bread-basket to the Chinese despite the utter failure of all agricultural operations other than perhaps sheep grazing, which was doomed to failure as the temperature continued to drop. That Australia is in the southern-hemisphere air-mass, and had taken fully six months longer than the northern hemisphere to grey-out, meant that grasses and other rudimentary feed-crops had continued to grow for a time, but even that marginal degree of production soon ended a year later.

The real treasures were the grain silos, cattle-yards, warehouses and orchards that had been brimming with commodities when the war had begun. The first thing that the Chinese had applied the civilian workforce to was the conversion of these bulk goods into products suitable for long-term food storage. The planners in Jinan had projected that the nuclear winter would last from eight to ten years globally, less so along the coast where livestock and dairy operations were expected to be viable again after five to eight years, at least minimally so.

That meant that culling herds, slaughtering and processing 90% of the animals, drying and storing the nuts and grains, and drying, canning and otherwise processing the fruit products had to be accomplished before these strategic commodities began to rot. To the Chinese, and eventually to the enemy, food was as vital to the war effort as weapons systems and ammunition.

And with the enemy agents largely neutralized in New South Wales – Fang's AOR – an efficient Chinese administration of the factories, warehouses, canneries and other food processing infrastructure was swiftly achieved. After the first few months, there was very little of the sabotage, assassination and other forms of resistance that so plagued his counterparts up in Queensland and down in Tasmania.

Fang had toured some of the warehouses himself lately. They were brimming with enough supplies to last, for the Chinese at least, for the next ten years. That the Australians who worked in the industry had behaved with a suitable degree of deference and obedience to their new masters he attributed to their desire to live, even if not free, in order to provide for their families. After all, word had gotten around throughout occupied Australia that women and children would be raped, tortured and murdered if their men gave the local administrators any difficulties.

The Chinese soldiers were particularly fond of the 'ANZAC biscuits' and canned 'Bully Beef', which one particular food processing plant had been producing in massive quantities. Both products were made entirely from local stockpiles of grain and beef and had extremely long shelf-lives. The ANZAC Biscuits were very hard, but the Chinese soldiers liked to grind them up into a porridge and flavour them with hoisin sauce. *That enormous red-haired manager at the Bully-Beef plant in Waga Waga – Mr. Blais –* Fang recalled his face and other details, from his archive-like memory, *had gone so far as to label the biscuit tins and pallets of corned-beef with Chinese-language labels, no doubt ingratiating his company with their local Chinese military commander and occupation administration officials*, he recalled. *We're getting it done despite the setbacks. Everything is going according to plan, but that does not mean that I can relax, the enemy is still quite strong, and no doubt will continue to try to make inroads into the Chinese communities*, Fang reminded himself, watching everything that was taking place in the busy restaurant.

And then, as he sipped his Oolong tea in a dark corner of 'The Seven Seas', the best Chinese restaurant in Dubbo, he picked up on something. It was only a tiny detail, one that had almost no meaning at all. But it was enough to catch his attention.

That young man sitting around that big table in the back of the restaurant just shook hands again. Completely normal, the way the old man had put his other hand on top of the young man's during the handshake, in a warm and welcoming gesture that was common in the Chinese community. No doubt it was meant to convey respect and friendship, like when you meet someone you have heard good things about, or the family member of a respected associate. Fang reflected to himself, becoming conscious of what his unconscious spy senses had noticed. *But the way the old man nodded his head, only slightly, as if in deference to the young man, meant that the young man was not only welcome and 'known' about, but that he was also extremely important. Such reverence from an old, well-established man directed to such a young man, a boy really, is strange…*

Fang worked it through in his mind. *Here in Dubbo? This crappy little cross-roads town in Chinese-occupied territory, with the Indian Army advancing relentlessly from the west…it can only mean one thing. The local Brown Pandas are finally, after almost four years of war, choosing sides. They are going with the allies. They can see the writing on the wall, and want to show some good faith for the allies before they arrive, so that they are seen as having been loyal Australians all this time. And this young man is their contact. He's one of Weir's spies!* Fang thought, excitedly.

He knew exactly what to do. With a few quick keystrokes into his secure cell-phone, he activated his rapid response team.

Ten minutes later, when he saw the black Mazda CX5 SUV pass by on the '1-minute warning' pass outside the restaurant, Fang moved into position.

Approaching the young Chinese from behind, he timed it perfectly, pressing his pistol into the back of the man's neck just as the front entrance of the restaurant erupted into gunfire.

The other customers attention was focused at the six men in black combat fatigues who had stormed into The Seven Seas, firing rounds into the air and shouting: "Get Down!"

The only men who did not move were Sunny Yao and the unseen man who had pressed the cold steel of his pistol into the back of Sunny's neck.

From the firm hand on his shoulder, Sunny knew that he was dealing with a professional; he did not move. *However this plays out, I have to finish what I came here for,* he thought, his mind racing through possibilities before he came up with the right words. When the local business leaders finally looked up at him from the relative safety of the floor under the table, he smiled at them, hoping to show more confidence than he felt.

"It was a pleasure to make your acquaintance, Li Ning. I must beg your permission to depart with the gentleman behind me," Sunny said, hoping that the unseen operative behind him would be curious enough to let him finish, "but I will be back this way one day to finish our conversation once and for all," he said, hoping that would be enough of a clue to tell Mr. Li that he would never see him again, that the next visit would be from the Australian military – in force, and that Li should carry on with the agreed upon plans. *Hopefully he'll be able to talk his way out of the interrogation that's sure to follow. Maybe his prominence in Dubbo's Chinese community and his commitment to the cause will be enough,* Sunny thought, of the man who he knew would probably be the last friendly face he would see before he died.

Sunny did not resist as he was man-handled out of The Seven Seas, thrown into the trunk of the waiting SUV and chained to cargo tie-down loops bolted to the floor.

As the SUV sped away, he looked out the rear window, half-heartedly trying to keep track of the direction of travel when his head was suddenly struck by a blunt object. Dazed, he felt consciousness slipping away. He was not surprised. *It has been a long time in coming.*

The brightness of sudden daylight hurt his eyes almost as much as Sunny's head ached when Major Fang removed the sack from his head. As he tried to get his bearings, Sunny remembered the beating, the shouted threats and the preliminary round of questioning that the scar-faced enemy agent had put him through before knocking him unconscious.

The initial attempts to get him to talk had been rushed, and seemingly in a place where his captors were uncomfortable staying very long. Some sort of warehouse, Sunny figured, but not an isolated one. There was lots of noise coming from adjoining buildings.

This time it was different. The other thugs were gone. The two men were alone, out in the snow-covered wilderness someplace. *What's he going to do, kill me and bury me here?* Sunny wondered, more curious than afraid. He had accepted the inevitability of his fate. He knew that the level of pain would continue to increase until he cracked. Hopefully he could hold out long enough to provoke an excessive, fatal beating before he gave up too much information. He had no other options. He simply knew too much, and could not allow himself to divulge the names of the Green Pandas he had cultivated, or disclose what he knew of coming operations in the Broken Hills sector.

"Young man, you have impressed me. You have taken it like a man, and held out well so far. That is to be expected, as I am sure that you're the one I've been looking for," Fang began. "You're the one who's been impossible to find, the one sent by Colonel Weir," Fang guessed, accurately. "The question is, what are you trying to accomplish in Dubbo?" Fang asked, rhetorically. "There's no way you're going to turn Li Ning against us, by the way. Don't you know how much he's enriched himself in the years since we took over here? He's one of us, an Orange Panda in your silly code-words. We've taken him from being merely a small warehouse and transport operator to being a very big man in Chinese New South Wales. By the way, did you know, I was the one who recruited him? And did he tell you that as a rite of passage into the ranks of the most privileged local contractors, he himself pulled the trigger, killing Mr. Calhoun, the former Mayor of Dubbo?" Fang said, gloating, but also in an attempt to provoke an emotional response out of Sunny.

And that was the opening he had been hoping for. Sunny pretended to be devastated by the news, and slumped just enough for his tormentor to notice without being obvious.

"That's right, my little Green Panda or whatever you are. You put your trust in the wrong hands, my friend. Li Ning told me all about what you told him, your plan to assassinate General Leung."

Slumping just a bit more as if the news was a physical blow, Sunny was actually elated by what Fang just said. *Li must have made that up, to have something to give to this scar-faced jerk. He gave me something to work with,* Sunny thought.

"I don't know what you're talking about. Who are you? Why are you doing this to me? I'm just a student! A nobody!, I don't know anything about what you're talking about," he said carefully in Mandarin, putting out a little more bait for the spy.

"Listen, little guy, your Mandarin is crappy, stick to Cantonese, you Hong Kong fucker. Is that where you're from? You signed up with the Aussies because you are jealous of real Chinese, mainland Chinese? – or did you have no choice?"

"What do you mean? How do you know that?" Sunny had him. He could sense that the guy was so full of himself, so culturally and intellectually superior to the defenseless kid he'd been beating on for the last 24 hours that he'd never see it coming. Sunny waited, patiently, as Fang carried on.

"I know all about you – your type anyhow. What were you studying, by the way?" Major Fang asked, happy to have his prisoner talking. He would soon have the kid singing like a bird, Fang hoped. *He does not stand a chance against me. What is he, twenty years old? He's just a kid. Maybe I can turn him, once I find out what makes him tick, what he needs...*

"Dentistry, at U of Adelaide. I was in third year when your lot came here," Sunny said in English, feigning the Australian-Chinese accent, hoping that none of his American accent came out.

"Dentistry?" Fang said, with sincere surprise. "I could use a good dentist. Are you any good?"

"Yes, I am. And I'm going to have my own clinic when this war is over, one way or the other."

"What's your name?"

"Dazhuang. My Aussie mates call me 'Dusty'", Sunny said, switching back to Mandarin as if trying to please the man standing over him.

"So just to get things off to a better start today than yesterday, just tell me something I already know, like who sent you, and what was your mission in Dubbo?" *Sing, little birdie, sing!*

"Look, I don't really know anything. I get my orders from different people every time. They really don't tell me much, just to travel to some shit-hole town, talk up the big man, and then report back with a summary of 'who's who in the zoo'. It never really amounts to much. I just give them the names of the players in each town they send me to, usually, that is."

"But not this time?"

"No, this time I was supposed to…Look, I don't want to tell you everything. Not until I know what's going to happen to me. I mean, are you going to kill me?"

"We'll see. It depends on what you do here, now."

"What do you want from me? What do I have to do?"

"Why did you become a spy? Don't you know how dangerous that is? It's certain death if you're caught, you know."

"I really didn't think about it. I was in Adelaide. The war had started and Adelaide was hardly even touched, unlike everywhere else. Everybody there thinks that China will ultimately lose, so I went along with them. What choice did I have?" Sunny looked up at Fang beseechingly. To ensure that he looked suitably terrified and anxious, Sunny thought of his girl-friend, Agness Blakely, and the prospect of never seeing her again. That led to a moment of capitulation, where he accepted that there was a good chance that he would not come out of this alive. *Agness was right, I take too many risks. Should have gotten assignments like Jake Weir, Melody's boyfriend. He never gets sent on dangerous missions like mine. Poor Agness, when she hears what happened to me. I sure hope that she does not blame Melody for her good luck, she'll need a good friend when she's grieving over me,* he thought, and then brought his attention back to his tormentor. Somehow, Sunny found himself calmed by the acceptance of his coming fate, even if it was somewhat contrived.

"Makes sense, kid. But now it's over for you. You're in some pretty serious trouble," Fang relished the way the boy seemed to cringe whenever Fang approached him, and decided the young man was in way over his head. *He may have been useful as a go-between for the allies, passing messages to Green Pandas in the NSW AOR, but he was not a trained operative. He was a dentist, not a soldier. Time to give him a scare, and then some hope, and see how he responds.*

Fang brandished a sharp knife in front of the boy, and then stared at him menacingly.

"You're going to kill me, aren't you? So why should I tell you anything?" 'Dusty' looked fearfully at Major Zhang.

"What choices do you think I have, Dusty?"

"You could let me go," Sunny said, looking meek.

"Would you go back to Adelaide if I did?"

"I don't know, should I? Would you let me go if I told you something useful?"

I've got him, Zhang thought. *The kid broke so easily. I'll need to toughen him up, give him some women and booze, or boys, or drugs — whatever his weakness — and then send him back in as a double.* Zhang cut the plastic zip-strap from the boys wrists. "Who's in charge of your unit?"

"What's the deal, first?" Sunny did not move, but began to breathe a little deeper, as if breathing easier, like a hostage who felt hope thanks to his bonds having been cut.

"Deal? There's no deal. You are in no position to negotiate. But if you give me something good I may let you live one more day. You give me more — everything you know — then maybe things could work out for you after all. So who's in charge of your little network?"

Sagging back onto his heels from the 'dog-begging' posture he had worked himself up to, Sunny felt the muscles in his legs tighten up under his buttocks; his feet pressing into the snow.

"Some American guy. They say he's a Ranger, whatever that is. He's the one always hungry for my post-mission reports. I've seen him in the debriefing area, getting all excited about the reports."

"Really? Like which ones? Be specific."

"He's really horny for reports about where your top officers are travelling to and from, any planned visits, hospitality being prepared, accommodation arrangements. Things like that. They're always telling us to listen for specific 'Time-and-Space' information on guys like General Leung," Sunny said, letting the enemy spy swallow the bait, hook, line and sinker.

"So it really is an assassination plot, like Li Ning said?" *Probably because they're having so much trouble making inroads into my*

AOR, they've given up on recruiting support, and are getting desperate – going the assassination route. Major Fang was so impressed with himself, thinking a mile ahead about how to seduce and turn the young boy, and of how best to use him as a double, that he momentarily dropped his observation routines. He took his eyes off the boy a bit too long as he cast his eye on the snowy horizon thinking of where to set the boy up for his indoctrination. *It'll take time, but I can shape this boy into whatever I want.*

Sunny leapt up, swinging his fist with all the force he could put into it. He struck the distracted Major Fang directly on the chin. Fang fell back into the snow, momentarily dazed.

Sunny hesitated for an instant, unsure whether to pounce on the man or head for the vehicle.

It was a mistake.

The scar-faced Chinese agent had begun to roll over, still clutching his knife. As Sunny ran for the tree-line, he felt his legs being taken out from under him. Fang had gotten his arms around Sunny's legs, like a football tackle.

In a panic, Sunny began kicking wildly, but his feet seemed to only slide off of the tightly muscled agent. Fang pinned Sunny's legs down as he climbed up on top of him.

Brandishing the knife over Sunny's face, Fang seemed to be making a choice, *kill or capture?*

Any thought of salvaging the boy and making a double-agent out of him soon evaporated, as Fang saw a murderous look in the boy's eyes. He knew the look, what many of his victims had shown him in the past. It was the look of sheer enmity. *There's no turning this boy, he well and truly hates what I am.* Fang thought, as he raised the knife for a killing strike.

Sunny threw a handful of dirt and snow up into Fang's face and reached up to grab Fang's jacket, and pulled hard. Smashing his face into Fang's nose and lips, Sunny felt the contact as the hard bone of his forehead smashed into the soft cartilage of Fang's nose.

Fang grunted, but quickly recovered, and stabbed his knife into Sunny's ribs several times.

Before he felt the pain, Sunny felt the solid contact as a rock in his hand made contact with Fang's head. Sunny had not even known that he had grabbed the rock, it was as if his body was fighting for its life, completely disconnected from his conscious mind.

Fang fell off of him and rolled to his back with his hands on his head, but he did not drop his knife.

As the pain hit him in his guts, Sunny became terrified that the man would recover again and continue stabbing at him, so he rolled away from Fang and painfully crawled a few meters away. The pain was terrible, but a surge of adrenaline flooded into him and he was able to get up and stumble towards the SUV. He got into the driver's seat and pulled the door closed behind him. Looking around inside the vehicle, he found a gun on the passenger seat, and reached across for it.

No more than a few seconds behind Sunny, Major Fang closed in on the vehicle, smashing the driver's side window into a hail of shattered glass with the tip of his knife. *Shit, I've brought a knife to a gunfight,* Fang thought, as he looked into the barrel of the Glock. He saw the boy's trigger finger tightening on the trigger. Fang's training took over, releasing the tension in his legs and falling to the ground in the same instant as the charge in the bullet casing exploded and sent the projectile past the space in the air where Fang's head had been a millisecond before.

Fang rolled, and ran a few strides before diving over the snow-bank at the side of the road. By the time he rolled to a stop in a kneeling firing position he had pulled out his back-up pistol from his ankle sheath. He took aim at the SUV before the spray of snow he had disturbed from the snow bank even came to rest. But rather than taking more shots at Fang, the boy had elected to start the vehicle, and gunned the engine.

Fang emptied the full magazine into the vehicle as he ran towards it, but he clearly did not hit anything important and was left watching his prisoner escaping, accelerating the SUV to the west, toward allied lines.

Shit. Well, he won't get far with those wounds, Fang thought. *The boy will be dead in twenty minutes or less. I got what I needed out of him. I know his identity and how he was being handled....and I've got his picture... Maybe I can use that, to try it out on locals. See if I can draw out*

any of his contacts up in Bourke; maybe use that to infiltrate some of the
Brown-turned-Green Panda underground....

In no time, Fang had convinced himself that mortally wounding the rookie enemy agent, had been a stroke of genius, and forgave himself for losing his potentially useful prisoner.

Two months later, after successfully turning the tables on a group of inexperienced Green Pandas in Bourke, NSW, thwarting an Allied incursion that the foolish locals were supposed to facilitate, Major Fang had been sent out of New South Wales on a dangerous mission deep into Northern Territory

The entire sector was a disaster, and General Ma was looking for better intelligence on enemy forces and plans in the area. With air resources so scarce now, ever since the Marines out of Darwin had wiped out the 42nd Group Army, Northern Territory and the western portions of Queensland were essentially a black hole to the PLA. Even now, after three years of careful advances across a more comprehensive front, the sole Division from the 41st Group Army sent in to salvage the situation had only progressed a few hundred kilometers west of Charters Towers.

With two full divisions of Chinese armor now in the hands of the Australians, and with the constant threat of raids by the Marines all along the front, the PLA had all but given up any hope of advancing as far as Northern Territory. Camooweal had been the offensive culmination for the PLA. The focal point now was on surviving the anticipated onslaught of Australian and Indian forces coming eastward from Adelaide. So far, the 41st and 38th Group Armies had been able to throw back the enemy incursions, but each action had taken a steady toll in terms of attrition, both of land force units and what was left of PLAAF air superiority fighters. Meanwhile, the Indian Army and Australian forces continued to build up larger and larger formations, and seemed to be preparing for a major offensive.

The planners in General Bing's command post back in China had ordered a resumption of offensive operations in the north, to draw some divisions from the Adelaide region and perhaps buy a little more time for General Ma to consolidate the gains north of Melbourne. The hope was that as the nuclear winter continued to wear down the Australians, the front lines might stabilize somewhat and allow the PLA to hang on to the eastern half of the continent. If they could do that, they would come out of the nuclear winter with the most productive agricultural lands, and be in a position to use food as a weapon. In order to accomplish this, they needed more solid intelligence on the disposition of the Australian forces in Northern Territory, and more importantly, on the Marines of MAFTFA, who were considered to be the most lethal opponent due to their expertise in battle-space-management, strike-and-maneuver tactics, anti-occupation warfare, and reconnaissance-in-force. So the mission was critical to the PLA cause, and Major Fang was pretty much the only man qualified for such a crucial task.

It was probably a suicide mission, he knew, but if successful it could turn the tide back in China's favor. All he had to do was get to Alice Springs, collecting intelligence on enemy forces along the way. Once there, he would find a way to send the intelligence back to the 41st Group Army. He was then to establish himself within the massive refugee camp near Alice Springs, build an identity as a helpful Panda, and then get close to just one particular person and find a way to kill him. Escape was a tertiary objective at best, and the least of Fang's worries at this point.

The most difficult part of the mission was not the culmination of it, but the starting of it. He had to bluff his way past enemy lines, playing a refugee from the Chinese sector.

The first checkpoint had been touch and go, but he bluffed his way past the checkpoint west of Emerald, Queensland.

Having insinuated himself into the vehicle of a mixed couple, befriending the Chinese wife of an Australian farmer, Fang had an easy ride most of the way. But when the couple asked him too many questions, and was forced to put his razor-sharp knife into their hearts just outside of the battle-scarred town of Mount Isa, his free ride was over.

The deeper he penetrated into Allied territory, traveling on his own after returning the Australian couple's kindness with murder, the more carefully the security forces checked him out. But he had woven together the seemingly plausible story he had adopted from the motorists who he had dispatched so recently, that he was headed to the refugee camp at Alice Springs to link up with his sister and her white Australian husband. He passed himself off as a landed immigrant who had lost his papers when he, his sister and his brother-in-law had fled the town of Emerald when it had fallen to the PLA 42nd Group Army three years back.

His acting and lying skills had taken him almost the rest of the way, until he came upon a simple checkpoint outside of Ti-Tree, just three hundred kilometers from the refugee camp near Alice Springs.

He had no idea that the area was an important source of potable water, nor the burgeoning production of grapes that the tiny town had been known for before the war. All he knew was that he was suddenly confronted by a chicane of concrete blocks which he had to maneuver through very slowly. Backing out was not an option, he knew, as his vehicle had already passed over the one-way tire spikes laid across his path. The final turn in the serpentine row of concrete blocks put his vehicle square in the sights two soldiers standing on either side of his vehicle, their rifles trained on him and their fingers on the trigger.

Major Fang remained calm, stopped the vehicle at the stop sign and kept his hands on the steering wheel as he waited for the soldiers to begin their protocol.

"Shut-er off, mate!" said the one on the left, his M-16 aimed carefully at Fang's head through the passenger side window.

"Yes, Sir!" Fang said, shutting off the engine and then brushing his left hand across his left leg, just to feel the reassuring hardness of one of his concealed weapons, in this case his favorite throwing knife.

"Who are you and where you going, buddy?" said the soldier.

In the instant before answering, Fang had taken a more careful look at the first soldier and saw that the man had a cigarette on the go. A tiny whiff of smoke rose from the unseen cigarette which the soldier must have laid on the sand-bag that he was using to support his left elbow. He had his rifle trained on the passenger side of the vehicle, from Fang's left, and was in a good position to watch Fang's every movement. *If I have to make a move, it'll have to be when that one takes a puff*, he thought.

"My name is…Dazhuang, but everybody calls me Dusty," Fang said, using the name used by the Allied agent who he had skewered outside of Dubbo. He had been using the alias at every checkpoint he had encountered, half hoping someone would recognize the name and give Fang some clue as to his fate. It was risky, but in Fang's experience using the real names and identities of people he knew something about was better than making up fresh lies. Imaginary identities are much harder to keep straight than real personalities, even to a man as organized and detail-oriented as Fang. But this time he got an immediate reaction. He saw the soldier on his right freeze momentarily, his eyes narrowing in concentration for a brief moment, followed by a resumed and seemingly casual conversation, but now accompanied by a subtly higher level of alertness.

"Dazwang, is it? Right. And where are you going?" the soldier asked, continuing the roadside interview.

"I'm headed for the camp near Alice Springs, to meet up with my sister and her husband – he's a farmer, or was, and I'm going to work with him when the war is over and the snow goes away," Fang tried to spin the back-story the same as he had a dozen times between Charters Towers and this latest check-stop. But his heart was not in the story telling this time. He had already decided that it was pointless. He had switched to combat mode, in response to the subtle change in the soldier's manner.

"And what was your point of departure?" the man, wearing the rank of a Master Corporal, his shoulder patch featuring a dagger through the center of a boomerang and the motto: *Strike Swiftly* was instantly recognized by Fang as that of 1 Cdo Regt, Australian Special Ops Command. The soldier seemed to have a strange accent, *perhaps American*, Fang guessed, assessing the soldier carefully as he wondered what had caused the man to tighten up like that. *Dusty! That must have been it. The guy must have known Dazhuang, or at least the name. Maybe he knows the kid is dead, so my turning up here using his identity is what he's reacting to. Not good!*. Fang decided he had to make a move, before the American-Australian could make a radio call.

"Hold on! Stop what you're doing, and get back into your car!" commanded the other soldier.

Fang had opened the door and stepped out, moving toward the front of his car with his hands raised, pretending to be a bit panicked. He was careful to keep his distance from the soldiers, so as not to make them think he was moving in on one of them, but he was equally careful to position himself in between the two, so that each of them was in the other's line of fire. They would know that they can't shoot at him without putting the other man in danger.

"I have documents – about the camp – from the Australian Red Cross in Longreach," Fang said, tugging some papers out of his shirt-pocket with his fingers, slowly so as not to alarm the soldiers.

The Master Corporal's attention was momentarily diverted to the papers in the Asian man's fingers. He leaned forward, over the top of the sandbags atop his concrete barricade as his eyes followed the papers falling to the ground. He watched the imposter fumbling to collect the papers and then rise back up, offering them to him. *That's not Sunny Yao, but he's using Sunny's cover name "Dusty". How many Panda's could have a name like that? who the fuck is this guy?* he wondered

On the opposite side of the road, Corporal Gillich could not see what the Chinese was doing, as the subject was bent over, with his rear end directed at the Corporal in the over-watch position on the left.

Get your arse out of the way, Gillich thought, and then saw the threat. Adrenaline rushed into his blood as he saw the subject hiding a knife with his left hand under the sheaf of papers he was presenting to the Master Corporal with his right. Unable to fire without risk of hitting his partner, Gillich shouted: "Knife!"

It was exactly the sort of thing that Fang had hoped for. The Master Corporal suddenly looked across at his partner on the opposite side of the road, and then back to Fang. He was just in time to see Fang lunging at him from two meters away, suddenly closing the distance enough to jab a knife sideways into the Master Corporal's right hand. The soldier heard the sound of metal on metal before he felt the pain in his hand, as the knife penetrated right through his hand and struck the stock of the rifle before the blade was yanked out.

As the pain reached his brain and he instinctively pulled his hand back from the rifle's hand-grip, he saw the Chinese whirl. Gillich was in the perfect vantage point to watch the knife tumble end-over-end towards him as it flew across the road, hitting him squarely in his chest. He squeezed off a few rounds in his death-convulsion, but the rounds simply kicked up some mud and snow, well off-target. Corporal Gillich was dead before he hit the ground, Fang's throwing knife having pierced his heart.

Half stepping, half falling backwards now in an attempt to flee, the Master Corporal on the right side had let go of his rifle when the pain had struck. He raised his left hand to grasp the microphone clipped to his breast pocket, and squeezed.

He heard the electronic 'beep-bloop-rip' sound that the Motorola 3,000 was ready to transmit, but he did not utter a sound. He had been frozen in place by the solid force of a man standing behind him. A man who had just reached over his left shoulder and grasped his jacket firmly on the right.

He felt a strange tugging sensation across his neck, and then his head seemed to tip back on its own and a warm wetness sensation spread across his chest. The Master Corporal was puzzled by the strange saggy feeling in the skin and interconnecting tissue of his neck, just under his jaw.

He dropped to the ground, his legs and torso suddenly having stopped resisting gravity, as if they were no longer there at all.

He knew that he had just been killed, and that the ugly, scar-faced man must have been the one that had carved up Sunny Yao.

He summoned up Melody's face in his mind, taking her image with him into oblivion.

Jake Weir no longer had to pretend to be a soldier.

20

AUSSIE RULES OFFENSE

The snow and ice were a mixed blessing, General Ma knew. While climate along Australia's east coast was moderated by the relatively warmer, five to ten degree temperature of the air masses coming inland from the ocean, the climate inland was altogether a different story. It was like two entirely different worlds. The coast was gloom, drizzly and grey but the roads were usable and it was easy enough to shift forces up and down the coastal highway, Highway A1, and use as many of the secondary roads as possible to move inland, but after about two hundred kilometers inland the moderating effects of ocean became overwhelmed by the deep freeze of the inland areas. After the third full year of nuclear winter the interior of Australia had been transformed from the rugged, dry bushland and sparse forest to a wintry tundra reminiscent of the arctic, with sustained winds below minus twenty centigrade and wind-chill values in the minus thirty range. – quite inhospitable to anybody caught out in the open. And that was the primary problem.

It had taken the PLA three years to stabilize the coastal region, despite brutal repression and at times outright massacre of the local population, there had been a spirited insurgency taking out units up to company size. Larger formations, such as Combat Teams and battalions had been relatively unchallenged, as long as they did not try to push too far inland.

As a result, at this point three years into the campaign, the Chinese had solid control of the first two hundred kilometers inland all up and down the east coast, and part of the way round the south coast towards South Australia.

General Ma, in command of the 42nd, 41st and 15th Group Armies, was responsible for everything north of the Queensland – New South Wales border, essentially everything north of what had once been Brisbane. Once the expected reinforcements arrived from Indonesia, he would reconstitute the 42nd Group Army out of the two Regiments of the 31st and one from the 15th. All that he had left of the 42nd was one regiment of the 372nd Division that was holding on to what little pride they had left, at the front-line town of Emerald. Reforming the 42nd Group Army was altogether unnecessary given the way he was operating the much larger formation designated Army Group North out of his Command Post in Rockhampton, he knew, but the effect on the Marines when they would ultimately be hit by a renewed campaign led by the 42nd Group Army was expected to be a deep insult. The US Marines had a long enmity with the 42nd, and were enjoying the sweet satisfaction of having wiped out the 42nd on the road from Cloncurry to Camooweal and the border regions of Northern Territory.

General Ma intended to take that away from them. All he had to do was shift his forces around up and down the east coast, enjoying the freedom of movement that the coast roads offered him. Ultimately, he knew that he would have to provide some assistance to General Sheung's Army Group South. Based on the 38th and 65th Group Armies, out of Beijing Military District – Sheung's force was concentrated in Victoria and was expected to bear the brunt of an expected allied assault from the Adelaide sector when the Indian Army completed its cross-continent deployment from Perth to Swan Hill. But that assault was not expected to take place for at least another three to six months, so General Ma had delayed transferring any of his regiments to Sheung. *When the time comes, I'll probably have to transfer the 2nd and 3rd Brigades, 121st Regiment, 41st Group army over to Army Group South. They're just sitting on their asses getting fat in Biloela and Gladstone anyhow, well behind the front lines. I'll hold on to the 164th Marine Brigade for myself, when they get here from Indonesia,* the General thought. Having the PLA's most elite, highly trained 6000-man brigade of marines with him at his base on the coast in Rockhampton would give him a highly versatile, ready-reaction force to deal with any mischief that the US Marines might try to pull on him. *It would be nice to throw our marines against the US Marines at some point,* the General commanding Army Group North thought with satisfaction.

In the Adelaide to Broken Hill sector, the Indian Army was having a great deal of trouble with the heavy snow and washed out bridges, and the PLAAF was interdicting their engineering units, making things even more difficult. The terrain from the border between Victoria and South Australia was littered with wrecked T-90's and Arjun Main Battle Tanks, albeit at a heavy price paid by the PLAAF. In committing so many aircraft to taking out the first effort of the Indian Army to bring the fight to the Australian state of Victoria, the PLAAF had lost much of their fighter force. The sacrifice of the Air Force had been worth it, however, as it had stalled the allied offensive in its tracks and bought the Chinese forces perhaps eighteen months before a larger allied force, and more air power, could be brought over from India to replace losses experienced by the first Indian Expeditionary Force.

The allies in the north had also suffered serious setbacks after their initial success when the Marines had led the Australians to victory in the Cloncurry campaign. Their troubles had started months later, when the Australians had tried to move east with their captured Chinese armor. They had moved first one, and then two full regiments made up of Australians outfitted with captured Chinese equipment, and had gotten as far as Longreach.

At that point, Colonel Yip had given the appearance of withdrawing from the key crossroads town of Barcaldine, drawing in the advance formation of US Marines, who had been clearing the path for two advancing Australian Regiments.

It had been a masterful stroke, General Ma had recalled, with Colonel Yip's forces turning on a dime and tearing into the Marines from three sides, and a well-timed air attack by the PLAAF fighter bombers. The company of Marines had been obliterated, yielding almost two hundred prisoners and certainly giving the MAGTFA a bloody nose. True, the Marines had gotten even somewhat by their daring raid on Emerald, capturing

Colonel Yip. General Ma had to give them that, *But the heroics of a few Marines and Special Forces with help from the Australians does not make up for the ass-kicking we gave them at Barcaldine. Colonel Ng, while philosophically much softer than Yip, would certainly be able to get a grip on Colonel Yip's regiment, restore their shattered confidence and keep the allied hounds at bay in the Emerald sector,* thought General Ma. *Besides, they're really screwed up now, all that armor stuck in snow and abandoned like that. The Australians just do not have the capability to mount anything larger than a combat team or perhaps a brigade. They're simply outclassed.*

The screw up that General Ma was thinking about was, according to the intelligence reports, a colossal screw up by the Australians. They had struggled for four months to build a road through the snow, over the harsh terrain east of Tambo. Why the Aussies had abandoned Highway A2, which should have been easy to clear of snow, was still not known. Most likely, they had been hoping to reach Mount Moffatt road on the east side of Carnarvon National Park. That was the only strategy that made sense, as it would have allowed the Australians to swing down onto the crossroads town of Roma from the north, and avoid the well-entrenched 364th Infantry Regiment of the 121st Motor Infantry Division, 41st Group Army at Charleville. With the 364th Regiment having a lock on Highway A2 from Morven to Charleville, and a battalion established as a buffer in the crossroads town of Augathella, eighty kilometers to the north, the allies could not make it very far by coming south on the A2. So if their strategy had been to travel cross-country around Charleville, it could have worked. The PLA, lacking any serviceable drones and with very limited air power now, had no more than a weekly reconnaissance sortie in the region. They had spotted the long columns of Australian-operated Chinese armor crawling cross-country, and had taken notice.

And then the Allies had run out of gas. Literally and figuratively. They simply abandoned the armor, engineering support equipment and fuel bowsers. Most likely these were empty, General Ma had decided. The effort to do an end run around the 364th Regiment had been a complete blunder, at least a full regiment's worth of armor and associated equipment had been abandoned in the snow.

Just in case the Aussies ever came back with fuel and men to recover the equipment, General Ma had a weekly surveillance flight take pictures of the abandoned column. And for the last three months there had been absolutely no activity. Many of the tanks were now so completely covered with snow that they were indistinguishable from the snow-covered, hilly terrain. Even so, if the allies did come back, it would take them weeks to extricate themselves, and the equipment would most likely be in need of major servicing to even start up, let alone be put into action.

What a shame for their commanders, Ma reflected, They had been only a few kilometers from reaching Mount Moffatt Road.

It had been a gamble, and most of the battle staff had been against the idea. However, General Adams had convinced the Australian High Command that it was worth the risk. Once the operation had been approved, the Marines as well as the Australian MARSOC had signed on and generated Branch and Supporting Plans. Colonel Weir had been one of the few who was on General Adams' side, and had been enthusiastic in coming up with a variety of ways that his Chinese spies and Australian Special Forces teams could support the operation.

Now, six months after the operation had launched with the preliminary phases, things were heating up. To be more precise, warming up would be a better term.

Within the Chinese community, Weir's spies had been instructed to warm to their Chinese occupiers, providing them with cooperative, if not overly enthusiastic service in support of the Chinese invasion.

With carefully crafted instructions delivered to the spies only when needed, there had been many months with apparently no activity, on the surface at least. If one were to stand back and re-read all of the intelligence intercepts, cross-check them with local news in the dozen or so communities that were ultimately involved in the Allied offensive, and with 20-20 hindsight, the pattern might look obvious. But at the time, General Ma, and all of the Intelligence directorate that supported him, had no idea what was coming.

The trouble was, he did not have any kind of understanding of the Australian sport of rugby, known as "Aussie Rules Football".

But 'footie' was at the core in General Adams' inspiration. The idea was simple, to lull the enemy into a false sense of security, and to distribute 'players' across the field. Just as in Aussie Rules, players can position themselves at any place in the field and can contact the ball with any part of their body. In General Adams' plan, therefore, war-fighting resources were to be strewn across the operational theatre, to be thrown into combat in a variety of unique ways. This would be in stark contrast to the set-piece manoeuver warfare practiced by conventional armies – which was much more like Rugby or American Football, with well-understood procedures for 'making yardage' and 'moving the ball down the field'. Aussie rules, in contrast, was all about freedom of movement, and considerably more physical contact – and without protective equipment. Put simply, the action would be a desperate, personally dangerous, unconventional and fast-paced sprint for the goal line.

And thanks to Colonel Weir's application of psychological warfare, and deep-selection of enemy commanders through assassination and other means, the enemy would be in a vulnerable position *at just the right time.*

The first moves in the campaign had already taken place a week before, with engineers and mechanics having surreptitiously returned to the snow-bound line of tanks, infantry fighting vehicles, fuel bowsers and engineering support equipment that had been carefully put to bed under snow-white tarps in the Mount Moffat Road area.

There had been a company of maintainers there throughout the four-month period, camping in snow caves and keeping themselves out of sight. So that the batteries of each and every vehicle were still fully charged, the engines had been run for fifteen minute periods on and off for several hours each night and were kept silent during the daylight hours so that any PLA drone or surveillance aircraft would not detect any smoke or other sign of activity.

The newly arrived engineers and technicians were needed to prepare the engineering support, earth-moving and other special equipment at the front of the column – and to operate it.

Over the next 24 hours, as the excavators, bull-dozers and other equipment resumed the road-building operation, others came in after them to stretch out snow-cover camouflage so that every day, for the next week, any PLA surveillance would not notice that the column was being prepared to move forward.

When the time came, eight days later, the road had been extended not just the five kilometers to Mount Moffat Road, but rather, fully thirty kilometers in an entirely other direction, to the north-east, and right into the hilly terrain of ridgeline between Expedition National Park and Carnarvon National Park. The first ten kilometers of this improvised road was through what should have been impassible terrain, and for that reason had been eliminated from the range of possibilities considered by the PLA analysts who had studied the potential lines of advance that the Australians might have been considering six months earlier. They had concluded that the Australians had intended to continue to the south-east, onto Mount Moffatt Road, which would carry them southward towards Roma.

But with the help of local guides, former park rangers and others who knew the area very well, the Australian Army followed a path through the terrain and into the flatland of Nuga Nuga National Park, on the far side of the impassable ridge.

Once in the Nuga - Nuga, road-building amounted to no more shoving the snow cover aside with a bull-dozer without stopping, with follow-on crews filling any low areas with hard-packed mix of snow and gravel. After that, water was sprayed to provide additional strength. One of the engineers commented that the operation reminded him of the ice-road construction done in the Canadian Arctic, building seasonal roads to service remote native communities and diamond mines.

This Australian "ice road" would support the advancing Australian 3rd Armored Infantry Division's Chinese pattern armor very well, as long as the temperature stayed cold, which it was, with frigid temperatures expected to continue for years to come.

A battalion of Marines from the MAGTFA had the honor of leading the advance, at least to the end of the improvised road through the Nuga Nuga. They did not encounter a soul, which was perfectly fine with them. But when they reached the A7 highway, the Marines split off on their follow-on task directly to the north, for unfinished business with the 42nd Group Army in Emerald, one hundred and fifty kilometers to the north.

The Australians, advancing at breakneck speed once they reached the tantalizingly clear pavement of Highway 60, moved in on the unsuspecting PLA garrison at Moura. Just as they arrived, Australian Special Forces and Green Panda agents sprang up out of the woodwork and interfered with the PLA battalion billeted there.

And just like in Aussie Rules Footie, the ball moved swiftly onward towards the coast, not pausing or delaying, and brushed right through Moura and on to Biloela, within one hundred and twenty kilometers of the Port of Gladstone – the goal line – and the east coast.

Colonel Weir's contribution to the ensuing battle at Biloela had been immense. He had sent in two spies, with devastating effect. One man, a veterinarian, had been pressed into the service of the PLA, taking care of the livestock which the Chinese intended to use as seed-stock for a rapid expansion of the herds when the nuclear winter was over. The rest, over 90% of the livestock in the region, had been slaughtered and prepared for long-term food storage by the local population, under the control of the Occupation Authority. The Chinese relied heavily on the locals, who, for some reason, were far less troublesome than the locals down in Victoria and New South Wales.

The veterinarian's task during the Australian offensive had been simple. He did something he had done a thousand times before, only on a much larger scale, and with a different population in mind.

In the past, before the war, one of his routine duties had been to attend to abattoirs and small slaughter houses where a particularly unruly species of long-horned cattle or other beasts had been acting up. The simple solution was to add a carefully calculated dose of Acepromazine, ACE. Normally used as a sedative to quiet and calm domesticated livestock, it was once used as an antipsychotic drug on humans. Normally administered by IV or intramuscular, it can also be given orally.

The challenge was how to deliver it to the PLA soldiers? Depending on how much wound up in a soldier's bloodstream, there could be acute side effects, such as phenothiazine-induced seizures. That was a risk that had to be taken, and even if the PLA medical community detected the ACE in the bloodstream of any of their personnel, the information would come too late. The soldiers will have been sedated in time to coincide with the Aussie Rules offensive.

It was all about timing. With just a four-hour effect, he had to time the delivery just right. As a result, the vet had been given specific instructions as to timing. He had been told to watch for a signal, a small plume of smoke rising exactly due west of his home, which would give him 12 hours advance notice.

The smoke signal had been coordinated with the Australian 3rd Division to coincide with their advance eastward out of the Nuga - Nuga. After that, the vet had eight hours to dump the 200 kilograms of powdered ACE he had prepared into the water-tank that served the town of Bilolea. With a brigade of PLA soldiers from the 371st Regiment all drawing their drinking water from the town's water system there was a good chance that when the alarm is raised a good proportion of the soldiers would draw water for their canteens, drink a few liters, and begin to be affected by the ACE just in time for the fast-moving assault of the Australians.

That a large number of local citizens of Biloela would also be affected could not be helped, as giving them any sort of warning risked tipping them off to the coming assault. The best the vet could do was to study up on what types of medications could counteract the effects of Acepromazine, particularly for anybody who went into a seizure. He intended to help mitigate the effects of what he had done, *if I live to the end of the day*, he thought.

The other man dispatched by Colonel Weir to support the assault on Biloela was one of the Red Pandas who had been turned. The man was not entirely trusted – however he did seem to have the best interests of his former colleagues in the PLA in mind. Without giving him any details, Colonel Weir had sent the man onward to the Biloela lines with the Australian 3rd Mechanized Infantry Division. His orders had not been conveyed to him until the battle was about to begin. At that point he was given a motor-cycle and a radio tuned to the frequency being used by the PLA Brigade stationed in Biloela.

His assignment was to ride out ahead of the advancing column of Australians, get close to the PLA security forces there, and to transmit in Chinese his personal account of how he had been treated after being captured by the Marines during the battle for Mount Isa.

The man proved to be loyal, both to the allies, who had given him a chance to save lives on both sides, and to his PLA countrymen whom he truly wanted to encourage to surrender.

Just as the Chinese T-99A2 Main Battle tanks, Type 4 Infantry Fighting Vehicles, modeled after the Russian MBP-3, and armored personnel carriers of the Australian 3rd Mechanized Infantry Division rumbled into range of the men of the 2nd Brigade, 121st Regiment, 41st Group Army, the soldier-turned POW – turned agent, Wan Shanyu, began to transmit on the UHF radio.

His message was simple: "Brothers, you do not want to fight. We have been lied to by the Generals. This invasion of Australia was a mistake. It was not about China. This is not something we Chinese want. It is madness, and China is being destroyed because of this. The allies are our friends, just as they were before the war. We just have to restore peace and all will be forgiven for China. Except for the Generals. They are the ones to blame. I call upon you to surrender, just as my unit did at Mount Isa. We were treated well, just as the Geneva Convention requires. And after the war we will be allowed to stay here and become citizens, or we will be given safe transport to China, to help with reconstruction. I am going home. I want to see my mama and my wife and my daughter. I want to help China put this madness behind us. Are you with me? Surrender now. Turn your weapons on your officers, or just lay them down. Do not fight. Brothers, you do not want to fight..." Wan continued the prepared text, transmitting continuously for the next thirty minutes, until the battle was over.

And it ended as swiftly as it began. About a third of the 2nd Brigade's men had imbibed enough of the ACE-laced water to feel the effects. These men were particularly susceptible to the idea of not lifting a finger. They also found no particular reason to take any action against their own officers, however. They just sat there, docile, like sleepy cattle.

About a third of the men actually put up a fight, but were poorly coordinated and not supported by their fellow soldiers, and failed to organize an effective resistance.

The final third, hearing the talk of surrender and seeing the confusion within their ranks, panicked. They had been terrorized by rumors of a massive assault of US Marines, and believed that the advancing formation was part of this terrible American force. Others had been effected by the stories of soldiers finding poisonous snakes and spiders in their equipment just when battle begins, a tactic that had been used to good effect in a number of small battles, and had been too afraid to enter their tanks and infantry fighting vehicles. These panicked men ran, on foot, for the presumed safety of Gladstone.

With the Australians mopping up what little resistance there was in Biloela, and the highly disciplined PLA security forces at Gladstone ahead of them, the panicked soldiers were soon unarmed and exposed on the long stretch of highway 60 to the coast. When they heard the rumbling of the advancing Australian armor they dove to the ground at the side of the road, expecting to be mercilessly gunned down.

As it was, they were not harmed. The Australians waved at them in a strangely friendly way, as if to thank them for not fighting. *Could it be true? We will be treated kindly?* Some of them thought as they sat watching the Chinese armored vehicles they knew so well being operated by these strange Australians advancing towards the coast.

At Gladstone, a highly disciplined brigade of the 121st Regiment, 41st Group Army had begun to mobilize their defenses. They were not entrenched, other than the base's security perimeter and military police post, as they were so far removed from the front lines as to be beyond any risk of attack. But they had considerable firepower available to them and a one hour warning.

All they had to do was hold out long enough for General Ma to send down a regiment from Rockhampton, just one hundred kilometers up the coast, to relieve and support the 3rd Brigade.

But an hour was a long time when faced with Aussie Rules offense, they soon found out.

The Australians appeared to be about to drive right at their lines, but then swerved to the right on the Bruce Highway, and carried on to the east to the coastal town of Tannum Sands.

"Shit! They've cut us off to the south!" the operations officer informed his Colonel.

"What do you mean, along Kirkwood road?" asked the PLA Colonel.

"No, Sir, they bypassed us altogether, and now hold the intersection at Highway A1 and the coast road, Highway 58, into Gladstone."

The major had no sooner given his report when new intel came in from the perimeter.

"Sir. It gets worse. It now appears that another element has swung to the north, up Callope River Road. That cuts us off from General Ma and Rockhampton. We are entirely surrounded now."

"Don't' panic, Major. Let's get some solid information. What else are we getting from the perimeter? What unit is it, the First or the Second Division?"

"That's just it, sir. We don't know. There are reports of this guy from the 371st Regiment of 42nd Group Army who surrendered at Mount Isa now transmitting on UHF Channel Six, encouraging guys to surrender. It looks like they must have surrendered in Biloela, or else how could the enemy have come this far so fast?"

"Doubtful. But they could have bypassed Biloela."

"No, sir, we would have still had comms with Colonel Chen and 2nd Brigade. They're off the air, so they have fallen. But there's more. Remember that action up in Emerald, Sir, that started an hour ago? Turns out it is the US Marine Corps, the MAGTFA. They're supported with air power! The brigade in Emerald has been ordered to withdraw towards Port Mackay."

"You kidding? Why not to Rockhampton?" the Colonel fumed. "What the hell is going on here, how big is this thing, anyhow?" The colonel leaned over to examine the map closely. His command post was abuzz with a panicky tone that he did not like. But he took the time to plot what was known of enemy units and their disposition. "Look here, Major. Is this about right?" he asked his Ops O, indicating the map symbols he had drawn with grease pencil.

"Yes, Sir, and we now know that the Australian force surrounding us is the 3rd Mechanized Infantry Division, that unit that was supposed to be stuck in the snow near Charleville."

"So what do we have, a US Marine force driving east at the remnants of the 372nd Regiment at Emerald – what are they down to now, Brigade size now, right? And we have the Australian 3rd Division already here on the coast. Where is their 1st Division going to strike? Shit, this is a Corps sized formation we are up against, if not larger. That's where all those Australian men in Queensland have disappeared to – they've been force generating quite an army, I'd say. They are attempting to – have in fact already done so – cut us off from the rest of Army Group North. They've cut our forces into two, for fuck sake! The question is, do we try to hold off here, or try to fight our way out of this box? If so, which way, to the south? – to join with the rest of the 41st, or try to the north? – to help protect General Ma, in Rockhampton?"

"I don't know Sir, but we need to act swiftly. The longer you delay giving the evacuation order, the more the enemy will be able to entrench. I say we go south, try to link up with the rest of the 121st Regiment down in Childers."

"What is Division saying now?"

"They want our sitrep, but also advise that there is a risk of a major allied offensive in our sector."

"Great timing, as always," Colonel Guo said, turning his attention to observing the mood in the Command Post.

So far, there were no reports of enemy firing. It was as if the enemy had already achieved their tactical objectives, and were waiting for his next move. *Should we fight our way out, or are we cut off now like the German Sixth army in Stalingrad? Who am I kidding? I'm just the Commanding Officer of a single Brigade, and still just be a major if it were not for the assassination of Colonel Luo.* Thinking back on that day, Colonel Guo still had not shaken the notion that the allies had ordered Colonel Luo's assassination to coincide with the absence of the Deputy CO, Major Yuan. Major Yuan and Colonel Luo were birds of a feather, entirely committed to General Bing's global ambition, and excessively brutal to the local population. With Yuan away, General Ma had elevated Major Guo to Acting CO, likely to hold the post until Major Yuan returned. But then Major Yuan was also killed, in an enemy ambush out on the highway. It had always seemed to be more than a coincidence. Perhaps fate, or some other grand design, but it was as if someone wanted him to be in command of the 3rd Brigade at this precise moment in history.

As Colonel Guo thought about the decision he had to make, he observed the way the Command Post staff were listening to the loudspeaker, where the repeating broadcast from the soldier from the 371st Regiment continued on and on, calling for his brothers to surrender, promising fair treatment and calling on the men to turn their arms against their officers.

Hope they don't turn on me, Colonel Guo thought. And then he explored the possibility of surrender. Certainly, he knew, his role as the Commanding Officer would put him at risk of being held accountable for the war crimes. Guo knew them to be war crimes, that some of his men had been forced to commit under Colonel Luo's orders.

Then he explored the idea of running the gauntlet through enemy lines, probably to the south as the Ops O had suggested. But that would be like the Falaise Pocket, Guo knew, where his men would be picked off by the Australian tanks just like the retreating German 7th Army had been picked off by the Polish tanks that had taken up firing positions on a hilltop overlooking the only escape route. It had been a massacre, and a turning point in the war with the destruction of the German 7th and 5th Panzer Armies.

Colonel Guo was about to give an order, when the phone rang. It was strange, and startled many in the CP. The phone was a local phone, part of the pre-war telephone network that still worked in some towns. In this case, the only person who could be calling would have to be his closest friend in the PLA, the CO of the 3rd Brigade, in Biloela.

Picking up the phone, Guo felt some powerful forces at work. "Guo here," he answered.

At first he barely recognized his old friend, the man was speaking in such a rapid, panicked manner. But it did not take long to be certain that it was Chen. But the reason for the call was simply unbelievable.

Chen was sitting in his CP in Biloela, surrounded by Australian and American military personnel, and apparently a few Chinese-speaking allies who Guo could hear conversing in English and Chinese in the background. Of course, both Chen and Guo could both speak perfect English, so he switched to English as much to ease the situation for Chen in Biloela as to keep his side of the conversation at least somewhat private in his own CP, where almost none of the personnel spoke very much English.

"Are you serious? How could they know that about us?"

Colonel Chen told Gou that the allies knew that Chen and Guo had been classmates when they attended university in America, both having been ordered by the PLA to pursue Bachelor's degrees in American Cultural Studies before resuming their careers in the Army. Part of a program of "know your enemy", the degree had taught both men a great deal about the western way of life.

Chen went on to say that the allies had a dossier on each of the Chinese commanders, and were compiling evidence for War Crimes Tribunals that had already begun to take place. Each and every captured commander would be accountable for his actions, with swift justice in the form of a firing squad or hanging for the most ruthless perpetrators. But for others, who had surrendered their forces and fully cooperated with the Allied authorities, amnesty had been given in a number of instances. At least that was the story being fed to Colonel Chen, who was inclined to accept the allies at their word based on what he had seen of how the Chinese community in Seattle were treated.

The notion that the Allies were holding those behind the global war accountable, but not directly attributing the madness to the Chinese people, rang true for both men. The same discussion had been taking place in private within the PLA, ever since the war had started. A great many PLA officers were uneasy with their role in the repugnant war, the attempt to reduce the human population by 95% and to have the new world under Chinese control. Guo and Chen discussed the situation for a few moments longer, until Chen was instructed to press Guo.

"So what do they want, exactly?" Colonel Guo said, getting out his notepad.

"I don't know how the men will respond, quite frankly. If I do as you ask, what assurance do I have that the Allies will keep their word?"

After a long discussion at the other end, Colonel Chen got the answer back to Guo.

"Well, if that is their assurance, it is good enough for me, I suppose. I will put it to the men and let them decide. I will call you back with our answer in under an hour," Guo said, and then hung up the phone as if it weighed a ton.

"Men, listen up. I have just been informed by Colonel Chen that many of his men have surrendered. Those who did not were quickly defeated and the Colonel himself and his command post staff were captured. The allies are offering amnesty to any of our military personnel who will surrender," Guo paused, to gauge the effect that this had on his personnel. They seemed to be pleased to hear of the option, as if relieved that surrender, unimaginable only a few weeks prior, was a good option.

He went on. "There's more. They also offer Australian citizenship to all personnel of any formation that switches sides, and engages in combat against PLA units loyal to General Bing that refuse to surrender."

The CP erupted in argument, with some saying that it was just a cheap trick, psychological warfare, no more. But from the serious expression on Colonel Guo's face, many of his staff understood that he was seriously considering the offer.

There was a long history of rebellion in Chinese military history, most of the men knew, and even as recently as the Tiananmen Square crisis of 1989, officially known as the 'June Fourth Incident', when an entire Army Corps had refused to move in on the pro-democracy protestors. Those soldiers had actually considered intervening to protect the civilians from the crackdown ordered by the Communist Party of China hardliners and Premier Deng Xiaoping. Guo imagined for a moment what China could have become had the nascent pro-democracy movement been taken up by the military. *Perhaps this foolish war would never have begun,* he thought.

He knew that his decision would have far-reaching consequences and that he would most likely be killed one way or the other. With nothing to lose, he went with his conscience.

"Men, we have been given a choice. As your Commanding Officer, I could make that choice for you, however the implications of this choice are very personal and profound. We are being asked to mobilize our forces, and engage the enemy. The question is, which one? Is the allied force that now surrounds us, the Australians and Marines who we have been fighting for three years now, are those our enemy? Or is General Bing and his command structure our enemy? Are they the traitors who have put China into the role of monsters, wrecking the world and utterly destroying China's reputation? We are being offered Australian citizenship and amnesty if we engage General Ma's formation, strike at his Army Group Centre' headquarters up in Rockhampton. Alternatively, we are offered amnesty but not citizenship if we simply surrender in place. The third option is to remain loyal to the cause of General Bing and his war. I believe that you all know me, and can guess at my answer. But you are free to express yourself on your own. Will all of you who wish to stand and fight for General Bing, go to the east side of this command post. Those who wish to surrender in place, come into the center of the CP. The rest, come and join me on the west side of this CP, and work with me on putting together a plan for an assault on Rockhampton. You have twenty minutes to decide." Guo concluded, and then made his way to a map table on the west side of his command post.

Pandemonium broke out in the CP, with everybody raising their voices to be heard over one another. With such din in the CP, nobody achieved very much verbally, however their body language made it immediately clear what the consensus was. Within two minutes, nearly everybody had migrated to Colonel Guo's side of the CP, with a small number standing uncertainly in the middle of the CP.

There was nobody on the east side of the CP.

News of the allied offensive spread like wildfire. Accompanied by incredulity and confusion in the PLA command network, the effect on the Australian population had been quite the opposite. After three years of Chinese occupation and brutal reprisals for any transgression, any attempt to interfere with the Occupation Authority and the PLA units in their towns, the remaining Australian population of Queensland now had hope. Most understood that now was the time to implement long dreamed-of actions which, on their own, would not have caused all that much trouble for the occupying forces. But now, with their forces cut in two and reeling in confusion, the PLA was vulnerable and very much afraid.

Rumors that an entire Army Corps formation of US Marines had landed in Darwin and were moving east to recapture Cairns had put fear into the hearts of the men of the 42nd Group Army.

In the Combined Joint Task Force Command Post in Katherine, General Adams and Colonel Ferebee discussed the altered battle space with the success of the Aussie Rules campaign and the capture of Gladstone. From intelligence reports it appeared that the Marines had been successful in their efforts to carefully nurture this belief by gradually increasing the amount of radio chatter, spoofing the PLA intelligence analysts into believing that a much larger force of US Marines had deployed into Northern Territory and were even now moving closer and closer to the front.

This had been a major operation of deceptive tactics, inspired by similar operations used to misguide the Germans prior to the Allied invasion at Normandy. Unlike World War Two, however, there was no massive allied force in the region.

The objective of the deception was to dislocate and confuse PLA forces and to pave the way for the assault on Emerald, where the Marines could settle an old score with the 42nd Group Army, while contributing to the Australian objective of cutting right across Queensland to the coast, just north of Brisbane. The real fighting force was provided by just two Australian divisions that were involved in the assault through Biloela to Gladstone.

It was a desperate move – and one that would end in utter catastrophe if General Ma and his Army Group North realized that there were no follow-on forces to worry about. However, if the Marines had done an effective job in the deception campaign, creating the legend of a larger force of US Marines bearing down on what was left of the 42nd Group Army, and with the prospect of the four regiments of the Australian 1st Division to worry about, General Ma would have come to the conclusion that his forces were spread out far too broadly to hold on to all of eastern Queensland in the face of such a large offensive. Once he realized that the allies had cut him off from Army Group South by having captured Gladstone, he had no choice but to pull back his outlying units to concentrate his forces – abandoning all of the inland towns in order to hold on to a much smaller pocket along the north east coast, from Cairns to Rockhampton.

The allied assessment of the re-allocation of PLA units in Queensland was that it would leave only a single regiment of the 121st Division in the extreme south of Queensland, south of the Biloela – Gladstone area now held by the Australians. As long as General Sheung was unwilling to reinforce the 121st, they would be unlikely to attempt to counter-attack at Gladstone and more likely to hunker down and try to hold on to the Maryborough sector. If so, then they could be tackled by the Australians once additional militia forces were raised from the liberated towns inland. That would leave just the PLA 364th regiment, now entirely cut off and isolated several hundred kilometers inland at Charleville, for the Australian 1st Division to deal with. Without resupply and so far inland, the 364th would be forced to starve or to surrender. If that could be achieved the bulk of Queensland would be liberated, and the Chinese would be on the defensive, at least in the northern part of the country.

Satisfied that their understanding of the battle space in the northern sector was up-to-date, General Adams and Colonel Ferebee, in cooperative command of the Marines of the MAGTFA and three divisions of Australian militia and regular Army, turned their attention to the southern sector to update themselves on what had been passed to them from their counterparts in the CJTFHQ in Adelaide, in Sector South. Unlike the CJTFHQ in Katherine, however, the Generals running the show in South Australia had the Indians. Not only the initial expeditionary armored corps that India had first thrown into the fray, or what was left of it, but now a fresh, fully outfitted and now fully deployed Army comprised of two additional divisions of the Indian Army, and four newly formed infantry divisions that had been stood up by the Australians. Organized into two nearly identical Corps sized formations, each with a mix of Indian heavy armor and armored infantry regiments supported by a flood of Australian infantry regiments, the two corps of the Allied South Australian Army advanced on separate roads.

The northern-most corps struck east into New South Wales along highway 32 from Broken Hill towards Dubbo; the second drove along the bottom of New South Wales along Highway 20, through Hay towards Waga Waga. The remaining forces, some five or six brigades of mixed origin, were held in reserve and as a blocking force on the remaining roads across Victoria into South Australia, and were well supported by artillery.

The only American contribution to the Allied South Australian Army was contributed by Colonel Weir, back in Perth, and his assortment of Special Forces resources, tactics, Chinese intelligence and counter-intelligence resources.

The most notable of these was the food-poisoning operation in Waga Waga, which resulted in a generalized reduction in the enemy's ability to fight over the entire two weeks of the dual offensive. It had taken the PLA that long to trace back the salmonella and other strains of food contaminants back to Mr.

Blias' factory in Waga Waga before they were able to identify the lot numbers and food types that had been compromised with Clostridium Botulinium. Eventually the PLA medical authorities had realized the implications of the surge in cases of blurred vision, difficulty swallowing, respiratory problems, nausea, constipation, vomiting, rapidly increasing muscle weakness and, ultimately for many who were not given prompt medical attention: paralysis that started with head muscles and then worked its way down the body followed by respiratory failure and death. Once botulism had been confirmed, they had tried to get the word out for the soldiers of the PLA's Army Group South, to have them test all of their food supplies and to treat for botulism toxin, but this had come too late.

The most heavily affected units, the ones specifically targeted by Colonel Weir and Mr. Blias, were the 112th and 113th Mechanized Infantry Divisions of the 38th Group Army, deployed to Cobar and Bourke in the north of New South Wales, and the 195th Infantry Brigade of the 65th Group Army, in Hay, NSW.

With over 60% of his front-line units suffering debilitating cramping and diarrhea at the critical moment, General Sheung, Commander of Army Group South, was suddenly faced with a catastrophe. Rather than being in a strong position to repel an understrength Allied offensive along the very predictable axis of advance into New South Wales, where at best the allies would have less than a 2:1 ratio in their favor, his forces were hit with this mysterious malady that had a 3:1 force-dividing effect. The end result was that the odds had suddenly changed to 6:1 in the allies favor.

The numbers did not come near the actual catastrophe that he faced in the simultaneous crumbling of his front-line brigades at both the north and central NSQ battle areas. The allies once again used that reckless tactic that had become known as 'Australian Rules Offensive", rushing across the battle-space with no structure whatsoever, as if throwing everything they had into the mad rush to reach their distant 'goal line' objective. After crashing through the ass-wrenched PLA soldiers at Bourke and Cobar, the northernmost Australian and Indian force soon swooped down to make contact with his reserve units in Dubbo. Meanwhile the second front crumbled at Hay as the Aussies outran their Indian counterparts while they sprinted through the lightly PLA held territory, liberating no less than a half-dozen small cities surrounding Waga Waga before an effective response could be put forward.

By the end of the assault, some two weeks after it had first began with the men of the 38th and 65th Group Armies falling prey to the sabotaged rations, General Sheung had lost over 30% of New South Wales. That the lost terrain was mostly snow-bound and of little use was not much consolation: *the enemy now had the initiative.* It seemed to General Sheung that the writing was on the wall. *We are going to lose this war,* he thought for the first time. *And if that's how I am thinking, imagine how much worse it will be for the troops. They'll be lining up to trade their surrender for amnesty. Fucking Americans and their psychological warfare or whatever the hell they are doing. Why can't they just fight like they are supposed to, with bullets and bayonettes?*

21

A FATE WORSE THAN DEATH

The war was not going well for his side. Major Fang could see it in the high morale of the Australian and allied soldiers whose faces he scanned. Every day he spent hours shuffling along the highway with other refugees, making his way towards Adelaide. Unlike the downtrodden remnants of a once comfortable nation that his fellow travelers were, Major Fang was not looking for a more viable place to live. He was looking for a particular face, the face of the man he blamed for helping Australia win the war – and win the war they surely would. It was evident in the cheerful, eager faces of the young men in trucks he passed, the men newly trained soldiers being transited to the front lines in New South Wales. They were eager to join the winning cause before the war was over.

What he had learned by observing Chinese soldiers he had seen in the same trucks, coming in the opposite direction on their way to the processing camps, prison camps and labor party camps – these men were scared. Scared that they had been beaten and were now at the mercy of their enemy, scared that the promise of fair treatment that had bought their surrender would prove to be a lie, and scared that somehow they would wind up back in the lines, suffering the hardship of being a soldier for so many cold years.

But most of all, Fang watched the faces of the white soldiers, looking for the face that he had burned into his mind.

He had seen the man on a few occasions in the years since he had begun this, his final mission, but had not been able to get close enough to kill him.

And then the opportunity presented itself to him on a silver platter on the day that Fang arrived in Adelaide. Fang had wandered around the bustling city in a state of bewilderment. He was occasionally stopped by police and some sort of citizens watch force, but his forged documents and well-practiced lies always satisfied them that this particular Chinese was 'one of us' and should enjoy the same freedom as any Australian or guest.

And then Fang stopped to admire the beautiful architecture and stonework of a very elegant old building he had come across. His trained eyes continued their incessant scanning, and came to focus on a man climbing out of a military vehicle. The man turned to look Fang's way, just for an instant, and then carried on towards the hotel.

There was no doubt in Fang's mind that it was him, the man that was responsible for great suffering, death, and defeat for so many PLA soldiers. The man whose actions often tilted the equation, subtly at times, more overtly at others, in favor of the smaller, less well equipped allied forces.

And now Fang was only a few meters from him.

Stalking like a predator, Fang followed the man as he walked into a hotel. He was out of uniform, and dressed very well.

Fang followed him into the lobby, and tried to press into the crowded elevator a step behind the man, but he was held back by an attendant who had extended a gloved hand: "Sorry, mate, this one's full, and for the wedding party only. You'll have to take another lift."

Fang backed off, and watched the antique yet functional floor indicating arrow that silently arced from "L" through "1" and "2" and so on all the way to "11", where it stopped.

After walking around the lobby for a few minutes to gauge the range of activities in the hotel, Fang had noted that there were few military personnel in the hotel, seemingly no more than 2 or 3 security personnel, and a great deal of well-dressed, likely very well-off, civilians.

He also saw a schematic of the hotel, and formed a mental picture of the engineering details of the old building before heading up a fire-stairwell, bounding up the stairs two at a time

432

with pure joy in his heart. *I'm going to get him this time, no matter how many others I have to take out in the process*, he thought.

Once on the 11th floor, Fang quietly opened the emergency exit a few inches to look down the hall. He was just in time to see the man disappear into a room near the far end of the corridor.

With nobody else in sight, Major Fang withdrew his favorite throwing knife, the one that had saved him years before at a checkpoint near Ti Tree, just north of Alice Springs.

He listened at the door for a moment, his hand grasping the door knob. Through the partly open door he could hear a soft, familiar voice. It gave him pause.

"You made it!" the beautiful bride to be said to the man who had just arrived. "I was so afraid that you wouldn't make it in time, Sir."

"Come on, Wendy, you can call me Peter. Have I missed it?" he asked, I must be an hour late."

"Nope. We're just about to start. We had a delay, the Blakely's and the Yao's were stuck in traffic, and there's no way Rick and I are going to start without our best mates," she said.

"So where's everybody else? I would have expected them to be here, but the concierge told me you were up here all alone. Jitters?"

"Nothing like that. Wardrobe malfunction, but I got it sussed on my own. I was just about to head back to the Edinburgh Room when you knocked"

Fang heard it. *The woman and the target are alone*, he realized. *The man could be a problem, if he's armed, but the woman will be nothing more than a nuisance. He pushed the door open quietly and moved in for the kill.*

Colonel Weir and Warrant Officer Wendy Hayman looked up just in time to see the sudden motion of the intruder's throwing arm and the flicker of something shiny flying through the air.

433

With a sickening sound, the knife struck Colonel Weir in the chest and struck bone.

As the Colonel fell backwards onto the dresser, Wendy sprang across the room, her wedding dress flowing out behind her as if taken by the wind.

Fang had momentarily fixated his eyes on his target, and had determined that the knife had missed by a few inches, striking the man dead center in his chest and becoming lodged in his sternum rather than into his heart as intended.

The look on the face of the woman flying at him surprised him. He had not expected a woman in a wedding dress to be so aggressive, and was a moment too slow in turning to face the threat.

Wendy smashed into him with her claws extended, tearing into his face.

Fang registered pain all around his face as he rolled backwards, falling away from his attacker. But she held on, her beautifully painted nails now digging deeply into the assailant's face, her thumbs digging up under his chin, slicing upwards in search of an artery. Falling on top of the man, Wendy felt pressure on her stomach as the man pushed up with his legs, trying to push her away.

Had he still had use of his eyes, now both out of action as Wendy dug her index fingers into his eyes, he would have seen the absurd sight of the inverted woman now doing a momentary hand-stand, her fingers all dug into his face and neck and her energy focused on pushing her index fingers deeper and deeper into the soft tissue of his eyes. But what was even more ridiculous was the sight of her dress falling 'down' around her legs and torso, completely inverted as she was suspended above Fang by his futile attempt to push her off. The large bell-shape of her dress's train now completely enveloped her attacker and her, with only her garters and stocking-clad legs visible.

For a moment, as Fang's struggles faded and Wendy continued the pressure on her fingers into his eye sockets, there was no movement.

And then suddenly the door opened an a massive black man, dressed impeccably in his finest US Marine Corps dress uniform, Top Sergeant Rick Rideout wondered *what the fuck is going on?*

"Wendy! Who have you got under there? Get off of him! Who is that? Is that you, Dickie!" Rideout shouted, as he pulled Wendy up by the ankles.

The sight of blood all over Wendy's chest and hands, and the terrible stains on her wedding dress were the first sign that something worse than a pre-wedding fling with her old lover was taking place.

He looked at the Asian man on the floor, and deduced from the dark blood flowing out of the man's eye sockets, and the blood on his bride's hands, that this was a fight to the death.

As the man tried to roll over, Rideout stomped on his stomach, and then stepped on one of the man's hands.

"You're not going anyplace, fucker!" Rideout said, then looked at Wendy. "You alright? What the fuck happened here?"

"I don't know. He threw a knife at Colonel Weir. He's an assassin, so I used my only weapon on him." Wendy said, now standing over Colonel Weir, who was clearly alive, but laying back on the dresser, trying to hold still out of pain.

Rideout looked at the man. "He's Chinese. Maybe an assassin from the PLA?" then he leaned closer, seeing something on the man's face. "That scar on his face. Could this be the guy who?"

"Tried to kill Sunny Yao? Yes, I think that's him," said Colonel Weir, through his pain.

"Mother fucker!" Rideout said, and then raised his foot high over Fang's face.

When Fang woke up he was in darkness.

He could not tell if it was because his eyes had been gouged out or if it was because he was in a box, but as he felt around with his hands and legs, he quickly realized that blindness was the least of his problems.

What is this, a coffin? Fang thought, as he felt the sides, top and ends of the softly lined rectangular box that he found himself within.

Fang was on the verge of panic at the thought of being trapped inside a coffin, buried alive. But the sound of rain, *no, shovels of dirt* landing on top of this box, captured his attention.

They're burying me alive! "NOOOO! HELP! LET ME OUT OF HERE!" He shouted, the strain on his vocal cords at the intensity of his scream was simply primordial.

Standing above the open grave, taking his time with the task, Top Sergeant Rideout thought he heard something from the coffin below. He paused to listen.

"Is that the effect you wanted, Sir?" he asked.

"Yes. Give him a few more shovel-fulls."

"No reason we can't just keep filling the hole. He killed Jake, after all, and cut up Sunny Yao quite badly," said Rideout. "On top of that, didn't he kill a number of your agents over the years?"

"Yes, he did. Quite a few, in fact. And Cheryl and I would take a small measure of satisfaction to know that he was dead. But we need him. We need him broken, ready to sing like a bird, to give us a watershed of names, dates, and facts. We need him for the war crimes trials back in the US, and to ferret out some of his kind still unaccounted for here in Australia," Colonel Weir said, soberly.

But the look on Weir's face told Rideout that the Colonel was deeply conflicted. For a moment, Rick thought of ways to kill the Chinese spy now desperately screaming and kicking in his tomb, but put those thoughts out of his mind when Weir waved a hand, indicating that's enough.

"Mr. Clarke, you can have him now. Just make sure you don't let him get away.

"Are you kidding, Colonel? The man's blind and broken."

"I don't think you know what you are dealing with here," Weir said, "Don't underestimate this man, he's capable of anything."

"Whatever you say. But by the time we're done with him, and after the trials, he'll spend the rest of his life blind, confined to a box not much larger than the one you have him in now."

"That'll have to do," said Weir.

22

DEPARTURE

The "package" had been a watershed. It had arrived on the Canadian maritime patrol aircraft, which made the round trip from Adelaide to the United States. For the extreme long-range mission, Captain Bass and his crew, Demon-72, had stripped the aircraft to the bone, removing some of the tactical work-stations and sonobuoy racks to reduce the weight and make room for a few extra passengers, barrels of fuel and essential spares. The Flight Engineer, Warrant Officer Poke, had carefully supervised the Australian technicians at RAAF Edinburgh to ensure that the removed equipment was treated with care, in case it would ever be re-installed in 'his' aircraft, but everybody knew that the age of antisubmarine warfare had long since come to an end. Not only was it likely that the world's fleets of submarines were all but destroyed, unserviceable or abandoned; but also the supplies of spares, armaments and other resources needed to maintain or repair these warships were also a thing of the past.

The aging antisubmarine warfare aircraft – tail number '111', or 'triple-sticks' - was one of the few long-range aircraft still in operation, and it was the only one with the sophisticated navigation and communications equipment needed for the dangerous mission. And in this, its age was an advantage, as it still had a functioning inertial navigation computer, which had been left in the aircraft when the avionics had been upgraded to include GPS, now a completely useless navigation system.

From the stories the crew told of their trip, there had been more than a few close calls along their plan-as-you-go itinerary. What made the mission so dangerous was not the risk of encountering enemy forces. The Chinese military expansion had long since come to an end and the contraction was well underway, so the enemy lines were now fairly well established and easily avoided. The real problem was that there was no way to communicate with the airports they needed to use along the way. Without knowing the status of airfields, they could not do their normal mission planning, and they did not have the support of the planning cell at their Higher Headquarters, the Canadian Air Operations Centre of the RCAF in Winnipeg, who would normally have taken care of coordinating diplomatic over-flight clearances for the required fuel stops. So they were going in blind. The vast distances involved in flying from Adelaide, in the South Pacific, all the way to the west coast of the United States, was such that they would arrive at many of their planned fuel stops without sufficient reserves to make it to any alternate. They would be fully committed. In this way, each leg of the journey was high risk and full of unknowns.

All they could do was rely on past experience, and land at places that had provided support in the past. In part for the purpose of bartering, they had brought with them two tons of food supplies, including some live sheep and an assortment of fruits and seeds that the farmers in the Adelaide region had succeeded in bringing back into production. The bulk of these goods had been traded in a tense negotiation-turned-armed-standoff with a gang of machete-wielding thugs operating Nadi International Airport in Fiji, for fuel and airport services. That they had showed up unannounced and landed unexpectedly at the crowded little airport had not been a good start, but the promise of future visits and the allure of increased power and influence for the gang's leader had tipped things in favor of commerce over outright piracy, and Demon-72's crew had been permitted to depart with full fuel tanks.

Their reception in Hawaii had been much better, as it had been coordinated on the fly over the HF radio. They had traded the remainder of their commodities with the local militia operating Port Allen Airport at Hanapepe Bay, Kauaia, and took a delegation from Kauai to Dillingham Airfield, on Oahu, as part of the deal. Landing closer to Honolulu was out of the question, of course, with so many military targets in the area, most notably the Joint USN – USAF Pearl Harbor – Hickam Base having been hit a dozen times when the war broke out. The devastation, suffering and loss of life in Honolulu had been staggering; however, the communities on the other Hawaiian Islands were largely intact, and eager to help with reconstruction. But with aviation resources largely worn out or destroyed in the years since the war, now most travel was being conducted by sailboats. So the air transport of officials from Kauaia to Oahu was the least that Demon 72's crew could do in exchange for fuel.

As it was, a group of military personnel from the new post-war base built at Waialua had come aboard for onward transport to Oregon, to meet with military officials coordinating the re-mobilization of the American military on the west coast..

For their part, the crew of Demon 72 satisfied their curiosity just at the end of their journey to the US by overflying the crater that had once been their home base, in Comox, on Vancouver Island. In a way, it was fortunate that most of the crew had been single, on the fateful day when they last departed their home base. By now, most of them had married Australians and now saw Adelaide as home. However, a few of the men had learned the fate of their wives and children who had perished in their military housing when RCAF Base Comox had been obliterated. Those men still grieved, but no longer had any wish to return to the devastated base. They had long since accepted their losses, and grieved long enough. It was enough to look out the window as the barren scar of land that had once been home, and face reality by permanently putting to rest any fantasy that there could have been survivors.

During the flight over Vancouver Island, the crew made radio contact with Canadian military personnel operating from Port Hardy, farther up Island, but were directed to carry on to the new military base in Astoria, Oregon, where some P3 Orion spares could be sought. This was great news to Bob Poke, the Flight Engineer, as he had a long list of compounding snags and other mechanical problems to rectify if triple-sticks was to remain airworthy.

Flying over Comox allowed them to take images of the disastrous effects of the detonations in Nanaimo and Vancouver, the devastation that had once been the Canadian Naval base at Esquimalt and the provincial Capital at Victoria. But the worst scenes they documented with their belly-mounted and hand-held cameras were the series of blast zones they overflew as they flew over US Navy, Air Force, and Army bases in Washington State. It was the same at each base. They had been hit several times, from the Naval Air Station at Whidbey Island to the Submarine and Naval base at Bangor, and the Naval Stations at Bremerton and Everett in Puget Sound. The military installations had quite simply been erased from the face of the earth.

Civilian targets were also hit, and the devastation they saw in Seattle and Tacoma and what had once been a sprawling Joint US Army – USAF Base Lewis McChord. As a personal favor to Major Blakely, they had tried to locate JBLM. Peering out the starboard aft bubble window, Blakely took pictures of the barren landscape that was in the correct geographical location, but he did not see anything on the ground to evidence that there had ever been a large military base there. *I sure hope some of those poor bastards got out of there in time*, he thought, knowing that it was more likely that few had escaped.

"You see what I mean?" said Dirty Dave, the copilot. "There's nothing left of any of the military bases, so it's not correct to say that they are 'rebuilding' the military capabilities. More accurate to say 'building anew', starting from scratch."

"I see what you mean. So all of the new bases, they'll be located in smaller towns, or out in the wilderness?" asked one of the crew over the intercom as they flew onward into Oregon.

"My bet is that they will be based on regional airports and existing infrastructure. There simply won't be the resources or manpower to start with virgin ground. So we should have approach plates and charts for these towns, in the civilian aeronautical database," he guessed, accurately.

After the horrors of the Pacific Northwest, the terrain in Oregon looked at first to be relatively untouched, until they descended out of 31,000 feet and got close enough to see that the forests had the unmistakable blackness of land ravaged by forest fires.

After a quick pass over the wastelands that had once been Portland, they arrived at the congested Astoria Regional airport. After landing and taxiing to the main apron it soon became apparent to Dirty and his skipper that their aircraft could be one of the very few operational aircraft. The airport was littered with aircraft in various states of disrepair.

Two USN P3C Orion aircraft, clearly being cannibalized and beyond repair, looked particularly inviting to the their flight engineer as a place he could harvest some fresh tires and other spares for the Canadian P3C Aurora aircraft.

Triple-sticks was in very poor condition by this time, riddled with bullet holes, undercarriage damage, and a few very messy looking oil streaks hinting at serious hydraulic boost package issues which the flight engineer had been working miracles with during the journey from Australia.

Once on the ground in Astoria, the crew and passengers were eager to figure out who to talk to about their lodgings, and to get some sort of orientation about the new base. It did not take long before all of their questions were answered, when a well-prepared Lieutenant from the US Air Force arrived with the "Ramp Taxi" crew bus sent to collect the aircrew and passengers.

They were all impressed at how well prepared the Joint Services Base' Astoria's operations support staff were for their arrival, but something about how the base was organized seemed unusual to the visitors.

With a robust international airport and port facility left intact, Astoria had been chosen as the location for Unified Joint Command, UJC, bringing all branches of military and civil defense under a single command. Joint operations were new and unfamiliar to some of the soldiers, sailors and airmen, and there had been a great deal of confusion at first, but ultimately they had found a good model around which to organize their efforts.

Major Blakely recognized it first, of course, as the Unified Joint Command was largely based on the doctrinal template of the United States Marine Corps. After all, the USMC had been refining and mastering the concept of joint Land, Sea Air, and

Special Forces and expeditionary power projection from the seas ever since their origins as the Continental Marines, in 1775, in the American Revolutionary War.

But that was not the only explanation for the efficiency and professionalism that they encountered. It was also that the war was now going their way, after eight years of hopelessness in the aftermath of the initial, incomprehensible devastation of the Nuclear Extinction War. And now that they were carrying the fight to the enemy, and growing stronger by the day, the Allied military forces were at the top of their game. The commitment to the cause of liberty – to the defeat of the Chinese forces around the world – had permeated throughout the military organization in a way that had not been seen since the later stages of the Second World War in the mid-1940's, when the Allies had finally overcome the shock and awe of the Nazi blitzkrieg, and put together a grand alliance that eventually had the power and effective leadership to turn the tide and defeat Adolph Hitler. Hitler was a madman who had wreaked much devastation on Europe. However, he was a mere vandal in comparison to General Bing, who had murdered literally billions of people and put the global climate into a nuclear winter that came close to exterminating humankind.

So it was into a beehive of highly purposive activity that the contingent from Australia engaged. Indian Air Force Group Captain Garwhal, Australian Army General Davis, USMC Colonel Ferebee, the former Ranger-turned Australian Colonel Weir and Major Blakely all had very productive meetings with the military brass, and a chance to get in contact with their counterparts. There was a welcome package prepared for each crewmember, the Marines, and the Australian and Indian military personnel onboard the Canadian P3C aircraft.

The powers that be knew full well how tenuous the battle for Australia had been, and how much damage the Marines of MAGTFA, the fighting power of the Indian armored formations, and the determined effort that the Australians themselves had collectively inflicted on the five Group Armies that China had thrown into their attempted conquest of Australia. That China had ultimately been defeated, at least in Australia, had been one of the most positive developments of the war, after the assassination of General Bing, when his bunker in China had been destroyed by dropping a few modified artillery round sized nuclear warheads down some hastily drilled shafts, converting General Bing, Colonel Hua, and the collective brain of Operation Winter Snake.

Since then, without the snakehead and his strategic staff to coordinate global operations, Chinese expeditionary forces had been cut off from resupply and left isolated. The operations to mop them up were a challenge for the Allies, with so little left in terms of resources, fuel, and munitions. However, they were conducting operations meant to beef up local opposition wherever they could, to interfere with the Chinese forces until a larger operation could be mounted at each theatre of war in turn.

And so it was quite fortuitous that the representatives from Australia had arrived in Astoria when they did, not only to give a thorough briefing on the status of the mop-up operations still going on in Queensland and New South Wales, but also to participate in planning for the next phase in the effort in their AOR, putting together an expeditionary strike force, task force Whakarewarew, pronounced 'Fucker-A-wa-ray-wa'.

Now that the Chinese had been defeated in a few key areas, the larger strategic plan was to deploy special operations teams to reinforce areas where the Chinese were facing persistent local opposition, and then ultimately to bring larger expeditionary task-forces to bear where the Chinese were more deeply entrenched. So the experience brought to the table by the Australian contingent – the tactics and strategies that they had honed over the last eight years – as well as their strategic location for mounting the anticipated operations, contributed to the Supreme Allied Commander's planning efforts.

However, after three weeks of participation it soon became clear to everybody that their work at the UJC HQ had come to an end. With their precious copies of the war-plans in hand, along with sets of modes and codes for secure HF and UHF communications, and with triple-sticks once again fully repaired, provisioned and preflighted, the Australian contingent of Indian,

Australian and USMC personnel rejoined the Canadian P3C aircrew and departed for home.

For their return itinerary to Australia, the planners at UJC Base Astoria had coordinated fuel supplies and a very friendly welcome for Demon-72, and what turned out to be a two-week stop at the Cassidy International Airport on the Kiritimati Atoll, formerly known as Christmas Island. They had planned to stop there for just one night, but had damaged their main landing gear when landing on the poorly maintained runway and had spent the next two weeks improvising an airworthy repair out of the limited local resources.

The price that the allies had agreed to pay for the communities' nearly exhausted supply of aviation fuel had been to deliver a precious cargo of urgently needed parts for the tiny island's reverse-osmosis water purification unit. They also brought spares for the communications equipment at the climatological research facility on the island.

Their final refueling stop was at Norfolk Island, one of the easternmost external territories of the Commonwealth of Australia. The small island territory had remained free throughout the war and was in surprisingly good condition. All that had been required to secure the aviation fuel was to bring in a complete UHF radio transmitter-receiver, and a pair of US Navy communications specialists who were up for an adventurous assignment.

The final leg of their flight was the most dangerous, with the risk of being shot down by Chinese patrol aircraft operating out of New Zealand. There was little doubt that the People's Liberation Army Air Force units operating from New Zealand would be sent to investigate the military aircraft that had suddenly arrived in their AOR, seemingly inbound from the United States.

As a result, Demon-72 made a quick, one-hour turn-around, staying just long enough to offload the two technicians and cargo, refuel, and continue their marathon flight to Adelaide.

Still firmly in the grip of Chinese forces with essentially all of the 38th Group Army - 190,000 soldiers - and a range of utility, air-to-air, fighter and early warning aircraft, the original Chinese force to land in New Zealand had complete control, and were by this time very well entrenched. In the final days before the complete capitulation of PLA's 41st and 42nd Group Armies in Queensland and New South Wales, fully three divisions had been evacuated to the relative safety of Chinese New Zealand, along with what was left of their fighter aircraft after the grinding attrition of the air war with India that had raged in the skies over Australia for the last eight years.

There was nothing left of the two other Group Armies that had been part of the million-man force that General Bing had thrown at Australia, with the air assaulters of the 14th Group Army being shot down by DDG 116 *Thomas Hudner* as they approached the Darwin Sector, and the 13th Group Army's initial wave of air-land forces having been defeated at the Battle of Carnarvon, when the Indian Amy's 10th Division drove up Highway 10 from Darwin to rid Western Australia of PLA soldiers. There were no follow-on forces to beef up the Chinese foothold in Carnarvon and Exmouth farther to the north. Even so, it had taken the Indians out of Perth and a brigade group of Marines from MAGTFA and Australians coming down from Darwin fully two years to mop up the beleaguered Chinese forces in the West.

On the east coast, with nearly 600,000 Chinese soldier having successfully deployed through the ports and airstrips from Cairns to the clean zone just north of Sydney, the Chinese had enjoyed a solid six years of control. But with the success of the Marine-led forces out of Darwin, and the victories at Julia Creek, Mount Isa, and Comooweal the tide had slowly turned. However, it had not been until the field-grade commanders of many of the Chinese units had lost the will to fight, or had come to the conclusion that the Allies were going to win that things really began to fall apart.

Certainly the betrayal by the Indonesians, converting the entire flotilla of ships that were supposed to transport the 16th Group Army into a floating prison, the ship's propulsion systems rendered inoperative by the Indonesian saboteurs. And with the Indonesian military having timed their rebellion to perfectly coincide with the Allied offensives in both Queensland and in

New South Wales, the Chinese were clearly on the defensive in the entire region.

The PLA was over-extended and on its heels, unable to hold the territories they had captured. The allied incursions penetrating deeper and deeper into New South Wales and Queensland had become an alarming trend. But the most critical failure was when the Allies had reached the coast, at Gladstone, and cut the two Chinese Army Groups off from each other.

After that, the writing had been on the wall.

Individual units of the 41st and 42nd Group armies continued to embrace the offer of Australian citizenship in exchange for handing over their superior officers and surrendering their unit en-masse, or, where their commanders were ruthless enough to hold them together to fight, the Australian 3rd Division and the MAGTFA moved in to cut them to pieces one and town at a time. The Allies now had momentum on their side, and continued to grow stronger while the Chinese forces withered with no hope of reinforcement and with abysmal morale.

In the south, despite having a much larger force, General Sheung wanted to find a way to avoid being prosecuted for his war crimes and ultimately hung. He led the evacuation of the strongest elements of the 38th and 65th Group Army, stripping out the core of his once powerful Army Group South after finally accepting that all was lost when his best subordinate commander, the field-promoted General Ma, had committed suicide after having ordered an entire brigade group to surrender en-masse just before what could have been a decisive victory for the Chinese. *I thought Ma was made of stronger stuff*, Sheung had thought.

By the desperation and haste with which General Sheung's men threw themselves into any seaworthy ship or serviceable aircraft in a panicked exodus to Chinese New Zealand, the Australians, Indians and Marines realized that victory was in their grasp, and were spurred on mop up the isolated and poorly coordinated units that remained – those who were too slow to flee Australia in time.

It was as if the Chinese were preparing for a last stand in New Zealand, or perhaps they believe that they could hold out indefinitely, what with New Zealand having everything needed to support over 200,000 Chinese soldiers, perhaps another 300,000 ethnic Chinese civilians, and another million or less Kiwis that had survived the privations of the nuclear winter and the horrendous treatment at the hands of the occupying Chinese forces.

In the two months after his return to Australia, Colonel Weir took care in the delivery of the two shocks he had to disclose to his wife, Cheryl. To do it in the right way, and in case he never saw her again after what he was about to do, he did the one thing that he had not done for her in over eight years – he took her on a vacation.

It had not been difficult to negotiate with the High Command in Adelaide, as he had continued to operate as the one and only US Army Ranger in Australia - still operating as an autonomous, free agent, providing leadership, training and advice to the Australian Special Forces. So he did not have to go through as many hoops as his USMC colleagues in the MAGTF. All he had to do was say that he needed two weeks leave, and that he would report for the assigned duty, ready to engage, when his personal time had been completed. He did not even have to bring up the troubles he had been having with his health ever since his sternum had been impaled by Major Fang's throwing knife.

Always thinking several moves ahead, Peter Weir had selected a secluded, Five Star resort, the Thistle & Clarke Vineyard Hotel in the Barossa Valley, just a few hours' drive north of Adelaide.

Cheryl had been through so much over her time in Australia – not just the loss of their only child, Jacob, at the hands of that evil Chinese agent, but also the unending years of toil and sacrifice of a military wife during wartime, the constant dread that she would hear that she had lost her soul-mate, and would be all alone in this strange land.

After a week enjoying the fine cuisine and extraordinarily good wines at the Thistle & Clarke Wineries, Peter had been working up the courage to break the news to her, and undoubtedly to break her, once again. But she beat him to it.

"I know that look in your face, Pete. I can see your ears wiggling. You're having one of those internal conversations with yourself, aren't you?"

He simply stared at her, unable to put words together.

"Come on, out with it. It must be a big one, this time," she said, and then burst out in tears when she saw the expression on his face drop.

"You're going away again, aren't you?"

"Yes," he said, simply.

"To New Zealand, right?"

"You know I can't say where," he began, and then dropped the 'Top Secret' bullshit. "Yes, I'm leading a special task force of Aussies, going in to link up with a Maori unit. You know, Major Collins and the boys from 1 Commando and other SOCOMD units, and much of the MAGTFA. We'll be the first to go in."

"You'll be with Top Sergeant Rideout? Well, that's a bit of a relief, that man always seems to have your back. I suppose Wendy will be staying behind, with the twins – at least I'll have her to pester for information on the campaign," she said, showing the strength and loyalty that Peter always appreciated, but never took for granted. *Maybe now is not the time to tell her*, he thought.

"What else? You're holding back something very bad, aren't you? Another mission, I can take, even you're going up against what everybody around here says is an impregnable Chinese force in New Zealand, I know you'll do your sneaky-squirrel stuff and slip in and do whatever terrible things you do to make everybody so impressed with your ruthlessness, but to me you're such a baby. Don't be afraid that I'll cry or something, just give it to me like a man," she said, becoming increasingly pissed off at whatever bad news was about to come.

But in her hostile tone, Peter saw that she was at the end of her rope, and would be devastated.

"We are not going home," he said.

In the silence that ensued, while Cheryl's face worked itself into a knot of confusion, Peter waited for her to fall apart, as he was certain that she would.

"We? Do you mean you and the men? Not coming home from New Zealand? What, are you on a suicide mission or something?" she finally asked, her voice shaky at the thought of her husband going on a certain death. The thought terrified her, as she always saw Peter as some kind of military superman, always aware of – and mitigating – every conceivable danger. That was what had made him so effective in guiding the Australians as insurgents, screwing with the minds of Chinese commanders so effectively that in many cases the mere report that Colonel Weir was active in their sector would make them pull back and turtle until he moved on to another sector to harass – or murder – some other poor bastard Red Panda.

"No. You and I. We're not going home, I turned down a place for us on a grain ship leaving for the US."

"Home? You mean Darwin?....Or do you mean the smoking hole that was Lewis McChord? Or do you mean 75th Ranger Training Brigade?" she said, getting angry rather than afraid. "Cause from where I stand, Colonel, we have no home other than our latest PCS. And as far as I'm concerned, Australia is it. This is our last PCS – whether you come home on your feet or in a box – 'cause we buried my baby here. I'm not leaving Jacob, and he's buried up there near Ayers Rock. He died trying to be like you, Peter. He wanted to please you, to have you spend more time with him as a soldier than you ever did with him as a child," she began to rant at him, throwing up years and years of missed baseball games, school performances, birthdays and late nights when Jacob's asthma had Cheryl afraid she would lose her little boy.

The reality of her son's death the price she had paid for encouraging her husband's career ambitions, and was now making her regret ever thinking of aspiring to be general's wife.

Peter held her in his arms as her shouting became sobbing, the two grief-stricken parents brought back down into the black hole of their staggering loss.

Parents should not outlive their children, and she's right, I was never there for Jake. It's my fault he tried to become a soldier, he just wanted to be closer to me, and now I've lost him. It's all my fault, Peter began to cry as well, for the first time in decades, he cried with the deep roar that one is only capable of when fully opening up to the pain and letting out a primordial scream of agony.

His cries were so deep and loud that Cheryl began to fear for his sanity, and could only hold him until it passed. It terrified her to see him this way, as though something awful had been released in him. She imagined that whatever it was that made him so ruthless when hunting and killing Chinese officers, his specialty, came from some dark place that now, for the first time in her experience, she was seeing a glimpse of. Only now, in his grief at having squandered his time with his son, he had turned his inner monster on himself. It was truly terrifying.

Eventually the monster crept back into its cave deep inside him, and he became silent, spent, and wrecked.

"There, there, Pete. I'm here. Jacob will always be with us, and we will always be with him. We are not leaving this place, Australia. Jacob has made this our home," she said.

"Cher, I'm not sure what just happened to me. Maybe I need to see a shrink," Peter said, chagrined from the magnitude of his emotional outburst, and afraid for his own sanity. *I should have killed Fang, the fucker,* Weir thought, grasping for something other than Jake to focus on.

"No, my love, you need to go to New Zealand and kill. Kill, and kill. Kill until there's no more monster left in you, and you can no longer kill. Then come home to me, and we'll visit Jacob, and then we'll do what he would have wanted to do if he had lived through this insane war, we'll leave the military and become farmers. Jacob would have liked that."

Feeling slightly stronger, and at peace, with the image of his young son riding a horse back at the stables in Sudden Valley, near JBLM, Colonel Peter Weir was beginning to feel that he was himself again, ready for the grim task of finding new and terrifying ways to hunt down and kill the leadership of the People's Liberation Army. His stony expression told Cheryl that he would once again channel that inner monster to a terrible, but necessary purpose, and she wondered if this time he might not go too far over the line, and no longer be the man she knew when he returned - or if he would return at all. But then, a few simple words came out of Peter's mouth that were enough to give her hope that her man would return intact, ready to give up killing, and ready to embrace the pastoral life that could have been, for Jake.

"Yes, Cher, he would have. Yes, he would."

Down at the dedicated grain berth pier in Adelaide's inner harbour, the USA bound dry bulk carrier that Colonel Weir had been offered a berth on was in the final stages of buttoning up the massive hatches, sealing up over fifty thousand deadweight tons of Durum Wheat, the first Supramax-sized grain shipment to leave Adelaide in over eight years.

But that was not the only cargo on MV *Thor Insuvi*. A one-time Singaporean operated bulk dry cargo ship, manufactured at Tsuneishi Heavy Industries in the Philippines, had been idle ever since it had been liberated from Chinese control by the Australian navy, its former cargo offloaded back into the very grain terminal from which it had been loaded just weeks before the war broke out – providing much needed food to South Australia during the long, cold, nuclear winter.

With food production having risen above the sustenance level, and grain silos from Perth to Adelaide now brimming full, Australia was back in the commodities export game.

In large part as a thank you to the contribution made to the defense and liberation of Australia by the Marine Air Ground Task Force Australia, the Australian government had offered the first grain shipment as a gift to the still struggling United States. With the American agricultural sector still struggling to produce meaningful quantities, what with the contamination of so much of the Midwest and the much more persistent continental snow-cover in the United States, food was still scarce. It would still be another year or longer before the US grain production could begin to meet the needs of the thirty million survivors in the United States.

With a crew of twenty five and additional quarters for a dozen or more passengers, the ship provided a rare opportunity for transport across the enormity of the Pacific Ocean. There had been over a hundred worthy applicants for passage, so the ship's crew agreed to improvise additional berths in suitable spaces throughout the ship, and to double-up most of the larger quarters, generating fifty additional spaces. More than that would have interfered with the safe management of the ship, which took priority over the opportunity to transport people to the United States.

Of the applicants, the majority were expatriate Americans or Europeans who had been displaced in Australia or Asia when the war had begun, and were looking for a way to get home. There were a few diplomats and businessmen, and two dozen military personnel and their dependants. Of these, three were Marines from MAGTFA – two who were convalescing, recovering from serious wounds, one a double-amputee and the other having lost an eye. The two combat veterans were the only Marines willing to leave the Australian AOR. They had agreed to return to America, having accepted that their ability to contribute to the cause had come to an end, but they were not happy to be leaving. There was still work to be done, for the Marines, and nobody wanted to leave their brothers – their bonds were stronger than ever after the long campaign to defeat China in Australia.

The Marines, once of the 3rd Marines, were now more strongly connected with Australia than with Okinawa or Hawaii. Many had taken Australian wives; all having buried countless friends in Australian soil. So when OPERATION WHUCKEREWREWA had been announced, to a man the Marines had clamoured for the opportunity to be part of the first wave to go ashore, to finish what they had begun in Darwin. And, somehow, the infusion of Australian soldiers into their ranks – as replacements into the original Brigade Group that constituted the MAGTFA when the war had begun, and later as additional battalions of Australians that were stood up as 'Australian Marines' to bring the MAGTFA to Divisional strength – had infected the once purely American unit with an unusual blend of Marine Corps pride and ANZAC traditions. So it was natural for Combined Joint Task Force New Zealand to see the liberation of the "NZ" portion of the "Australia and New Zealand Army Corps" tradition to be unfinished business that was profoundly important to the original MAGTFA Marines as it was to the native Australians and New Zealanders who were force-generated for the operation.

The operation had been named "Whuckerewarewa" in honour of the men, women, and children who had been massacred by the Chinese forces when their community of Rotarua, on New Zealand's North Island, had been wiped out by the PLA in reprisal for their having given material support to the Maori "terrorists" who had been so effective at conducting guerrilla warfare against their Chinese occupiers.

And then there was one very unhappy Marine, along with his wife, who had been ordered to return to the United States. Despite the loss of international telecommunications, satellites, and other means of communicating, the USMC had not forgotten about Major Robert Blakely. They had been forced by the doctrine of personnel administration to hold him back, and not promote him to Lieutenant Colonel, and with good reason. Due to the nature of his PCS to Darwin as a Liaison officer, and his lack of the conventional Professional Development credits that he would have chipped away at if he were back in garrison in the US, he was not technically eligible for promotion. To do so would have required reassigning him out of his LnO function, and throughout the campaign in Australia Major Robert Blakely had proven himself invaluable as the conduit for all military coordination between the Australian military and the MAGTFA.

His deep understanding of Special Operations, along with his study of the Chinese order of battle before the war had even begun, had been instrumental in the successful cooperation between the normally self-contained Marine Air Task Force construct and the Australian Army.

The very survival of the Australian Army as a fighting force, reeling from the devastation of the opening months of the war, when fully 80% of Australia's fighting force had been obliterated, was due to the heavy load that the Marines took over from the Australians, and the shocking setbacks that they inflicted on the

PLA. This had given Australia time to reconstitute a viable force, which by the end of the eight-year campaign had swelled to a half million fighting men and women, fully two Group Armies comprised of 7 Divisions.

And throughout the campaign, Joe Blakely had provided subject matter expertise to the Australians, on everything from accelerated training, based in large part on what he had learned as a young Captain while training USMC recruits at Paris Island. And teaching them the structure, tactics, and the very mindset of the enemy.

His expertise on the Chinese military had only grown, as he mastered Cantonese so as to be more effective when debriefing Brown Pandas, when extracting information from Red Panda deserters, and when examining captured documents from over-run Chinese command posts.

And this was what had been of greatest interest to the USMC. They had identified Blakely as the most competent expert the Marines had on the Chinese military, and the USMC – the United States in fact – had pressing need for his expertise. Their intent was to extract Blakely from the Australian AOR, debrief him and then shape him into a policy wonk, an "S5 Planner", to plan and then to deploy so as to help adjust the plan in execution, for "OPERATION MARINE SEOUL HAILSTORM" – OPERATION MASH.

The audacious plan was to send Combined Joint Task Force Korea to the unforgiving, mountainous terrain of Chinese-occupied Korea, landing at a half-dozen locations along Korea's east coast, in places like Gangneung, Yangyan and Donghae, and then piercing through the Chinese units along Highway-50, to liberate Soul. If all went well, the concept of ops was to then repeat what had been accomplished by the allied force in the 1950's, by British, Australian, Canadian armies, supported by the US Navy warships and aircraft, by US Air Force Bombers, and, leading the charge at places like Chosin Reservoir, the United States Marine Corps. Korea, where the Chinese had swarmed over the border like so many cockroaches, more numerous than the allies had bullets. The place where the world had come so close to nuclear war, and where the US Marine Corps had first come into combat against the Chinese 42nd Group Army. Known then as the 42nd PVA, it was the very unit that spearheaded the Chinese invasion of Australia; the unit whose commander, General Leung, had escaped to New Zealand. And the Marines had decided he would be dealt with soon, by OPERATION WHUCKEREWREWA, where the Marines would finally close the history books on the 42nd Group Army.

As for bringing the fight all the way to the enemy's doorstep, to bring the Winter Kill War to an unequivocal end, Korea must also be liberated before China would ultimately be forced to submit to the final reckoning. But for OPEARTION MASH to be mounted swiftly, and with the best chances for success, Major Blakely's expertise was needed back home.

He had no choice.

He had tried to convince his daughter, Agness Yao, and her husband, Sunny Yao, to come with them, but they had declined. Australia was where their heart was now, and they were so deeply involved in helping rebuild relations between the Anglo-Irish-Scotch Australians and the ethnic Chinese Australians who had fought alongside their white comrades to throw off the Chinese invaders. But in the larger civilian population, the six million survivors out of the original twenty five million Australians when the war had started, there was a great deal of hostility against all things Chinese.

This antagonism would have resulted in a bloodbath of recriminations and 'pay-back', were it not for the support that Sunny Yao had cultivated from the military, amongst whom Sunny was legendary for his contribution to the counter-intelligence and psychological warfare contribution he made during the war. He was a hero, as much for his effectiveness as an Allied spy as for the story of his courage and suffering, his will to survive after having been carved up by Major Fang, the war criminal whose testimony had put the nail in the coffin of so many PLA superior officers.

Ultimately, Sunny had decided to become a politician, to stand up for the Chinese Australians, the Brown Pandas, and to commit his life to healing the wounds that the uninvited Chinese invaders had caused in the expatriate Chinese community. He saw it as the culmination of his efforts during the war – making peace between Occidental and Oriental.

Agness's father, Major Blakely, had suggested that maybe his wife, Tannis, might want to stay on in Australia with Agness and Sunny while Major Blakely went on the long trip back to the United States. After all, he knew, he would return to the Asia Pacific theatre, and to the ongoing war, so having his wife safely tucked away in Australia seemed to Blakely to be a good idea. But Tannis decided to go to America with her husband, hoping to track down their extended family: her brother in law, Warrant Officer Matt Blakely, who had been serving at the Mount Weather Emergency Operations Centre in West Virginia; the MacInnes's and so many other family and friends whom Tannis wanted, and in a sense, needed, closure about. *They'll probably all have headed for the Upton's, in Altoona. That's where I would have gone,* she had thought, *they'll be so surprised to see me. I miss mom and dad so much. I have to know what happened.*

Saying goodbye to Agness was the hardest part, of course. Not only because they were so close as a family, but also because of how much the world had changed, and they knew it. There would be no long-distance telephone calls, no 'Skype' video calls, no e-mails, no intercontinental commercial flights, not even letters. Once *MV Thor Insuvi* pulled out of the port of Adelaide, they would most likely never see each other again.

It dawned on Tannis that this was how it must have been a century before, and throughout the ages, when the world was larger, before the interconnectedness of the modern age; before the madness of the globalized economy. A romantic age, when life was lived with humility and thrift; when farewell truly was goodbye, and when each day was greeted with grace and gratitude. *Much like how it has become again,* she thought with a sense of nostalgia and hope.

The End

ABOUT THE AUTHOR

Gene has served as both a civilian and a military pilot from 1988 to 2012. He has studied an eclectic range of subjects, and has a degree in Philosophy from UBC in his home town of Vancouver. Father of four, Gene has taken up writing books as his retirement activity. Gene is also a founding member of Flea Circus Books Inc. To find out more about Gene, explore his page through Flea Circus Books. www.fleacircusbooks.com

Check out these other Gene Skellig books:

$3.50 off *Winter Kill – War With China Has Already Begun:*
www.createspace.com/3537111 enter code PAC6SETA

$2.50 off *Homestay – A Japanese Girl's Romantic ESL Adventure In Vancouver,* **Canada**:
www.createspace.com/ 3715916 enter code 9JGPMV3B

Lost Child (Volume One) - Anguish in the Nantahala
http://www.amazon.com/dp/B007IK2MBA

Lost Child (Volume Two) - Retribution in the Nantahala
http://www.amazon.com/dp/B0089Y0PEA